KITCHEN MUSIC

KITCHEN MUSIC

a novel by

Charles Foran

Cormorant Books

Published with the assistance of the Canada Council and the Ontario Arts Council.

Cover illustration from a drawing of Simey Doherty, Ballybofey 1977 by Eamonn O'Doherty from *The Northern Fiddler*, published by Blackstaff Press Ltd., Dublin, courtesy of the artist. Cover design by Artcetera Graphics Inc., Dunvegan, Ontario.

Edited by Gena K. Gorrell.

Published by Cormorant Books Inc.
RR 1, Dunvegan, Ontario
Canada K0C 1J0.

Printed and bound in Canada.

Canadian Cataloguing in Publication Data

Foran, Charles, 1960-

Kitchen music : a novel

ISBN 0-920953-73-5

I. Title.

PS8561.0633K48 1994 C813'.54 C94-900414-6

PR9199.3.F67K48 1994

For Mary

CONTENTS

And my nightly slumbers end wherever I think of her
I could court her vision in America

Irish emigration song

Go out every day and you will learn
You'll be wiser and wiser the farther you roam
Go here, go there, go everywhere—
How can you be smart by staying at home?

Vietnamese song of welcome
for newborn child

OVERTURE

OVERTURE

"Is there no end to it?" Michael asked.

"What?"

"The weather."

"Awful business," Seamus agreed.

Michael abandoned the rectangle of window-light shading the pub floor. He crossed the room, went around the counter, brought out a fiddle case and opened it. Then he took two glasses and, pumping the beer tap, filled them until foam trickled down their sides.

"But tomorrow will be better," Seamus said. "It's bound to clear by morning. It's bound to—"

"Cheers."

"Good luck, Mickey."

Michael drained a quarter of his pint. Though the sentence on Seamus's lips—"A bit early, isn't it?"—was never in danger of being spoken, he coughed and rolled his cigarette back and forth in an ashtray. But Michael was again at the window, seated on a bench with the fiddle.

"A couple of tunes," he said, "and we can be on our way."

He wedged the instrument under his chin. Leaving it suspended, he used both hands to tighten the bow hairs and coat them with rosin. Michael sounded the E, secured the peg, then moved through the A, D, and G. He down-bowed all four strings. Repositioning the fiddle, he settled his gaze on the neck and raised the bow above the bridge.

"Tommy will be back shortly," Seamus said. "He'd be dead keen to hear you. Better to play for a crowd, eh?"

"A crowd?"

"Well. . . . "

"Friday and Saturday nights at MacDonagh's?" Michael asked, anger in his eyes. "Ninety minutes the one evening, ninety minutes the next? A half-dozen of us squeezed into the corner, unable to hear ourselves for the chatter?"

"I don't know!"

"Two numbers, then we're off."

"Off? You're not thinking—"

The first set consisted of Kerry slides. Though they were familiar pub-fare, Michael's treatments lent the tunes fresh personality. His style was clean, grounded in a strong rhythmic accent and long, almost leisurely bows. Stretching quaver values and breaking up triplets, Michael cut and rolled through the slides with characteristic restraint. Only now the restraint was matched by an intensity that threatened to propel the music out of time. Anyone familiar with his playing would have raised an eyebrow at such recklessness. Still, the final note struck fierce but clear, the bow lifting off without a stutter.

The pub thrummed with silence. A sound lingered in both men's ears, the *ssshhh* of surf receding from a shoreline. Seamus reached for his glass. Strangely overcome, he barely managed a curt "Good job." Michael also drank, never looking up, and plucked the A string with his thumb.

"What about a song," Seamus said. "You know, something sad and lovely?"

"Huh?"

"A lament, maybe."

"Fuck sad," Michael said.

"Ah."

"Fuck lamentation."

He played a jig instead. From the start, Michael's

fiddling was still more aggressive. Early bars emerged edgy and hard. These were followed by a series of cross-bowings that shifted the accent to the second note. Modal drones, introduced midway, further coarsened the texture, and by the final round the music was turbulent. Michael's demeanour changed as well; his lips pursed and the lines on his forehead creased then relaxed in step with the phrasing. In a rare physical expression, his upper body lunged downward during a double-stop. But when "The Walls of Liscarroll" ended, the timing was flawless and the jig had been played without a note missing or misplaced.

Neither man moved. Eventually Seamus tipped back his empty glass. He coughed again and glanced at the door. "That was brilliant."

"Thanks."

"You should give Tommy a listen. He'd be delighted to hear such playing."

Michael returned the fiddle to the case, and the case to a shelf below the counter.

"Not this afternoon," Seamus pleaded.

"Why not this afternoon?"

"You've drink taken, and so have I."

"It means nothing."

"Please," Seamus said, crossing the room despite himself. "We'll stop around at your aunt's for a sandwich. You haven't eaten all day."

Michael's hand was on the door.

"What about the bar? You promised Tom Daly to mind the place until half-two. We can't just abandon it, can we?"

Directly across from the pub was the pier; among the dozen trawlers moored along its eastern flank was the vessel owned by Michael and Seamus. The morning sky had been dolorous, a ceiling of ashen clouds that permitted a gap between its lowest swerve and the summits surrounding Dingle town. By early afternoon the gap had closed and the hills were obscured in a mist creeping across the harbour.

The drizzle had intensified to a downpour and the surface, choppy an hour ago, was now organized into militaristic waves hurling themselves against the shore. Boats, roped both to the pier and to each other, pitched bow to stern in the shallow water.

"I'd appreciate knowing what this is about, Mickey."

"Come on, boy," Michael answered, passing into the street, "let's bring in the pots before they're torn out to the Skelligs."

Part I

ONLY CHILD

ONLY CHILD

Chapter I

When I was a child I loved to disappear into closets. I would slip inside the one off our front hall, shut the door before my mother noticed, and seal the seam with a scarf. Then, on my back among the shoes and boots, I would extend my arms into the void to caress and be caressed by jackets and coats, a garment bag locked at the top. I stayed in there for hours. Everything—the darkness, the silence, the enclosure—was absolute. But I never felt scared. Quite the opposite: the darkness was a cocoon, the silence a carapace, the enclosure a bower that held me in mid-air. I was also driven by the vague but consuming purpose that possesses kids. What did I do? I can't recall exactly. The sensation I remember is similar to that achieved by rubbing closed eyes; images and outlines are resolved behind the lids, ripples of psychedelic colour, rivers of smoky light. In the closet I saw such things, saw them in flashes, often blurry, occasionally clarified, and with my eyes wide open.

Though she teased me, my mother never outlawed these "shell" sessions. (She claimed I was crawling inside a seashell to hear the ocean within my own head.) Of course she knew where I was. If she needed to talk to her son, share plans regarding dinner or homework, she simply stood in the hallway and spoke. Jig and Reel, meanwhile, scratched at the wood and meowed. Sometimes I acknowledged Mother's monologues by rapping on the door: the knock, I assured her, of a hungry ghost, a phantom who had finished his arithmetic. The cats I ignored.

My seashell days ended the night my mother accidentally abandoned me. I was seven years old. I had arranged during dinner to stay over at a friend's house, and then had vanished. Assuming I was gone, she left for her weekly bridge session. But I was in the closet, deep in an underwater sleep. When I awoke my shirt was soggy and my eyelashes had crusted together. Still groggy, I listened for the reassuring murmur of the television, hearing instead rustlings and whispers, the squeals of hangers sliding along the rod—all within the chamber. Suddenly, the darkness ceased to be buoyant. It was now an anchor around my neck, and I was drowning. Crying out, I seized the doorknob. It refused to turn. I shouldered the wood. It repelled me back into the coats. Charging again, I plunged from the closet into the hallway, only to discover yet another sea of black, less pure, more encompassing. At the foot of the front door lay a parallelogram of twilight, its beam fed from a diamond window. I curled into a ball and, certain I had been forsaken, gazed at the light.

I was just a lonely boy, lonely and blue; I was all alone, with nothing to do. Actually, Mother's version of the Paul Anka song—which she sang to me at bedtime every evening, both of us squeezed into a rocking chair, even after I had graduated from a toddler into a monkey-limbed youth—her version featured lyrics that were various, and unpredictable:

I'm just a lonely boy
Lonely for you
I've waited so long
But my heart is true.

Or else, on days when her mind refused to function in her second language, she chanted absently:

Je suis un lonely boy
Seul, but *sérieux*
All I *besoin*
C'est toi, merci Dieu.

Years later, a freckly kid soured into a pimply adolescent, I mocked Mother's imperfect English listening skills (I had an uncanny memory for melodies) by devising my own lewd versions, and declaiming them in the kitchen. But again, no matter how crude my parodies became, Mother never frowned, never grimaced, never wagged her finger. Her benevolence was disconcerting. Had she failed to get the jokes? Was she paying her son only scant attention? The pattern—her mangling lyrics, me mocking her botches—persisted. A favourite:

Felix, nothing more than Felix,
Trying to forget my Felix of love.

Mother's ditty, based on the AM hit "Feelings", conjures up an entire decade for me. The 1970s were calmer around our house: fewer closets, less sleepwalking. More ordinary stuff, too—voice changes and growing spurts, high school, girls. No longer a Lonely Boy, now I was Felix of Love. In my memory, Mother stands at the stove stirring a pot of beans, a pan of hamburger mush, a skillet of fried potatoes. Arch-tailed cats dance escadrilles around her legs. Birds flutter on the windowsill. She is a tall, thick-calved woman in the uniform of female middle management: printed dress and high-heeled shoes, demure sparkles of jewellery (wedding band still worn). Her long face is framed by permed black hair. Her eyes are vivacious, her ski-jump nose as telltale as the *th*-less accent, the Franglais malapropisms. My mother is so striking, so unusual: a district manager for a national department store chain with its head office on Bay Street, a tower full of men named Jones and Simpson, and she a refugee from northern Ontario whose disregard for the dominant language of the city borders on the wilful. This woman, at the stove in her suburban bungalow on a weekday evening, her thoughts gliding in an updraft of fatigue and hunger, her feet throbbing, a run in her stocking—this woman is my mother, cooking for her son the simple foods we liked to eat.

Such was our household. Constrained, comfortable, full of holes you could have driven a truck through. I was, after all, the only child of a single parent in a neighbourhood where procreation measured optimism and singularity of circumstance or disposition was held in high suspicion. Hia Thi Loi, my companion these last five years, maintains I am not just an only child but, temperamentally, a youngest child too.

"You are the last child of large family," she says, hammering at English the way a blind man hammers a nail. "Used to being in a room of older brothers and sisters. Used to watching others. Liking to watch, and listen, and wait for growing up. But also needing more attention than you will admit. Needing to not be in the centre, but still near the middle."

"I'm like that?"

"You are youngest child."

"Waiting for growing up?"

"A person cannot see these things himself. The duty of a loved one is to remove the, you know, those glasses horses wear—"

I provide the word.

"Blinkers, yes."

"You are a dutiful loved one, Hia."

"I know," she replies.

Her theory is, of course, both ludicrous and staggeringly insensitive to any anguish my mother or I might feel about our situation. The fact is that if I am the youngest of a brood, then all my siblings were aborted. My brothers and sisters were aborted and the room that Hia refers to, likely the bungalow kitchen with its arborite table-for-six, is cluttered with phantoms.

The remark is typical. Obsessively visual, monomaniacal in her obsessions, Hia summons images that dictate how she views the inanimate world, and how she doesn't view, closely or carefully, the animate—i.e. other people. The room she presented to me had appeared before her only moments earlier, and her awkward verbal rendition of it emerged unimpeded by considerations of propriety. She is what she is: an artist. I respect that. I respect her concentration, her determination to resolve the shapes that haunt her, waking or asleep.

I am my mother's boy, through and through. Also lanky, also friendly but remote, also inclined to address my feet when confronting people I would rather not confront. But Hia, who knows my mother (aka Francine) well, disagrees.

"Francine is a strong person," she says. "Full of confidence in herself. You get this tendency from someone else."

"Who, the cats?"

"Like your tall forehead. Like your bad sight, which you refuse to fix."

"My sight doesn't need fixing."

"Glasses."

"I'm too young."

"How many fingers am I holding?"

I can't resist. "How many fingers do *you* think you're holding?"

"Like your walk."

"I've explained that already."

"Story behind the story, Pat. You explain the superficial, but never the deep."

"Holes you could drive a truck through," I agree.

Hia wrinkles her nose. "Not all Francine," she repeats.

"No way you are just her child."

But I am just Francine Keane's child, even if we briefly did not share the same last name. The date was May 15, 1976, my eighteenth birthday. I was opening gifts at a dinner party in the kitchen. For once, the table was full: myself and Mother, Davey Russell, a school friend named John Macdonald. After the final package was unwrapped, I made a speech. From this point onwards, I announced, in order to officially close the thin book on the Keane "family", I would be referring to Mother as Francine, or Fran, if she liked. I would also be using her maiden name, Ferron. Born within my heart the moment I allowed those hurtful (and unrehearsed) words to escape my lips was an anger, inchoate and unpredictable, that clenched my hands into fists. I had no idea I had it in me. I had no idea what it *was* I had in me.

Certainly Francine Keane, née Ferron, was unprepared for the outburst. She stood, eyes welling, and excused herself from the table. Davey Russell shot me a murderous look before following her down the hallway. John Macdonald reached for the wine bottle. And the feisty birthday boy? He stared stupidly at the jacket of an album that had been among the gifts, brooding on the folly of pronouncing strong opinions when one's disposition was basically mild, even simpering.

Which it was. And still is. And I don't mind.

Hia minds, though. A couple of years ago, relating the anecdote to her, I admitted to feeling nostalgia for that bitter teenager. He seemed, in retrospect, an interesting guy; I wished I had known him longer. When Hia piped in with her own lament for that brief incarnation of me, I lost my temper. But could I fault her? I am still Pat Keane, despite the fact that I know no other Keanes anywhere, and still my mother's son, despite that Hia calls her Francine and Davey Russell calls her Fran, and people at work, at least her staff, refer to her as Mrs. Keane, in deference to her short temper and the gold band.

What I am definitely no longer is a copy editor at Toronto's largest newspaper. The job, which I had held since graduating from university eight years ago, and probably would have clung to for the rest of my career—I have always liked working with words, so long as they aren't mine—ended abruptly. Hia is to blame. It was her idea that I apply for a position as section editor, that I go head to head with another underling for the job, a man with half my skill but twice my ambition. He won, became my boss, and told me I was "overqualified, undermotivated, and doomed to wear my trousers rolled". I got the allusion. (My degree is in English and history.) When the man started calling me Prufrock around the office, I did what I really didn't want to do, but felt pushed into: I quit.

I also turned thirty-one. Crow's-feet patterned the corners of my eyes. The skin around my mouth started to tighten. I squinted constantly, as if into a raw sun; my voice dropped a half-tone, as if from too many unfiltered cigarettes. Several people commented on it; my face, that of a landlubber who had never been on a boat except to cross Toronto harbour to Centre Island, appeared to be slowly transforming itself into the visage of an Atlantic fisherman.

More serious than this genetic plastic surgery were the first faint pangs of unfulfilment that began to act as an alarm clock on weekday mornings. The issue wasn't professional stagnation or personal unhappiness. Simply, I found myself staring at the walls of my apartment, decorated with framed posters from art exhibits, most of which I hadn't actually attended, and deciding they were bare; that my bookshelves, stuffed with paperbacks and college texts, the majority of which I had either skimmed or never even opened, were empty; that my stereo, surrounded by neat columns of cassettes and stacks of records, many embarrassing rock dinosaurs, others unmemorable jazz sessions, still others middling stabs at the classical canon, was broken, the discs cracked and the tapes all blank.

Hia, meanwhile, was also flirting with a crisis. Her experience of the eighties could not have been more dissimilar to mine. She came to Canada from Vietnam in 1980 with a smidgen of French, a smattering of English, and an ear so tinny it was a wonder she had ever mastered her mother tongue. Language proficiency should have been a priority. But when I met her five years later the French had vanished and the English—hours of government-financed and church-supported tutoring notwithstanding—was a disaster. Granted, she was busy: full-time student, part-time guardian to her younger sister Nhung, nocturnal office cleaner. She was equally consumed by her search for her parents (one had just turned up in California) and, less dramatically, an addiction to television (three sit-coms, two game shows, an hour of news per day). Still, other Vietnamese who had arrived the same year, including Nhung, all were making progress in their adopted tongue, while Hia, confident she already had a language, wreaked havoc on it.

I was smitten instantly. Nurtured on my mother's haywire grammar, I associated fractured speech with trustworthy speech, incapable of deceit. I also thought it protean compared with the hackneyed diction of journalism. Though outwardly stern with Hia—at one point I threatened that all thoughts of "serious things" would have to wait until she got a grip on English grammar—inwardly I was delighted. So delighted, in fact, that years passed without progress on either front. Hia spoke broken English and our relationship remained unserious. She was completing a degree in computer science. I was editing articles on immigration policy and the "new" Toronto. She was a technician for a software company by day, an art student by night. I was working directly with a journalist on a four-part series concerning the emigrant experience. She was a sales assistant at a fashionable art gallery and assembling a portfolio to show her boss. The journalist was nominated for a national newspaper award. The gallery owner loved Hia's work and invited her back to his place for a drink. The writer won the award, I lost the promotion. Hia threw orange juice at the owner and fled his townhouse.

Then, to deepen her dismay, she had confirmed a personal loss she'd half known about for a decade, but refused to believe. Devastated, she exercised her privilege as a Catholic convert and entered a belated period of mourning. Hia's bereavement included quitting the gallery, burning her folder of (I thought privately) tedious abstracts, and expressing a sudden desire to go abroad. Not just abroad, but "back".

I asked.

"Back to our past lives," she clarified.

"Bishop Avenue?"

"We must return to where we are from. See how much of us is still there. See what must be stolen for use living here in Canada."

"I was born here in Canada."

"Vietnam is impossible. Too much politics. Ireland is possible. Tickets for Ireland cost $649. We can leave on April first."

I smiled.

"Dingle is only six hours from the airport where we land. Dingle is where your people live. Dingle is where your bad eyes and curly hair belong. Also your thing about scratchy fiddle music."

"My thing about fiddle music?"

"We should go to Dingle."

"Have you been talking with—?"

"Francine is my friend."

"Also my mother."

"You need a passion to explode your imagination. To go deep into something and come out changed."

"You want me to change?"

"Don't you?"

"I've never thought about it," I lied.

"But you can be so bland!"

I rarely rise to Hia's taunts. (They are contradictory: she stays with me, doesn't she?) "I'm a good copy editor," I said mischievously. "I salvage bad articles, make decent ones even better."

She was prepared for this. "This is not your own work. Not your own passion."

"And scratchy fiddle music would be?"

"Sure. Your—"

She stopped, bit her lip.

"Ah," I said. "You *have* been talking with Francine."

"It is the right thing. Trust me."

The matter was settled.

"Can I ask one question?"

"Of course."

"I can see why I might benefit from this trip. But what will going to an Irish fishing village do for you?"

"I have a project."

Hia has a project. I have an ultimatum to explode my imagination. We have a flight for April first, 1990, returning at the beginning of June. Two months "back" in Dingle: to order our pasts, Hia thinks aloud, to face the reality of serious things, I think to myself. Either task will be more difficult than she envisions. History, I was once taught, can be conceived of as contrapuntal, control and inevitability in eternal exchange. Instinctively, I side with the inevitable; wilfully, Hia opts for the control. A private history I would rather avoid giving air time to, but which we are about to turn up the volume on, certainly aspires to the counterpoint, if not the condition, of music. (Did Francine mention this detail to her young friend? I suspect not.)

I am steadfast in love, Hia promises.

Chapter 2

The pots Michael and Seamus had to collect lay in coves along the north face of Inis-na-Bro, an island twenty-five kilometres southwest of Dingle and nine kilometres off the coast of the westernmost point on mainland Ireland. Michael had shot them there shortly before dawn, two lines of fifteen pots tucked into crevices beneath the cliffs. The crevices were ideal for fishing in good weather but dangerous during a storm. Few Dingle boats bothered to venture so far for lobsters. Michael O Cathain had special cause: his father had shot and hauled in those coves for four decades, and his grandfather for a half-century before him, and as a boy Michael had accompanied his father and uncles in the boats on long summer evenings, helping sort the catch and plunging into the water to free wedged ropes.

Inis-na-Bro was the smaller neighbour of the Great Blasket island, where Michael had spent the first twelve years of his life. Barely two dozen people remained on the Great Blasket in October 1952. In the villages along the tip of the peninsula, however, in Dunquin, Ballyferriter, Ventry, and Dingle, there lived a hundred more like him: men and women delivered by a midwife in an island house, raised hunting rabbits and robbing petrel nests, and perhaps grown into adulthood eking out a living from the sea and the stony fields, all the while gazing across the three-mile sound at the mainland or squinting westward into the vanishing point of ocean.

Now the community had dispersed, and soon it would be rendered extinct. What could exiles do? Stare from Dunquin back at the Great Blasket. Visit, weather permitting, the stubborn few (including Michael's father, Tomas O Cathain) who were determined to die on the island. Set sheep to graze on the Blasket slopes. Make a point, if a fisherman, of working the seas around the group. The catch was still bountiful in those waters and the risks were no greater than elsewhere.

Michael had convinced himself that he needed to reach Inis-na-Bro and haul the pots before they were swept away. Laying them had probably been a mistake, though if others had also misjudged conditions they seemed resigned to the loss. The men approached an empty pier. Two figures huddled in the shelter beside the landing, but they were lifeless, apparently dozing despite the rain. Strand Street was equally desolate: doors closed, blinds drawn, lamps turned on in front rooms. The rest of the village was shrouded. Only the spire of St. Mary's, its bell pealing the hour, protruded above the mire.

The day felt heavy on Michael's shoulders, the rain skirting the open water to sting his cheeks. He understood the insult and made a point of walking with his head upright, his manner haughty and scornful. Often he would stop and light a cigarette, striking the match in cupped hands and protecting the flame even when it singed his palms. On this afternoon Michael would gladly have burned his skin. But twice he forced Seamus to halt while he fumbled with a match, and twice the wind snuffed it out.

Stopping beside a row of trawlers, Michael stepped onto the foredeck of the first, crossed to the second, nearly lost his footing when the bow nosed down, leapt to the third, then slid along a gunwale into his own vessel. He issued an instruction to Seamus and primed the engine. Once in Dingle Bay, he asked his friend to take the wheel.

Seamus hugged the coast until they reached Ventry harbour, where he dipped inland to catch the waves at their ebb. Blatant warnings flashed near Slea Head: foam rushing back from submerged rocks, breakers erupting against the cliffs, air currents visible hundreds of metres away. The men had also to contend with a roar that dissolved the engine but failed to drown the squawks of seagulls, who hung over the trawler like paper airplanes.

"Angle her out towards the Blasket," Michael said, blowing funnels of cigarette smoke from his nostrils. "You're holding too close to the shore."

Seamus frowned.

"Will I take over?"

"I'd prefer to cut straight across the head."

"But it doubles the time Seamie. Best to angle to the island right away."

"I can't even see the Blasket."

"You know it's there."

"I can't even see it!"

The Great Blasket, a ridge of purple sandstone starkly defined on days of middling visibility, was now cloaked in mist at sea level and in cloud higher up. Both men could discern its outline, but their perceptions were conditioned—the island was etched into their retinas.

"Let me have a go at the wheel," Michael said.

"Are you sure?"

Michael grinned.

"What's this about?" Seamus asked again.

Intent on meeting the waves head on, Michael opened the throttle and steered southeast towards the emerging land mass. Once astride the Great Blasket's eastern flank, he veered inland to draw parallel to the cliffs.

Suddenly the boat passed from under the protection of the island and into the gap. Michael directed the bow into the first swell and sensed the trawler impact and rise, rise, until sinking back. The narrowing interval between major waves left the boat rocking, the stern either pointed up at the sky or down at the seabed.

Seamus was on his feet.

"Better to draw a line," Michael said. "If we're broadsided, we'll turn turtle."

Inis-na-Bro was a deserted clump of rock. The trawler slowed approaching the coves gouged into its north face. Michael was anxious to pull under their shelter, but also leery of being drawn into the eddies of foam. He had to get near enough to the pots to use the grapnel. Only their boat, a nine-metre vessel with a thirty-horsepower engine, gill and trawl netting, and space in the hold for two hundred kilograms of catch, was inadequate; even a medium swell from the rear could have lifted the trawler and dashed it against the cliff. If that happened, planks of wood and pieces of equipment would wash ashore the next day on the strand at Clogher, to be followed by bodies bloated with water.

"I'll have to back her in," Michael said to Seamus. "I can't haul from the bow."

"But the propeller?"

"I'll slip the engine out."

"How will we control her?"

"No control," he admitted.

A swell erupted. Though the boat stayed in the sea it pitched sideways, the hull scraping bedrock. Seamus braced himself against the cabin.

"I trusted you, Mickey," he shouted.

"What?"

"We all trusted you."

"Why me?"

The question startled Seamus. "Well," he said, "I mean, you were the man—"

"I only had this craving for the music," Michael

interrupted. "Nothing else. Honest."

He began with the line of pots furthest along the promontory. Sidling up to an overhang, Michael cut the engine and used an oar to rotate the hull. The first marker bobbed in a configuration of swirls. He poled the trawler closer to the cove, then caught the buoy in the grapnel and began hauling rope. The work was treacherous and the men reeled about the cockpit. Michael was forced to lean over the stern to pull in pots, submerging his arms. Seamus stood near the wheel stacking traps and tossing lobsters into a basket. He saw the watery mountain first.

The boat was lifted and flung back. Seamus landed on his knees but Michael remained upright, paying out rope and sidestepping pots being yanked back overboard. Again the hull ground against rock and the stern shipped water. Both men lurched towards the rear gunwale to wedge themselves between the trawler and the cliff face.

"To the bow," Michael ordered.

"But—"

"Stay up there!"

Seamus could not believe his eyes. The cockpit was actually beneath the overhang, and Michael was once more hauling pots. Then he was at the wheel, opening the throttle wide despite the risk of flooding.

The action saved their lives.

The second swell was even more lethal. The boat hung suspended in mid-air, like a child on a swing at the top of its arc, before plummeting into the foam. Pots and lobsters were sent flying. Seamus cracked his head against a winch and Michael, a hand still gripping the wheel, tumbled to the floor, his forearm burning with pain. The trawler stood on its side, teetered, then straightened.

"You're bloody mad!" Seamus said, probing the cut above his eye.

"We'll swim for it."

Seamus gaped. Neither of them *could* swim.

Next Michael crossed the island to the other line. Going further out and running before the wind would have reduced the chances of being broadsided, but Seamus kept silent. The ensuing scene was equally harrowing. The difference now was Michael's demeanour, which was openly, absurdly joyful, his desperate efforts punctuated with laughter and promises to "swim for it" if need be. Twice the engine came close to swamping. When it started to miss the second time Seamus blessed himself, only to have his prayer interrupted by the stench of diesel. Finally, there was the moment when Michael, struggling with a line, chose not to cut the rope but instead extended his leg across a chasm, planted a foot atop a rock, and manoeuvred the rope until the pot sprang free. He shoved off just as a rebounding wave propelled the trawler forward.

The pots were in. They could leave.

Recrossing the gap proved no less perilous. Too light to assail the larger swells before, the boat was now too heavy to sit properly in the sea. Ordering Seamus to the wheel, Michael began shoving the lobster traps over the side with such abandon that he nearly fell in himself. Seamus also conceded a smile, in punch-drunk amusement at this latest problem. With the final pot dispatched, the trawler rose.

Michael's mood underwent yet another transformation alongside the Great Blasket. He wandered the cockpit in a daze, scrubbing his face with his hands. "You've every right to be furious," he said.

"Thanks."

"It was cowardly to drag you along. I'm not half the man you all think I am."

Seamus softened. "I'd suggest visiting your da," he said, motioning towards the island village. "Only I'm not convinced we could land."

He went on to navigate Blasket Sound. Two men waiting on Dunquin pier indicated he should anchor beyond the landing. They rowed a smaller boat out and brought Michael and Seamus ashore. Michael had to be helped onto the cement. He accepted a cigarette from his cousin, Maurice Guiheen, and stood facing the island while Seamus explained their misadventure.

"It's time," Michael said suddenly.

No one responded.

"I'm dead serious."

"I know you are," Seamus answered.

"But it's *time*."

"Only for some, Mickey."

Michael flicked the butt into the water. Any hope of shrugging the incident off and buying his mates a pint was in vain; his every word would be scrutinized for weeks afterwards in pubs and houses around the peninsula. Michael O Cathain might be a fisherman (he had the rasped contours and burned cheeks to prove it) who had been raised in town by his Aunt Moira, and now was an under-employed twenty-four-year-old, too poor to move out, too feckless to court a woman, alcoholic, depressed; but he was equally a fiddler, and possessed the spindly fingers, graceful posture, and severe manner characteristic of musicians. Unknown outside Dingle, he was revered within the tiny community that had nurtured him, and from which he had so far never strayed. At six foot five, he was also reputed to be the tallest man in Munster province.

When he turned around, the despondency had vanished and Michael wore a sheepish smile. "Right you are, Seamie," he agreed. "Only for some."

ONLY CHILD

Chapter 3

The thirty kilometres between Tralee and Dingle is a desert of bracken and gorse. Barren hills and cratered valleys display a sheen as bright as the glare of sand; the effect of sun and light is at once negligible—the hue appears unchanging—and marked, in great shadows that roll off the slopes. When not socked in, the sky is climbing; when not blanketing the road, mist caps the hills. The impression since Hia and I landed at Shannon airport six hours ago has been of deepening withdrawal. Villages have grown scarcer the further west each bus has headed. Houses are few and far between; sheep graze at precipitous angles; the rare human silhouette, sighted above the highway, is indeterminate.

But the hills, called the Slieve Mish mountains, also function as fortification. The Irish republic and province of Munster, the county of Kerry and tourist region of Killarney-Tralee: these abstractions recede in the rear window, narrowing the world (my guide-book informs me) to a town and scattered hamlets, a couple of neolithic ruins, dizzying cliffs and barren crags, one large island, the ocean.

Actually, we could be driving down Yonge Street for all I know. A drizzle has steamed the windows, leaving only the swath of the driver's wiper to peer through. Clearing an eyehole is feasible, but awkward; Hia demanded, as usual, the window seat, and proceeded, also as usual, to fall asleep on my arm. The bus is crowded with elderly people boarding along the road, and smells of damp wool and pipe tobacco. I like watching the other passengers, like the smells and intimacy—everyone smiles at everyone else, offering greetings in a foreign tongue—even the blindness of fogged glass. Eventually I turn my attention to Hia's *phung thi chin* face.

Phung thi chin, woman warrior, is one of a handful of Vietnamese expressions to have entered my vocabulary. It was I who first suggested the term, based on a book I had read. Hia blanched at my innocent reference, supplied the phrase, and then confessed to having modelled herself on the woman warrior as a girl.

Her face is indeed fierce. Hia's cheekbones do not evolve from the lower curve of her eyes so much as explode; an artist drawing her would do well to use a single unbroken line, and then reinforce the figure by matching the arch of her brow with that of her chin. For eyes, two semicircles would suffice. The challenge would be to suggest their ability to fluctuate between ovals (when she is animated) and teardrops (when she is more pensive), as well as the brilliance of her whites, how they contrast with her black hair and tawny skin. Hia's mouth is small and her lips are thin, but she possesses perfect teeth and a clown's repertoire of smirks and grimaces. Her fierceness is, in other words, not the sort one associates with myth. Traditional renditions of *phung thi chin* tend to be generic. Even their beauty is uniform. Hia is untraditional and, in the opinion of most, unbeautiful. Interesting, singular, even arresting—but not a beauty.

I used to agree with this assessment, comforted by the fact that I was equally plain in appearance, and that she seemed determined to undermine clichés of femininity. Hia has always kept her hair cropped, worn no makeup or jewellery, and dressed androgynously: sweat-tops and t-shirts, jeans and shorts, black boots and running shoes. Her body is, admittedly, ill suited to fashion. She is short, almost squat: short legs, squat torso, small breasts, curiously broad shoulders. I might hesitate to describe her in such terms were she not so indifferent to matters of physical beauty. Hia doesn't give a damn, and I take heart in her aesthetic rigour.

But a confession: more and more I am finding her, if not beautiful, then elegant. Her hands, for example, are lithe and long-fingered. Hia moves them slowly, gesturing with precision, often for effect. Besides her chameleon eyes, the hands are her most striking feature. Equally elegant, to me, is the quality of distillation in her expressions; they seem condensed, without waste or excess.

On the bus, however, her hands are stuffed into her jacket pockets and her forehead is filmed in a jet-lag sweat. Eventually, I stretch across to the window, clearing a portal with my cuff. My timing is perfect: the Slieve Mish are levelling off; the continent is running down.

In Dingle, we are deposited at the intersection of two roads, one following the curve of the harbour and the other climbing a gradient. Both streets are immediately swallowed by fog. Filaments of cloud brush the top of my head; genies stagger over the pavement, dissipating if we draw near them. I hear water lapping against a breaker. I sense the bulk of buildings and guess, from the inclines, that much of the village lies uphill. A sluicing rain does little to clarify the setting.

"Nice," Hia says.

I gather the bags and set off in search of 50 Grey Lane, our domicile for the next two months. In February I wrote a letter to a name my mother provided, James Sullivan, asking about accommodation in Dingle. Three weeks later I received a reply from Eily Murphy of 50 Grey Lane. Mrs. Murphy, it turned out, had a flat in her house that had come available due to the passing away of her tenant of thirty years, Joan McGreevy, aged ninety. In a note requesting the apartment I expressed condolences about Joan McGreevy, and also asked, at a certain someone's insistence, about a television. We left Toronto before our landlady could confirm the presence of an idiot box in the flat. The suspense is killing Hia.

I stop an old man buried to the nose in his overcoat collar. His accent is thick as the fog. "Two rights," he instructs, "a short jaunt, and you're home. Eily Murphy is expecting you, sure."

Eily Murphy is expecting Pat Keane, not Hia Thi Loi. It is Hia, however, who reaches 50 Sraid Ghrae first, a blue rowhouse with a white door to one side of a curtained window. Ignoring my entreaties to wait, she sounds the bell.

"Mrs. Murphy?"

There is silence.

"I am Hia. Sorry to be soaking."

"I don't do bed and breakfast, dear," a voice declares imperiously. "Try Mrs. Lynch around the corner."

Hia turns to me. "Pat?" she calls. "She doesn't do bed and breakfast."

I introduce myself.

"Why didn't you say!" Eily Murphy asks.

"I did say," Hia answers.

"Jimmy told me to expect you before noon," she tells me. "Early afternoon at the latest."

"This is Hia," I offer, grabbing her by the shoulders. "My companion."

"He-uh?"

"Pleased to meet you, Mrs. Lynch," Hia says. There is punishment in her voice.

"Murphy," our landlady corrects, unwrinkling her nose. "Your hand is like ice, dear."

"The rain," I say.

"Beg pardon?"

Hia catches raindrops with her tongue.

We are ushered into the hallway and up a set of stairs. Eily Murphy is a middle-aged woman with a round face, watery blue eyes, and hair so white it might have changed colour from a shock. Her gait is stiff and varicose veins bulge through her stockings. Hia and I are privy to her medical problems by virtue of our laborious ascent of the stairwell. Our landlady leads the way, stopping every few steps to clarify a point in her monologue and to apologize for keeping us on the front step. Her speech is slow, marked by a metronome-like steadiness of stresses and orotund vowels.

"Jimmy said you were a couple. He said Pat wasn't coming alone. These days, people see no reason to formalize their commitment. A relationship hasn't any need of a stamp, has it? That's what Jimmy says. Only we were taught so different. Your father too, Pat."

"I wouldn't know."

"Of course."

"Pat hates fathers, Mrs. Lynch," Hia says.

Eily Murphy corrects the name, resumes her speech. "Taught it should be done properly, formally, in the eyes of God and the community. The old way of doing things." She rests at the top of the landing. "We are all so different, aren't we?"

I nod.

"That's my only point."

"Yes?"

"To what I was saying. . . . I tend to lose the line of my thoughts, the direction of them. What I mean to say, well, I don't always *say* it. Memories are the worst."

She sighs.

We don't ask.

"Joan McGreevy's flat," she announces, opening the door onto a wave of curiously ripe air. "May she rest in peace."

Joan McGreevy's flat has a kitchen and bathroom, a spacious main room overlooking the street. Carpeted in gloomy red shag and papered in faded blue, the room is most notable for the quality of the framed sketches decorating the walls—they are uniformly ordinary—and the quantity of furniture smothering the carpet: a couch and two armchairs, a coffee table and press, empty bookcases, pots of brittle paper flowers. Beneath the window hulks a cabinet television; atop the press rests an ancient radio. A flying-saucer fixture centres the ceiling, its basin spotted with insect corpses, and there are lamps at either end of the couch. Conspicuous by its absence is a bed.

"Did Joan McGreevy sleep on her feet?" Hia asks.

"A cot, dear. Hardly suitable for a man and. . . . A couple, I should say. The couch pulls out into a bed. There are sheets and blankets in the closet."

"Nice radio."

"It hasn't worked in ages."

"Big TV."

"Joan was nearly blind her final years," Eily Murphy admits. "We never got around to getting the tube fixed. . . . " She is rattled now.

"The flat is fine, Mrs. Murphy," I say, squeezing Hia's hand.

"Eily, please."

"Is Mr. Murphy—?"

"Mr. Murphy died in 1979."

We are silent.

"But Jimmy—James Sullivan, I mean—mentioned that your visit here isn't solely for family reasons. I understand that you have a project."

I pause to let Hia enter the conversation. She demurs, arching an eyebrow in mock anticipation. "Hia has a project," I answer sourly. "I have some free time."

"But I thought—?"

"I might do research into the local music scene."

"Do you play the fiddle?"

"No."

"You know your—"

"I know."

"I heard him once."

I cross deliberately to the door. "We're a little tired," I say.

Eily Murphy hands me a key for the downstairs lock. "I work mornings at the chemist's, but am still at home a good deal. Please feel free—"

"We will," I promise.

She is about to add a thought when a sound from the kitchen, of an object hitting the floor with a grunt, cuts her off.

"I should mention—"

A shadow darkens the carpet.

"—one other occupant."

A massive Persian cat, belly listing from side to side, ambles into view.

"Carolan," she says.

"Carolan?"

"The cat. He lives here."

"Lives here?"

"Has for nearly fifteen years."

"I see," I say.

"In the kitchen, mostly. Loves the padded chairs. Eats relatively little, despite his girth."

Carolan has a softball for a head. He raises it to probe the air with a bow tie of whiskers, then issues a plangent meow, his neck arched dramatically.

"He wants you to draw nearer."

The cat's great age is apparent up close: his orange coat is drab and wiry, and his green eyes, halved by cataracts, are glazed. Carolan has a moist black nose, a ruffled brow, a double chin of fur and fat.

"Will he be bothered if we move in?" Hia asks.

"He'll be delighted for the company. The creature has been lonely these last few months, locked in the flat with only birds on the windowsill to sustain him."

"He eats birds?"

"Watches them, dear. For hours on end."

Twenty minutes later, Eily Murphy calls from the stairwell with a tray of tea and biscuits. Though her face is less pinched, she still stares at my leg as I descend. "I fear I've made a mess of things," she whispers.

"The cat is fine."

"I mean with your friend Hia. I was a little surprised. Shocked, even. But I meant no offence."

The hallway fixture casts a gentle light; her face is more vibrant, and youthful, than at first glance. But her eyes are sad. "I'm delighted to have you in the house, Pat," she adds. "To have you both."

Hia is waiting for me at the top.

"Mrs. Lynch . . . ," I joke.

"She is a nice woman. I can tell."

"You were mean to her."

"She deserved it. We work things out later."

Hia always keeps her promises. Satisfied, I change subjects. "Sorry about the television."

"Sorry about Carolan."

"I don't mind cats."

"I don't mind missing TV."

"You mind."

"And you hate cats."

"Only when they're surrogates," I say, thinking of Jig and Reel, and their offspring.

"I'll watch television in other places."

Hia proposes we try the bed. Without waiting for my consent, she extracts the mattress, shouldering the frame when it refuses to unfold, and lays out the musty bedding. Then she rescues a terrified Carolan from beneath a chair and deposits him atop the blankets. My turn comes, and I undress. But Hia's enthusiasm isn't primarily sexual; she is by nature a snuggler, a proponent of the partner as foot-warmer and masseur, story-teller and therapist. The job description is lengthy, duties are somewhat vague, and the order of operations is unclear. Though willing to accept the position, I am also cautious, leery of giving offence, acting crude.

"In love . . . ," I say.

"Shh."

" . . . you and I . . . "

"Shh, Pat."

She hates it when I talk.

We gaze out at our new aerie. Jet-lag, sex, a lack of solid food leave us both languorous, too relaxed to even venture to the toilet. Twilight dims within the room; the curtains, rocking on their wooden hooks, are fully drawn but still six inches short of joining. Noises from the outside—dogs barking, tires over wet pavement—enter freely. Odours are pungent. I smell low tide, cut grass, cooking meat. Hia smells apples.

"All the furniture in this place smells of apples," she says, tracing my eyelids with her finger.

"What would your ancestors think?"

"About apples?"

I wait.

"My ancestors are dead."

"But still with you? Still watching over the living, protecting them from harm?"

"You know official story."

"Unofficially?"

"Still with us," she agrees. "But very weak and ineffective. Too many miles separate where they are from where I am now."

"Worlds apart?"

"Worlds destroyed."

Carolan's bold leap back up from the ground sets the

mattress springs squeaking.

"Even your—?" I ask.

Hia sighs.

"I didn't mean—"

"Even her, yes."

As always, we leave it there.

The fog lifts overnight. Dingle town is set in a vast, sculpted landscape. The largest stretch of level ground skirts the shoreline. Otherwise, the village is a network of lanes that climb, level, and sometimes end before rocky inclines. Protecting it on three sides are the same hills that rib the peninsula. While a few brick bungalows scale the slopes, and a few masonry farmhouses crumble near the summits, most habitations, wary of the isolation, huddle on more solid terrain.

The sky above the town is perpetually in flight. On a clear day, it both vaults into infinity and recedes further into the ocean. The pull westward is strong, as is the sense, gathered from the layering of colours in the middle margins, of staggering dimensions. The blue closest to land is icy, dark; a few miles out it lightens to aqua, then to pastel, then to a shade too ephemeral to describe.

Our day is spent mocking conventions of domestic bliss. Hia supervises my tidying of the flat, dictates rearrangements of the furniture (she soothes Carolan while I topsy-turvy his world), banishes to the closet all but one of the artworks, and then accompanies me to the supermarket, where her advice on what to buy is pithy—food and tea. She does not cook. For years she hated to cook, but did. Then her sister turned eighteen. Nhung was now an adult; adults could look after themselves. Adults could cook, if they wished, or not cook, if they preferred. Hia preferred sandwiches, tins of soup, reheated fast food. I, however, wished to cook. Not gourmet, necessarily, but hot dishes, fresh vegetables and salads. In Dingle, I will prepare these modest meals, and offer to share them with her. She will accept my offers; about all things less than vital to her spiritual diet Hia is indifferent, acquiescent in a distracted, faintly condescending way. The problem is that she will also bite the hand that feeds her. She will bite it regularly, gleefully, on the not-so-faintly condescending assumption that the hand will never fight back.

In the evening, we settle in separate rooms. While boxing up my belongings for storage in Hia's apartment (I gave up the lease on my place), I had to decide which books and cassettes to bring on the trip. To my surprise, the decision was easy: no books, one tape, and a photocopy of an album cover. Now, ignoring Hia's grumbles, I pin the photocopy to the wall outside the bathroom.

It is a sketch of a fiddler, set against a sea of musical notation. Barely an outline, the sketch renders up few details: the musician is seated, wears boots and a bulky sweater, and holds the instrument high, like a violinist. The score behind the man—he floats atop a crest of dotted notes—belongs to the slip-jig that lends the album its title: "The Drunken Butterfly".

The slip-jig was composed by Sean O Conchuir, whose solo performances of his own tunes, and some twenty other pieces, make up the record. According to the linear notes, O Conchuir was a legend in Irish music circles, a reclusive genius who permitted only this single recording of his fiddling. The album was taped during a session at O Conchuir's house in 1973, when he was seventy-four. (He must be long dead.) I came into possession of *The Drunken Butterfly* three years later, among the gifts at the notorious birthday dinner. How my mother obtained the record remains a mystery. *Why* she gave it to her son, at that stage a lukewarm rock-and-roller, is easier to fathom: Sean O Conchuir lived his entire life in and around Dunquin, the village across from the Great Blasket island.

I was unimpressed. Even at eighteen, I could recognize

a parent's attempt to provide her child a link with a dispossessed past. (Francine has never been to Europe, never mind Ireland.) For years the album languished, cellophane intact, at the back of my bin. Then, on a spring night during my final undergraduate semester, I awoke from a rare dream—I almost never dream, or don't remember if I do—to discover an image printed on my eyelids. Recognizing it, I jumped up, tore off the jacket wrapping, and switched on the turntable. For a moment I expected a voice, like God in movies, to blast from the speakers. What I heard instead were bursts of bristly melody, as alien to my ears as atonality would have been to Handel.

Among the worst offenders was a "A Lament for Paudeen Bawn." Listed in the notes as an air composed by the collective "traditional", it had three parts built around three core phrases, used almost no ornamentation, and repeated itself with only faint variations. The third part was especially skeletal, more silence than sound, and simply dissolved back into the opening. No resolution: just fifty-eight seconds of aggrieved experience. The plainness of the piece seemed wilful, an impression nourished by O Conchuir's terse rendering.

I was even more unimpressed. The album cover, though, was now integral to my dreamscape, and became a decoration in my bedroom, then in the apartment I rented after graduation. I also developed a taste for O Conchuir's cerebral reflections—he wrote of his art as being his *heart's delight* and a *pitiful echo of the eternal music that is the Lord*—and took to summoning head-shots of this invisible (no photo was provided) and clearly eccentric man. The O Conchuir of my imagination was one part Samuel Beckett, one part Barry Fitzgerald, two parts Davey Russell. While his music was not appealing, he played it with great seriousness and devotion.

Finally, at around the time I met Hia, the music began to resonate. The unaccompanied fiddle can be scrupulous.

Sean O Conchuir's brief treatments—no tune lasted longer than ninety seconds, and several featured bizarre interpolations from Bach and Mozart—were so intense they sounded less a rendering of the melody than a baring of its essence. The fervour approached prayer; several cuts repeated key phrases with a gathering urgency only to diminish on a single sustained note. "A Lament for Paudeen Bawn" ended with a note of such gravity I could never be sure if the air was empty or if my ear had failed to track the thinning sound. The lament affected me strangely. With each listen of it I sensed I was being watched. Once or twice, I sensed even that I was being noticed.

Hia also unpacks: sketch pads, boxes of pencils, sticks of charcoal, rulers, a large and small compass, an abacus. No books either, no photographs, no teachers. By evening she has begun to work at the kitchen table and I have begun to brew her cups of tea while disciplining my gaze to avoid the open pad. Hia knows what she seeks. Her contours are already defined. She will strive towards clarity: of method, result, resolution. I will seem a muddle by comparison. I will seem—

Why would I compare us? I dabble. She draws to save her life. At the end of the day, the work doesn't matter to me. At the end of the day, nothing else matters to her.

Chapter 4

Michael O Cathain left Dingle on April 11, 1953. He boarded the Tralee bus, transferred to a train to Killarney, then switched again for Cork City. During the longer ride he read through the journal he had kept from the spring of 1948 until the previous October, when a near-calamity at sea had convinced him to emigrate. Except for a few passages recounting music sessions in homes around the peninsula, the journal consisted of reminiscences about Michael's childhood on the Great Blasket island. Faithfully written and dated each week, the entries reconstructed with exacting detail the first twelve years of his life, on the apparent understanding that the following twelve years were either inconsequential, or lacked the urgency to compel his pen.

One passage concerned the Second World War. For the older islanders, the war was a rumour of disturbance in England and of fratricide on the continent, similar to the earlier commotion that had bestowed upon the Great Blasket a grim harvest of goods, washed ashore from torpedoed supply ships. Youngsters, though, were fascinated by the fighting, racing down to the harbour to pepper visitors with questions about the Blitz of London and the occupation of Paris. In November 1940, a German bomber went down near the most westerly Blasket island. Unbeknownst to villagers, the plane's crew survived the crash and spent two days on Inishvickillane, before deciding to assail the waters in their dinghy. Believing it was attached to the mainland, the three Germans stopped at the eastern face of the Great Blasket, scaled treacherous Hawk's Cliff, then marched the five kilometres into the village. Hence their assault from the rear, and the shouts of the women at the well above the settlement that the island was being invaded. The enemy, startled to discover more water below the village, pacified the natives with cigarettes and chocolate. Children were especially impressed by the leather-jacketed visitors, and took to following the men around, imitating their loping strides and guttural speech. Michael had a conversation with the crew leader in English, a language both spoke poorly. You are a prisoner, Michael told the officer. You must go to jail. To which the German, grinning and gesturing at the surrounding island, answered: Boy, it is *you* who are the prisoner. But what a beautiful jail!

The officer crossed to Dunquin the next morning to officially surrender. Two days later an Irish naval vessel anchored in the sound and arrested the crew, who spent the remainder of the war in a POW camp in the North. Michael even wrote a letter to the German at a camp in County Armagh.

Another entry concerned a tape recorder that belonged to an English scholar who had visited the Great Blasket regularly when Michael was a child, to record a woman famous for her story-telling. Known on the island as the "talking machine", the tape player ended up in the house of Michael's boyhood friend Gearoid O Se. The journal catalogued the O Se home with the thoroughness of a museum guide. The main room, which functioned as kitchen, living room, and sleeping quarters, measured twenty by twelve feet, and had whitewashed masonry and a wooden floor. Pegs on walls held paraffin lamps and framed holy pictures, photos of relatives in America, a mirror placed near the door to reflect incoming light. Above the fireplace was a clock; below the only window stood a table, with a long bench across from it for visitors. In an island home, the centre of the room was kept free of furniture for social gatherings and dances, where, Michael explained, musicians gathered by the fire, spectators lined the walls, and the middle area dissolved into a dervish of high-stepping heels and swirling petticoats.

But in the O Ses' it was the tape recorder, perched atop a table by the entrance, that held sway. Guests tended to comment on it, and its long-absent owner, even before greeting the woman of the house. Gearoid's mother polished the machine religiously, and children snuck in to twist and turn the knobs, in the hope of hearing their voices seize the air. Except the tape player never worked. It was also never collected by the scholar, and by 1939 the majority of the people who could account for its presence on the Great Blasket were either dead or living abroad.

The entry concluded on a rare autobiographical note. When the island school closed in 1941, Tomas O Cathain sent his only child to live with Moira Burke in Dykegate Lane, Dingle. Years later, while a student at the national school in town, Michael was assigned a new book in Irish class. The book was a collection of tales recorded on the Great Blasket in the late 1920s, and was worth reading, the teacher intoned, for both the quality of its language and the timelessness of its insights. Though Michael knew the storyteller personally (she had assisted at his birth), and had heard all the tales before, told in an island house with a fire blazing, friends gathered, the ocean in a rage and the wind piping through a derelict building down the lane: tales told differently each night, as alive to flights of fancy as seabirds were alive to updrafts; despite possessing this wealth of detail, flesh to the bone of the text, the sixteen-year-old merely flushed with embarrassment and anger. In hindsight, Michael's anger matured into self-loathing at his perceived failure to "defend" the story-teller, the tales, the island, even himself. Defend them against what? The journal failed to outline the charges.

Many of the entries kept returning to the same childhood scene. In this episode, which ran through the text as a leitmotif, the boy lay on a mattress of heather and spring flowers in a gully so steep that, from flat on his back, his vision was evenly partitioned into sea and sky. Only sea and sky and, if he turned his head, hares scurrying from holes and birds that swerved upwards, drawing so near that he stretched to touch their wings. (*Like trying to cup smoke in your hands,* he wrote.) The gully was tucked above the Lochar Rocks on the north side of the island. Most villagers preferred the gentler slopes of the south face, its views of the Skelligs and the mainland. Along the entire length of the opposite side, in contrast, the vista was monotone. What was Michael looking at? Passing ships were rare, and the next land mass, Newfoundland, was four thousand kilometres to the west. The north face of the Great Blasket was isolated from even the remote community and exposed to elements so harsh, dimensions so ineffable, that a healthy mind would have been tempted to deny them. Still, it was here the boy came daily and, burrowing into the heather, allowed the emptiness to fill him.

Michael made a final entry into the journal from a hotel room in the port of Cobh.

Evening, April 11

Stood on Reenbeg Point at dawn this morning and watched a seagull plummet from the sky, like a torch from a cliff, to be extinguished in the darkness below. Kept waiting for the bird to emerge. It didn't, or else I lost sight of it in the racing sea.

Got jarred with Seamus last night. He offered me cash for my half of the MR. Keep it, Seamie, I said.

Payment for putting up with my foul moods! Poor man shed a tear in the snug, claiming it was sweat. Hope he marries a local girl and settles.

Have I any choice but to leave? Father doesn't need me, that's certain. Even coming to Dingle for the farewell was a bother. They'll evacuate the island soon, next spring at the latest, and house the old ones in Dunquin. Sooner the better, I say. Clear the thing, then seal it, like a crypt. Skirl in the ear. Pounding in the skull. *Ta rud eigin in easnamh anseo.*

Left the fiddle with Seamus. The music is the moment, surely. Rooted in time, as a life, and in place, as a graveyard. Even a vain man knows his body can travel while his heart stays behind.

Blather. To the new island, so.

Early the next morning Michael O Cathain boarded a ship that had arrived during the night from Liverpool. When the ship sailed two hours later he stood alone on a deck. All the other passengers had chosen to bid farewell to family, and country, from portside; only Michael preferred the starboard view. Not until the vessel was well out to sea did he remove the journal from his jacket and, bending over the railing, allow the book to slip through his hands.

ONLY CHILD

Chapter 5

James Sullivan has asked us to join him for a drink this evening. Eily Murphy climbs the staircase to relate the message. Our breathless landlady frowns on naming the venue, then extends apologies, on Sullivan's behalf, for him not having greeted us at the bus. The apology is unnecessary. When she provided James Sullivan's address, care of a grocery shop in town, my mother explained that he had once sent her a letter of condolence, and therefore constituted her sole living contact in Dingle. Given that the letter must have been written decades ago, even receiving an answer was lucky.

The pub is located somewhere near the pier. Grey Lane, nestled above the harbour, runs parallel to the town's waterfront boulevard. We follow Strand Street, admiring the painted exteriors of buildings and smiling at the stares of locals. The stares are innocent; even I would gape at the sight of a North American redwood swinging the arm of his bonsai Asian companion, gaits dissimilar, steps out of synch. I am basically a stroller, predisposed to dawdle. Hia, in contrast, thunders through landscapes. Her rhythms range from the trot to the sprint, and she marches to one drummer only—her own. Holding hands obliges me to keep up, her to slow down.

Arriving a few minutes early, we wander out the cement jetty to watch trawlers navigate the harbour. Crews unload the larger ships at the end, separating catches into bins for pick up by a local plant. Smaller boats, relegated to the eastern flank, moor side by side, forcing skippers to straddle successive bows to reach solid ground. Birds divebomb the waters, making tidy splashes. The air is acrid and the sun over Mount Eagle—the ridge stretching across the southwest side of the harbour—is an aureole, flecks of purple and red above a saintly head.

Our search for a bar called, rather plainly, "T. Daly", is brief. The pub sits at the foot of the pier, a drab building with two windows and a railing that runs the length of the glass. Both windows are blinded; one boasts a CLOSED sign dangling from a string.

Inside, all is dim and hushed. A bell clangs as I close the door, the floorboards sigh beneath Hia's footfall. The bar, a wooden counter with a pole as baseboard, extends down the room until encountering a snug at the back. Stools huddle near the front; aluminum beer kegs stand at attention below one window. The ceiling is high, a floral inlay centred by a brass fixture, and the walls are decorated with Guinness advertisements and photos of football squads. Behind the counter, amid shelves of glasses and rows of inverted liquor bottles, are Bank of Ireland calendars, one for June 1985 and the other, faded to parchment, for May 1958.

In front of the counter are two men who belong to the 1958 calendar: caps and jackets, pipes and pints, green wellingtons to their knees. Neither figure turns at our entrance. A third man, dressed in a suit jacket and bulbous tie, makes a gesture—half nod, half wink—that I assume is a nervous tic. He also humphs, his eyes hooded by folds of skin.

Hia is fascinated by the calendars. "Wrong years," she tells him. "Wrong decade on that one."

"You're Hia?"

She confirms it.

"And you," he says to me. "It's himself."

"Whose self?"

"The very man."

"The man?"

"We won't talk here," he decides, taking my arm. "Not in public."

The "public", as far as I can tell, are mannequins propped against the wood. No one even bothers to serve them; the bar area is vacant. Still, James Sullivan (I presume) insists we retire to the snug. He asks about my limp.

"A long story," I answer, stunned that he also noticed.

"Happened when you were a boy?"

"Right."

"Accident?"

"Right."

"Two accidents?"

I tense.

"Broke the same leg twice?"

We squeeze through a narrow door into the chamber. I roll my eyes at Hia.

"It's barely noticeable," I add.

"Absolutely."

"Few people even realize—"

"The secret is ours."

"Pat likes secrets," Hia says.

"I'd say he does."

"I'd say I don't," I reply. "No more than the next person."

"Who would that be?"

"What?"

"The next person—who would that be?"

"Me!" Hia says.

"I'd say so."

The snug is a roofless closet, bench seating for four maximum, with frosted glass halfway to the ceiling, and a slot, like a ticket window at a racetrack, to service occupants directly from the bar.

"Now," Sullivan says.

"Small room," Hia comments.

"Cozy."

"You *are* Mr. Sullivan?"

"Mr. Sullivan is dead these thirty years. I am his mere shadow—his son Jimmy."

"Joan McGreevy is dead too," Hia says.

"It's in the air."

What is in the air, besides the weird camaraderie between Hia and our host, is smoke from the cigarette Jimmy Sullivan lights. He is a slight man, nearly as short as Hia, his actual size betrayed by the way clothes hang from his frame and the delicacy of his neck and wrists. Only when he hitches up his pants is an egg-shaped paunch revealed. Determining his age is equally difficult. The bristle covering his chin is white and his bushy eyebrows are grey, but his hair, long and thick and combed close over the skull with gel, is a silver-shocked black. Likewise his eyes, often a murky blue, that suddenly take in light when the conversation is animated. Sullivan has the slouch and shuffle of a pensioner. In the snug, though, he sits ramrod straight and jiggles a foot, occasionally grasping it to harness the energy. Keeping still for even a minute is a struggle; he crosses then uncrosses his legs, tugs on his ear, scratches his scalp.

"You'll call me Jimmy," he commands.

"Okay."

"You'll call me any time, day or night. I'm only up the road. John Street, number sixty-seven."

"O'Shea's grocery shop," I say. "We walked by there yesterday. Didn't see you, though."

"My imitation of a shopkeeper is barely passable."

"I'm sure—"

"A feeble anchor, I'd say. Something to hold me down, keep me here—lost, unhappy, and at home. That sort of thing," he explains breezily.

I nod.

"But have I even offered you a drink?"

"It isn't necessary."

"The hell it isn't."

He stretches across to the slot beside my head and raps on the wood. "Now," he repeats.

We wait in silence. Jimmy rolls his cigarette against the rim of an ashtray. A clowning Hia stares at the window, her mouth an anticipatory O. I feel like William Tell's son: apple on my head, Father's pistol pointed in the general direction. The slot opens. I jump.

"Jimmy?" a voice calls.

"Introductions first. Tommy, this is Pat Keane. And Hia, ah, Hia. . . . "

Hia provides her family name.

A face fills the book-sized window. It belongs to a rugged man with a crooked nose and a swollen lower lip. The visage is replaced by a hand that juts into the snug. "Pleasure," the hand says.

I shake it. The grip is acute.

"He-uh, is it?"

Hia receives a gentler shake.

"Not from around here, Hia?"

"Dublin," Hia says.

"I figured."

"I thought you were from Vietnam?" I oblige.

"Vietnam?" the voice says with a whistle. "That's no joke over there, I'm told."

"You think they're laughing up in Dublin, Tommy?"

"What about me," I ask. "Don't you want to know where I'm from?"

Both men chuckle.

"Toronto," I say.

Jimmy humphs.

"Ontario."

"Lad," he says, shaking his head.

"Canada."

"Will you listen to this?"

"Crazy," Hia agrees.

I turn on her. "You don't even know what we're talking about!"

Hia, an infrequent but amusing drinker (she turns pink immediately), orders a glass of beer. I ask for a pint. Jimmy requests a Britvic.

"Beg pardon?" the barman says.

"Beg nothing. You heard me."

The window closes. Our host flares another cigarette, offers the pack. Hia takes one, dangling it from a corner of her mouth á la Humphrey Bogart.

"You don't smoke," I say.

"Only when I drink."

"You don't drink."

"Only when I smoke."

I jump again. Calming, I distribute the glasses that materialize in the slot. One glass contains orange juice. By process of elimination, I ascertain its owner. Jimmy's enthusiasm is unconvincing.

"Cheers," he says, wincing at the taste. He also wishes us good luck. Then: "Come here a minute."

We are close already. So close that I only just gave up looking for the motor causing the bench to vibrate. Jimmy's foot jiggles; my stomach churns. Still, Hia and I slide over.

"Is the old hen treating you decent?"

"The old—?"

"Eily's a wily one," he elaborates. "She didn't try anything, did she?"

"We have a cat," Hia says. "Carolan."

"Carolan? I thought he was dead."

"Just fat," I say.

"I recollect being told the animal passed away shortly after Joan McGreevy. Are you certain?"

"She's dead. He isn't," Hia summarizes.

"I wouldn't be so sure," Jimmy says, cocking an eyebrow.

"Sure about what?"

"I'd ask questions."

Hia isn't following.

"We will," I promise.

"But you're settled, are you—set up comfortable, ready to get down to business?"

"Ready," Hia agrees. She would offer more, but her first drag on the cigarette induces a coughing fit. She also tips back her glass. "Phew," she says, touching her florid cheeks. "So warm in here."

"An oven," I concur.

"You can't pass wind in this town without it being announced at the eleven o'clock mass."

"Watch out," I warn. "Hia's a good Irish Catholic."

"I'd say she is."

"And Pat's a funny Vietnamese Buddhist."

"Is he?"

"Am I?"

"I'd say," Hia says.

"Cheers," Jimmy says.

I rap on the window, more to encourage air into our cell than to order again. The noise level in the pub has been rising steadily; the ceiling fixture was recently switched on, throwing shapes against the back wall. Viewed through opaque glass, the figures outside are puppets in a shadow theatre, kneeling and standing, laughing and crying, all on command, their strings skilfully hidden.

"Jimmy?" the voice says.

"The same?" I ask the others. Hia nods eagerly. Jimmy shrugs. "The same," I order.

The same arrives a minute later.

"Another Britvic for the Father," Tommy the bartender announces.

"Father?" Hia says. "Where is your son?"

Jimmy pales.

I hold up a five-pound note.

"You're going nowhere, lad," the voice predicts, refusing my money.

Our host waits until the window closes. "Gobshite," he mutters. Then, again: "Come here a minute, you two."

Any closer, and we'll have to sit in his lap. Though we bend forward, Hia and I still strain to hear Jimmy's words. His face does not benefit from the scrutiny. A moment ago it was vital, eyes mocking, eyebrows in exclamation. Suddenly he seems an old man: features shrivelled, skin translucent, red capillaries behind both cheeks. The transformation coincides with an equally abrupt change in demeanour.

"The business," he begins. "Tell us everything."

"What's to tell?" I say.

"Everything!"

"Be more specific."

He addresses Hia. "Do I have to pound it into this lad's skull?"

Hia isn't sure if she should laugh.

"You of all people ought to understand," he resumes. "What glues us together, I'd say. Keeps us afloat. Stops us from drifting."

"Out to sea?"

"A perpetual diaspora," he sighs.

Hia stares into her beer for a translation.

"Live and let live, eh?" Jimmy says with scorn. "Other people's lives are other people's lives?"

"I don't read minds, Jimmy."

"I don't understand this English," Hia says.

"You understand full well."

"I do?"

"Not you. *Him*."

"Me," I say.

Jimmy tries to hold my gaze. I look at my feet.

"Do you have God?" he asks.

"Do I *what*?"

"Answer my question."

"No."

"I figured."

He turns back to Hia. "In the eyes," he says, speaking in abbreviations, as if his thoughts, fretted over too long, have been pared of their grammar. "The manner of the walk, the speech, even the inward smile. If not God, then what? Other extremes. Other implosions."

Hia's bewilderment is acute.

"Damned if you have him," Jimmy concludes, "damned if you don't."

I have had enough. "Hia is working on a series of drawings," I say loudly and clearly. "Her subject is an ancient temple complex in Cambodia."

"Sounds great," he answers blandly.

"And Pat wants to—" Hia begins.

"The music, right. Don't I know all about it."

I refuse to be baited.

"The family inheritance. A father's legacy to his son. The great old tunes. The rare old melodies. That dead horse," he concludes, crushing a cigarette in the ashtray.

My voice is tight. "My mother is from northern Ontario. She gets the lyrics wrong to most songs."

"What do you think you know about him?"

"Who?" Hia asks.

"Nothing at all," I reply, reeling from the shifts in the conversation. "The man is a stranger to me."

"And what do you think you know about it?"

"What?" Hia asks.

"I know only a little."

"But you want to learn more?"

"Hia wants me to learn more. My mother wants—"

He stares.

"I suppose," I say.

My feeble answer seems to please him. The anger vanishes and he stretches across the snug to touch my arm.

"Can we leave now?" I request. "Maybe drink in the main bar, with everyone else?"

Jimmy's eyes fix on me again. So intent and affectionate is the gaze that for a moment I envision him and me somewhere else, alone, set against a colossal landscape, an ocean sky. I close my eyes to ward off the image.

"How much?"

The figure escapes my lips. "Six foot four."

He nods.

"A hundred and seventy pounds, soaking wet," I add.

Hia's eyes bulge.

"Anything else?"

I ponder. "Good pitch," I say. "Never forget a melody once I hear it. Never confuse one tune with another. Play no instruments, though. Heard the fiddle for the first time when I was twenty."

"Near-sighted, by any chance?"

"Possibly."

"Doing anything about it?"

"Not so far."

He opens the door. "Welcome back."

"Thanks," Hia answers.

"And you, with the rosy cheeks!"

"Sweet Molly Malone," she agrees. (She did background "research" in Toronto.)

The room is wall-to-wall revellers, mostly male, mostly elderly. The area behind the counter, where Tommy the bartender should be, is once more empty. When I turn around, Jimmy Sullivan has also vanished; even on tiptoe, a full head above the crowd, I cannot locate him. The interrogation appears over for the night. Hia, whose bloom is rapidly fading, begs to leave.

"Phew!" she says on the street. "What language were you and him talking?"

Though I have an answer, the response is, like so much else I've said this evening, not mine. I did once earn my living with other people's words. But other people's words from my own mouth?

I sing:

In Dingle's deep ditches
Where girls speak with glitches
I first talked of love
To sweet Hia Thi Loi

"You're weird."

"This night is weird."

"I'd say," Hia giggles.

"Do I have God?" I say in exasperation. "What kind of a question is that?"

"I do."

I ask.

"Have God."

Besides tanning to lobster, Hia also gets painfully literal-minded when inebriated.

We cross the unpaved parking lot separating one section of Strand Street from the harbour. Though the rain stopped in the afternoon, it left a legacy of deep, uncharted puddles that glimmer in the dark. Hia is in trot tempo. She curses each splash, refusing to avoid the puddles, take my hand, or answer queries regarding her health. But an answer is soon provided: before the looming shape of a boat stranded ten metres from shore, she drops to her knees, gasps, and vomits.

I slip around the trawler. It is a derelict old tub, reeking of rotten wood and stagnant water, and I hesitate to slide my hand along the runner. Cloud-veiled moonlight, reflected off the harbour, illuminates the prow. I glance idly at a name painted on the side while listening to Hia dry-heave and spit. I would help her, of course, in any way I could, if only she would ask. I need help often, and have no trouble calling on loved ones. (I don't think they mind.) But Hia is different. She never needs help. Certainly she never asks for it.

ONLY CHILD

Chapter 6

On a deck four levels above the matchbox cabin he shared with three other emigrants, Michael spent much of the week at sea draped over the railing, watching water surge against the hull. The dimensions of the ship distanced the experience from him, as did its function: a boat built exclusively for transportation seemed an alien, faintly ludicrous thing. Michael also pinched Sweet Aftons between his fingers and played gin rummy. His partner was a Tipperary native named Davey Russell. While the majority of passengers were dissuaded from the open decks by wind and rain, Michael and Davey were indifferent to the weather, and actually liked the bracing air. When not chasing blown cards, they talked. Mostly, Davey Russell talked and Michael listened, his features permanently tense.

"There won't be too many more," Davey predicted one afternoon. "It's all aircraft now—Vanguards, DC-4s. Fourteen hours, London to New York. They'll render these behemoths extinct in no time."

"I'm feeling rare myself."

"I'm speaking of the boat."

"Are you?"

"A man would be a fool to rot on board a ship when a plane will get you there in a flash."

"Surely."

"Are you listening to me, Michael?"

"I'm thinking this," Michael answered. "What kind of madness is it to be locked in a metal machine that blasts across the sky, at the mercy of strangers, in the hands of a God whose benevolence is far from certain?"

Davey Russell grinned. Popping a mint into his mouth, he offered the roll.

"I don't care for sweets."

"Any sweets?"

"Not to my taste."

"Cream-cakes? " Davey said, feigning dismay. "Flan or meringue, chocolate éclairs—none of it?"

"I don't mind a hard licorice, now and then."

"Hard licorice?"

"Now and then."

"You are a piece of work," Davey said.

In Montreal, where the liner discharged its passengers, Michael was quizzed by an immigration officer about his name.

"O-Kath-ayn?" the man tried.

"O-Ka-hoin."

The official, whose nametag read "Lucien Fortin", rubbed the bridge of his nose. "Maybe you can help us a little?"

"K-E-A-N-E," Michael said. "Family name, Keane. First name, Michael. Middle initial S, for Seosamh."

"Show-what?"

"Joseph."

"You don't mind if I change the form?"

"Why would I mind?"

"People have strong feelings about names," the officer explained. "In this town, for sure."

Michael Joseph Keane, born Micheal Seosamh O Cathain on October 9, 1928, in Dunquin parish, Kerry, Ireland, had his passport stamped with a six-month visa, commencing on May 3, 1953. The visa allowed him to travel within Canada and to seek temporary employment. Once the period was up, he could apply for landed-immigrant status with the help of a sponsor.

"I haven't any expectations," Michael assured the man.

Encouraged by Davey Russell, who had determined that his fellow émigré needed both his friendship *and* his guidance, Michael travelled on that same day to Toronto, where English was dominant and winters were less harsh. The men boarded the train at Windsor Station at midnight and pulled into Union Station in time for morning rush hour. Davey's brother was waiting for them at the gate. He loaded their bags into a maroon Buick that climbed University Avenue at the speed of the Tralee-Cork Express. The ride took twenty minutes. While Davey and his brother chatted in the front seat, Michael kept wiping the rear window with his cuff. What he glimpsed—office buildings and apartment blocks, the Provincial Legislature, low-lying suburban sprawl—was fascinating at first, then ordinary, and finally of no interest. He let the glass fog over.

Within a week he and Davey Russell had rented an apartment on Church Street that had a refrigerator, hot and cold taps, mice. Davey liked a clean flat, but was untidy; Michael was indifferent to the state of the lodgings, yet fastidious about his own hygiene. Davey loved to eat, but couldn't toast bread; Michael didn't mind frying up a few rashers and eggs, roasting a piece of beef, even though his appetite tended to abandon him when he sat at the table. A modest drinker, Davey enjoyed the Irish bars that were springing up in the downtown; Michael, who kept whisky in the cupboard and beer in the refrigerator, detested them.

The flat was three blocks north of Davey's favourite watering-hole. The evening he dragged Michael to the Shamrock to enjoy a session of "genuine traditional music and song", Michael lasted through fifteen minutes of rebel ballads and whistle tunes.

"Is it the nostalgia of the place?" Davey asked.

"Not the nostalgia."

"The sentiment?"

"Hardly."

"Then it must be the music. . . . "

"What music?" Michael snapped.

Davey Russell, a pigeon-chested man with an easy smile and a warm laugh, gazed at his taciturn friend as if for the first time. "Do you play?" he wondered.

Michael was silent.

"An instrument, Michael—do you play?"

"Don't be daft."

Davey turned to the others at the table. "Mr. Keane is an islandman."

The men, mostly Dubliners who had never ventured west of Phoenix Park until compelled by unemployment to cross the Atlantic Ocean, nodded appreciatively.

"Was it a poet who said, 'No man is an island?'" Davey continued. "Well, let me tell you, he'd never met up with these lads."

"Enough, Davey."

"Raised by seals. Learned by puffins. Reared on saltwater and fattened on kelp."

"Enough!"

They looked for work together. Michael's impulse was to seek short-term jobs: construction, bartending, road repair. But Davey, on the advice of his brother, insisted they apply for the salaried "lifer" positions that were appearing around the city. The Toronto Transit Commission, Ontario Hydro, public works, police and fire departments, even the library systems—all were advertising for staff. The police had an advantage over the rest. If the force wanted a recruit badly enough, they took care of immigration: citizenship in twenty-four months, guaranteed. For Davey Russell, secure in his family connection, the enticement meant little. Michael was ambivalent about police work, ambivalent about getting a proper job (he kept thinking he already had one), but he also knew of no relatives in Canada, no connections, no one who could help.

He got as far as the medical examination. The doctor had a list. His right arm, which had bothered him since the boating incident with Seamus, had in fact been fractured, and then healed incorrectly. The damage was permanent; he would never be able to fire a gun accurately. Michael was also colour-blind, myopic, and prone to inner-ear infections that could threaten his balance. The doctor apologized for rejecting him, and recommended he make an appointment for glasses.

Both men were eventually offered positions with the TTC. Davey, who had an Irish driver's licence, was put in a program for bus operators. Lacking specific skills, Michael was assigned to the Eglinton division. Beginning in August 1953, he laboured eight hours a day in the catacombs beneath the Yonge-Eglinton intersection, cleaning and painting around the construction crews, then working on tunnel maintenance. As a teenager, Michael had shuddered at newspaper reports of Welsh coal miners trapped in collapsed shafts a kilometre below the surface, the air thinning as the hours, then days, passed. Panicking, the miners would claw at the walls, cause the chamber to cave in. They would drink urine and eat dirt. They would gag, bite their tongues, gouge out their own eyes. Airplanes floating above the earth and humans scurrying in tunnels within it struck him as equally nightmarish, equally unnatural. But Michael now earned his living underground, and soon, according to Davey Russell, air travel would render transatlantic passenger ships obsolete.

Every morning Michael stood at the street corner taking a final drag on an Export. He would pinch his tongue for tobacco, don his hardhat, then stride down a dark passageway. Only in the evenings did he reel from dizziness, and sometimes vomit.

Chapter 7

Funny, I didn't ask for Jimmy Sullivan's help, but I'm getting it anyway. Eily Murphy ascends the stairwell again this morning with another message: I have an "interview" with a fiddler in an hour, a meeting arranged, on my behalf, by Jimmy. At first I am miffed. I had no plans to accost Dingle musicians with questions about their craft or queries regarding local history. Of course, I had no real plans at all, which makes me susceptible to the schemes of others. ("I have a life philosophy," Hia once told me, "to make sure no one, except God, tries to act my father.") Hia thinks I'm afraid of being original. She thinks I should take risks, make changes, develop a life philosophy. I think she goes on about the importance of change in other people because she is incapable of it herself. I think I ignore the matter because I am incapable of not adapting, not doing what is needed to get by minus the disasters that pass, in the minds of some, for passionate living.

There I go again: comparing us.

But the interviews might serve a purpose. My interest in my father's music has always been private, a family secret, and silent, a family shame. Unlike Hia, who comes by the language of her compulsion so naturally she couldn't be bothered with the grammar, I am challenged in the tongue.

As a result, I am more concerned with not misusing words than with using them newly, freshly. Still, the vocabulary of the form, both the technical jargon and its offspring—terms that aspire to explain what is mysterious yet primal to human experience—is one I am instinctively drawn to speak. It isn't mine, exactly, but then, coming from where I come, being who I am, what language is? The issue shouldn't be proprietorship. The issue should be a commitment that is more than passing, less than obsessive. Eight years of copyediting taught one lesson. While language can always be acquired and parroted, it rings false unless in the service of an identification with the subject that is urgent, complicit. Not a possession: just a relationship. For whatever reason, I identify with Irish music urgently, despite a lack of particulars, and feel complicit with it, despite the absence of an accomplice or even a crime.

I should do fine.

Eily Murphy has, however, brought more than Jimmy's message. In her oven-mitted hands is an olive branch, an apology to Hia: a fresh-baked apple tart.

"I heard you had a sweet tooth," she says to me, glancing around the room in obvious dismay.

"Who told you that?"

"I heard."

Hia is uninterested in sweets, except sugary tea, but also hasn't eaten today. She cuts herself a slice.

"Before lunch?" Eily asks.

"Mmm."

"Hia pays no attention to meal times," I say. "They interfere with the creative process."

"Good cake," Hia says.

The apology is, I gather, not accepted. Eily Murphy absorbs the jab meekly. I am steering our landlady towards the door when Hia invites her to stay for a cup of tea. The offer appears sincere. Eily, who hasn't yet gotten over the changes in the room—she stares at the blank walls as if a text is scrawled across them—is momentarily stunned. We both turn around and return to the kitchen.

"You can go," Hia tells me.

"Sorry?"

"No need to be here."

Am I being told to leave? Can't be.

I go anyway, just in case.

John Bagley is a dentist. He lives in one of Dingle's finer townhouses, and keeps offices on the ground floor. Married, with three children, Bagley is a fit fifty-one-year-old, an avid golf and tennis player who has the placating voice common to doctors. We meet in the office reception room, amid Kerry Tourism posters and pamphlets advocating oral hygiene. He apologizes for not inviting me upstairs; his wife, Fiona, is still in her nightgown, reading the Sunday newspapers.

PK: Thank you for agreeing to see me, Dr. Bagley.

JB: Jimmy Sullivan said you were a fan of the fiddle, and a Canadian no less! I felt it my duty.

PK: Why?

JB: Well, I don't imagine you've much exposure to the music over there. Also as a favour to Jimmy. Fiona does a good deal of our shopping up in his place you know.

PK: When did you start to play the fiddle?

JB: At the age of sixteen. About the time I was awakening to the need for the preservation of, and participation in—the 'P&P', we call it—the culture of this country. I joined Comhaltas Ceoltoiri Eireann, and began spending summers at an Irish school in Waterford.

PK: You're not from Dingle?

JB: Dublin, born and bred. My father was a barrister. He met my mother in Trinity College.

PK: Were they fiddlers?

JB: (*laughing*) Not likely!

PK: Then you learned . . . ?

JB: Taking lessons at the Ceoltoiri. It was an electrifying experience. I began to understand how beholden we are to the traditions of our past, the song and dance. All through college and dental school I continued to play at the club, and on weekends in a ceilidh band. Never a doubt, never a hesitation, regardless of the opinions of certain colleagues.

PK: How did you end up in West Kerry?

JB: There was an opening, and my father helped me purchase the practice. Then Fiona and I fell mad in love with the countryside.

PK: Do you join the sessions at MacDonagh's?

JB: I am *not* a believer in pubs. They've done more harm to this country—cost more lives—than emigration or the Troubles ever will.

PK: Right.

JB: I saw a need for better organization within the ranks of the Dingle Ceoltoiri, and set about the task. The resistance I met with! Some of the locals out here. . . . At any rate, soon enough I was leading the band as well as instructing youngsters, helping choose the finest prospects for the regional *fleadh ceoils*.

PK: Do you still play?

JB: Of course. Most Saturdays during the winter months.

PK: Why only then?

JB: Beg pardon?

PK: Why do you only play in the winter?

JB: Eh, well, what with the miserable peninsula weather, you'd be a fool to miss even a single decent day on the links.

PK: The links?

JB: Golf, lad. Out in Ballyferriter.

PK: Which tunes do you play?

JB: Ceilidh tunes. The popular jigs, reels, and hornpipes. Things people can dance to.

PK: Slow airs?

JB: You can't dance to an air! The music is for dancing. You have to be practical.

PK: Would you play me a couple of your favourites?

JB: Now?

PK: Because it's Sunday?

JB: It's not that. . . . I wouldn't feel comfortable on my own. Jimmy mentioned that you'll be in Dingle for a spell. Why not come out to a ceilidh? They're brilliant, and we serve scones and tea during the break.

PK: Do you practise?

JB: I'm a busy man, understand. And I get all the practice I need with the group, and through teaching the rare child who expresses an interest. Dingle is *not*, I regret, a positive environment for cultivating the traditions.

PK: Are you—

JB: I should add, however, that there is no greater satisfaction than helping a youngster learn the music. The 'P&P', you know.

PK: What about influences: Michael Coleman or Sean Maguire. Maybe Denis Murphy?

JB: You've done your homework. Good job. Fiona has the run of the stereo in the house, and she's big on the classics—James Last and Phil Coulter.

PK: Sean O Conchuir must have influenced you?

JB: (*puzzled*) The name is familiar. . . .

PK: Right.

JB: I do listen to Raidio Na Gaeltachta in the car on the way to the course. The station isn't too far from here. We own a good deal of the land around it, in fact. An important part of Irish life.

PK: Buying land?

JB: Radio in the native language.

PK: Is traditional music important to you?

JB: Of paramount importance. I associate it with my profound awakening as an adolescent, and I still enjoy it today.

I return to Grey Lane in despair. Actually, I keep thinking I *should* be in despair—the interview was a disaster—but can't muster the gloom. On the contrary, I feel loose, almost light-headed. Deciding that I am in shock, I don a dour face for Hia.

She is seated at the kitchen table, sketch pad open, pencil gliding across the page. Looking up, she smiles vacantly, lowers her gaze. "Let me finish this," she says.

Carolan is curled on the chair next to her. The cat yawns when I pet it, stretches a hamhock leg. I fill the kettle and gaze out at the backyard. Eily Murphy is no gardener; the grass is shaggy and the fence is matted with vines. Behind the yard lurks Dingle's equally neglected public green, buried in the basin of a square block of houses. Facilities include a derelict swing set, benches missing half their boards, and a doorless caravan used by teenagers for nocturnal trysts. The park is an odd place, grotty and ingrown, and though geographically the centre of town, it is treated as a bad memory, a communal failure. Our knowledge is a fluke; the kitchen window opens onto the upper village.

Hia tries to conceal one of her own secrets while I make tea. Propped against the wall on the table is a piece of sandstone the size and weight of a brick. To the naked eye, the object *looks* like a brick. On one face, however, are faint etchings, clearly made by a chisel, clearly part of a design. The face is smooth and the markings are almost worn away, perhaps have been erased. Hia claims the sandstone fragment is from Angkor, the great temple-city in northwest Cambodia that is the subject of her endeavours. She maintains, moreover, that the fragment belongs to a bas-relief of an *apsara*, the celestial dancers of Khmer myth.

These are astonishing contentions. The etchings are, first of all, formless: one line curves upward, another cluster of lines intertwines in knots. How Hia could connect these scribbles with a shape is beyond me. How she could then designate that shape to be human, of divine origin, and female, of distinctive beauty, constitutes a major leap of faith. Whatever the content, if the fragment is indeed from Angkor, then it is a thousand-year-old artifact—rare, valuable, pillaged. She bought it from a black-marketeer in Saigon shortly before fleeing Vietnam, on the man's assurances the article was genuine. Hia then lugged the treasure into exile and smuggled it into Canada, where the brick stood for a decade atop her bedroom dresser. When she confessed her plans to transport her shard of Cambodian history to Ireland, I had a fit. (Even assuming the piece was a fake, Customs people would still have given her grief.) I lodged my protest despite sensing that the fragment was related somehow to her loss, her grief, even possibly to her recovery. Our discussion ended inconclusively, and I assumed the matter was settled. It was: our first night here, she unveiled the carefully wrapped booty from within *my* suitcase, thanking me for breaking an international law on her behalf.

But the presence of the fragment in Dingle is not the secret. Hia disclaims visual aids in her work. She loves the blank page: the terms of success unyielding, the probability of failure high. With the Angkor drawings, the disclaimer is even more remarkable; assuming she visited the site once, probably as a child, and glanced at a few books, she is still calling forth images directly from her imagination. This relationship appears healthy—she possesses the images, they possess her. Still, there is a slightly clinical feeling to the project. The truth is that Hia uses the artifact as a mnemonic device, running her fingers over the etchings every few minutes, as if the texture of the sandstone, the sensation of exploring its grooves, helps to conjure up the lines and curves she is seeking. The first time I caught her in the act I was strangely moved, overwhelmed by a tenderness towards her, towards us. I remain reassured by it. Hia, in contrast, is ashamed of this need, or else is simply too proud. She disguises all contact, becoming flustered if I notice her, ordering me from the room.

Now, jerking her hand back from the totem, she accepts a cup of tea. "How was the interview?" she asks, her eyes still on the page.

"He was a dentist."

She nods, not listening.

"It didn't go well," I elaborate. "He wasn't insightful or interesting."

"Too bad."

"I didn't mind. The man was so banal, and so smug, that I got angry, and started sniping back at him."

Hia looks up.

"I knew I wasn't being polite. I knew, but I didn't care. Suddenly it seemed too . . . "

"Yes?"

" . . . important."

She grins.

"But it isn't, really. I don't even know why I did the interview. I shouldn't get carried away."

Hia has filled the page with a latticework of lines, like an aerial photograph of a delta. The forms are concise, the divisions are proportional. While no dominant shape emerges, and the plan seems yet a blueprint, the overall impression is unified, despite a daunting scale.

"I draw the entire complex first," she explains. "An area twenty by eight kilometres. Also there are four reservoirs and many canals, many fields. To settle the geometry of Angkor in my mind is important."

"Where is Angkor Wat?"

"Too early to think about temples. Angkor is not just some wats and statues. It is a city, a civilization, once. Most buildings were of wood, so the jungle could take them back. Only palaces and temples were of sandstone. For Khmers, some things lasted for ever, others did not. But," she adds, touching the pencil to her lips, "for me, even if the structures all crumbled, Angkor would still exist."

"In memory?"

"In dream."

I think about her answer.

"The jungle is so hot the buildings hover in air. Like the reflection of mountains in a lake, like snow when it falls. Not of this world."

"But of your dream?"

She shrugs.

"Do you have any photos to help?" I ask, glancing at the artifact.

"I have several of her. You know this."

"I meant Angkor."

Hia reddens. "I don't need photos," she answers quickly. "My interest is not to draw perfectly the temples. I wish to *create* Angkor. . . . Wait. Wrong word. To create an image of it."

"Your image?"

"An image."

"Is there only one?"

"Explain," she says.

"Can't Angkor be seen a thousand different ways by a thousand different artists? Can't someone's interpretation of the complex be so personal it's almost unrecognizable, yet still be valid?"

"No."

"No?"

"Angkor has a shape. I try to draw image of it. My eyes, my imagination, but not my shape."

"Then is it your art?"

Hia extends her hand to make contact with the fragment. "Don't trick me with English. I need discipline and clear thinking. Your questions confuse me."

I retreat to the doorway. "Did you go to mass after I left?" I ask.

"I had decided not to. So uncomfortable to be in a new church, with people staring and whispering. But Eily Murphy asked me to join her."

"And . . . ?"

"Simple, elegant exterior. Inside is cool and full of natural light. Nice stained-glass windows. Unusual altar. There is a statue of the Virgin Mary showing comfort to Baby Jesus and another child."

"I'll have to peek inside."

"But you have no God."

"It's just a building."

"Leave, please."

"How's your head today?"

"Out!"

Exiled to the living room with tea and apple tart, I recline on the couch beneath the sole survivor of Hia's purge: a sketch of St. Mary's church, Dingle.

Chapter 8

Michael received his first letter from Seamus O Suilleabhain in December 1953. Seamus had planned to wait until the new year to write, in the hope that his descriptions of Christmas in Dingle, the church activities and Wren parade, the pageants and choral performances at the schools—all somewhat cheerful, somewhat gay, and certainly not as unrelentingly bleak as the other feast days—would boost both their spirits. He mailed the missive early to pass on two newspaper clippings. When the clippings fell from the envelope, Michael put the letter aside and examined them. The first, from *The Kerryman* for November 21, was entitled "Blasket Island Evacuation Impeded by Heavy Seas".

> The Atlantic, which dominates the lives of the Blasket island people, asserted its supremacy on Tuesday, the day appointed by the Irish Land Commission to have this community of 22 people and their furniture transferred over the Sound to four newly built cottages in Dunquin with three acres of arable land attached.
>
> About 9:30 on Tuesday morning Dingle harbour was placid and the fishing boat St. Lawrence O'Toole left the pier and proceeded towards the

> Great Blasket. Weather conditions looked ideal except for the troubled sea which broke into white foam against the Blasket group and the headlands.
>
> When approaching Innis Mor on the Blasket Mor, Mr. Michael Brosnan, skipper of the fishing boat, shook his head. It was doubtful, he thought, if the islanders with their furniture could be transferred to Dunquin, owing to the heavy seas.

The second article, from *The Cork Examiner,* was dated two days later, when the evacuation finally commenced. The newspaper ended its coverage of the event:

> Even when the last of the islanders have settled on the mainland (in two or three days' time), their link with the Great Blasket will not be entirely severed. Not only do all their new homes look straight across the waves at their old, but it will be necessary for the menfolk at least to cross those waves quite frequently in their "naombogs" to tend to their flocks of sheep, which will be left to graze on the island.

Michael's response to the news was to return the clippings to the envelope (along with the letter, scanned only for word of his father), drop the envelope in the bin, and then bring the trash down to the alley, a day before pickup. A month later he had trouble recalling why he knew the Great Blasket had been emptied, telling Davey Russell he must have dreamed about it. He also told Davey that the silence of his best friend in Dingle, Seamus O Suilleabhain, meant Seamus had finally come to his senses and emigrated, probably to England. Davey Russell had sat at the kitchen table watching Michael unseal the letter, deposit it in the bin and remove the liner, and head for the door. Now, on hearing Michael's version of events, he kept silent; his roommate, he kept telling himself, was a piece of work.

The men hosted a party, inviting a dozen friends, mostly Irish. The guests in turn brought along another twenty people, mostly Canadians. The evening, an open house where the refreshments consisted of a pail of gin, a tub of beer, and trays of cigarettes, and the smoke grew so dense that Davey had to insist everyone march around the room, was successful enough for a neighbour to lodge a complaint. When the police arrived, Davey invited them in. One officer looked ready to accept; the other threatened to cite the men for disturbing the peace. Among the guests was a fiddler from Dublin who sang *while* he played the instrument, a feat that earned applause. Though Michael kept to a corner the entire evening—kept, as usual, to himself—Davey still questioned him afterwards.

"The way you eyed the one from Dublin. Your gaze locked on the fiddle, frowning when he missed a note. . . . Are you sure you never played?"

"Maybe years ago."

"How many years?"

"Sometime in the last century."

"Do you own a fiddle?"

"Not in Canada."

"Back home?"

"This is home, Davey."

Davey Russell nodded in disbelief. "But you were a fiddler?" he asked.

"I was many things once. Now I work for the TTC. Now I live here."

"But—"

"Now I'm a lifer," Michael added, his attempt at a smile collapsing.

Michael's position with the Toronto Transit Commission was permanent only if he obtained his papers. His second six-month visa was due to expire, and renewal, officials had hinted, was not guaranteed. Davey Russell lectured him while walking to mass one Sunday morning in

May. The men strolled down Church Street towards the cathedral, both in tie and jacket, neither terribly interested in celebrating the mystery of the covenant. Davey went to mass because he was Catholic and wanted to meet Catholic women. Michael went because he loved the acoustics of the building, the incantations and murmurings, voices in prayer and song, that resounded and lingered, hung suspended in the air, like the susurrus of waves in a cove. When he closed his eyes during the ceremony, it was to imagine how a fiddle might sound in St. Michael's: a sweet timbre and rich inflection, chords full and sharp; and how he would love to launch a note towards the vaulting ceiling—itself a margin between earth and sky—with a single great stroke, running the bow from the point to the nut, modulating, holding steady, so the tone would at once contract while ascending, as a starling recedes against a widening empyrean, but also expand on contact with the open space. The note would keep climbing, keep resonating, keep contracting and expanding, for all eternity, world without end, amen.

Davey's lecture focused on two themes. First, Michael was antisocial. The quality was inherent, and likely could not be redeemed. What such a person needed, lest he become progressively more inward (the thought of which, in Michael's case, made Davey shiver), was an alter ego, a mediator. A wife, in other words: Michael had to find a wife, fast. The second theme was related. This wife should be attractive, of course, not too tall or skinny, young, in good health. In addition, she should be supportive, patient, and, for his sake, gregarious and outgoing. Oh yes, and Canadian. A Canadian citizen, with the birth certificate to prove it. Otherwise, Michael could find himself back in Dingle by summer, wandering the deserted streets, gazing at the barren hills, hands in empty pockets.

"You are the hard man," Michael said appreciatively.

"Not me," Davey answered. "The world."

Unbeknownst to Michael, during mass Davey Russell

exchanged glances with a woman in the next pew. He approached her on the church steps afterwards, veering away to drop a few coins in the St. Vincent de Paul Society box. The woman, a pretty twenty-year-old with red lipstick and a beehive of black hair, fished her purse for change. When Davey offered the woman a mint, and she accepted, Michael settled in for a wait. Birds nested in the cathedral tympanum. Pigeons waddled across the cement. Nearby, also abandoned, was a fourth parishioner: a young woman in a blue dress and white shoes, with a purse that she clutched in both hands. Her face was open, and when she smiled—at the pigeons who circled her—it was crooked but sweet. The way she stood there in a sea of bobbing birds, not fidgeting, not embarrassed, reminded Michael of the manner of Kerry girls: a little awkward, yet also graceful and self-possessed. Differences were, however, notable. The woman in Toronto was five foot nine, thin (almost skinny), and, as he soon discovered, ill at ease in English.

Davey introduced Michael first to his new acquaintance, Karen Williams, and then to Karen's friend, Francine Ferron. He had a plan: ice cream, in a restaurant, immediately.

"Michael hails from West Kerry," Davey said to the women, "and is, consequently, unintelligible in English. Expect only nods and exclamations."

"Fuck off, Davey," Michael joked.

Karen Williams covered her mouth coquettishly. Francine Ferron blushed.

"Lovely," Davey sighed. "In any case, as I understand it, Miss Ferron is also uncomfortable with the language. Karen and I insist you both accompany us, but want it known that there is *no* obligation to make conversation."

The hint was broad, and Michael, mortified by his slip, fell mute. The foursome strolled to a coffee shop on Yonge Street. Failing at a collective rhythm—Davey and Karen surged ahead—they quickly divided into pairs, one couple flirting, the other tongue-tied. Across the restaurant table, Francine Ferron observed Michael sip milky tea while he stole glimpses of her stabs at a sundae. Michael also noted her tall forehead and prominent nose, the way her smile wrinkled the skin around her eyes. Though these exchanges remained nonverbal, Francine seemed to inhabit his silence with him, her eyes glazing over at the courtship banter. Only when Karen Williams excused herself and Davey went to pay the bill did they dare words.

"Why did you leave your home?" Francine asked, her English slow and meticulous.

"Poverty."

She nodded.

"And yourself?" he said.

"Small town in north Ontario. Nothing happens there. Nothing for me."

"Is your family still in the town?"

"Of course. What about you?"

"Me?"

"Your family . . . ?"

"No family, except for my father. He won't last much longer, either."

"Sad."

"Lamentable."

Francine furrowed her brow. "My English," she said. "Not so great."

"I have trouble myself," Michael assured her.

The couples parted at the corner of King Street. On the way back to the flat Davey rubbed his palms in delight; he had a rendezvous with Karen Williams that same night. Davey also apologized to Michael for dragging him along to the coffee shop, and then forcing him to endure an hour with the "tall French bird". Michael told his friend to go to hell. He hadn't minded the restaurant. He hadn't minded the tea. He hadn't even minded Karen Williams. As for the tall French bird, Michael's reaction was, he admitted, stronger: he had a date with her next Friday evening.

Chapter 9

We spend the day mapping, appreciating, but never actually climbing the hills around Dingle. Hia's determination to explore the outlying areas is idiosyncratic. Her enthusiasm has little to do with the flora and fauna, less with the birds flitting from shrub to shrub, and nothing whatsoever to do with the ruins of farms and towers that dot the slopes. I find the ruins fascinating; she calls them "broken rocks". I tell her the sites are about all that is legible about the topography. She replies that ruins, and ruined things, not only unnerve her, but have the power to make her physically ill. I would challenge this extraordinary remark—she is, after all, embarked on a study of one of the world's most famous ruined things—if it did not ring true.

Fronts roll off the Atlantic. Watching them is exhilarating, like standing beneath a river to observe it flow overhead. The sky can be smothering the town, draping the church spire, while remaining split wide open a few kilometres to the west, shafts of light searching the countryside. Judging from our first week, the volatility is permanent; the weather is always changing, always in the process of evolving and devolving, dying and being reborn. The only vantage point from which to appreciate these rhythms is on the outside: at Reenbeg Point, partway up a slope, along the road that climbs to the Conor Pass.

Ordinance map open, poncho draped over her head, Hia leads the charge out highways that narrow to lanes and often end up as boreens, marching against the breeze, into the rain, sweating beneath the sun, until we arrive at gullies affording panoramas of hills and lakes, valleys of checker-board plots. Humans set in the landscape—a farmer walking his land, a tractor puffing up a road—seem irrelevant. Again, the verdancy of the peninsula is luxuriant, even in mist, rivalled in brilliance only by the washed blue sky when the cloud curtains part.

Hia loves the mouth-filling names of the mountains: Ballynabooly, Knocknoylemore, Chroaghmartin, Brandon. She revels in the patinas of the words, a rare indulgence on her part in a sense other than the visual. What delights her about the hills, besides the contours she traces with her hands, is the illusion of their accessibility. The ranges are so round and compact, so like the shapes a child might sculpt at a beach, and, though largely devoid of inhabitants, so clearly tamed—abandoned houses, fences that ascend to the summits. No peaks, few stark faces. The mountains are, Hia stresses, grim and desolate and quite beyond our comprehension, but they mollify by their dimensions and endear by their photogenic severity. Croaghskearda, she intones. Knockhahoran. Ballyma— Ballymac— Ballymacadoyle!

In the evening I drag her on a pub crawl, promising she can watch television, assuming the bars have them, while I investigate the music scene. We begin furthest along the promontory at Tom Daly's. The door is unlocked but the room is deserted, almost dark. I am about to turn around when a figure emerges from the snug.

"Now," Jimmy says.

I cross the floor.

"Who are you looking for?" he asks.

I poke my head inside the chamber. A glass of wheat-hued liquid sits on the bench; a cigarette burns in an ashtray.

"No one," I answer.

"Where's T. Daly?" Hia wonders.

"Up the road a minute. I'm minding the place until half-eight." He focuses on me: "Were you expecting something?"

"I haven't any expectations."

"I want to ask T. Daly a question," Hia says, leaning against the counter. "Those calendars up there—they're all wrong!"

"How's Carolan?"

"Still dead," she answers.

"We're after live music," I say. "Preferably not played by a dentist."

Jimmy's smile etches parentheses around his mouth. "Apologies about John Bagley. Eily mentioned he bored you to tears."

"Eily?"

"Bagley has brought tears to many an eye. Half with his awful fiddling, half with his murderous drill." He hooks a cracked front tooth in his fingernail, as illustration.

"I'm confused," I tell Hia. "How did Eily Murphy know about the interview?"

"Church," she confesses.

"Old hen!" Jimmy concurs.

I ask for suggestions about pubs. Though doubtful of our chances, he names three bars. Back outside, I press my face to the gap in the glass between the window-frame and the blind. Jimmy stands in the middle of the room a full minute, arms limp, head bowed. Then he turns and retreats to the snug, as if heeding a call. The door closes.

Our first stop, a pub along Strand Street, welcomes customers with a backdraft of cigarette smoke in the entrance. Two men in their twenties, one on accordion and the other on guitar, are regaling the crowd with ballads. The vocals are lusty, the guitar is amplified out of tune, and the accordion, a bouncing baby against the man's chest, exhales chords that wash over the audience. Patrons not singing along must shout at each other to out-decibel the performers. Hia contributes to the screech by lingering before a television perched above the counter until the bartender, taking pity, offers to raise the volume. Ignoring the stares and bemused smiles, she proceeds to bask in fifteen minutes of prime-time American TV.

On the street again, the rain tapered to a drizzle, we continue to Dykegate Lane, stopping at a corner to observe an entire cloud formation, perhaps twenty-four hours of weather in Dublin and a week in Toronto, sail by in the twilight sky. The next pub, MacDonagh's, is a high-ceilinged room with musical instruments on the walls and a stove in the corner. Near the stove, separated from the door by a subway car of bodies, are a banjo player and a fiddler. The musicians appear ready to play. Only after I have elbowed close enough to the bar to bellow an order, been handed the beers, entrusted money to relays, and muscled back to Hia, spilling a third of the contents onto my jacket, do I realize that the musicians *are* already playing, probably as loudly as they can. The gulf between us is unbridgeable without fisticuffs, and the absence of amplification, which I'd smugly approved of, deals the session a fatal blow. We watch, glasses against our chests, as the man and woman ply the necks of their instruments, respond to phrases, the fiddler raising her bow with a flourish—all to no avail.

It is now dark. It is also raining again. We sprint up the street to a pub at the foot of the Conor Pass Road, where we find a concertina player performing to a small crowd. I sit by an unlit fire for an hour while Hia, perched on a bar stool, watches a mute television (the bartender ignores her entreaties). The musician is a bearded man with scraggly hair and eyebrows that stitch into a line when he sings. The concertina is delicate and emotive, especially when extended, air racing through the chamber to produce a soft, sad drone. His voice is rough, but the songs, especially one in Irish, are lovely.

"How was the program?" I ask her afterwards.

"Clint Eastwood movie," she answers. "I saw it before."

I wait for her to question me about the music. I want to tell her it was awful; that what I heard in these pubs has little to do with the records I've listened to for years; that either the music is gone, or else I am looking for it in the wrong places; and that I am anxious to figure out where the problem lies. She doesn't ask, however, and we walk home in silence.

Carolan greets our arrival with a doleful meow, stretching into a drawbridge on his chair. The rain starts back up shortly afterwards, a murmur at first, then raps on the roof and against the window. Hia fixes tea while I arrange the room: dim the light, plug in the space heater, centre three candles on the coffee table.

Once she is seated, I lower the cat onto her lap. His position is invariable: backside against Hia's stomach, front paws curled over her knees, head bowed in contemplation of the abyss below. I also cover her slippers with a towel. She commences her nightly massage, each dragging stroke pulling the pink skin back from his eyes and pressing a groove down his spine. Beginning between his ears, Hia finishes by tugging on Carolan's dancing tail, a fur Brillo materializing in her fist. He purrs, syncopated music in time with the flutter of the flames, the beat of the rain. The animal also drools, globs that inch down his chin, dangle from tufts, then plummet onto the cloth.

I pour the tea. Hia takes milk, spoons of sugar: one, two, three. I take mine black.

"What did you look for in that closet?" she asks.

I pretend not to understand.

"In T. Daly's. Jimmy comes out of the room, you immediately look inside it."

"The pub was empty," I answer, checking my voice for cracks. "Why would Jimmy have sat in the snug?"

"Meditation."

"Jimmy's Catholic."

"Confession."

"I just wanted to see if someone else was in there."

Hia sips her tea. "You should write your mother. Tell her all this."

"What's to tell?"

She stares at me.

"My mother and I don't talk about him," I explain. "We never have."

"You won't let her."

"What has Francine been saying?"

"You blame her for things she never did. You punish her, treat her unfair. You are a bad son."

"A bad son?"

"I respect my mother. I never hurt her. I never hide things. How could I? My mother wraps me in her wings."

The imagery shocks me into an unkind thought. "Are you sure about that?" I ask.

"Who talks about your father?"

"Not me."

"Fathers, fathers, fathers. Always this stupid business with men. Phew! What about mothers? What about—"

"Hia."

"— her?"

"Hia!"

Her eyes narrow with anger.

"You're torturing the cat," I say.

The fury of Hia's massage has driven Carolan deeper between her legs. His body is now level with her thighs, his head dangling off the couch in a weird death pose. Only the motor of his purring suggests the animal has survived.

"You still miss her?"

Hia raises a hand in frustration at my question. Caught in candlelight, the hand is projected onto the far wall. "I remember her," she answers. "I remember everything about her, about me and her—every detail. I have those details, in my head, like shapes."

"I didn't ask—"

"You must remember your father better. Otherwise, you will remain unformed, unfinished."

There is a complication. I have never told Hia the exact date I was pried from my father's embrace. My hunch is that Francine has also been evasive about this point. "I never said I knew nothing," I answer. "My mother tried telling me things when I was a kid, at the dinner table, before bedtime. I remember names, like Seamus and Moira, and places, like Dingle and the Great Blasket; stories about here, I guess, stories about him. But I was just a boy. They didn't stay in my memory."

"Not true."

"The point is—"

"You don't care."

"I don't care enough."

She sighs.

"I hate all this stuff," I say, avoiding her gaze. "None of it makes sense; none of it relates to me. I almost never think about it."

"But it *is* you."

"It was me."

"Then why are we here?"

"You wanted to come."

"Liar."

"I'm older now. Less likely to be overwhelmed. I can handle myself better." I examine the floor. "No more nightmares," I say. "No more accidents. It's how I want it."

She sighs again.

"Mothers, mothers, mothers. Phew! Always this stupid business with women."

"More tea, please," Hia says.

I have a theory about Hia and sweet tea. Unless I am mistaken, each guzzled cup corresponds in her with a rising vocal inflection, an increase in histrionic gestures and provocative opinions. Compound this addiction with a haphazard diet of sandwiches and biscuits, and her nerves must jangle. I dutifully stir the poison. The rain strikes even harder, and the candles jump, throwing unresolved, violent shadows against the wall.

"God is a cathedral," Hia announces. "God is perfect proportion, perfect light. He is structure. He is order."

"Design?"

"I don't care who created the universe."

"But—?"

"Things from the past, Pat. He is only the present. He just is."

"Or else?"

"I could not draw."

"And?"

"I could not love."

This is new. I ask her to repeat it.

"Without God, there would be no shapes. Where there are no shapes, no order exists. No order, no chance for love."

"Does God show his love?"

"You know my answer."

"But does he?"

"God is in the sky, on the page, in my head. On the earth? No, not here. But—" Hia stops, lowers her cup to enlist both her hands to coax thoughts to the surface. "I know only myself," she continues. "That the forms exist in my imagination, not in my eyes, not in my pencil when I work. As a child, landscapes and skies held fascination, especially skies. I saw things in clouds: outlines, images. These shapes existed for me, no one else. That was okay. Because I believed the shapes were the truth."

"Truth about what?"

"I don't know."

"You must."

"I am not a college professor. My ideas are not in books.

If I say I don't know, you should respect."

"Okay," I agree, sensing how fragile the conversation is. Pushing it would be foolish.

"*Truth,*" Hia says passionately. "Not lies, not deceptions. Not broken, ruined world—whole, full, beautiful world. Full of light. Full of—"

"Churches?"

"Dignity."

"What about the churches?"

She frowns. I push it.

"Explain the cathedrals in the sky," I say, referring to a vision Hia experienced during her flight from Vietnam. "Explain Santa Maria and St. Stephen's."

"That was ten years ago."

"Explain the domes and spires."

"You think I saw cathedrals above the ocean because of security? You think I value structure because of need for safety? Churches, God, Cath—li—cism, all to protect over me, poor boat girl whose life before Canada was episode from television show?"

Now Hia is really angry. I can tell because she is suddenly still, her face inscrutable. Also her English, normally a monotone, has assumed the cadences of Vietnamese—rushes of vowel sequences, scores of misapplied tones.

"It is demeaning," she says.

"How?"

"Cheap biography. TV movie, newspaper article. Not me. Not respecting of my intelligentness. Not resp—" She slaps her thigh. Carolan emits a *prrrt*. "Now I can't even speak English!"

We both pause.

"You still miss her?" I ask.

Her look is lethal. "This music," Hia says, wincing at O Conchuir's fiddling on the tape player. "It is all scratches and squeaks."

I nod.

"You still listen to it?"

I heed the warning. "I bet Carolan misses Joan McGreevy," I say, moving from a chair to the couch. "I bet she visits him every night in his dreams."

Raising my arms, I initiate a shadow play against the wall. Joan McGreevy occupies the left side of the stage. She is a gnarled phantom: curled fingers as ears, a recoiling wrist as body. Carolan is on the right, his ears my thumb and pinkie, his nose my extended knuckle. The play, which I improvise, is a pantomime dramatizing her death and his slow awakening to the loss.

Imagining he hears his name called, the cat scours the flat, finally locating his mistress in her favourite chair. Carolan listens for her cooing, but hears only silence. He tests the air for her perfume; the air is stale. The cat jumps into Joan McGreevy's lap. She always helped secure him as he landed. When he receives no support, the cat opens his claws. He anticipates a bop on the nose. Joan McGreevy is motionless. He climbs her sweater. She remains still, chin on her chest, breathing imperceptible. The cat licks cold flesh.

While I clear the tea, Hia also makes shadow theatre. Hers is a dance, a solitary performance set to music I cannot hear. Her limbs sway to the melody, sometimes intertwining, like birds in airborne combat, most often dancing in isolation. I watch from the kitchen door. Alternating between Hia's sculpted face and fluid limbs, I become absorbed by *her* absorption, delighting in the rapture so apparent in her features. I also identify for the first time what she is doing with her hands. Years ago, when I first learned that Hia had done her senior thesis on Angkor, and actually possessed an artifact from one of the temples, I spent an afternoon in a library reading about the site. (Her identification, even complicity, with the ruins baffled me. After all, she was Vietnamese, not Cambodian.) Among the photos of wats and *barays*, statues and panels, a single figure kept reappearing, second only to the Buddha in prominence. The dance is not of her imagining; does Hia know whose outline she occupies?

ONLY CHILD

Chapter 10

Michael proposed to Francine Ferron in the kitchen on Christmas Day, 1954. Davey Russell was spending the holidays with his brother in York Mills; Francine had told her parents she could not get time off to make the trip home. What had kept her in the city was a feeling, based on the number of sentences Michael had swallowed and the blood that kept flooding his cheeks, that he had something to ask her. In the apartment, festive music on the radio, snow brushing the window, Francine basted a turkey with her cardigan sleeves drawn to the elbows. Michael stood at the counter peeling apples, his tie tucked into his shirt.

"It would be grand, wouldn't it?"

"What, Michael?"

"You and me, together. A family."

"Grand," she agreed.

He cleared his throat. "Have you any objections to the idea, Fran?"

"Objections?"

"I want your mind at ease. Confident it's not for the immigration business. That it's for real."

"It's real," Francine said.

He sliced the apples.

"Are we settled then?"

She permitted herself a smile. "Do you also want raisins in the pie?"

"I'm not fussy," he replied.

Francine suggested a spring wedding at a church in North York, where she planned to put a down payment on a house with money saved during two years as a department store clerk. In the new year they registered at St. Gabriel's parish on Sheppard Avenue, an hour north of the cathedral by bus, in order to qualify to hold the ceremony there. Francine also lugged Michael up to the church for obligatory sessions with the priest. Her desire to settle in North York was based on her understanding of how life in Toronto should be: entirely different from the drudgery of her home town, exciting and fast-paced, but still comfortable, communal, a house for her family on a street of unlocked doors and open invitations, neighbours who were also friends. Colleagues at the department store, especially those in management, where Francine intended to eventually work, described the suburbs in such terms: not only modern and efficient but welcoming, peaceful, permanent.

For Michael, who rarely ventured beyond the city limits, and who had never given a thought as to where he might settle, Francine's vision was lovely—her eyes glimmered as she spoke—and the plan sounded fine. When sketching their futures in North York, Francine was careful to emphasize certain qualities to her fiancé. The area was miles from the nearest Irish bar. Life there was anonymous; streets were not designated by race, not ghettoized. People were free to do as they wished, in solitude, without interference or approbation. Though the neighbourhood would constitute a community, it was a contemporary arrangement: based on convenience, not tradition; grounded in private desires, not public welfare; rooted in happenstance, not history. Each family occupied, Francine stressed, a separate unit, with space on four sides and a yard out back—an island in an archipelago. Regardless of the proximity of its neighbours, an island still had to be approached, still had to be landed on.

Francine insisted on house-hunting even before the May wedding. Borrowing Davey Russell's car, the couple visited three properties before making an offer on a newly finished bungalow a block east of the Yonge-Finch intersection. The house cost $11,200, minus the $1,200 Francine put down. (Michael, whose wages at the TTC were higher, hadn't a penny saved.) The date of possession was in June, but they were allowed to begin moving in a month before. Michael's first acquisition was two kittens he'd found in a box behind his building. While Francine was unhappy about the animals—cats belonged in barns, not living rooms—she was relieved he was taking an interest. Jig and Reel, so named by their rescuer, had the run of the bungalow until the newlyweds arrived.

The night before the ceremony Francine finally asked Michael to talk about himself. It was twilight, and the couple were strolling through Allan Gardens. Michael was nursing a work headache. Francine's promotion off the floor was a week old, but her excitement at the position, the wedding, the house, had left a spring in her step, obliging him to keep up. Her decision to press the issue was not giddiness. Nor was it born of doubt. Quite the opposite: assuming Michael's silences to be the result of shyness, a lack of confidence, Francine believed he needed to talk, to hear himself define, with pride and satisfaction, who he was, where he had come from. Hoping to establish a tone, she offered a summary of her own biography.

She came from a town north of Sudbury that was minority French-speaking, majority poor. Originally a Gaspé peninsula clan, the Ferrons had emigrated west at the turn of the century to work the copper and nickel mines, the pulp and paper mills, drinking beer, fighting world wars (her grandfather was killed at Verdun, her father wounded at Dieppe), attending mass, raising enormous families rife with more miners and mill workers, plus the token priest and maverick hockey player; and the daughters and grand-daughters who stayed on in the town, despite knowing better, to marry second cousins, high school drop-outs, trappers who drank at the Star Inn on Friday nights, and then to take jobs teaching kindergarten or in the bank, until they got pregnant, married, plump. Francine's brothers were those men and her sisters were those women. Not her, though; at fourteen she had set her sights on Toronto, a persistent rumour—few locals had ever been there—from the south. Her friends thought she was arrogant; her father called her ungrateful. Only her mother understood, and started to put aside a few dollars every month towards her daughter's flight. A week after her eighteenth birthday, her diploma wrapped in cardboard, Francine kissed her grim father, hugged her weeping mother, and boarded a bus for Sudbury, with a connection to Toronto. That was three years ago, she summarized. That was another lifetime.

And Michael?

Only child of a late marriage, he began, the words catching in his throat. His mother died when he was five. His father, now seventy-one, lives in a village called Dunquin. He and Michael don't get on well: nothing to say to each other. Michael was raised by his aunt. She runs a chemist's shop in Dingle. He boarded with her for twelve years. Went to middle school. Even applied, at the insistence of an Irish teacher, to the University College, Cork. Was accepted into an undergraduate program, but never acted on it. Co-owned a trawler with a friend. Did some fishing, some bartending, some construction work. Got out of Dingle in the nick of time. Moribund town: no future, little present, too much past.

Michael stopped. Francine encouraged him to relax on a bench, to lie in the grass—anything to keep him talking. Davey Russell had already told her about the fiddle and the Great Blasket; why was Michael avoiding these subjects?

Francine pleaded with her eyes. *Please* mention the music. *Please* speak about the island. Michael agreed to a rest for a minute. He lit a cigarette, positioned it on the edge of the bench, then absently lit another.

"You should know, . . ." he said, pinching tobacco from his tongue.

"Yes?"

"I can't explain it."

"Try."

Michael rubbed his temples. "I've a fierce headache tonight," he confessed.

"I can make it better."

His grin was bemused. "Let me tell you about a dream," he said. "A dream I keep having."

"Please do."

"God you're young."

"Not so young!"

"I'm a boy in the dream, lying on my stomach at the Lochar Rocks, gazing down at a ledge. Below me is the sea. Above me is the sky. Ahead is the sea dissolved into the sky and the sky dissolved into the sea. Guillemots sketch halos above my head and puffins—"

Francine asked what a guillemot was.

"Small birds," he answered impatiently. "The Blaskets are swarming with them." He dragged on the first Export. " . . . sketch halos above my head and puffins fall through the air, the way seabirds do. The slope is sheer, running down to the precipice, and though the ground is solid underfoot, I no longer feel it. Like I'm between heaven and earth—rising, rising."

"Yes," Francine said.

"Anyway, as I'm perched there, three seals appear on the ledge below. The animals begin to low, soft and plaintive, snouts twitching in the salt. Do you know how a moaning seal sounds, Fran?"

"No."

"Like a child in pain."

Francine's smile wavered.

"A seal raises its eyes to me. The animal seems to indicate something, so I inch nearer the edge. Sure enough, there's a staircase carved into the cliff. Why haven't I seen it before? I'm at Lochar daily. How could I have missed a mossy staircase?

"I'm delighted, naturally, and resolve to climb down to the cove. Only there's a problem: a ten-foot drop onto the first step. I look to the seals for advice. They're dissolving in mist, though their lowings are still clear." Michael paused to crush one cigarette, begin another. "I sink to my knees, turn around, spread my elbows, and lower my legs over the edge. My shoulders tremble—"

Closing his eyes, he extended his arms in demonstration. Francine's face lost colour.

"—as I slide, until I dangle, cheek flush against the rock. I seek the first step with my toe. Too far below. Determined to drop onto the stair, I crane my neck, left shoulder slumped, to locate it—the step, the staircase, that will lead me down to the sea."

He stopped.

"Finish," Francine said.

"You're sure?"

"Finish the dream, Michael."

"It's what you expect," he said. "I'm too extended to pull myself back up, and there's no stairs beneath me. No stairs, no ladder: a sheer drop to the ocean. I keep searching for the step, thinking my sight must be bad. But the truth is I'm losing my grip, clutching at crumbling earth, grabbing at thin air. . . . "

Afterwards, Francine rationalized her reaction to the end of the story. She had fled the park with barely a good night, boarding the College streetcar for the rooming house where she was staying until the wedding. In her room she had wept, wrapped herself in a blanket, and cursed not only dreams but people who took them seriously. Francine rarely dreamed, and counted herself lucky, like a thin person who could gorge without gaining a pound. The comparison reminded her that she and Michael had planned to have dinner at Fran's restaurant (a sentimental favourite). Hunger vanquished her brooding, and she descended to the kitchen to fix eggs and toast.

Francine did believe she could cure Michael's headaches and dizzy spells. She believed equally that she understood his doubts, and that he had, in effect, told her about the fiddle and the island, obliquely but implicitly—the best he could manage. Her Michael was a thinker, someone who felt deeply but could not express the depths of those feelings, leaving him frustrated. She would help him. She would explain him to himself. Love explained people to themselves. Love, Francine maintained, was a set of magical glasses; without them, blindness ruled. The glasses had two sets of lenses. The first set allowed the wearer to see herself more clearly. Not only to see, but to like: the tint revealed how basically decent human beings were. The second set permitted the viewer to recognize those same qualities in others. Know yourself, and you could know other people; love yourself, and you would be capable of love for someone else.

Her confidence regained, Francine sat at the kitchen table for an hour daydreaming. She dialled Michael's number, but he wasn't home. Perhaps he had walked over to the restaurant to find her, and then decided to eat there anyway. More likely, he had set off on a ramble. Michael might have dropped by the apartment to confirm a barren fridge. Probably he had stopped at a greasy spoon for a hot sandwich and french fries. A bite of food, a cup of tea, and he was content. Michael had repeated the phrase so often that Francine now believed it implicitly; he just wasn't fussy.

Chapter 11

On Sunday morning I escort Hia to St. Mary's for eleven o'clock mass. We are merely two pilgrims in a procession that climbs the street and disappears through the church's gaping doors. The spire is set against an enthralling sky. Before coming to Dingle, I would never have imagined that a single heaven, viewed from a single point at a single moment, could embody such contradiction. It is simultaneously sturdy and sagging, cinereous grey and crystal blue; raining over town while pouring sunshine across the harbour; perpetually moving, perfectly still; threatening, calm. Little wonder most parishioners walk with their heads bowed.

I leave her at the church and continue up Green Street. At the request of the musician (via, as usual, Eily Murphy), the hour of the interview was changed last night from three o'clock to "mass time", the question of which mass being left up to me. I knock on the door of a rowhouse across from the national school.

"I'm looking for Mr. Walshe," I say to the young man who answers.

"In the flesh."

I am supposed to interview a sixty-year-old musician named Naill Walshe. "Is your father in?"

"The old man's up in Listowel caring for his sister. I'm the stand-in. Francis—Francis Walshe."

We shake hands.

"Can you play?" I ask.

"Like Paganini."

"Maybe I'll try again later this week."

"Chat about the fiddle?" Francis Walshe says, pulling me inside the house. "The Celtic roaratorio, the bog-hole singalong? Baby, I'm your man!"

He motions into the living room.

"Beer?" he asks.

"Too early."

"Fuck it. I always open a can of stout at precisely half-eleven Sunday morning, the moment the sheep below in St. Mary's are preparing to gnaw on the Party wafers. Hair of the dogma, you know."

Francis Walshe is a lanky twenty-eight-year-old with rust-red hair and sallow skin. His muddy green eyes, so round they are almost protuberant, belie an otherwise manic personality. He speaks in clipped tones, abuses the air with his hands, and bounces up and down in his chair at his own witticisms. Besides collecting dole, Francis tells me he tends bar at a local hotel, spins records at dances, and sometimes "fucks off" to busk in Cork. He is, for some reason, quite familiar; I have probably seen him around Dingle.

PK: Did your father teach you the fiddle?

FW: I was initiated into the fraternity at a tender age, lessons every Saturday and Sunday, and then carted off to hear the da jam, with a few well-jarred comrades, at the local shit-been. Hedge school, like.

PK: Hedge school?

FW: You know, the "P&P". *(Voice deepens.)* "Handing down the traditions is the life-blood—"

PK: John Bagley, yes. I met him.

FW: What a gombeen man. Dire at the fiddle, too. Couldn't play to save his—

PK: You were talking about your father?

FW: My father taught me the instrument, that's right. I also learned a few tricks doing three years of music at UCC.

PK: You studied formally?

FW: The lecturers were certainly formal. So were the west Brits in the class who prattled on about Moh-zarr and Bay-tho-ven. I was less formal, interested enough in the classical stuff, but not gone on dead Austrians who wore wigs.

PK: Do you play classical violin?

FW: I know a tune or two. *(Picks up the fiddle.)* "Can I play?" says Stevie Wonder. "Can I play?"

(Francis down-bows the D string. He offers two strong phrases, definitely not classical.)

PK: They taught Jimi Hendrix at UCC?

FW: Hardly. More this tempo: *(He plays a single volatile phrase.)* Guess who?

PK: I don't know. . . . The Pogues?

FW: Béla-fucking-Bartók! Now there was a composer with some juice. Sounds like the feedback when you smash your guitar into an amp, the way Townsend used to.

PK: Very interesting.

FW: The old jigs and reels, right. "Toss the Feathers" and "Drowsy Maggie" pounded out on a thousand and one accordions and a wall of tin whistles played by pink-cheeked nine-year-olds.

PK: Just solo fiddling.

FW: All you foreigners want—

PK: Solo fiddling.

FW: What about your father? I know about him.

PK: Sorry?

FW: I grew up in this backwater, remember. Time *is* an abstract out here—1958 or 1985, it's all the one. Put that in your pipe and smoke it, Paddy Keane!

PK: I know about him too. Now I want to learn about your experiences as a fiddler.

FW: You're serious?

PK: I think so.

FW: Well, if that's the story.... I spent last summer in Edinburgh, busking outside a department store in Princess Street. The Scots were mad for Irish music, so I played it for six hours every day, until my bow was in tatters. Mostly I ghost-walked, more concerned with ogling some bird than the music. But the occasional melody would draw me back: the beauty of the structure, certain phrases. I'd be standing there on the sidewalk, watching tenpence coins drop into my box, people rushing past, dogs sniffing my leg, and I'd be thinking: you hand-me-down Brits, you highland culchies, I am here playing a work of art, a singing thing, and all you can do is scramble to buy a jumper or scoff a bun in a café!

PK: And?

FW: And nothing. That was maybe once a day. The rest of it, I was too knackered or jarred to even be sure which tune I was playing. It's all hereditary. All political.

PK: Political?

FW: Status quo, son. Paddy in the cap and wellies stuck in some squalid hole of a pub, where the jakes are a wall to piss against and a photo over the bar of De Valera keeps a close watch; Paddy the no-abortion, no-divorce, good John Paul II Catholic, good subsistence farmer yanking spuds from the fields and chasing pathetic cows about the place;

Paddy the half-arsed Republican who sings "A Nation Once Again" and "Tom Barry" but is, in actual fact, a Free Stater down to his breeches, has never been to the North, doesn't *know* any Northerners, doesn't *like* the Northerners he doesn't know, their accents, their nasty habits, the crises of guilt and bad-fucking-faith they're causing him—THAT'S the Paddy who's playing the music, you see, slumming it through "The Pigeon on the Gate" all fat-fingered and out of tune.

PK: Why blame the music for the people who play it?

FW: The music fits the patter.

PK: Tired ideas, Francis.

FW: I wouldn't expect you to understand.

PK: Then why do you play?

FW: How do you mean?

PK: Why not join a rock band in Dublin and perform parodies of traditional songs on electric guitars and synthesizers?

FW: Don't be daft.

PK: Why is it daft? You said yourself—

FW: I said the music was brilliant. I said, or should have said, that the fiddle can be lovely. It's great gas to play it. Hell is other people; not some poor instrument. . . .

PK: Okay.

FW: You'd have to live here to understand my thinking. It's not fair to come waltzing in for a fortnight, son of the local legend, and pronounce upon the colourful wildlife.

PK: I never—

FW: Besides, all my brothers and sisters have emigrated or fucked off to Dublin. My parents are on their own. Everyone has responsibilities. Everyone carries a ball and chain.

PK: Of course.

FW: Let me tell you a story about our beloved Dingle. There once was a man who owned a house along the Tralee Road, near where the football pitch is now. Thatched cottage, like: two rooms, an outhouse, a shed. Right. One morning the man is chewing on his brown bread and greasy eggs, listening to the wireless, the rain on the roof, when he decides he's had enough. Enough of what? The poor fuck hasn't a clue. Wouldn't recognize his own shadow. Wouldn't join a club that would have him as a member. Typical Kerryman, in other words.

Anyway, he puts on his jacket and cap and walks up the road towards Tralee. Leaves the breakfast on the table and the radio turned on. The man tells no one, understand, and packs nothing. Just up and vanishes.

Right. People in Dingle, meanwhile, trot past the house and stare through the window at the bread and eggs. What's up? they ask themselves. So-and-so must have gone to visit his mother in Tralee. After a few weeks, one neighbour is bold enough to cross the doorstep and switch off the radio. Otherwise, the locals leave the place be. Years pass. Five, six, seven, eight, nine, ten, *eleven* years go by without so much as a postcard from the man. Maybe he was kidnapped and murdered? Maybe he jumped into his trawler one night, opened the throttle, and piloted west towards Canada? Eleven years! Even Dingle folk are growing inquisitive.

Then one morning Paddy or Mick or Liam is ambling past the house when he notices a familiar fellow washing the same plates and cups at the kitchen sink. The local doesn't knock or anything—

that might seem nosy.

But he runs into the ghost later that evening at Tom Daly's. Sure enough, it's himself, back from the dead. "Are you well?" asks Paddy or Mick or Liam. "Fine," answers the man. "Things are all right?" says the one. "Never better," replies the other. Then, to be sociable, the lad adds: "Will I see you at the eleven o'clock this Sunday?" "I'd say so," says the man.

Happy ending: God in heaven, Paddy back in church, on his knees, praying to be forgiven for the sin of being alive.

PK: Yes?

FW: Ask Jimmy Sullivan about the story. Ask him if it isn't the truth.

PK: One more thing. How come you know about . . . ?

FW: Your da?

PK: *(nods)*

FW: The Great Man once deigned to give my fiddling a listen. He ridiculed my technique, mocked my style, then went on for an hour about music and art, heaven and eternity. Senile rubbish. Your father figured in the rant.

PK: The Great Man?

FW: I'm sure Jimmy has plans for you and him. Assuming, of course, the old codger is still breathing. Even *he* isn't immortal.

I am halfway up the stairs to our apartment when Hia calls from the sitting room off the hallway. She is sipping tea with Eily Murphy. Both women smooth their skirts over their knees at my entrance. Hia always dresses for mass: red shoes and dark nylons, a black dress or plaid skirt. Her choices in sabbath apparel mirror uncannily those of her friend and mentor, Francine Keane. In Toronto I had to get used to Hia emerging from the bedroom every Sunday morning transformed into a miniature version of my mother, a weekly flirtation with aesthetics fundamentally alien to her. (She dismissed my criticisms as Freudian.) Today she wears the skirt below a white turtleneck drawn to the elbows. With her jet-black hair and serene brown eyes, her eloquent hands and coffee skin, Hia is a portrait of decorum, a study in controlled dignity.

Eily Murphy is equally demure in a wool dress, knotted orange scarf, and a phoenix-shaped brooch pinned to her chest. Her hair is fastened with a clip, strengthening her profile and highlighting the freckles on her forehead and cheeks.

The sitting room itself is cosy. A Victorian couch is bookended by matching chairs. On the mantel of an unlit fireplace is a vase of daffodils; along shelves are rows of black-and-white photographs, mostly of family, but several of fishermen on Dingle pier or in the cockpits of trawlers. Eily Murphy's walls boast a half-dozen unsigned sketches—of the harbour, Reenbeg Point, the view from the Conor Pass—whose resemblance to the drawings that Hia closeted upstairs makes my palms sweat. If Hia shares my dismay, she disguises it. Avoiding even a glance at the artwork, I run my eyes over the photographs while politely refusing tea. I also notice a colour television flashing soundless images from a corner.

On my way upstairs I stop and listen to our landlady's explanation of her wedding day in St. Mary's (a wedding portrait is prominent amid the collection). She is detailing a point of difference between the restored church and the pre-1962 structure, a distinction that is valuable if Hia is to visualize the ceremony. One too many asides, digressions, and dangling sentences, and I climb the remaining steps.

Hia appears an hour later. "We met at mass. Nice of Eily to ask me for tea and biscuits. But her English is so knotty. And the accent!"

"Could you follow?"

"Mostly. If not, I watched the TV and looked at things in the room."

"Did you avert your eyes from the sketches?"

"Different walls," she answers with a shrug, "different tastes."

"Any idea who the artist is?"

"What artist?"

I switch mediums.

"Why so many photographs of fishermen?"

"Her husband fished."

"Really?"

Hia's smile is inward. "Eily has something important to tell us," she says.

"Us?"

"Don't be so self-absorbed. Not everything is about your father."

"I never said—"

"How was the interview?"

The question is such a pleasant surprise that I drop the other business. "Awful," I answer. "Again."

"Why?"

"It was off centre, off topic. Actually," I say, analysing my hour with Francis Walshe for the first time (on the walk back home I was once more euphoric), "there *was* no centre, no topic. It was like this man and I had known each other in a previous life, and had to resolve all these old tensions before getting down to business. We never did."

"Sounds good."

In a way it was. Very good, even.

"You had to be there," I answer. "But I do have the tape of the interview, if you'd like to listen."

She ignores the offer. "Tension is important. Makes you sharp, gives your work edge and clearness. Tension is also opposite of, what is the word, for person who is unsure, who hesitates?"

"Tentative?"

"Opposite of tentative, right." Hia indicates the top sheet of her work pad. "Look at these drawings," she says. "Not great. Not to be content with."

It is difficult to agree with her. The sheet has been quartered with a ruler, each box housing the outline of a temple. The sketches are simple, but clear and professional; I still have trouble accepting that Hia can work without visual aids. Next to the pad is the abacus, the large compass, and a stick of charcoal to darken images.

"Name the temples."

"Top left is Phimeanakas. The very old one, Phnom Bakheng, is below it. That temple is weird: long and low, like a tunnel, with no interest in the sky. My favourite," she continues, running a finger over the outline, "is the Bayon. So orderly. So mystic. At the bottom is a temple called Phreah Khan. It is just okay."

"What about Angkor Wat?"

"I cannot draw Angkor Wat yet. I have no right. I must be worthy of it."

Each temple lurks on the page behind a scaffolding of faint lines. The sketches all use ruler marks and compass arcs, though the predominant shape is the square. While the work is not rigid, it is conventional: more an architect's model than an artist's rendition. The abacus has been shifted and calculations clutter the margins.

"Do you use ratios?"

"Only to make the temples have the same size. For the moment, I need them to be clear."

"They are."

"But too tent-at-ive. Too much working with the subject. I must get inside Angkor. I must get to a place where I no longer see anything; where the lines come out by themselves, each time new born, each time perfect."

"These drawings are not tentative, Hia."

"Maybe skilled. Maybe accomplished. But still wrong."

I glance at the Angkor Wat artifact propped against the wall. Hia has turned the etched face away; the exposed sandstone is blank.

"Eily tells me Jimmy has interviews for you with better musicians next week," she remembers. "She says he contacts men with no phones."

"No phones?"

"She says."

"How does our xenophobic landlady know so much about Jimmy Sullivan's plans?"

Her eyes change shape. "I have forgiven her," she says.

"So I should too?"

"*I* have forgiven her."

"How come she knows?"

"In the village where we lived everyone knew when you had sex, bad bowels, your first period. Privacy is not possible in small towns."

Later that evening I step out to buy milk. Something Hia mentioned earlier, about the need for tension in creativity, stays in my mind. Where, I wonder, is the tension in her work? Where is the tautness and trembling, like a cocoon pecked by predators until it bursts open? When Hia's project is completed, will the creature that emerges from the shell be what she envisioned? What she wants? What she needs?

I nearly collide with Jimmy Sullivan in front of the house. He coughs, slips a key into his pocket. "Imagine it," he mumbles. "Meeting you, out here in the open."

He invites me into the landing. To do this, he must retrieve the key and unlock the door. Given that the night is dry, the sky is glittering, and the landing is narrow and dark, the invitation is eccentric.

"Apologies about today," Jimmy says, breathing whisky. "I meant for Eily to tell you that Naill Walshe had been called up to Listowel. She thought you and Francis should meet."

"He was interesting."

"A bit chuffed with himself, I'd say. But a decent boy. Far too talented to be languishing here. Francis is the only child of six still in Dingle, and he's devoted to his parents. His mother is seriously ill, you know."

I thank him for arranging the interview.

"Now, Pat. Come here a minute."

I stand my ground.

"I'm delighted with this project of yours. Truly I am. Never mind my poor form the other evening. Never mind the botch with Bagley. Your father would—"

"Would he?"

"Surely."

I hold his gaze.

"I mean," Jimmy stammers, "it's fitting and proper, a sign of respect. A sign of commitment and—"

"Would he, though?" I repeat. It's happening again: words are fleeing my mouth before I can stop them.

"How would you know what he'd think?"

"I don't. I'm asking you."

"The hell you are. You're accusing. You're pointing fingers at others instead—"

"I have to get to the shop before it closes."

Jimmy's fine-boned face, reverting from animation back to lethargy, momentarily loses all expression. The blankness is startling.

"The pleasure is mine," he says blandly, "to help get the business off the ground. We'll have her going in no time, I promise."

Back outside, he flattens his palm against my chest, then pushes, fondly, but with a dormant aggressivity. Jimmy announces he is home to bed. We part. At the street corner I hide behind a wall and observe him turn around, check for witnesses, then reinsert the key into Eily Murphy's front door.

Agreed: Jimmy Sullivan is more than a stranger who

once wrote a letter to my mother and helped arrange our accommodation. He and I *are* connected. The story hovers around Dingle, like a bird circling over a chasm, and I should work to draw it closer. Eventually I will, or else, more likely, the bird will be tempted by fatigue or curiosity into descending. But where's the rush? It isn't that important. It isn't about me.

When I was twelve, a girl in my class was rumoured to have no father. Her name was Ellen Peters. She was pale and sickly, her curly hair matted, her fingers yellow. Because she was often absent for weeks, often forced to leave class at midday, her mother pulling into the driveway at Holy Ghost Elementary and waiting until her daughter was escorted from the office by Sister Anne-Marie Lincoln, and because it was always the mother who collected her, an unsmiling woman in sunglasses and a shawl, and the father was never present, never referred to, and Ellen had no real friends at Holy Ghost, suffering recesses in a corner of the playing field, where she read or watched other kids play, and rarely spoke out (her illness had caused her to fail a grade already), and teachers, probably fearful of embarrassing the child, sometimes passed over her name at attendance even when she was there; because Ellen Peters had hollows beneath her eyes and wore shabby clothes and was pudgy, and ill, and so desperately unhappy she gave off a warning scent, other kids acted ruthless towards her. She was Peters the Pig. Peters the Pig, Peters the Pig, a face like an ass and an ass twice as big! Her dad was so disgusted he ran away. Her mother was so depressed she drank all day. Ellen Peters had an illness. She was gross. Touch anything she had touched and you got cooties. Touch her and you got them the most.

In the playground, my classmates would dare and double-dare each other to sneak up and brush against her. Then they'd scream and flee laughing, contaminated until a hot bath washed the germs off.

I acted neutral towards the girl. Never did I jibe her, either to her face or behind her back; nor, however, did I befriend her or come to her defence. What I managed, once, was to wait until she had dropped her milk carton into the garbage, make certain no one was watching, and then fish the container out, daring a malicious infection to spread.

In June of that year, I followed Ellen Peters home from school. On reaching the corner of Bayview and Finch, where a ravine crossed the intersection through a culvert, she veered from the sidewalk onto a path down the slope. I was surprised—the culvert was for necking during daylight and drinking at night—but scurried after her. The stream was ankle-deep. It wound around a bluff, straightened before the hillside, then vanished into the gaping cylinder that had been wedged, like an eyehole, into the embankment. Flat stones formed a causeway. Ellen Peters straggled to the mouth, scanned the slope where I crouched in tall grass, then entered. By the time I reached the entrance she had negotiated a bend; reluctantly—I had been inside once with Judy Dillon, once to smoke cigarettes with John Macdonald—I went in too.

The tunnel was four metres in diameter. Being round, its sides were easy to knock against, useless for gripping. Water seemed to gather force over the surface, unfettered by rocks or branches. It was how I imagined miners might feel a kilometre into the earth. Air was damp. Light meshed with dark. The stream, barely a murmur above ground, was now a roar. The deeper I penetrated, the stronger the darkness, the greater the noise. Near the middle of the culvert, I stopped before a bend and squatted. A grey shadow, cast with sunlight from the opposite entrance, stretched against the wall and up over my head. The surging water fell silent, and I locked onto the sound of a small, high voice.

I went to school all day today, Ellen Peters was saying. Mommy said I should try. Just this once. I felt bad in the morning. Mr. Martin told me it was okay if I left early. He said everyone understood. I lied, told him I felt good. Mommy talked with Sister Anne-Marie on the phone last night. I never ever cry, no matter what. Kids call me fat. Mommy says it's because I can't exercise. I wish I could eat chocolate. I wish you were here. I wish—

Suddenly the shadow shifted, plunged into the current. I looked up and saw her across the tunnel. Her head was cocked in my direction; her limbs were frozen at her sides in fright or dismay. Panicking, I leapt back over the flat stones, not daring to check over my shoulder. At the mouth I squinted into the sun, splashed through the water, scrambled up the embankment to the road.

My first impulse was to race home. But the house would be empty until six o'clock; Mother was inspecting stores in Mississauga all week. Instead, I hid in the ridge of oak trees that covered a shoulder of the ravine, drying my shoes on a branch. An hour passed. I calmed. Another hour went by. Mother would have the table set for two, food cooling in bowls, cats stalking my glass of milk. Twilight deepened. I grew bored. Also anxious: I would be grounded for the weekend, maybe longer. Why hadn't Ellen Peters come out? She was a weird girl. Lingered in tunnels. Talked with her dead—

At midnight, I crossed Bayview Avenue and slid down the far embankment to where a streetlamp illuminated the culvert's opposite mouth. The hole was, as I well knew, fenced off: no one could have entered or exited at that end. I ran home to a distraught parent and a livid pseudo-parent (mother had called Davey Russell) with full knowledge that Ellen Peters was still under the earth.

She was. I wasn't. That's how I understood it.

Ellen failed to appear at school the next morning, and was officially "withdrawn"—a word students mouthed in hushed tones—a week later. In the fall, her name was not on the class lists.

I was reminded of the incident after nearly two decades by the shadow Jimmy threw into the lane the instant before he slipped inside the house. From my spot behind the wall, backlit by a streetlamp, I also cast a form, which Jimmy would have noticed had he glanced up the street. What finally occurred to me was that if Ellen had been a flicker against the culvert wall, so must I have been. Worse, since she was addressing an absence, might my shadow have been mistaken for its incarnation?

I should return to the apartment, but prefer to haunt the Dingle streets for an hour, admiring the moon adrift behind clouds. Parted curtains offer up the interiors of houses. Front rooms, aglow in television light, are full of people I don't know, who don't know me. The night ensures this anonymity.

Chapter 12

In the fall of 1957, Francine made an appointment with a young doctor in his office at the corner of Finch Avenue and Yonge Street. The day was blustery and the overcast sky hosted a flock of noisy seagulls, infrequent visitors to the suburbs. As she walked to the meeting, Francine observed the birds spread their wings and be blasted upwards, bodies arched like bows, until their plumage blended with the clouds. Dr. Reynolds confirmed her intuition: she was six weeks pregnant, due in mid-May. Francine rushed home in peace—the seagulls had circled back towards the lake—to ring Eglinton Station. Michael was at lunch. She called her mother. The line was busy. Thinking she would burst if she couldn't share the news, Francine dialled Davey Russell's number, knowing he was working nights. Davey toasted the prospective parents with his tea.

"Michael will be thrilled," he said.

"I hope so."

"In his own way he will, sure."

Francine sobbed.

"Now, now, Fran."

"I'm so happy!"

"I'll be there for you."

"You don't—"

"Count on it," Davey Russell said.

That evening, once the news had been spread up and down their street, the length of the Eglinton division, and across a swath of Northern Ontario, Francine seized upon Michael's delight to ask him a question. They sat in the kitchen picking at a dinner of take-out fish and chips. The question had lived in Francine's heart for as long as, perhaps longer than, her desire to fill the other four table chairs with hungry children. She could not, in fact, separate the two things, though she was equally unable to connect them consciously.

"Why won't you play the fiddle?"

Michael lowered his celebratory glass of whisky. "Have you been talking to Davey again?"

"I talk to you, Michael."

"The question is a bit off. You should ask why I stopped playing the fiddle."

Francine didn't agree, but waited.

"I stopped because I stopped living in Dingle. I stopped because I was dead as a fiddler. Dead musicians are pitiable creatures."

"When did you . . . ?" She left the sentence unfinished.

"The moment I left the island, most likely. Once in Canada, at any rate, I heard no sounds."

She asked.

"The sound of wind," he said uneasily, "and birds, and surf over a shoreline. You can't play with a head full of car horns and subway trains. You can't—"

He shrugged.

Francine studied his eyes. Disliking what she learned—Michael could convert his eyes from windows into walls instantaneously—she did something she had never done before: refilled his glass.

"I ask again—why won't you play the fiddle here, in Toronto?"

"There's no one to play for, Fran."

"No one?"

"No barn dances. No kitchen sessions. Not even any other real fiddlers. There's no *reason* for the music. It hasn't any purpose in this country."

"You need a reason to play?"

"What a question," he answered.

The conversation ended unhappily.

Francine was advised to quit her job before the Christmas season. Anxious about her career, she requested a year's leave of absence, which was granted in December. On the first of February, Michael ordered her to stop all housework; he and Davey would give the bungalow a cleaning each Saturday morning. They did, and afterwards, when the house was quiet, Francine repaired the damage. In March she stopped repairing the damage, and began to watch more television. By early April she was confined to the couch, back aching, feet pillowed; the baby was a gymnast, specializing in somersaults. Michael was not surprised. Their child, he predicted, would be a daredevil. Their child would be a "little man". Never considering a girl, Michael assigned the foetus a name: Patrick John. Did Francine mind the choice? he eventually asked.

A telegram addressed to Michael O Cathain was delivered to the house on April 18. The spelling of his last name convinced Francine the message was both urgent and unwelcome. She debated whether to open the envelope. For a brief, shameful moment, she even considered destroying it.

TOMAS PASSED AWAY LAST NIGHT. WITH HIM DURING FINAL HOURS. SINCEREST CONDOLENCES. FUNERAL SATURDAY IN DUNQUIN. NO NEED FOR YOU TO COME. ISLAND IS EMPTY, DINGLE IS GRIM. WAIT A YEAR, THEN BRING FRANCINE AND THE CHILD. NO NEED TO COME NOW. SEAMUS.

Francine struggled with her emotions. The conflict within her was so volatile that for an hour she didn't trust herself to pick up the phone. Instead, she washed the dishes, made dough for a pie, and then finally got around to separating their winter clothes into two garment bags, for storage in the front closet. Once the trembling had subsided, and once the baby had ceased tumbling, she called. Michael took a taxi from downtown. He sat at the kitchen table with the telegram open and his eyes closed, fingers drumming on the arborite. Francine was too upset to sit, despite her back. She buried her hands in her sweater.

"Did you read it?"

"Only to know your father died."

"Not the rest?"

"It was to you, Michael.

He shut his eyes again. "I should return home for the funeral," he said quietly.

Francine failed to speak.

"Do you mind?"

The words, when she managed them, pounded inside her skull. "What you think best."

Michael folded the telegram. "It's best," he sighed.

The arrangements took a day. Francine's mother boarded a bus in Sudbury for her second-ever visit to Toronto. Michael phoned five travel agencies before finding a ship sailing from New York in thirty-six hours, with a dozen passenger berths and a port of call in Cork. The train to New York departed Union Station every morning. Davey Russell straightened matters out at work. He also drove up to Willowdale and asked his friend to sit with him in the car.

"Why the car?"

"More privacy."

"Privacy from whom?"

"Only for a minute, Michael."

They sat in Davey's car.

"It makes no sense . . . ," Davey said, offering his pack

of mints.

"You won't hear me disagree," Michael answered. "We could just as easily have gone around to the back garden."

Davey ignored the crack. "There's a flight to London this evening," he continued. "You could catch another to Dublin, or else a train to the Holyhead ferry. As it stands, you haven't a chance of making it."

"Making what?"

"The funeral!"

Michael was confused. "Sure I can't be home for that, Seamie. The boat won't dock for eight days."

"Fran is due when?" Davey asked, noting the slip.

"Three weeks."

"How in the world—?"

"I'll be back in time."

"What, are you going to make like a bird?"

"I said I'd be back."

The men exchanged glances.

"You must be keen to see Dingle again," Davey offered, conceding to his friend's illogic. "I know I'd love a holiday in Tipperary."

"It is nothing I am looking forward to."

The couple had only a few hours to decide. Francine, however, was serious about Michael doing what he thought best. Other people's lives were other people's lives. Even if that person was her husband; even if in a few weeks that person would be her daughter's (in her opinion) father. She spent the afternoon brooding. Her companion remained a stranger to her. Unfailingly gentle and polite, he was also as remote in many ways as on the day they'd first met. She had failed to penetrate the carapace that both protected and incarcerated him. Francine had extracted enough details about the Great Blasket to formulate a theory. Michael had, she believed, internalized the island: its isolation and inaccessibility, grandeur and aloofness. Now, tasting bitterness, she theorized further: his face was actually an island bluff; the cliffs of the Great Blasket were Michael's features.

She caught herself. They had good lives: jobs, a house, soon a child. These were tangible successes, tangible rewards for patience and perseverance. Francine was barely twenty-four years old. Her mind hummed with delightful plans and her body, even in the third trimester, was strong. Looking around her, she saw only newness. Half her neighbours were pregnant. The street rattled with prams; people on the block were petitioning the city for sidewalks so mothers could stroll in safety. Every week there was a baby shower to attend; every other week a glassy-eyed father knocked on their door to announce his newborn. Francine had helped decorate three nurseries in the last month, and had invited friends over that weekend to discuss wallpaper for the spare room. She would still welcome the women, still serve tea and cake, still gossip and laugh. Michael would simply miss the fun.

Davey Russell drove the couple to Union Station. Crossing the main hall to the platforms, they stopped momentarily to observe the skitterings of two starlings trapped inside the building. The tiny birds, caught under a cement sky, spanned the room in a flash, only to then veer from a wall, loop back, climb until confronted by ceiling.

At the gate, Davey lingered behind.

"Dreams are not us," Francine told her husband.

"Don't I know it."

"Not our lives. Not our future. We are not responsible to them."

"I'll be back with days to spare, Fran."

"Patrick John will never forgive you if you're late."

"Not for the world would I have my son angry with me," Michael said, kissing her. "Not for the world."

Davey knew of the plan, and approved. He would explain it to Francine in the car. Michael had been unable to even mention the word aloud. But he would follow through:

at a travel agent in Tralee he would book, and purchase, a ticket for a modern transatlantic journey. Michael would be flying home to Canada.

ONLY CHILD

Chapter 13

Hia thinks of lovemaking as a vessel that must be filled to capacity before it can spill over. She assigns only a single receptacle to the experience; both partners naturally share the same expectations. The vessel is fed with clear, icy water poured in gradually from a pitcher held high above the mouth. Foreplay fills the bottom third. First embraces bring the level halfway, the surface uneven, rising imperceptibly. The act grows solemn as the mark climbs towards the rim, until the liquid crests, levels, then seems to hold steady, despite still more water. Even the climax should be an act of will, trickles down the container walls, puddles at the base, rivulets that meander off like dripping paint.

For me, lovemaking involves two vessels, each filled to the quarter mark. Partners commence by pouring water from their container into the other. (Hia's vessel is serviced by an unnamed third party.) The exchanges are light, even silly: spills and splashes, liquid wasted in play. No need to worry about the supply; regardless of the intensity, the volume remains constant. Back and forth it goes, vessel to vessel, thirst to thirst, the level rising like a melody that trips into double time, the musicians playing on instinct. When the containers are topped and tip, when it rains sweat, showers oblivion, then a miracle, more impressive than the water into wine, has occurred; *both* vessels are brimming; *both* partners have been transformed.

As for Hia's contention that I am a latent Buddhist, which approach to lovemaking is more meditative? Which is truly Eastern, grounded in enlightened passivity and stoic virtue?

"I want to—" I say.

She groans.

" . . . want to tell—"

She groans louder.

" . . . tell you that—"

"You ruin it!" Hia says, pushing me off her.

"How?"

"I lose my concentration."

"They're just words."

"It is like there is someone else in the room."

"There is."

She is saucer-eyed. "Your father?"

"Carolan."

She hits me with a pillow.

Hia likes to recount her dreams after lovemaking. I don't mind hearing them, but feel under pressure to come up with my own, which, thankfully, I can't do. Tonight, though, I have prepared a story—half dream, half legend—to offer as a substitute. She goes first.

"I had the Chac dream again," she says, referring to her dead cousin. "I am burying him in a grave next to his father. I dig the hole myself, in order that the son and parent can be properly reunited. There are rules: too shallow in the hole and Chac's spirit will be unsettled; too deep and the *hon* will be unable to re-enter the body."

"I thought you didn't believe in *hon* and *via*."

"I don't."

"What about the *ma da*?"

"Same."

She gathers Carolan, who has joined us, into her arms.

"It rains hard in the dream," she continues. "The ground is wet, and I watch mud rise between my toes. Beside the grave are flowers and an incense pot. The flowers are wilted and the pot is filled with water. I dig and dig until the hole is ready—near his father, far from the jungle. Then I go to collect the body."

Though she lies beside me, Hia floats in a trance. "I have left Chac under a tree in the village. Wrapped him in white cloth, put rice ball in his mouth, studied the *cao to* to be sure he would not suffer from a bad spirit. Now, I race up the lane. The village is destroyed. Houses smoke from fire. Water buffalo rot in flooded fields. When I reach the tree, there is no body. I run from ruin to ruin, calling, the rain and my tears becoming one."

She pauses. "I return to the grave to throw myself in. Look down into the hole. There is a body already there. A body *not* prepared for funeral. . . . "

"Same ending."

"No change," she agrees.

Hia's sudden rise scares the cat. Throwing on her dressing gown, she disappears into the kitchen. I hear her rustle around in a cupboard.

"My turn," I say.

"You?"

"More a story—something my mother told me when I was a boy."

"And you remember?"

"I think so."

"Pat remembers his life before eighteen? Impossible!" Hia says, emerging with a stack of objects wrapped in newspaper.

"People used to believe that dreams were the adventures your soul had while you slept," I say. "The soul took the form of a butterfly. Once you were asleep, your soul crept up your throat, pried open your mouth, and fluttered away. *It* witnessed all the weird, impossible things you recalled the next morning. The butterfly slipped back in the mouth before dawn."

"I know this."

"Do you know what happened if the butterfly didn't return to the body?"

"Death."

My eyes widen. "Nothing so serious. Just no dreams that night."

"Death," she repeats.

"Are you sure?" I ask, trying to recall how mother ended the tale.

"It is logical. The butterfly is the human soul. No soul, no life. No life everlasting, either."

Hia's Old Testament spin sours the story for me, and I turn to her activity. She has unearthed six black clay dishes.

"I bought them from a pottery shop in town. Not perfect, but they will be okay."

"Okay as what?"

"Four for me," she says, lining up the bowls on the coffee table. "One for you, one for Carolan."

I am dumbfounded. Hia has always refused to have anything to do with ancestor shrines. Other Vietnamese in Toronto are openly critical of her apostasy, and her younger sister keeps a shrine in her bedroom closet. Hia's reasoning—that, as a practising Catholic, she believes the souls of the departed ascend into heaven—seems airtight. But her fellow countrymen dismiss her religious inclinations as irrelevant. For all her love of certain of her culture's more arcane ceremonies and obsolete customs, the gulf between how Hia, as a Vietnamese, is supposed to act, and how she actually lives her life, is often large.

"What else do we need?" I ask.

"Incense. Flowers. Oh yes, and photos."

"Ah."

"I have photos for all my pots. Four photos, four pots. What about you, Pat?"

She knows the answer. Defeated by her seriousness, I lower my gaze.

"Maybe we can find one," Hia soothes. "Of him, and also of Joan McGreevy."

Later, having transferred the pots to their home atop the television—Hia claims, without irony, that it is the ideal site for a shrine—I rise from the bed. Her breathing is regular; Carolan's wheeze is punctuated by snorts and gagging noises, as if he is expelling a furball in his sleep. The night is preternaturally still, and I cross the kitchen to the window. The village green is flooded in moonlight. The illusion of visibility is strong, but I can barely distinguish the caravan stranded near the south end of the park. I hear, however, clear as a culvert soliloquy, the *sshhs* and giggles of the teenagers who smoke cigarettes and neck inside the trailer, unperturbed by the mounds of garbage and broken bottles that must litter the floor.

I drink two glasses of water. The butterfly legend, told for innocent reasons, has triggered another, not so innocent memory. I don't know why I know, or who told me (or even why they told me), but I am fairly certain my father's body was never recovered. His grave in Dunquin is unoccupied. This should hardly come as a shock. When an object plummets from the sky, like a torch thrown from a cliff, like a jet obliterated by a bomb, it sometimes vanishes before reaching the earth. The fallen thing becomes the sky, the sea. Imagine a man who, waking from a dream, observes a bird emerge out of a wall of fog to perform loops and figure-eights. Eventually the bird returns to the obscurity. The air is again hollow. Heaven is once more a void. Question: is the man a man who observes a bird dance in the air, or is he a bird who watches a man observe a rolling heaven? And what about the earth?

The earth is empty. No body (to paraphrase Hia), no death. My father, therefore, must not be dead. My father must still be alive.

Part II

SHE WHO IS NOURISHED BY GOD

SHE WHO IS NOURISHED BY GOD

Chapter 1

My first recollection is of my mother. I am being held by her, held to her breast. She is beautiful. Of course she is; my mother is (*was*, I must learn to say) a beautiful woman. She had aristocratic looks, a few generations faded: a sculpted profile dominated by high cheekbones, short, blue-tinted hair, eyes set in swirls of liner. A beautiful woman, my mother, but the beauty of a victim, one who is doomed to be wronged. I inherited none of her looks and only a little of her passivity. I inherited everything from Thuy Thi Ngo *except* her lovely face and her sad, slightly forlorn ways. Certainly I have her image. I have her image, and I keep it well. Not in a painting, not in a photo, not even etched onto my retina. I keep the image where it cannot be erased: in my heart, my imagination, with God.

I recollect gazing up from Mother's chest to her face. Her narrow chin was set, her cherry lips were pursed. Strands of hair fell over her eyes, in fatigue, perhaps in despair. Someone was speaking to her, and from her furrowed brow I would guess the language was violent. From my vantage point, she is less a woman in a room with her husband and their baby, a room in a flat in Saigon in 1962, than an artwork in a museum: perfectly realized, perfectly displayed. My eyes cast beams to backlight the piece. My love calls corners from shadow.

Apparently, I consumed Mother's milk so voraciously that she ran out before I was a month old. Even in the cities, few children survived without this sustenance. A doctor prescribed the milk of calving water buffaloes as a replacement. My father found a supplier, and Mother began to feed me with dots of fluid from her finger. I was expected to die. When I didn't, when, in fact, I flourished, a neighbour nicknamed me *con troi nuoc*: she who is nourished by God. My younger sister, Nhung, less greedy, nursed for fifteen months from Mother's breasts, but was still sickly.

I got sick once, when I was seven. The war raged then, and Saigonese often linked private traumas, like an ill child, with the republic's misfortunes. I was suffering from headaches and dizziness. After a week of medicinal sweet rice and bitter tea, I was hauled off—at Father's insistence (he was from the highlands)—to a black-toothed shaman, a betel addict and con man, who spooked the neighbourhood from a shack off a busy thoroughfare. Mother was aghast; she was both city-born and Catholic. Nevertheless, I was presented to the wizard, along with the dried-up navels of all three children, for his inspection. The navels he examined closely, pronouncing those of both Nhung and me to be of living souls, still secure, in effect, within the womb. The navel of my fourteen-year-old brother Bo, however, was grey; the shaman could not see his future clearly—a bad omen. Mother scoffed at the prophesy. Father blanched.

The old man turned his attention to my malady. Noticing how I winced when a passing truck made the shed tremble, he asked if I had been exposed to any loud noises lately: bombings, land mines, helicopters. I perked up at the mention of helicopters. An American *may bay chuong-chuong* had landed in our schoolyard eight days before. This "fearful dragonfly" had swept down from the sky without warning, blasting an announcement only as it corkscrewed above the field. Classmates fled the terrain. Teachers scooped up the tardy. Only I remained in the shadow of the beating wings, determined to observe the mechanical insect up close. The helicopter was both dreadful and magnificent; I was frozen with terror, prickly with exhilaration. Waiting as long as it could—smoke billowed from the engine—the dragonfly flopped down ten metres from me. The wind whipped my clothes and a noise, like a gigantic vacuum, shattered the air. My ears started to ring.

Two soldiers were expelled from the wounded machine. They wore helmets and mirror sunglasses. One man jogged over to me, dropped to his knees. His face was hairy. His nose was enormous. I answered his babble with a question about the wisdom of blind people flying helicopters. To illustrate my point, I removed the glasses from his face. How blue his eyes were! How round, like marbles! At first I thought the man would strike me for exposing his deformity. But he only smiled and, probably relieved I hadn't been crushed, hoisted me into his arms.

I never mentioned the incident to my family, for fear of Father's bamboo stick. Now that the shaman had guessed it, though, I confessed to a buzzing in my head, the result of a shattered eardrum. My parents were furious. But the old man clapped his hands in delight, revelling at my impertinence with the sunglasses. The wizard declared me a young *phung thi chin*, an appellation, he assured my mother and father, he did not affix lightly. Nor was the status of woman warrior without its responsibilities, he lectured me. Honour, valour, and vengeance: these would have to be the standards by which I lived, and, if need be, died for my family and my country.

Being pronounced a member of a mythic sorority did not spare me a beating that night. Father drank rice wine before lacerating the flesh behind my thighs with his stick. Not to beat a child was not to love her, he intoned piously. My father's wisdom belonged to his ancestors; his venom could be traced to the wine.

But I was now a woman warrior, and the pain meant nothing. For ten years I embraced the myth. Never mind that the *phung thi chin* was a jumble of folklore and legend, or that famous women warriors, like the Trung sisters, were likely apocryphal; I was committed to living the aesthetic, and my aesthetics have always been consuming. At age eleven, while the Americans were scurrying from Saigon, I tried to join an attachment of the Phu Nu Cong Hoa, a female republican defence brigade. The brigade turned out to be in disarray, like the army, like the republic, and my application was ignored. Then, when Bo was killed in December 1974, among the final senseless deaths of an exhausted conflict, I flailed about endeavouring to avenge his lost honour.

From whom should I seek revenge? The Yankee dragonflies were a memory for most, a faint ringing for me. Defending the nation against outside enemies had long been problematic (the Americans were our allies). Once they had fled, however, the issue became even more murky. Bo was killed by his brethren. My family sacrificed its honour to our neighbour's. Unification under the Communists only heightened the confusion, especially once father was declared a miscreant and Bo's spirit, that of a fallen hero, was vilified. Humiliated, unable to locate a target for my heroism, I felt my fury turn inward: I loathed myself for failing my family, failing the myth.

I remember sitting by the window in our flat the morning in 1975 when the Vietcong marched on Independence Palace, watching as a republican soldier stripped himself naked, left his boots and helmet, olive fatigues, and dismantled rifle in a pile, and then removed a pair of pants from a clothesline and slipped them on. Three months later, Than Van Loi, a merchant with military connections, was sentenced to ten years in prison. Mother, Nhung, and I moved south to a Mekong Delta village called Can Duoc where distant, and unwelcoming relatives, took us in. Their reluctance was understandable; we were strangers, outcasts, and, to make matters worse, practitioners of an alien religion. The village was almost entirely Buddhist, but still featured a tiny Catholic church, raised on stilts to avoid the monsoon.

The church remained open for six months. Once the priest fled to Singapore in a boat, our family constituted the sole surviving Catholics in the area. Nhung and I were barred from school. Mother's clerical job was terminated. Her upper-class cheekbones and patrician ways—the Saigon accent, finishing-school manners, her knowledge of French—all were held against her, against us, both by Party bullies (cadres who wanted to sleep with mother particularly treated us like filth), and by the peasants who resented, more than ever, our presence in Can Duoc. By 1977 she was preparing bowls of noodles at the village pier, and Nhung and I, barefoot and friendless, were her assistants.

Women warriors did not serve noodles to gap-toothed fishermen. Women warriors did not keep an ancestor shrine, featuring photos of a disgraced brother and class-enemy grandparents, behind a cupboard. Women warriors certainly did not kneel every evening, after Mother had checked that no one was snooping around our hut, and after she had rehung the crucifix—hidden below a floorboard—on the wall, and pray for forgiveness from a vanquished God.

What gave way was the legend. I had gotten it wrong. The woman warrior had failed me, not the other way round. The myth was a useless antiquity. It could neither engage, nor combat, these modern complexities. The values the *phung thi chin* espoused were equally bankrupt. People did not avenge honour; people endured humiliation, smiling. People did not sacrifice for the country's good; people mangled their nation, brutalized each other, destroyed themselves. Why, in any case, should archetypes have always emphasized death and vengeance? What about life? What about creativity and procreation?

Other creeds imploded quickly. I no longer wished to

be Vietnamese. I no longer wished to speak the language. These were sunglasses that had blinded *my* eyes for too long. Flight from the country—the subject of whispered discussions between Mother and me from the moment we arrived in the delta—became a flight from an inherited selfhood to one that was, or would be, wilful. The open sea and the endless sky south of the Mekong would constitute a new sea and a first sky. I would stare with my own eyes at my own reality, and see, clearly, what was there. As usual, I adhered to this aesthetic with the same passion that I had applied to the woman warrior. A person can't help who she is, can she?

On the sea, though, I discovered still something else. On the sea, in my despair, the world changed yet again. All this happened, understand, before I ever saw Canada.

The problem is that I don't tell Pat enough about my past, and what he tells me about his is garbled in metaphor. Pat looks at the sky and sees what is within himself. He anthropomorphizes heaven because he fears order, fears what cannot be undone. But, like it or not, the sky over Dingle is a completed cathedral. Tonight, as we trample the hoof-rutted paths towards Reenbeg Point, the rain suddenly stops and the sky splits open above the storm clouds. Light filters through the strata. It is undulent, like sun through stained glass, and the air is crisp. Still further up, several tiers over the earth, is a ceiling, similar to a planetarium roof. You must look hard to see it, but it is there. Everything below the ceiling is protected. Everything, and everyone, is permanent: is, ultimately, still. Pat's emotional weather belies simple observation.

Low tide exposes forty metres of harbour bed. The shore is strewn with kelp and crawfish and the sand near the breaker is patterned with dog prints, the hieroglyphs of birds. Towards the point I spot a lamb washed up in the rocks. The corpse is bloated, one eye gone, a blue tongue between its teeth. Around the animal's neck is a rope. Vomit rises in my throat; my mind links events brutally, unfairly, until I look away. Happily, Pat is busy admiring the Ring of Kerry.

A tower stands on a rise a quarter-mile before the headland. Beyond it is a jetty of sandy grass, thickets of bracken and purple buddleia, networks of rabbit holes. The jetty is an excellent place to observe incoming ships. Most trawlers return to port at sunset. The day's catch is easily measured by the number of seagulls above the boats. Hundreds of pesky birds wheel over the large trawlers, squawking in jealousy, with dozens more surfing over their wakes.

We continue out to a lighthouse perched at the headland. Cement stairs descend to a launch carved into the cliff face. Pat hates the launch—he climbs down step by step, though there is little danger of stumbling—and sometimes waits at the top. This evening, my ambush carefully planned, I drag him onto the rock. The mountains of the Ring have emerged across Dingle Bay. Hills of a thousand metres vault up from the sea, their grandeur dramatized by the filaments of cloud that necklace peaks and caress slopes. Unfolding the map, I recite, trippingly, their names: Beenmore and Mullaghnarakill, Killurly and Slievagh. Further south, visible only on clear nights, is the castellated shape of the Great Skellig island. I crane my neck to peer around the cliff across the harbour.

"Any other islands to be seen?" I ask. "It would be nice to see other islands, don't you think?"

He plays dumb.

"One month we have been here, Pat. One month, and still we have not seen the Great Blasket."

"I like it in town."

"What about your father?"

"What about him?"

"I want to see the island," I repeat.

"Why?"

"Don't be so ego-centred."

Pat grins his your-English-is-terrible grin. I ignore him. "People say the Great Blasket is beautiful," I resume. "A natural wonder. People say the whole edge of the peninsula takes your breath."

"Which people?"

"Eily Murphy."

He considers a snipe. I dare him to.

"Okay," he mutters.

"She says we can rent bicycles. Bike to Ventry, then walk over a mountain to the village that faces the island. She says your family is in a graveyard near the village."

"She says all that?"

"She wishes only the best for us," I say, trying out some Kerry English.

"I've been told the Great Blasket isn't such a friendly place," he offers. "Even dangerous along some of the paths. Besides, you have to cross some pretty rough water to get to it."

"So?"

"You don't mind riding in a boat?"

"Why would I mind?"

"Even if the sea is high?"

I stare him down.

"I was planning to go out for a day," Pat insists. "I just want to be prepared."

A monstrous breaker, thundering into the rock, hurls spray up at us. I love the salty taste. Pat recoils in fright, nearly stepping back off the ledge.

"I don't like it here," he says.

"Does your leg hurt?"

He stops rubbing his thigh.

Now that he has acquiesced to the Dunquin trip, and now that the letter I secretly wrote to his mother is in the mail (Francine and I are friends; *she* will answer my questions), I feel more in control. The walk home is less pleasant. All at once we are beneath a trough of cloud and the rain, blowing horizontally, rasps our cheeks. Mistlethrush sing *sesesah* from their nests. Cows sigh in the fields.

Poor Pat, his hands are so stubby, so poorly designed for the fiddle. I would lend him my spindly fingers if I could. Did you know that a butterfly moving through the air still casts a shadow? I didn't, until recently. I can't tell him what he wants to know. I can't because it would destroy us. A person with five prayer pots should not live with a person who needs only one. (I know I put out just four cups: I can explain.) A person with five prayer pots is exhausted, ruined. I come from an exhausted country. I am a ruined temple.

SHE WHO IS NOURISHED BY GOD

Chapter 2

Hia Thi Loi was sent to Saigon a week before the departure date to buy a piston for the trawler engine. Chac had chosen her for the job. A young woman in a straw hat, peasant blouse, and black slippers, with a gift of crabcakes for relatives in the city, would stand a better chance of slipping past checkpoints. Than Van Loi's bank account had been confiscated after his arrest, but he had stashed away some cash. The ten thousand *dong* Thuy Thi Ngo provided her daughter for the purchase were sewn into the lining of Hia's pants. In her pockets were identification papers, a lunch of rice balls, and enough money for bus tickets.

Though it covered barely a hundred kilometres, the three-hour journey to the former capital was epic: transfers and tire punctures, delays while the road was cleared of vehicles, police-checks. Four years had passed since Hia last glimpsed her home town. Avenues in the suburbs looked scruffy. Blocks of unrepaired buildings hid behind brown eucalyptuses and palms. Fenced-in villas stood guarded by armed sentries. Traffic islands were deserted, streetlamps had been smashed. Except for soldiers, Hia saw few living people. She saw few people, fewer animals, and heard none of the sounds—shouting and singing, church bells, radios blaring in doorways—that had provided background music for her childhood.

Sidewalk commerce was more brisk along the downtown thoroughfares. Stalls sold cakes and soft drinks, cigarettes and magazines; outdoor cafés, usually a tiny table centring a ring of low stools, served *tra* and coffee. Awnings billowed in the scorching breeze. Buses and motorbikes spewed fumes. Potted flowers, a favourite decoration, wilted in the heat.

Saigon appeared to Hia to be inhabited exclusively by black-marketeers. Her clothing prevented her from being accosted often, but she was nevertheless approached to sell American dollars or buy Japanese televisions. Old women grabbed her arm and proclaimed themselves relations, willing to help her locate lost loved ones for a price. Aggressive teenagers with eyes that folded up and down, like Westerners, tried to hustle her into alleyways. Hia remembered her Amerasian classmates in elementary school; back then, they'd been exotic, and untouchable. A man with a bulging belly told her she was pretty, and should work for him, all within earshot of a group of soldiers sipping juice at a stand. "Country girls go cheap," said one of them.

Finally, Hia flagged a *siclo* and called out an address in Tu Do market. The ride carried her past the former presidential palace to a laneway off the market, renamed Dong Khai street. Once the purveyors of Cambodian Buddhas, porcelain from south China and jewellery smuggled out of Laos, Tu Do merchants were now mostly soup sellers, with more shady transactions relegated to booths set back from the street and defended by men in sunglasses. She located the booth, the dealer, and, again using a slip of paper, negotiated for the engine part. The dealer wanted twelve thousand *dong*: Hia haggled until the price was eight thousand. Wrapping the piston in newspaper, she slipped it into the sack and ripped open the seam of her pant leg for the money. As she was leaving the alley, she was confronted by a figure who whispered her name. Only after a minute of awkward conversation did Hia recognize him. An octogenarian twelve years before, the shaman was now a skeleton encased in brittle skin.

"Bo is dead," Hia said, touching her ear unthinkingly.

His face showed puzzlement.

"My brother," she explained. "You prophesied it."

The man waved his hands. "Superstition," he said. Then, dragging her into his stall: "You like treasures?"

"No."

"I can tell."

"I don't want anything."

The booth was the size of a detention cell, stuffed with rags and newspapers. Unwilling to turn her back to the alley, Hia stood in the doorway while the former wizard fumbled among the junk. He pulled out a brick caked in dirt.

"Cambodia," he said, grinning.

Hia loathed his grin.

"Khmer Rouge," he continued. "Rat-tat-tat—kill everyone. Only ruins now. Like this."

She had no intention of buying the artifact. Hia did, however, agree to hold it.

"From a temple. Not just any—Angkor Wat. A treasure, but not just for any."

"Why me?"

"*Phung thi chin.* Strength to strength. Immortality. Things that cannot be broken."

She was about to object.

"Four thousand *dong,*" he said.

"Crazy."

"How much?"

"It is junk," Hia heard herself say. She was already bargaining.

"A treasure to those who understand."

"I understand junk."

"Three thousand, okay?"

Suddenly the shaman's eyes darted from her face to the

alley. "Don't look," he warned.

Hia looked.

"They're coming. You must decide."

Her heart raced. She would be arrested by the police, sent to a re-education camp. She would humiliate her family. Still, she saw no uniforms in the alley.

"Well?"

"It's a fake."

"Genuine. You know it."

"How do I know it?"

"*Phung thi chin.*"

"Crazy," Hia repeated.

"Decide!"

The police were coming. They would detain her, confiscate the piston, unravel the scheme to flee. She had to leave. The brick was still in her hands. *Leave*, she told herself.

Hia threw her remaining money at the shaman. He counted it. "Hey," he shouted, suddenly unconcerned by his imminent arrest. "Not enough!"

But she was already out of the alley with the artifact inside her sack. Hia ran past more black-marketeers, more leering soldiers, more haggard locals with outstretched hands, until she was within a mile of where she had grown up. The spires of Saigon cathedral loomed over the neighbourhood. How many hours had she spent there as a child: inhaling the wax and incense, listening without comprehension to the priest's intonations, watching sunlight soak through stained glass, shadows unfurl across the floor; hours spent as well on the bustling front steps, sometimes with friends, most often alone, admiring the cathedral's alien exterior, watching the sky pass overhead. Now the sky was low and the only smell, besides exhaust fumes, was of noodles cooking in a nearby stall.

That evening, after they prayed together in thanks for her safe return, Hia told Thuy Thi Ngo the piston had cost ten thousand *dong*. (She repeated the story to Chac shortly afterwards.) The first serious lie of her adult life tasted less sour on her lips than she had imagined, and she believed she would eventually be forgiven for it.

Once night fell, she crawled into the space between the floor of the house and the ground, where she buried her treasure among the stones supporting the stilts. Though the piece was quickly swallowed by the soil, Hia felt certain she would unearth it, when the time came.

Chapter 3

Dingle pier stinks by the end of each day. Pat likes to walk out it in the evening to watch trawlers disgorge their catches. Fish slither in plastic bins, gills palpitating. Heads and guts, claws and tails litter the cement; nasty birds swoop and swirl, divebombing, pecking. Though we are both city people, I am the seafarer; a veteran of twenty days on a boat. Why then do the odours nauseate me rather than him? Why does the churning of the sea make me dizzy while he can stare at the surface for hours? Even tonight, the sky is placid; the ocean, however, cannot stop moving.

Jimmy Sullivan hails us from across the road. He waits, his back against the railing, outside T. Daly's pub.

"How's the cat?" he asks.

"Dead," Pat answers.

"Deader," I add.

"Who's for a drink?"

"Is Tom Daly in there?" I say, craning to peer between the blind and the wall.

"I'm sure he is."

"I want to ask him about the calendars."

"A conundrum," Jimmy agrees.

"A what?"

"Riddle."

"I have to interview Charlie MacDonagh," Pat says, standing in the road.

"When?"

"In twenty minutes."

Jimmy nods. "Get yourself focused," he advises. "Focused, but not obsessed. A man with focus is a man on course. But an obsession, now, that's another business. Too alienating, I'd say. Too solitary."

Jimmy Sullivan is an interesting person: too bad he speaks in tongues.

"I'll keep that in mind," Pat promises.

"Religion is the great balance. Forces you onto the straight and narrow. Gives you something to fix on, but nothing too taxing. Something to occupy your thoughts, but simple thoughts, sturdy things."

"An anchor?" Pat asks.

"Right."

"A rudder in a storm?"

"There you have it."

"Guys. . . . "

"Your man Jesus Christ did all the crazy business," Jimmy says. "We just pray."

"To be forgiven for the sin of being alive?"

"To make sure it doesn't happen to us."

"I want beer," I announce.

Jimmy opens the door. The pub is dark, empty. Pat won't even cross the threshold.

"I'll meet you later on," he tells me.

I change my mind about the beer once Pat leaves. Jimmy seems hurt, so I spend a minute talking about my project. I tell him I am obsessed by Angkor Wat, but am having trouble bringing it into focus. He tells me he is, perhaps always has been, adrift on the ocean. What disturbs him most is that the sea isn't volatile, isn't storm-tossed, but is eternally flat as glass, silent as melting ice. The one moment in his life the ocean was wild and he was at its mercy, a moment that was, or should have been, incantatory, he was too busy being terrified to sense the wonderment.

Later that evening, while Pat is in the bath, I glance at his notes, sprawled across the kitchen table (atop my sketch pad), and play the cassette, which has been rewound, inserted into the machine, and the machine also deposited over my work.

Charlie MacDonagh lives in the third of ten rowhouses along the high road above Dingle. The house is spartan but untidy. He is a thirty-seven-year-old bachelor with tousled black hair, puffy eyes, and a stocky body dominated by a soccerball paunch. During the interview, MacDonagh holds his fiddle and bow upright in his right hand, the strings facing the table. He works for the telephone company installing new lines. His home, however, has no phone.

PK: When did you start to play the fiddle?

CM: The old man messed with the melodeon, see, and he bought me a starter fiddle for my seventh—no, eighth birthday. An uncle in town gave me a few lessons that same summer.

PK: You were raised in Dingle?

CM: My da worked for the telephone company as well. I spent two years in Cork City without ever taking to the place. Better music there, though.

PK: Better than here?

CM: No question. But listen, Jimmy never said you were American.

PK: I was born in Toronto.

CM: He told me you were Michael O Cathain's son. Seemed immensely proud of the fact, like you were *his* boy equally. I figured you for a Dubliner, or maybe London. All the way from Canada, eh? I half thought of emigrating there myself.

PK: Why didn't you?

CM: The last decent thing the old man did was get me the job with Telecom Eireann. Once I signed on with that crowd, I knew I was a lifer.

PK: So you've played the fiddle since you were a boy?

CM: I couldn't get enough of it. Did the competition circuit, the regional *fleadhs*, the national finals three years running. Found the business too stiff, though, too bloodless. I only wanted to learn and to play.

PK: Is your style particularly West Kerry?

CM: How do you mean?

PK: Influenced by the East Kerry musicians, maybe. Employing a long stroke and a minimum of ornamentation. A concise sound, almost plain.

CM: I played with musicians from that part of the country down in Cork. They were brilliant. And I recall listening to Padraig O'Keefe and Julia Clifford on the radio, and immediately picking up the fiddle to see if I could copy them. But I did the same with Coleman, and the first Chieftains records. Plus O Conchuir, of course.

PK: *The Drunken Butterfly*?

CM: The record, sure. But more the man. Sean O Conchuir alters the shape of a room when he plays.

PK: When he *plays*?

CM: It's been a decade since anyone heard him, true. A fucking genius, he is. Wicked old codger, mind. Fierce.

PK: I didn't think . . . never thought he'd still be alive. . . .

CM: O Conchuir? When he dies, that's it. Time to get a telephone. Time to buy a video machine.

PK: What about younger musicians, like Tommy Peoples and Kevin Burke?

CM: I listen to them, sure. But I was in my twenties when all that got going up in Dublin. I already had my style.

PK: That's what I'm asking. Your style: what distinguishes it?

CM: How should I know?

PK: What kinds of tunes do you like?

CM: I'll play anything. The standards—"Drowsy Maggie", "Pigeon on the Gate", "Toss the Feathers"—are boring, and get done more because the Bothys recorded them than because they're important to a region. The problem is that if you're in a pub with a piper and a whistle player, you have to do the tune that everyone knows. That's why I keep away from sessions here in town.

PK: Because the musicians play only the standards?

CM: Because they're mostly young lads, and those tunes are all they *know*. They've been raised on records, not local music. The older men in the back beyond—Ventry, Ballyferriter, Smerwick—now, they play fiddle and pipe tunes I've never heard before.

PK: And they teach you?

CM: I listen. The sessions are better out there. Not as many chattering people. Not as many tourists. You should be looking west of Dingle for the music. This town will reveal nothing.

PK: Name some of the tunes played in those pubs.

CM: Things like "Miss McClouds", "Callaghans", "Keane's Romance"—I wonder was that your da's?—"The Harlequin Hornpipe", "The Rising Sun". Remember there are hundreds of them, and most have two or three names, and twice as many versions.

PK: Why did you say my father might have written "Keane's Romance"?

CM: Why wouldn't he have?

PK: Did he compose?

CM: I associate his name with certain tunes, all right. You didn't know that?

PK: I know very little.

CM: No way of telling for sure. And it really doesn't matter. Once a tune is out there, it belongs to anyone who does it well.

PK: Could you play something?

CM: I suppose. *(Positions fiddle.)* I'll have a go at a jig common to West Kerry—"The Gander in the Pratie Hole". Don't think Michael O Cathain had anything to do with it, though.

(CM down-bows each string, tuning the D and A. He holds the fiddle in a formal position, the scroll nearly at eye level. His fiddling is strong, with a firm accenting of stressed notes and a neat, if conservative, varying of a triplet in the second round.)

PK: That was great.

CM: Thanks.

PK: You use a lot of your bow.

CM: It produces a fuller sound. I know musicians in Clare and Sligo only bow with the hairs up near the tip. But they go for a squeaky, sharp tone in their fiddling.

PK: Your playing is clean. Very little slurring or cross-bowing. The triplets are all staccato.

CM: *(laughing)* Is that right?

PK: I was only—

CM: I've just never had my own playing explained to me. No question, the Sligo and Donegal styles are brilliant. But they just aren't the way down here.

PK: Not the way *you* play?

CM: Not the way I was taught. To be a good musician you have to be a good listener. The best knowledge is passed on.

PK: I noticed you used droning. On the D string, I think.

CM: You could probably use a drone note the whole tune. Take any D in the melody, cross-bow the open string, and you have a drone below.

PK: Is that common?

CM: It suits the tune. A good fiddler does things with specific tunes rather than as a matter of course. You have to play the music. My style, see, my fiddle, but not my melody.

PK: When you're playing . . . I mean, what do you feel?

CM: Feel?

PK: It must be incredible to be moving through a tune, sensing its structure, making it your own. . . .

CM: Is that a question?

PK: Is playing the fiddle an emotional experience?

CM: Sorry?

PK: Aren't the best musicians those who internalize the music most deeply?

CM: I wouldn't know. . . . Listen, good playing means being precise and professional, having a comfortable style, an easy sound. You can't be all over the place, droning on one tune and then using only single bows on the next. You have to know what you're on about.

PK: You have to know yourself?

CM: Right.

PK: Know who you are, who you aren't?

CM: *(impatiently)* Jimmy Sullivan told me he's

got you lined up with Joe John Sheedy next. Ask Joe John these questions. He's mad about laments and slow airs, and plays them like they're fucking hymns. Joe John's a queer old one.

PK: Is he?

CM: A lovely fiddler, mind. Just odd. Ask him the questions. You two should get on grand.

The tape ends. The click startles me—my thoughts have scattered—and I pour a second cup of tea. One, two, three teaspoons of sugar, then, why not, a fourth: I need the fix. Pat emerges in a bathrobe.

"Well?" he says smugly.

"Well what?"

"What did you think?"

"Think of what?"

The smugness vanishes.

"Not bad," I answer. "Full of detail. He was impressed by your knowledge."

"I was thrilled by his."

"The stuff at the end was weird, though. All this emotion talk."

"I was trying something."

"What?"

"I'm not sure."

"How can you expect success if you don't know where you're going?" I ask. My tone is oddly aggressive.

"I haven't any expectations."

"And this talk about your father—why do you keep making circles around him?"

His expression clouds. "What do you want me to do, Hia?" he asks.

"Nothing."

"Who do you want me to be?"

"Leave," I command, reaching across the table to touch the *apsara*. "Let me work."

"You worked all day."

"I need discipline. I need focus. I don't need you cutting up my character."

"I didn't—"

"I *don't* need you transferring your mixed feelings about your father to me."

Until recently, Pat's face could display only so many emotions without pinching. To sketch him, an artist needed a hundred brush strokes, all clean, none memorable. Even so, the result was a portrait more or less finished, an image more or less resolved. Part of the problem was the collapse that always accompanied anxiety or confrontation. Part of the problem was simple heredity: lots of soft-boned Francine, little of the apparently chiselled Michael. But in recent weeks the collapse hasn't happened. I first noticed it in Toronto, at about the same time others were discerning in Pat facial qualities of a type, a cliché, completely outside (I assumed) his physical and imaginative realm. Now, strong lines across the forehead and from the cheekbones down to the mouth serve as supports, lending his countenance the strength, almost hardness, of someone accustomed to daily confrontations with death, nightly anxieties about everything else. A fisherman, I suppose.

"Sometimes, . . . " he murmurs.

I flounder for another hour. Having to listen to that awful music from the front room doesn't help, and excuses my lack of productivity. All the temples are drawn, except Angkor Wat, and I am ready to move on to studies of individual statues and busts, some of the more important bas-reliefs. Honing in on specific sites will liberate me from the tyranny of design. Details are by their nature engrossing. They are also meaningless, referring only to themselves, intimating nothing. Perfect for a mind too easily drawn to vague intimations and elusive meanings.

Already the sketches are ordered in my head, and are, each and every one, luminous. Some repose in shadow, others in shade. Sunlight is rare; rain is inexhaustible. These objects display the sorrows of history. Statues stand decapitated, busts are pocked with bullet holes, bas-reliefs have been erased. Still, the outlines remain perfect, unperturbed by their troubled ancestry. I want to gain access to their form, understand their stillness and indifference, even borrow a little for myself. That is what artists do: steal (as I stole the panel) so they can divine for themselves a new shape that is merely the old one (the *only* one) repackaged.

"One bad night," I announce, joining Pat. "No big deal, right?"

"Lets make love."

The bed is already open.

"It's still light out," I say.

"We'll draw the curtains."

"I drank too much tea."

"The bathroom is through that door."

We make love. I don't like to be rushed. I don't like any light in the room. I don't like it when Pat talks, and I hate it when he tries to make me do new things.

"Why do Western men want gymnastics in bed?"

"Western *men*?"

"I read books."

"Gymnastics is a bit of an overstatement, Hia."

"I prefer old way."

"What about Vietnamese guys?" he asks, still kissing me.

"Rude question."

"You raised the issue."

"I told you already," I say. "I slept with only one man before you."

"In Vietnam."

"Right."

"All those friends in Toronto. . . . You never had—"

"It does not work that way. There are—"

"Rules. I know."

Even after I met Pat, I still figured I would end up marrying a Vietnamese. It would have been easier: no need to change myself, no need to explain my ways, no embarrassing conversations (like this one). But those boys all wore mirror sunglasses. When I was with them, I could not see their eyes; often, giving up in frustration, I donned glasses as well, so we could at least share the condition.

"What about the man in Vietnam?"

"He was a boy also."

"Did you and he—"

"Pat!"

"I think we should talk, Hia."

"You always want to talk. Lovemaking needs no words. It is a picture, not a song."

He smiles.

"Why do you smile?"

"I've heard you sing. . . . "

He is trying to make me laugh. "You should not talk, not sing," I say. "Love should be quiet, peaceful. Like an empty church. Like an uncloudy sky."

He rolls over.

Carolan, who seems glued to his kitchen chair these days, decides to join us. The leap up is too much for him; he ends up clinging to the side of the mattress. I watch him struggle. Pat stretches over me and hoists the cat onto the bed.

"He is old," I comment.

Pat resumes brooding, showing me his shoulder and back, the slope of his ribcage down to his waist. When we first slept together, I could not bare to look at his skin: his freckles reminded me of burns and birth defects. One reason I insisted we make love in darkness was to shield my eyes. Now, I prefer the dark out of habit, and because I am ugly.

I trace the freckles with my finger. There is a pattern, especially on his right shoulder, an arrangement of blotches, some faint, others bold, similar to oriental garden designs. Normally, my meanderings cause him to shiver with pleasure. But tonight he is stone. "There are rules," I confirm quietly.

My admission is an explanation, not an apology.

"You are a good daughter, Hia," he says over his back. "Experiencing pleasure, having fun, doesn't make you any less dutiful."

"You are wrong."

He is wrong. He is hurtful. But then, I ask myself, what is the use of cursing the rocks that bruise you when you're tumbling down a river?

Whose expression is that? Not mine, I swear.

Chapter 4

The piston fit. Chac installed the part the evening before their escape, making Hia hold the flashlight over the motor while he worked. The trawler was normally moored off the village pier, but in recent weeks Chac had anchored it further upriver, telling friends he wanted to sleep in the boat, and needed quiet. That allowed him to provision the vessel without attracting attention. Thuy Thi Ngo had already paid two bribes to local officials who had guessed the family's intentions. What little money was left went for supplies. Five tanks of diesel fuel, purchased litre by litre over a period of months, were stored inside the cabin; plastic containers of fresh water lined the hold. Cloth sacks of cooked rice, bags of dried fish and fruits, and a kerosene stove went into a cupboard at the bow. Food and fuel, Chac estimated, for seven days at sea. Plenty of time to reach Singapore.

Chac Dinh Che was a fisherman. He had the licence, flashed to soldiers at the checkpoint near Can Duoc each morning, to prove it. Though he co-owned the boat with another man, his partner had disappeared eight months before after trying, unsuccessfully, to unload his half of the operation. Now Chac had the vessel, a nine-metre trawler with an oil-thirsty engine and a warped tiller, to himself. He had fished the delta since he was a child, first with his father, then with his father's partner. The mouth of the Mekong was a tessellation of rice-paddies and waterways, fields of muttering bamboo and whistling reeds. The delta was also a junkyard of unrepaired dikes, barbed-wire fences, stilt houses in various stages of collapse. Chac knew every tributary, every creek. He needed no maps or compass to navigate the labyrinth. But he had also never piloted beyond the river's mouth. He had never used a compass, never consulted a map, never had to read an ocean sky.

Most people slipped away at night. They poled trawlers through the shadowy delta, cramming passengers into the hold, muffling children with cloth. Government patrols scoured village piers after sunset and boarded vessels. Patrols also inched up waterways with search beams trained on the banks. In the mornings, however, only the checkpoints were manned. Chac's face, and easy laugh, were known at the first guardtower. The soldiers would wave him on. At the checkpoint further upriver, where the estuary widened, he would throttle down, flash the paper, smile and wait. Chances were they wouldn't inspect the boat either.

Those chances would be improved, Chac reckoned, if Hia was his partner. For weeks she had boarded the trawler with him each morning, learned how to start the engine, cast the net, empty the catch into the hold; how to pilot, add fuel and oil. Her teacher had endured the razzings of soldiers and the jokes of other villagers who considered a woman coworker a loss of face. Chac had pleaded helplessness. What could he do? His real partner was gone. He had no money to hire help. Hia wasn't much, he admitted, but she was better than nothing.

By the morning of September 2, 1979, it was an established routine: Chac Dinh Che ambled down to the pier shortly after sunrise, where he was met by the noodle girl, Hia Thi Loi, now eighteen, and sometimes by Hia's twelve-year-old sister, Nhung, who hitched a ride to buy cheap flour at the next village and then walked home with a five-kilo sack on her back. The departure of this crew would cause little stir, only the usual jokes, the usual gossip. Meanwhile, if Thuy Thi Ngo left her house a few minutes ahead of her daughters, to visit relatives in a river hamlet thirty minutes north by foot, probably to beg and borrow, even to proselytize, this too would be normal. No one would be suspicious.

Hia lay awake all night. Shortly before dawn, with the rage of cicadas diminishing and woodpeckers commencing their *hoop-hoop-hoop*, she sat up on her matt. Her mother slept next to her. Thuy's profile, bathed in window light, was porcelain. For the thousandth time, Hia traced the contours of her face, the forehead and eyes, the cheek-bones—a temple rising from a plain—the nose and chin. In repose, the face wore, for Hia, an expression of aching love for all things lovely but fleeting. The line of the mouth highlighted the sadness, while the brow, furrowed even in sleep, seemed weighed down by both intelligence and fatigue. Though just four years had passed, Hia had no recollection of her father's appearance. It was Thuy, and Thuy only, who mattered.

They were alone at daybreak.

"*Con troi nuoc,*" Thuy said, using the expression for the first time in a decade. "Look after Nhung. And Chac. . . . "

Hia could not bear it. "We will meet you in an hour," she answered.

She wanted to hug her. To be hugged, even more. But the door was open, and the path was bustling. Families did not embrace at the outset of an ordinary day. Families went about their business in the usual exhausted trance.

Hia was on the pier, helping Chac load the cockpit, when she remembered Angkor Wat. She had intended to crawl under the house before sunrise to retrieve the brick, but had fallen under her mother's spell. The rendezvous was ten minutes upriver.

She told Chac she had forgotten a photo of her grandparents.

"We'll be late," he said.

"I'll hurry."

"*Don't* hurry."

She walked evenly, head bowed, the brim of her hat cloaking her apprehension. Fortunately, the path outside the hut was clear, and Hia ducked under the floor and crawled to the pole. Her first choice, a heavy, jagged rock, was obviously wrong. She chose again. Wrong also. The rear of the house lingered in shade. Hia brushed hair from her eyes and repositioned the hat over her back. The next brick, which she'd been certain was it, showed no etchings. What had they looked like? She had barely glanced at the artifact three weeks before. It had rained since. Digging the earth, she pulled up stones, chunks of cement, glass. Her fingers bled. Sweat stung her eyes. Wiping them, she smeared herself. The sting burned.

Suddenly, as if someone had whispered the words in her ear, she knew she had to leave. She knew people she loved were in danger, and she knew it was her fault. Hia scrambled back out. Noticing a darkness within shadow underfoot, she grabbed it. On the path, she slipped the object under her blouse, and returned to the pier. The thing felt comfortable against her stomach; she carried the extra weight easily. Her breathing, however, was short, and her face felt singed with heat.

"Go," she told Chac.

Had anyone noticed her? Chac motioned the sisters to squat in the cockpit, then untied the rope. The trawler belched gas, stained the convulsing water behind the stern.

The channel was a rippling ribbon, its surface tinted by sunlight and lily-pads. Chac nodded to other boatsmen and slowed to chat with a cousin in a sampan stacked with crushed sugarcane. The cousin made a joke about the aroma, which Chac laughed at. But the moment the trawler had the tributary to itself, he turned on Hia.

"We're behind schedule," he said.

She bowed her head.

"And what is that?" he asked, indicating the bulge in her belly.

The honest answer—that it was likely a worthless brick—perched on Hia's lips. She lacked the courage to speak, or to confirm her error. Instead, she lowered her gaze even further.

"Open the hold," Chac commanded.

Nhung opened the hold. Without waiting for the order, the girl stepped into the shallow chamber and, contorting herself, lay flat on her back.

Hia lowered the trap door just as the trawler rounded the bend below the next hamlet. The water near the pier was crowded with boats and sampans. Chac smiled, exchanged barbs with friends, lit the cigarette that would dangle between his lips until they reached the checkpoint. One fisherman shouted to Hia that he had seen her mother in the village a few minutes before, walking with her relatives.

They heard the shots a kilometre further upriver. Chac thought they had been fired from the left bank, the shore with the path buried in reeds: the route that Thuy and her nephew and her nephew's wife had to take to reach the meeting place. When more gunshots rang out, and Hia heard the bullets tatter the vegetation, and distinguished shouts—garbled, as if in a foreign language—then there was little doubt.

She tried to jump overboard. Chac restrained her. She tried a second time. He knocked her to the floor, his face twisted. But a split second later, Hia watched his expression harden to stone, like a soldier resolved to kill. "We cannot stop," he decided.

"My mother. . . . "

"They must have been caught."

"What about the bullets?"

"Maybe she tried to run."

"My mother!"

Nhung began to scream.

"Shut up!" Chac shouted, pounding the floor with his foot. Sensing the trawler lurch, he grasped the wheel. "Can you see anything?" he asked, peering into the reeds.

Hia was crawling towards the side to throw herself into the water. She could not swim.

He caught her again. Squeezing her arm so hard that the bruise turned crimson afterwards, he dragged her to the hold, opened the door, and shoved her into the opening. "Another boat—" he began.

The approach of a trawler moving down the channel saved them. The boat passed between the starboard and the bank, attracting the notice of the soldiers who had slashed their way to the shore. A smattering of gunfire into the water off the trawler's bow convinced its pilot to cut his engine. Chac, meanwhile, sped ahead to a bend and, not even glancing over his shoulder, steered their vessel out of sight.

At the first checkpoint, only a hundred metres away, he braced himself for a search. To his shock, the guardtower was empty, sunlight fissured between bamboo stilts. It might be a trap; legally, Chac was supposed to dock and wait for a guard to appear. Had the sentry left his post to meet his replacement, and stumbled upon Thuy and the others by the river? Destiny, Chac thought: we have no control over it. Grinding the cigarette underfoot, he opened the throttle.

Chapter 5

"Perman*ence*," Pat says, correcting me.

"Things have no permanence?"

"I never said that."

"You implied."

"I said they are permanent within time. They exist while we are experiencing them. Then they vanish."

I groan rhetorically. I sip tea. I stroke Carolan, who is looking more and more like a furry Buddha. "Musicians create things that are permanent," I counter. "Their music lives on for ever."

"I don't think a fiddler worries if a reel he is playing will endure beyond his lifetime. I doubt he cares if it lives beyond the two minutes needed to play it."

"Crazy."

"Evanescent."

Trying to rattle me with big words: a cheap trick. "If a composition or sculpture or painting does not have permanence," I say, "then it is senseless. It is like wind music—comes and goes, without anyone hearing the sound."

"Wind music is beautiful."

"But no one hears it!"

His smile is also designed to unnerve me. I focus on the candles.

"Performance is rooted in the moment," Pat says. "Each time the musician performs the tune, it is different. Its shape is changed."

"Bah."

"That's what fiddlers are telling me."

"Crap. I heard your last tape. That man said nothing of the sort. He only talked about drones and bows and the names of tunes."

"You're not listening closely enough."

"You're hearing voices in your head."

Finally, I get him.

"Change makes permanence impossible," I continue. "Change reduces all life to a movie: images flash, one after another, without order, without meaning."

"Maybe that's how it is."

"Maybe you want it that way, so you won't have to think hard about things that are everlasting, things beyond what you can understand."

I request more tea. Tonight, for once, we do not have to listen to the galloping rain. Tonight, for once, I do not have to suffer that squeaky fiddle. The sky is a vault inlaid with constellations whose names I know only in Vietnamese. (Some have no names; they were invisible from the South China Sea.) The tape recorder plays a cassette that Eily Murphy, realizing I was being driven insane by Pat's mania, lent me. The music, a choir chanting hymns, is unobtrusive.

"One, two, three," Pat counts, doling out sugar. "A fourth, maybe?"

"Why not."

"The everlasting is great," he says, "until it ends. Things change because they haven't any eternal meanings. We affix meaning to music, or to art, or to the sky, because the need to do so is within us. When the need disappears, or changes, then the music, the sky, changes, or disappears."

"If nothing lasts and nothing is eternal, if God is nothing and Angkor is nothing, then why bother to learn?"

"I'm not talking about your mother, Hia."

I tense.

"The difference between you and me, . . . " he begins.

"Yes?"

He sits back in the chair. "This music is making me sleepy," he says.

I am silent.

"No rain tonight."

I am silent.

"When you work," Pat offers, "you are praying. When I work, I am practising."

"What instrument do you play?" I enquire coldly.

"I know it sounds phony. The idea is new, and I'm not sure what to make of it."

"What idea?"

"That these interviews are. . . . " He looks at me. "Please don't take it personally."

"Creativity is my apprehending of the sacred. It is my meditation with God. This isn't personal?"

"Sure. I meant—"

"You know your problem, Pat? You think art is an accident. You think it always ends. You want it to be over soon, so you will not have to be questioned. But you are wrong. It is a careful construction. It is a lifelong labour. A commitment, a family."

"I swear I'm not talking about your mother."

"But I *am* talking about your father."

In my lap, Carolan attempts a rare back-to-belly roll. Twice the cat rolls; twice his girth acts like a magnet, pinning him down. I stroke him to allay his wounded pride. Should I also run my fingers down Pat's spine?

"Music is too crazy," I say, shifting on the couch. "You can't see it, can't touch it, can't enjoy its physicalness. I must be able to see what I work with. I need contact, touch, smell."

"With Angkor?"

"In my mind's eye."

Pat should laugh. (These kinds of comments always make him laugh.) No laugh, though; not even a smile. I drain my cup.

"It's easy for you," he says. "God is just some weird architectural cult. You still have the Buddha. You still have being Vietnamese."

"You insult me."

"You patronize me."

"This conversation is awful."

"Because it's not under your control?"

"Pat!"

"Because it's moving too fast? Because it's untidy and threatening to be incomplete?"

We spar some more, then fall silent; still in the chairs, still sipping tea, still not listening to the choir.

"Let's make shadows," I say, a peace gesture.

"Any requests?"

"You create. I'll interpret."

Pat adjusts his chair to intersect the candlelight. (He doesn't even get the joke.) He turns towards the wall and lifts his arms.

"It's a structure," he hints.

"Like a building?"

"Right."

I study the shadow. Pat has formed a helmet with his hands, fingertips touching, middle fingers arched, with the thumbs webbed below.

"Think of clouds."

"But you said—?"

"Think of that book."

"What book?"

"*Les grandes cathédrales du monde.*"

I sigh sincerely.

"You don't want to guess?"

"I'm tired."

He throws up another shape. This building, constructed

by pressing palms together and then widening the base, is so vaulting that its steeple is severed by the ceiling, like a tower that bumps against the floor of heaven.

"More familiar?" Pat asks.

"Don't be mean."

"We're just playing."

I stand up at the exact moment Carolan bolts from my lap, hits the carpet running, and charges the wall. He lunges at Pat's cathedral, his claws flailing the wallpaper. We both look on in astonishment as the cat jumps at shadows a second, then a third time.

"I'm going downstairs," I announce.

Television is not a stimulating medium. Though addictive, it is dull and maladroit: too bright and jarring, too self-impressed. I rarely come to its defence aesthetically. The reasons I like TV are banal. First and foremost, television is something to occupy the eye, numb the senses. Voices talk at me, or better, don't talk at me; strangers (usually attractive white people) chatter among themselves. The process is akin to finally getting invited to one of those parties you've always heard about, and then discovering that you are invisible and can infiltrate whispered conversations, slip between bedsheets. Of course, TV also passes the hours when one is too exhausted to do much else, except sleep.

For nine years my sister and I shared a five-room apartment. To Canadian acquaintances, this seemed liberating; to Vietnamese friends, it smacked of punishment. I always assumed our solitude *was* punishment for my sins. (Nhung was innocent, but nonetheless had to suffer.) Pat, who desperately wanted me to move in with him, understood that I couldn't because of the situation. Which left me and Nhung on our own. She was in school, or learning English at church; I was in school, at language lessons, or cleaning office floors. Having the television on served a simple function: company.

Eily Murphy keeps her set on every night. The glow of the tube is visible through curtains from the street, and is, I now understand, an invitation. When we first arrived in Dingle, I couldn't help notice how she left the door to the front room open, despite drafts. We'd pass by on our way upstairs, and wish her good evening. Always our landlady was seated in the same chair. Always the room was empty, lit only by a lamp beside the couch. (In April, with the air still sharp, she kept a fire scented of earth and herbs.) Always she was either reading or knitting, and always, without fail, the television murmured from the corner.

I visit her often. Pat joins me sometimes, but he usually prefers to take a walk or go to a pub. Eily is delighted by the company, and I am delighted to sit in the cosy room. We drink tea, watch television in snatches, chat.

Tonight I tell her about Bo and the waterfall. Pat's silly shadow trick reminded me of the story. When I was ten years old, Bo and I visited a village a hundred kilometres west of Saigon. People did not travel for pleasure back then; the war's boundaries shifted unpredictably, often between sunset and dawn. Rarely had I ventured beyond the city suburbs. Certainly I had never been to a contested area. Much of the upper Mekong Delta was a Vietcong stronghold, a recalcitrant swath of marsh and jungle that stretched perilously close to the Cambodian border. Bo, however, had unspecified, likely republican army business in a village (he was involved from an early age), and he persuaded my mother to let me tag along.

Successive bus rides brought us to Chau Doc, twenty kilometres south of Cambodia. Our destination was deep in the paddy quilt surrounding the town. The landscape was pockmarked. The thatched roofs of hamlets shared roadsides with rusted tanks and burnt-out trucks. Farmers planted crops around bomb craters; flooded fields reflected the sky. Clouds were tall, aloof. At one village, Bo made me wait at a noodle stand while he went into a hut. The woman who ran the stand offered a coconut to drink. With her dark skin and square chin, her thick lips and long-lobed ears, she did not look Saigonese. I suddenly found myself in a foreign land inhabited by men swinging hoes and scythes, children ankle-deep in water, a land flecked with water-buffalo and rice paddies, fertilized by steady rains and nourished by wats shimmering on the edges of jungles. When I asked the shopkeeper a question, and discovered we did not even share a language, I flushed with secret pleasure.

Afterwards, Bo and I left the road, navigated a dike path, and entered a forest of coconut and mangrove. The jungle was dense, knotted. A pungent bouquet, blended from rotting vegetation with new growth, coloured the air. Sunlight speckled the ground.

A few minutes into the grove, I detected the murmur of water over rocks: faint at first, then more urgent, and finally a resounding *ssshhh.* The waterfall stood in a clearing, fed by a narrow stream that plunged into a pool. Releasing Bo's hand, I raced to it, my slippers flying. Mist condensing at the base of the fall formed an iridescent glass chamber that tickled my skin. Too shy to lie on my back, I squatted in the pool tracing light with my finger. The glass filtered colour into the sun; above me was a rainbow, a cobalt-blue sky. When I rubbed my eyes, the quality of the light changed. I closed my lids, waited, then opened them again: another sun, another sky. Once or twice, gazing down at the surface, I saw the waterfall and the clearing and my own slight figure.

The world was topsy-turvy. I didn't mind.

Suddenly two black beads glared up at me from under the surface. Believing it a *ma da,* the ghost of a drowned person who could find no peace until it had located a replacement, I screamed. The *ma da* grinned fiendishly and grabbed my leg. I screamed louder. Bo burst up from the pool, roaring at my terror. I bawled. Wiping away my tears, he kidded me about the propriety of a woman warrior scaring so easily. Then he counselled that in order to resist, you had to believe. In order to accept fate you had to change it, to respect the past while ensuring the past was not repeated.

On the bus back to the city, the sun bleeding orange into a delta waterway, I gazed at my brother with a new and disquieting reverence. He was an adult; I was merely a child. It could never be any other way again.

"You are a sentimental person, Hia," Eily Murphy says once I have finished.

I am stunned by this interpretation. "People say we are a sentimental race," I answer blandly.

"Do they?"

"I disagree."

"Love is so demanding," she sighs.

"Families are worse."

"Pat, I suspect, would concur."

How does she know we argued? My mother used to guess not only my moods, but their reasons. I am uncomfortable with the thought that I am so transparent.

"Pat would disagree if *I* said it. I say watch, he say listen. I say sleep, he say wake up."

"A phase, I'm sure."

"I hate that word!"

Eily smiles. I love the way her smile wrinkles the corners of her eyes. "An American invention—the phase. Here, we call it history."

"In Vietnam it's known as fate."

"Well then," she says, "compared with the other two, phase sounds harmless. Temporary, too."

I'm not sure I agree, but I pretend to be cheered. We brew another pot of tea and watch a British drama until midnight. Outside, butterflies flutter through the air. I cannot hear them, cannot guess their flight, so they must be there.

Chapter 6

The boards were less than a foot above Hia's face, but she could not see them. Gaps between planks had been grouted with dirt; scant sunlight seeped through the cockpit floor. The fact that there was wood above her, against her back, and that, with Nhung pressed to one side and nets stuffed on the other, her escape was blocked; all this gave Hia the unshakeable sensation that she was not in the hold of a trawler, not beside her younger sister, but in a coffin—buried alive. Hair matted her forehead. A muscle cramp fired slivers up her spine. The engine rattled the hull so violently that vomit rose in her throat. Hia squeezed her eyes shut, relaxed, squeezed again.

She was underground, under water, in hell. What crimes had she committed? What sins?

"Quiet!" a voice commanded.

Who was whimpering? Hia didn't think it was herself. She found her sister's ear.

"Think of something else," she whispered.

Nhung trembled. Hia trembled also, though for a different reason; her mother used to brush her lips against Hia's ear, chant her name, and sing. . . .

"Think of a waterfall," Hia said.

She thought of the waterfall. And of Bo, who had

terrified her by pretending to be a *ma da*, his face distorted by bubbles. Her brother had died under the earth. The Vietcong had surrounded a field that was latticed, according to informers, with tunnels. Conscripts filled the chambers. When Bo's commander refused to surrender, the field was shelled. So much earth, so onerous and so unyielding, even for the quick-witted (Bo among them, surely) who might have prolonged their lives a few seconds by curling into a ball, some air to breathe, the darkness a cocoon. Hard to believe you were no longer on the planet, but *within* it; no longer feeling ground beneath your feet, but all around, like a bird feeling the sky. Next came a taste, a smell, a pressure against the skin, eyes blinded, ears deafened, don't try to talk, don't move, just rest, think; then the gagging, the stench, a pounding on the back of the skull, don't bother to cry out, don't bother to—

"Hia!"

Nhung was elbowing her. "Chac will be angry with us," the girl said.

Chac? Who was Chac?

"Think of God," Hia counselled.

She thought of God. Her ruminations were general: his benevolence, our selfishness, the grace he bestowed, the grace we rejected. Though designed to comfort, these thoughts only made Hia uneasy. Worse, they were mundane, unengaging. Her mind began to revert to other subjects, and she realized she was in danger. If she lost control, she would panic. If she panicked, she would hurt herself, hurt others, again. Clenching her fists, she prayed for a structure. She prayed for a structure that would house her imagination so the discomforts would cease to matter, and she would be transported to somewhere else, sometime else, and be alone, engaged, self-contained.

When Hia was eleven the priest at Saigon cathedral, where the family worshipped, gave her a present for her first communion. Titled *Les grandes cathédrales du monde*, with a stamp identifying it as the property of a defunct city library, the book was tattered and stained, with twenty single-page chapters describing twenty European churches. Also included were black-and-white photographs of buildings that struck the girl as strange and ugly. She glanced at the photos with mild curiosity, but then sold the book on the black market shortly before the city fell.

Now, four years later, the images resurfaced. The cathedrals were before Hia, and she studied them avidly. Actually, what came into focus were shapes; memory had reduced the structures to outlines on a page. Each church existed as a single, unbroken pencil line, black on white, light on dark. The lines were exact and unchangeable. She was dismayed. What had happened to the original photographs? Where were the elaborate portals and ornate transepts, the choirs and side-chapels, the faithful who naturally came and went from the site? Lines intersecting space in a fixed pattern could hardly satisfy. Still, her imagination kept conjuring up these images, distant from her own tradition and disassociated, it seemed, from human experience; and, despite herself, she was captivated.

But, Hia reasoned, it was wrong to be attracted to things that were remote, removed from other people. It might even be unchristian. She thought about being Christian, and about being close to other people. Like who? Her father, in prison? Chac, with his soldier's glare? Her mother, now that—

Nhung.

"Shh," Hia said.

"My legs . . . ," the girl whimpered.

"I know."

"I'm so thirsty!"

"Think of . . . ," Hia began. She was about to say churches, but caught herself. " . . . a song."

"Quiet!" the voice snapped.

Who had said that? Hia sought a face to accompany the

command. She couldn't conjure one up.

"I'll sing," she said.

The girl was shivering.

"Listen to the song, Nhung."

Hia chanted softly:

Go out every day and you will learn
You'll be wiser and wiser the farther you roam
Go here, go there, go everywhere—
How can you be smart by staying at home?

Time passed. It must have. But for Hia, absorbed by a sensation—she vowed never to wash her right hand, in order to retain the sensation of Thuy's skin—this passage mattered as little as the advance of the trawler up the channel to the river mouth. The boat might be moving through time and space, but she was, and for ever would be, motionless.

The engine was cut. There was a thud, a sagging of the boards above Hia's head, and voices. For a moment she thought the wood would snap, crushing her and Nhung. She found her sister's hand again. Would they search the hold? Chac had been confident they wouldn't. It was too cramped for human beings. Just some equipment, some nets—

Light penetrated the netting. Nhung shifted, and Hia tried to wriggle a few centimetres further from the door. A rifle barrel plunged into the chamber. The barrel caught in the net, hesitated, pushed on. It jabbed her thigh.

"Down there?"

"Nothing," Chac replied.

"Something," the voice said. "Give me the flashlight."

A flashlight could not be found.

"Crawl in."

"In there?"

"I said—"

A hand continued where the barrel had left off. When the hand touched her arm, she opened her eyes, which burned from being squeezed so hard.

"See?" Chac said. "Just junk, like this. Useless."

He heaved something into the air. Hia had to guess: Chac had been ordered to search the hold himself, and he'd grabbed the object positioned at her feet. Had there been a splash?

"Why so far out?" a different voice asked.

"Big catches."

"On your own?"

"I work alone."

The answer seemed to satisfy them. The door to the hold dropped. Darkness swarmed back in.

Twenty minutes later, lullabied by waves, Hia perched at the edge of sleep. Just as she nodded off, light flooded the chamber again, and a head dangled upside down in the opening. Both sisters screamed at the apparition.

"We're safe," Chac said sourly. "You can come out now."

Her heart hammered.

"Hia!"

Chac stretched into the hold and slid her over until she was below the door. Then he hoisted her up. Hia knelt on the wood, her muscles burning, her eyes webbed in fingers.

"It was destined," he offered once Nhung had also been rescued. "I knew it from the start."

"Water," Hia said.

"Plenty of that around here," he answered, daring another chipped-tooth smile. Then: "No control, no fixing. Life happens to you. Good or bad—it happens."

"Water," she repeated.

"Huh?"

Her lips were raw. Was he blind?

Chac uncovered a plastic water jug. While Hia and Nhung sipped from it, he went into the cabin, returning with an even broader grin, and a new hat. The cap was blue and white, and bore an insignia, like a target, in the middle of the forehead: DODGERS.

Hia sat at the rear gunwale until sunset. To the south, land receded and thinned, then finally blurred. She charted the hues of the South China sea. The water was an eggshell-blue in the early afternoon, a turbid aquamarine, a whitecap-shocked sapphire, and lastly the colour of spilt ink. She also pondered the sky, a dome above, around, and even—when the horizon united textures—below the trawler, confirming her impression of the planet as a circle, with the ocean a point on the circle, and the boat a dot within the point. When night fell, the sky consumed the sea and her eyes were raised. The heavens slowly brightened and stars began to throb. If her gaze was steady, then the sky, though actually fixed, would start to move. If her gaze was dutiful, fervent in respect and devotion, then the sky would even console—warm her body, soothe her soul.

Chapter 7

We are going to Dunquin today, going to see the island, and Pat will not set the agenda. I have a plan, a three-point plan, and it will be carried out. Each point is a question I will ask and he will be made to answer. I had hoped Francine would have replied to my letter by now; I didn't want to make the trip without more information. But she hasn't, so I must be aggressive. I can be aggressive, even when I don't feel well (bad nights, no appetite), even when my work isn't any good.

We pedal our rented bicycles through a stretch of rowhouses at Dingle's western outskirts, cross a bridge, and spin past the town cemetery towards Ventry harbour. The fields are sunlit and the road is bowered where trees have meshed their upper foliage. On flat stretches we gather speed—Pat's lanky frame gives him an advantage—and I lean over the handlebars, legs pumping. Mount Eagle, a fortress mountain with a limestone gate called Slea Head, looms behind Ventry village, its eastern slope trellised with stone fences. Halfway around the harbour we lock the bikes beside a shop and set off along a road that will carry us, according to Eily Murphy, over a pass and down into Dunquin. Eily was firm regarding the itinerary: drag Pat over the pass, allow Dunquin to unfold below, note the archipelago, highlight the largest island, affix a name to it, find the graveyard—extract details.

The road climbs sharply, distancing itself from the farms that cling to the slope. By the top, the back of my shirt is drenched. The pass is a transversal between three mountains: Mount Eagle, Rahinnane, and Croaghmartin. Desolate and wind-blasted, it affords stunning views of valleys and headlands, cliffs exposed to the ocean. The sky is so huge I expect to see another one reflected above it. The sky is—

"Enough!" Pat says.

Sheep nibble at fuchsia along the path until we come near, whereupon the lambs cower and the ewes scowl in retreat. Vistas shift dramatically, but Dunquin remains hidden. Though we are descending to sea-level, it is akin to strolling into heaven. The road appears destined to dissolve into the sky; the illusion is so strong, the pull so forceful, that I am relieved to be far from any precipices. Sunlight and shadow chase each other down the valley. No humans or even sheep are in sight. That is odd; the Dingle peninsula may be remote, but it is stubbornly inhabited. I do hear a voice, though, a farmer calling to his dogs: "Come back! Come back!"

I see no dogs, either.

Time for the first question. "When did your father leave this place?"

Pat smiles. Okay, so I telegraphed a little.

"Nineteen fifty-three."

"Fifty-three?"

"He returned five years later."

"Why did he—?"

"Emigrate at all?"

"No. I mean, yes."

"Because of this," he says with a sweep of his arms. "Can you blame him?"

The scene fills out. Farmhouses emerge, burrowed into

copses or centring rocky fields. The sea sparkles below the rim of the land. Then the road curves and an island appears, then a second, until the group is before us.

"Are they real?" I ask.

The ocean is a sheet of blue ice and the Blaskets are sculptures arranged atop it. One island is an arrowhead, another a crown. A third and fourth, tucked behind their mates, resemble saddles, while Blasket Sound is littered with tiny crags, like stone fragments from the slab. Even collectively, however, the smaller islands are no match for the Great Blasket. It lacks a single acre of flat land. The slope directly across from us, where a village lies in ruin, constitutes the northern face of two undulating hills. The larger hill is sheer and casts a shadow over miles of water.

I trace the Great Blasket with my finger. "Stones arranged to assist contemplation," I decide. "A shallow pool, patterns around it, light and dark—a Zen garden."

"Where?"

"The islands are gardens of glass."

"Hunks of rock."

"Planned nature."

"Random occurrence."

"To come from such a place would make a person strange. Eily was wrong. This is not a scenic spot, not a wonder of nature. This is. . . . " The words fail to form.

"A nightmare?"

"Don't be melodramatical."

He smiles.

"It must have been so painful for your father. To have this as his landscape. To have this, and then to lose it. Once you lose something, it is gone."

"Even if you return?"

"Probably."

"Want to go back to Vietnam?"

I ignore the snipe.

"Why haven't we come here before?" I ask. (A version

of my third question, but I am improvising.)

"We're here now."

"You have a stone heart."

"Do I?"

"To not be moved by the islands, to not be full of grief and understanding. Isn't so much suddenly clear?"

Dunquin is a feeble confederation of houses spread along two kilometres of road. Farms teeter at continent's end, then drop off. At either extreme of the village, like the claws of a lobster, headlands thrust into the ocean. The Great Blasket consumes the seascape, commandeering even the most digressive eye. To stand at the crossroads in Dunquin and not be overwhelmed by it would be akin to visiting Chartres and never noticing a cathedral in the town.

"It's so empty," Pat comments, turning up his jacket collar.

"So full."

"So grey."

"So verdant."

"Wow."

One month I have waited to use that word! "It's the only way to describe this place," I say casually.

"What's next, Hia?"

"Next?"

"The itinerary—what's up?"

"A walk, maybe. A walk to a cemetery, with interesting residents."

"Did Eily mention where this cemetery was?"

I bat my lashes.

"Did she instruct you to wait until we are at the foot of my father's grave before asking about his death?"

I frown in puzzlement.

The road winds out of Dunquin towards Dunmore Head. As we emerge from the hollow where dwellings huddle for protection, the highway swings nearer to the cliff. An earlier incarnation of the road literally drives off it, the cracked asphalt sprouting weeds and grass. At this point, beyond the settlement, the world consists entirely of configurations. The scale of the landscape is enormous and the tone is austere. But Pat is wrong; it is far from empty.

The graveyard is a rectangle of bracken wedged into the face of Mount Eagle, as if to prevent it, too, from sliding off the edge. The incline is steep and winds, blasting down the slope, stagger any who approach. We hesitate at the gate. Better, Pat hesitates and I, distressed by the ringing in my ears, acquiesce. Keeping my back to the cemetery, I watch the ocean roll. For all its senseless movement, the sea reminds me of a computer screen programmed to explore variations on a geometric paradigm. The apparent formlessness of each representation is deceiving; once the viewer understands the program, understands that every line has been designed, or at least originates from a formula, then what appeared random becomes purposeful, what seemed pure nature turns out to be pure artifice.

My stomach still churns after only a brief gaze.

Pat hunches below the wall. I am annoyed—he is clearly stalling—but see the wisdom in it. My hands are pink with cold.

"His body isn't even in the grave, Hia."

"What?"

"They never recovered my father's body. He fell from the sky and was swallowed by the sea."

"How can you say such a thing?"

"Because it's the truth."

"But so disrespectful!"

Pat kisses me on the cheek. "It's still interesting, though," he says.

I wait.

"To mess around in Dingle. Feign commitment, pretend to care."

He betrays himself. Not by his words, but by the tone of his voice: steeled, as if a bolt of lightning could strike him down at any moment.

Until a few minutes ago, the landscape was sunsoaked. Then clouds dragged a dark horizon in from the sea. The rain curtain was visible first on the Great Blasket, in the sound, on the caved-in road, at our feet. Pat pulls his poncho from the knapsack. I urge him on. I tell him—

We get drenched.

A car, the first in a half-hour, approaches from the village. Eily Murphy's directions featured a hitch: we had to get a lift around Slea Head and back to the bicycles. She was sure that would be no problem; she clearly had not hitch-hiked in Dunquin recently. The alternative is the walk back over Mount Eagle. These thoughts run through my mind as the car nears, along with the depressing fact that we have yet to visit any graves, yet to discuss the ferry to the Great Blasket, and most important, I have yet to properly ask my questions.

Pat springs up, strides to the roadside, flags down the driver. The vehicle stops.

"Come on!"

"Wait," I stammer.

"A question?"

"Yes."

"Number two?"

"How did you—?"

"Come on!"

The car, a ricketty Mini with a cardboard floor in the back, is driven by a bearded farmer whose sweater reeks of sheep. I share the back seat with a dog, also sheepy, considerably larger than his master. The animal's panting steams the window, so I miss the scenery. No matter: my thoughts are mired. Rain on the roof, against the windshield, and underneath the sagging cardboard—water is all around me.

But the ride is still harrowing. When not executing hairpin turns in the road with his eyes fixed on me in the rearview mirror, when not pointing out the window as the vehicle brushes the squat stone railings, the farmer is telling the tale of a ship impaled against the eastern flank of Dunmore Head. On its maiden voyage in 1984, the Spanish tanker *Ranga* veered into Dingle Bay to escape an Atlantic tempest. Unprepared when its anchor dragged in Blasket Sound, the tanker lurched, stayed upright, then swept against the headland. Only the ship tower remains. It rises crookedly, a rust-red pagoda housing colonies of seabirds and the rare yapping seal.

Sunlight parts the clouds the instant we disembark at the shop. It would be lovely back in Dunquin, the air redolent, the light new. Pat and I would have the cemetery, and probably the pier, to ourselves. But he is delighted with the day's events. I am less thrilled. Three points, none taken.

I have adopted a persona in my work, a medium that will guide me into Angkor, allow me to sketch the complex from the vantage point of an inhabitant, not an interloper. Having abandoned large-scale drawings, I am focusing on specific sites. I sketch temple entranceways, like the Buddha heads above the southern gate of Angkor Thom, the north portal to Preath Khan, the cruciform entrance to Angkor Wat. I sketch the relief carvings in the covered gallery on the lowest level of Angkor, mostly tales from the *Mahabharata* and *Ramayana*, with Vishnu in his various avatars and the cycles of reincarnation explained: the good anticipating better lives while the bad look ruefully forward to returning as dogs or despots. I draw battle scenes of rearing horses and plodding elephants, warriors in stances more elegant than belligerent, as if mythic combat is gentlemanly. Borrowing from bas-reliefs on the second level, I draw the full-breasted *devies*, consorts to the Gods, whose sarongs cascade to their feet. I draw smiling Buddhas, dour Vishnus—the two religions co-exist at Angkor—kings and courtiers, animals and serpents.

And I sketch the *apsaras*. Seventeen hundred of these creatures inhabit Angkor Wat alone; perhaps five thousand more are chiselled on the walls, entrances, and staircases of other temples. In Khmer lore, they were "the ones who go through the water of the clouds", appointed to sing and dance for the elect. *Apsaras* wore headgear and jewelled collars, brocaded skirts and bracelets. Their physical beauty was robust: round breasts, round bellies, firm jaw and cheekbones, brows doming eyes often closed in contemplation of the joyful existence after the last reincarnation. In dance, they employed supple gestures—the bending of a single finger was choreographed—to embody the rhythms and colours of rushing water.

But meditation was also central to the dance. *Apsaras* were, after all, both human and divine. Though incarcerated in a mutable form, they were liberated from decay by the permanence of sandstone, and thus became eternal—enlightened, vigilant, all-seeing.

Tension through detail. Tension, like my certainty that the artifact is from the panel of an *apsara*, based on my determination to continue the detailings beyond their surviving parameters. Tension, like my need to assert my mother's inviolability, maintained through the details of her face that anoint my fingertips.

"*Apsaras* are everywhere in Angkor," I tell Pat the next evening. "And so they can take me everywhere."

"How?"

"I must be one of them when at work. Know what they know, see what they see."

He examines my sketch. "Her eyes are closed," he says.

"So?"

"Is she pregnant?"

"Their stomachs are always round. This does not mean they are pregnant."

"Don't they also have swollen feet?"

"Swollen feet?"

"I read that somewhere."

"You read about Angkor?"

"It's a beautiful drawing, Hia."

"Just as example. Not—"

"It's still beautiful."

I shrug. Beautiful or ugly, accomplished or rough: these attributes mean little unless the sketch is integral to the larger design.

"The *apsaras* will not be part of the final series. The final must be a capturing of the whole of Angkor, the totality of it. Anything less is a failure."

Why does he stare at me?

"I just need a map," I say, biting my lip. "The site is too massive, and I am not able to fly to Cambodia tomorrow to make inspection, as you are able to visit a fiddler or listen to a tape."

"Maybe you should try paints. The colours might give you some ideas."

"You think I need ideas?"

"I was just—"

"You think I am not succeeding."

"I think I'll go for a walk."

"Paints take you too far from the subject," I answer, trying not to sound defensive. "Pencil and charcoal are right at perception. That is where I want to be."

"With the celestial dancers."

"Who live in Angkor," I agree.

"What kind of music did the Khmers play?"

"Many of the bas-reliefs show musicians with flutes and instruments that have keys, like a xy-lo-phone. Also, they used beautiful chimes."

"But aren't you tone deaf?"

"I will follow the lead of others."

It won't be easy; my impulse is to dote on the spatial composition of the complex. My pencil seeks those dimensions. To resist, to focus on a particular, will be a challenge.

As discipline, I spend the rest of the evening drawing a single panel, and then nod off to sleep, when sleep finally comes, with images of the Bayon ordering my dreams. The temple is so numinous: three tiers, shady courtyards, and umbered galleries, with the massive Lokesvara statue gazing out from the axis, his four faces affixed to the four cardinal points of the forty-nine turrets and towers. Incense sticks smoulder at the base of the statue. Red flags deck the galleries. Monks tend to the shrine, ancient men with shaved heads and robes. Clouds of butterflies flutter between temple tiers; woodpeckers hollow treetrunks; parakeets weave between arches.

Living things! People, even. See: the *apsaras* have led me to them. They will show the way.

Chapter 8

The brick was still on board the boat. Chac had tried to lob it into the channel to distract the soldiers, but it had struck the roof and slid off, landing at the bow. Hia found the object the next morning. She picked it up and wiped both sides with her sleeve. One face was definitely blank. But the other revealed, to the touch, designs carved into the sandstone. Dampening her shirt, she scrubbed through most of the morning, unearthing two patterns of chiselled lines. By noon, Hia knew the brick was the artifact she had bought in Saigon, and that it did belong to a temple panel. What had the shaman claimed—Angkor Wat, in Cambodia? The old man was a fraud. He would have told her anything for a sale. But why Angkor, and why had he remembered her name, her *may bay chuong-chuong* anecdote, and then stood in the alley, filthy hands trembling, cadaver face lit, as if he had been waiting all those years to complete the transaction so Hia could claim her inheritance and he could.... What? Die in good conscience?

On their second day out, the sea began to race and the wind stiffened. The light, bright in the morning, paled by mid-afternoon, and the sky bore down upon the surface. Spray drenched the prow and cabin. Instead of skimming atop the ocean, the trawler rode within it; the result, a rhythm of rise, crest, and pitch, tested constitutions. Chac was unaffected. He claimed to enjoy the storm, his first as a skipper, and stayed behind the wheel, cap on backwards, a cigarette between his lips. Consulting his land compass, he continued to pilot the trawler due south, except when a swell forced a correction. Nhung was wobbly-legged but functional. Hia suffered. The queasiness that had bothered her worsened into blurred vision and bouts of dry heaving. She lay on the cabin floor with a towel over her eyes, oblivious of everything except the hisses and roars, the grinding of wood. Nhung held her hand. Chac sang her songs.

By midnight, the waves were heavy and the bow thrust headlong into each trough, drenching the cockpit. Chac, determined to keep a bearing, refused to be relieved, his fingers cramping around the wheel. Nhung and Hia huddled together. Sleep was furtive, interrupted by drenchings and plunges into bottomless swells. The cockpit shipped more water. Bedding, cooking utensils, and a gas container were washed overboard. Eventually, Chac stopped singing; eventually, the sisters prayed.

Their prayers had a cadence. *OurFATherwhoARTinHEAven*, Hia and Nhung chanted. *HalLOwed-BEthyNAme.* When Chac had heard enough, he cajoled them into singing a wedding song about a hamlet tucked among orange-tree groves, where teenaged couples, their marriages arranged at birth, were wed by priests and welcomed into the community with showers of blossoms, banquets of fish soup and barbecued beef.

The storm exhausted itself overnight. Though the light at dawn was still bleary, the sun behind thinning clouds made everyone squint, their skin tingling with warmth. The sea settled back.

Chac asked Nhung to take the wheel. "I have to piss so bad!" he said.

Nhung assumed the duty with solemnity. Her sister

struggled to her feet.

"Where are we?" Hia asked.

"Chac knows."

They waited, eyes averted, until Chac returned from the stern. Hia repeated the question.

"Halfway to Singapore," he answered. "Halfway to America. Can we eat?"

Hia hooded her eyes. She wasn't looking for Singapore, but was curious to see if she could intuit a direction from the ocean. Examining the horizon to the bow and stern, and then fixing the sun in the sky, she tried to position their course beneath it. That didn't work; according to her calculation, they were actually heading northeast. Next she sought an outline that could serve as a reference point. Again she failed; nothing was fixed on the sea—not the gulls circling the boat (Hia was surprised they ventured so far out), not the receding horizon or climbing sun, and certainly not the cloud formations that sauntered past, stately and indifferent. After a while Hia understood that even Chac's trawler was itself such a reference. Were another vessel to spot the boat, it would be equally useless as a marker. They too were moving through the sea, a motion within greater motion, a motion without end.

"Food's ready, Hia."

The nausea worsened.

"Coconut rice," Chac said to encourage her. "Dried fish. Fresh tea. Nhung did well."

The girl beamed.

"Grab some rice in those beautiful hands of yours," he kidded. "Mess up your pretty fingers. Or do you want chopsticks?"

Hia tried to speak.

"Chopsticks for the *phung*," Chac ordered. "A napkin for the Saigon lady."

"I am sick."

Wiping his hands against his shorts, Chac crossed to

her, grasped her shoulders, and awkwardly kissed her. "Better?" he said.

Nhung's eyes widened.

"You promised—?" Hia said, feeling burn at the back of her neck.

"Does it matter now? Nothing matters out here. We can do as we like!"

Hia was too ashamed to speak. She sulked at the rear gunwale for an hour. Despite her mood, she was the first to notice a string of vessels to the starboard side. The ships were tiny and faint. They also appeared, in opposition to her earlier speculations, frozen on the sea, like a backdrop in a theatre. The gulls hanging over the trawler cast further doubt on the accuracy of Chac's piloting. A question loomed: if not near the Indonesian archipelago, where were they?

Two small islands materialized. A telltale fog had crept over the water, obscuring details, tricking eyes. Hia, trying to recall a classroom map, speculated that the islands might be part of a disputed group, which would have placed them halfway into the South China Sea. Chac was furious; maybe the storm had blown them slightly off course, slightly to the north, but towards the Philippines?

The fog thickened as they neared land. A sound, like a mortar firing, scattered the birds into invisible formations. One island was rimmed in trees, the other in scrubby vegetation. Chac thought it best to land where the enemy, if there was one, would be in plain sight. Hia and Nhung didn't want to land at all. The trawler had already avoided a sandbar, and scraped bottom, when a structure built on a cement promontory emerged fifty metres to starboard.

A guardtower?

Closer examination revealed humans scrambling on a beach, pursued by uniformed men.

Soldiers?

Suddenly the water near the trawler was filled with bodies, some face down, others clinging to planks and containers. The scene was incomprehensible, and for a second Chac and Hia stood fascinated, unable to imagine a connection between these activities and themselves.

"People in the water," Chac said.

More figures on the beach were turning to confront the sea, and were now swimming towards the boat, screaming, begging for help. Soldiers fired at them.

"Chac!" Hia shouted.

"Are they trying—?"

Wood from the cabin splintered; a *ping!* reverberated as a bullet ricocheted off the engine compartment. Hia and Nhung dropped to the floor. Chac, who only crouched, plunged face first when the trawler lurched violently. A hand, then two hands, grasped the leeward gunwale as a man pulled himself on board.

Chac crawled over to assist him.

Bullets jumped in the water, sending wood fragments flying, shattering the cabin glass. Recoiling with each impact, like a boxer absorbing a punch, the trawler also listed side to side as swimmers tried to board it. A man was almost over when his head exploded and he fell away. Nhung was splattered with his blood. Chac was helping a woman climb the gunwale when she clutched her leg. Her pants darkened, and she moaned in pain. Once the woman was secure, he crossed the deck to someone else. Hia grabbed him.

"We must leave!"

The assault intensified as a machine gun, nested in the tower, opened fire. Bullets shredded the cabin and pocked the hull. Ricochets killed a man who had raised his arms on the bow, as if to surrender, and had been shot in the neck. It was so strange: Hia, struggling to pull Chac, who was himself struggling to drag a teenage boy up over the stern, was abruptly, absurdly seized by the clarity of every stone, every sand ripple under the water. . . .

"Please," she begged him.

"What, just leave?"

"Yes!"

The boy was safely on board.

Hia and Chac scrambled to the cabin and, hunching behind the wheel, opened the throttle. To pilot, Chac would have to raise his head. Hia told him to take off the baseball cap. He grinned and reminded her of his vow not to remove it until they reached America.

"Stay down," Hia said.

"Crazy, huh?"

"Stay down!"

He stood up.

Chapter 9

We are in the snug. Of course we are; the pub was forlorn on our arrival—no customers, no lights, no T. Daly. Only Jimmy Sullivan, waiting at the counter in a short-sleeved shirt and the same onion-knot tie. I asked about Tom the barman, my interest piqued by a development in the calendar conundrum. The relic from May 1958 was unchanged, but the other Bank of Ireland calendar had leapt two years, to June 1987. Why 1987, why June, why now? But Tom had stepped out for a moment, and before either of us could object, we were ushered into the closet. I was counting on Pat to stall, even to refuse; he merely waved me through the doorway.

"Now," Jimmy says.

"Should I?"

"Please."

Pat raps on the window.

"But no one's out there." I say.

"You never know, do you?"

"Know what?"

"Other people. What goes on in their heads, their hearts. In their lives, even."

"Where are you going to take us tonight, Jimmy?" Pat asks.

Jimmy lights a cigarette, offers me one. (I've quit.) For a man of his age, his arms are surprisingly sinewy. On his left forearm is the outline of a tattoo. "No place you haven't been before," he answers.

The slot opens. A peep escapes my lips.

"Good to see you, Tommy."

All any of us can see of Tom the barman, even when he presses his face into the space, is a mouth and stubby chin, a battered nose sprouting nostril hairs. "You two again," he comments. "Jimmy lured you back?"

"Promises of revelations," Pat says.

"I bet."

"Dark secrets."

"He has one or two."

"On the subject, . . . " Jimmy says. "Hia here is anxious to question you regarding the decor."

I blanch.

"You mean the chandelier?" Tom asks.

"Never mind."

Directing comments at empty air is weird: I need to look at the person.

"A pint of Harp, please," Pat says.

I order a ginger ale (I've quit drinking too) and Jimmy once again requests, to the bartender's bemusement, a Britvic.

The slot shuts.

"Come here a minute."

"Don't move!" Pat orders me.

What?

"Tell us your secrets, Jimmy. I bet you're dying to share them."

"Tit for tat, lad."

"No problem."

Jimmy's eyebrow flares. "Guests first," he says. "House rules."

The drinks arrive. As usual, no money changes hands.

"Ask," Pat says.

Jimmy asks.

"You know the story already," he answers, unsurprised by the question. "An accident when I was a boy. Two accidents. Broke the same leg twice. Lucky guess—remember?"

"A few details wouldn't hurt."

I have to smile.

"Between the ages of seven and nine," Pat says, "I was a sleepwalker. Once a month I rose from my bed, climbed out the window and up a drainpipe onto the roof, crossed to a huge maple tree beside the house, shimmied along a branch, and then tried to stand. Twice I fell, both times onto the driveway, both times breaking this leg." He grasps his thigh.

"What were you dreaming about when you jumped?"

"I didn't jump. I fell."

"Is that what you said?"

"What did I say, Hia?

"You said you fell," I confirm. "But didn't the—"

"The psychologist who treated me thought I was actually jumping off a cliff."

"Tree," Jimmy corrects.

"What did I say?"

"What did he say, Hia?"

"You said—"

"Whatever I said, it was definitely a tree that I jumped—I mean fell — from. The maple tree beside our house. It's still there, if you don't believe me."

"And did the doctor have any theories?"

"It related to what Pat was dreaming," I offer.

"Hia!"

"Details, details," Jimmy says happily.

Pat guzzles his beer, his Adam's apple bobbing. "I didn't remember any of it. But under hypnosis, I explained to the doctor that I was on an island, near a cliff, the wind at my back and birds overhead. . . . "

"Were you alone?"

"All the time."

"In the dream, son."

"Alone," Pat confirms.

Jimmy slams his fist into the palm of his hand. The sound, a fleshy thwack, startles us all. "Where is the justice?" he asks. "A young lad. Innocent. Unknowing. Paying for another's weakness."

His gaze, aimed squarely at my lover's face, is intense. Eventually Jimmy's look wanders downward, to where Pat is massaging his bad leg. "You can't tell, you know," he says gently.

"You could."

"It's imperceptible. Am I right, Hia?"

"When I met him, I thought he walked a little funny to match my step. Never did I guess he was injured."

Pat raps on the window again. My soda is half full; Jimmy has yet to touch his orange juice. "Have you noticed anything peculiar about the way I walk?" he asks the barman.

"You're sitting down."

"When I'm not."

"I wouldn't know, would I?"

"Right. I forgot."

"Your father, now, he had a loping stride. Sort of jouncy, nervous. A nice change from the shuffle common in these parts."

"You knew my father?"

A frown creases Tom's nose. "What's your man here been telling you, anyway?"

"Nothing."

"So I gather. Jimmy. . . . " he says sternly. "Jimmy!"

Our host, busy rolling the tip of his cigarette against the ashtray, starts. "I'm grand, Tommy," he answers, displaying the Britvic.

"Another pint," Pat says.

The window stays open. I am dying to peek through it. But Pat is in the way, and he isn't budging. Jimmy, meanwhile, jiggles his foot and coughs into his fist.

"Sounds like fun out there," I comment. The chandelier has been switched on in the main room. The bell above the door jingles. Voices rise and fall.

"Out where?" Jimmy and Pat wonder together.

I shut up.

"My turn," Pat announces.

"Ask," Jimmy says.

Pat asks.

Jimmy is not surprised by the question; he is appalled by it. Pat, stone-faced, twists the knife.

"Bodies *always* wash ashore?" he continues. "On the strand at Ferriter's Cove, or further north at Sybil Head or Ballydavid? No matter how far out to sea the accident is, the victim is returned to land by the tides?"

"How would you know?"

"Is it true?"

A look of great weariness comes over Jimmy Sullivan. I use the pause to study his tattoo. It is bluish-green, the size of a wristwatch. The figure has almost disintegrated; I will have to redraw it mentally.

"Where is this going?" he asks.

"No place you haven't been before."

"I need a drink."

"Your orange juice is right there."

Jimmy turns to me. "What's with him tonight?"

"You guys talk in private language," I answer. "I understand only the English words."

"Cheers."

"No body, no death," Pat says.

"Ah Jesus!"

"Nobody what?" I ask.

"A corpse means fuck all, pardon my language," Jimmy says. "What matters is the loss, the months, even years of bereavement. What matters is ardent memory. What matters is love everlasting. If you still can't see that. . . . "

Tears well in my eyes.

"I can't see anything," Pat interrupts. "Not from in here, anyway."

Who *is* this man?

"I am steadfast in love."

Now who said that? Judging from the looks on their faces, apparently I did. The snug, not the bar, is suddenly crowded with strangers.

"Come here a minute, you two," Jimmy says. "Come here, and I'll tell you a story."

I am under water.

"Many years ago I owned a fishing trawler—"

"I just found out my mother is dead," I announce.

Pat flinches.

"Three months ago," I add.

"I'm very sorry," Jimmy says.

"She died in September."

Someone takes my hand. No use; I am drowning.

"September 1979. Killed by soldiers while trying her escape."

The men keep silent.

"My father informed me in Toronto. He came up from California to visit his daughters. Brought his new American wife and new Vietnamese American children. His two letters from before, since 1985, when he became a boat person, never made clear—"

"They made it clear, Hia," Pat interrupts softly. "You just didn't want—"

"No! Never made clear what had happened that day. Never made clear that she was dead. How could I assume? How could I say for sure?"

"You are steadfast in love."

Drowning.

Pat wraps his arms around me.

Jimmy excuses himself. The door is cracked partway; voices and lights flood the chamber. I look for a face, but see only jackets and sweaters, smoky profiles. For the rest of the night I concentrate on the phantoms projected against the rear wall of the pub, impressed by their theatricality and grotesqueness.

Once he senses that I am comforted (as if he has a clue!), Pat knuckles the window again. Funny; he could simply step through the door, turn left, and present himself, in person, to Tom the bartender. "What is Jimmy supposed to be telling me?" he asks the slot.

"Ah."

"He's gone to the washroom."

"Thanks for the tip."

"I just thought—"

Tom clears his throat. "You're right, sure. Jimmy's had too many years to prepare for your arrival. He's frozen up."

"How can I unfreeze him?"

"Not with Britvic orange."

"Jimmy drinks whisky?"

"Jameson."

"A double, please. My tab."

The barman roars.

"But it's not really my place, you know," Tom adds after a moment.

"No one will mind."

"Not a matter of minding. More of propriety and respect. This is Jimmy's business."

"Mine too."

"In his own time. . . . "

Now I know what they resemble: Pat on one side of the barrier, hands in his lap, gaze fixed on a blank wall; the barman on the other side, whispering into a narrow slot. Who is the sinner confessing his misdeeds, and who the priest absolving all trespasses?

"Nature called," Jimmy says, clicking the door behind

him. On his way past, he squeezes my shoulder. His grip is powerful.

Pat serves another ginger ale to me, a pint to himself, a tumbler of iceless whisky to our host.

"What's this?" Jimmy asks.

"Antifreeze."

"Sorry?"

"Cheers, lads," Pat says.

"Tommy?"

The slot closes. Jimmy continues to stare at his glass, as if watching the play of light in liquid.

"You were saying, . . . " Pat says.

"I was?"

"'Many years ago I owned a fishing boat. . . . '"

"Did I order a whisky?"

"'Many years ago, . . . '" Pat repeats.

"Cheeky bastard."

"' . . . I owned a fishing boat. . . . '"

"With another Dingle man," Jimmy sighs. "A small trawler, fine for local waters but unsteady on the open sea. Not a vessel for a storm, I'd say, at least not the kind we are subjected to in the autumn and winter."

He sniffs the liquid. "But this man, a friend, was a special case. Inclined to depression, disinclined to struggle with it. On the afternoon of a particularly foul day he decided we should collect some lobster pots shot early that morning. I was not keen. He insisted. We walked out the pier and boarded our sorry little boat. An act of madness, pure and simple.

"Eventually, we brought ourselves to the base of an island cliff. The pots were buried deep in cracks, meaning the trawler had to crawl right into the shallows to free them. There was no way a boat should have gone near rocks with a storm raging. Only this man wasn't concerned with the conditions. He was intent on taking the risk, skirting the edge. *He* was lost in his own darkness; I was fighting to save our lives."

Jimmy sips the whisky. The taste is not unpleasant to him. "So we hauled the pots," he resumes. "Below the cliff, scraping rock, we stacked pots half empty because even lobsters wouldn't venture out. The man was at the stern having his upper body submerged each time he hauled a line. Once, I scrambled the length of the cockpit to keep him from tumbling overboard and then opened the throttle before a breaker landed. Had I not, we'd have been finished. And what was his mood? What was going on inside his head?"

The question is posed directly to Pat. Even stranger, he receives it without complaint. Both men drink while I study the tattoo. The shape is definitely not a woman's body. Nor is it an anchor.

"He was laughing," Jimmy answers. "His eyes were narrowed, but it had nothing to do with the pots. And he was laughing! The man was displacing something, some deep anxiety another person couldn't begin to fathom, regardless of his interest and concern. And, really now, who was suffering the more? Some of us haven't aspirations beyond healthy, reasonably happy lives. Was it so wrong not to want to die?"

He tips back his glass.

"Who is not wayward?" he adds in a rising voice. "Who is not adrift on the sea?"

"A perpetual diaspora," Pat agrees.

"There was a moment," Jimmy says, turning to me, "a single, defining moment that has stuck in my memory, like the death of an infant. Imagine it, Hia: a figure poised with one leg on the stern and the other on a rock, the water foaming beneath. The gap suddenly widens and the man hangs in the air—a waver of light, a chord of music. Astonishing, I'd say. Passionate. Totally deranged."

"Did the man die?" I manage, my heart back in my throat.

"Over a period of years."

Pat's conciliatory tone vanishes. "Is that really the whole story?" he asks. "All there is to it?"

"He played before, if that's what you mean."

"Played for you?"

"For himself."

"Do dying men play the fiddle?"

"With consummate elegance."

"He was twenty-four years old."

"He chose his age."

"And later—?"

"Later it was all elegy," Jimmy mutters, brandishing his cigarette. "Later it was all lament."

Pat and Jimmy are locked in telepathic combat, and I am a shadow on the wall. "You guys move too fast," I complain. "Want to tell me what goes on here?"

I think, for some reason, of my final night in Toronto. A freak storm had postponed spring. Outside the apartment building were filthy snowbanks and tree skeletons. My sister was at work and Pat was in Willowdale visiting Francine. Fidgety, uneasy about the trip, I wandered from room to room flaring joss sticks borrowed from Nhung's shrine. All the lights were off, the TV was dark, and the high-rise, normally thrumming with voices, was still. I had been taught from birth that ghosts were simply people we could not see. That night, I paced the apartment with an awareness that I was not alone. But what could the spirits do? How could they help? Unseen, our ancestors protected us. Unquestioned, the tragic circle of life drew us back in.

"A drowning man," I say suddenly, "will grab at his own hand in the hope of being saved."

My comment, which left my mouth unexpectedly, earns stares.

"What was that?" Jimmy asks.

"A Vietnamese platitude."

"I thought you were from Dublin?"

"I thought so too."

Tom the barman opens the slot to announce last round. Pat orders more alcohol.

"Hia has a question about the calendars behind the bar," he says.

I punch his arm.

"What about them?"

"Nothing," I stammer.

"They're wrong, Tommy," Jimmy summarizes.

"In what sense?"

"The dates," he says on my behalf, "the years, the circumstances—it's all off."

"I didn't realize."

"You didn't *realize*?" I ask.

"Well, . . . " Tom answers, his voice neutral, "I mean, I hadn't checked lately."

"Let me show you," I say.

The main room should be vast, should be cool and fresh. Instead, I confront a forest of men, thick-trunked, gangly-rooted. Foliage filters the light. Cigarette fumes block the moon. I weave, ask politely, and finally muscle my way to the bar. When I reach it, the area is dark and the slot into the snug is shut, a rag dangling from the ledge.

A young man at the counter smiles at me. He has a long face, protruding eyes, and orange hair that has run over his skin, blotching his neck and hands with freckles.

"What's he got that I haven't?" he asks.

I step back

"Baby, I'm your man!"

His smile reveals stained teeth. I am not frightened, but hasten past him anyway. "I need to leave," I announce at the snug door.

What a pair they make: drinks on the floor, cigarettes burning in an ashtray, with Jimmy's arm extended forward, as if to give blood.

"He's showing me his tattoo," Pat explains.

"It's a boat," I announce, having just resolved the shape in my mind.

"Clairvoyant!" Jimmy says.

"A fishing trawler. Forty-horsepower engine, nets and pots, a hold below the cockpit for catches and refugees."

"This girl is special."

"Let's go," I repeat.

Pat drags on a cigarette.

"You don't smoke," I say.

"Only when I drink."

"And you drink . . . ?"

He grins drunkenly.

We leave. My search for the freckled man who called me his baby is half-hearted; Pat probably knows him; they probably hang out together in pubs. The rain has paused. Rectangles of light angle from windows onto the sidewalk. Shop signs creak in the breeze. The pier, where Pat appears headed, is deserted, masts tilting like compass needles.

"I'd love a chip," he says.

"You're drunk."

"Sausage and chip."

"How about a piece of fish?" I suggest sarcastically.

"I'm not fussy."

"Where are we going, Pat?"

Changing his mind, he crosses the lot between the drydock and a row of buildings. I sidestep the puddles; Pat keeps a straight line, his limp worsened by each plunge into a crater. Twice he reaches for my hand. I keep my distance. He thinks we've finished arguing. He thinks we've fought, scratched, even wounded each other, but now are back on the best of terms. Why does he believe this? Because the latest spat happened a day ago, and a day ago, for Pat, is a useless memory, a closed book.

"Where are you going?" I repeat.

"To the island."

"You drank five beers."

"I thought you wanted to go."

The trawler is still up on blocks. Pat stops beside it. "We'll visit the Great Blasket," he boasts. "The ancestral sod, the soggy ancestral sod, the besodden—"

"Don't even think it."

Hoisting himself up, he tumbles on board. A bird shoots up from the cockpit, passing so close to my face that I sense its beating wings against my cheek. Wood grinds; strakes snap. I half expect the cockpit to collapse through to the ground. I fully expect the trawler to capsize.

Pat pokes his head over the side. "We'll sail the high seas," he says. "The B flats and D minors. Ride the crests of rolling G chords into the troughs of major keys. . . . Do you think the engine will start?"

"Get out of the boat."

Rising, he walks wobbly-legged to the stern. Floorboards sag under him; he panics, reaches for a gunwale. "No anchor," he reports.

"Get out of the boat."

"*Phung thi chin,* hah! Try cultural bureaucrat. Try devout Catholic sheep."

The cock crows a third time.

"Fine," Pat answers. "I'll get out of the boat."

He falls out of the boat. Endeavouring to raise a leg, he clips his foot on the side and somersaults, ending up under the rocking hull. I hear the cement blocks grind. If even one support collapses. . . .

He groans.

The rain surges.

I turn and stride towards the road. He calls my name, once, twice, then decides to sing.

Ferme tes jolis yeux
Car le sommeil approche
Du pays merveilleux
Du beau pays des rêves. . . .

The apartment smells of mildewed carpet. Carolan greets my return with a *purrt* from within his near-perpetual sleep. I check the clock: midnight. I fix tea, change my clothes, stare at the top page of the sketch pad—a Buddha head, indifferently executed—and sit in the dark listening to animals stomp on the roof.

Swollen sky.

Babies never die.

Mothers won't lie.

Darling, don't cry.

Pat is swimming beneath a trawler. The hull is an apparition in fonts of light, explosions of bubbles. He is below the light and must surface for air. Only he cannot climb; around his ankle is a shackle attached to a chain. He yanks at the chain. Pull! Until the links snap. Pull! Until his leg is—

I revive with a jolt. Immediately I check my watch: 2:35 a.m. Forgetting my jacket, I fly down the stairs and out the door. The trawler has vanished. Pat is gone. Then, stepping cautiously—the darkness cloaks my own hand—I bump into the bow.

There is a body under the hull. I shake it.

"Hia?"

"You were asleep."

"Was I?"

"I shouldn't have left. I am sorry."

"I had this dream. . . . " He sits up. "What time is it?" he says, still groggy.

"I'm late."

"That's okay."

"I'm late!"

"I think I bit my tongue."

"Get up."

"I turn thirty-two next week," he tells me, extracting himself from the muck. "I am sleeping under a boat. I have no wife or family, no job or home—and I am sleeping under a boat! What a disaster."

"You have me."

"God bless you, Hia. God keep you safe."

I help him to his feet.

SHE WHO IS NOURISHED BY GOD

Chapter 10

Once the trawler was beyond rifle range, a man who had climbed aboard during the attack took the wheel from Hia. Bon Dran Ly was a sixty-year-old former army colonel, the only one of the three new passengers not wounded and not in shock. It was he who had dragged Chac from the cabin into the cockpit and covered him with the tarpaulin. Bon Dran Ly had then escorted Hia past the corpse, past strangers lying in pools of water and blood, past her own sister picking at a sliver of wood embedded in her arm. The twilight sky, containing both sun and moon, was tranquil, the blue of the higher recesses full of light. These margins of transparent air were so radiant that everything seemed to Hia to become clearer, more visible. A body of seabirds spanned overhead. Water slapped against the hull.

"I don't feel well," she told the man.

"Sleep," he said.

Hia slept alone at the stern.

At dawn Bon Dran Ly roused her to urge a quick burial. Hia's knowledge of the *cao to* was sketchy, but the woman with the thigh wound, a widow from Haiphong, offered to lead it. Ordering the sisters to turn away, Dung My Chung withdrew the tarpaulin and hid the face under a red handkerchief. Hia's only dress was knotted and tied to the chest.

The hands and feet were bound. Next, the woman pried open the mouth and slipped in a ball of rice with a penny buried at its centre. All Chac's belongings were put in a sack, which Bon Dran Ly strapped to the waist using fishing net. Dung My Chung, wincing in pain from her own injury, complained that adults should be dressed in white. She bemoaned the lack of incense and paper money, *cao vong* silk and catafalque. The ceremony was incomplete. Fanning the body with her shawl to catch fleeing *hon* and *via*, she ordered the women to sit, the man to stand, then closed her eyes and began chanting sutras. With the sun half risen and no birds in sight, Dung My Chung commanded the adults to clasp their hands together and bow three times. "Feet first," she ordered Bon Dran Ly. "And may his spirit find fulfilment."

The body was dumped overboard.

The situation, as outlined by the former officer with the salt-and-pepper hair and the small, piercing eyes that fixed directly on Hia, was desperate. The trawler was somewhere northeast of the Spratlys, a loose federation of islands and reefs two-thirds of the way to Palawan, the westernmost island in the Philippine archipelago. They could proceed due east to Palawan, where they might be welcomed by authorities but more likely would be raided by pirates. Manila Bay, a safer destination, was only forty-eight hours further north. Though the cabin had been damaged and the hold was a foot deep in water, the engine sounded fine. Of the five gas tanks, three had been hit. But two tanks should be enough, Bon Dran Ly maintained. He had, admittedly, little experience as a navigator. He was also charting their route from memory and piloting based on the position of the sun—risky for amateurs.

At midday, Hia finally thought to ask what had happened. Dung My Chung, a broad-faced woman with a booming voice and a thick country accent, shrugged at the question. Her son and mother had been killed on the island, her leg throbbed, her heart was torn: that was what had happened to her. Now if she could only die. . . . The colonel interceded. He was wiping the brow of the teenager shot in the chest. The boy, pulled on board by Chac, had yet to regain consciousness; no one expected him to live. Bon Dran Ly responded to Hia's query by wondering if Chac had smoked and, if so, where he might have stashed any extra packs. Hia catwalked around the cabin to the bow. In the cupboard, now dimly lit through bullet holes, she sifted among the burst rice bags and hacked fruits, the unscathed Angkor Wat artifact, to where Chac had kept his cigarettes and matches. One package was intact. Bon Dran Ly tore it open.

"Bad habit," he admitted.

The colonel, Dung My Chung, and the teenager had been among fifty fugitives on a trawler departing the coastal city of Qui Nhon three days before. Their journey had been uneventful until the captain, blinded by fog, struck a sandbar. Thinking they had already reached the Philippines, many passengers jumped overboard and struggled to the shore. More than half, including women and children, were huddled on a beach when a searchlight trapped them. Soldiers stepped into the light and ordered everyone to line up. The commanding officer demanded to talk with a spokesman. Bon Dran Ly came forward. The commander listened to his explanation (a transparent lie), claimed the refugees would not be harmed, then went off to consult with his superiors.

Moments later an explosion rocked the lodged boat. A second mortar shell blew it up. Panicking, people on the beach dashed for cover, either into the scrub or back to the water. Soldiers began firing. Bon Dran Ly first hid in the bushes, then recrossed the beach and fought the surf. The shoreline was a shooting gallery: survivors were picked off by marksmen who stood in groups, comparing expertise. The surf aided the soldiers by dragging their targets back into range. For the colonel, a strong swimmer who clung to a plank of wood, submerging himself at intervals to confuse his attackers, it was basically over; his luck had run out; fate had willed that he die.

Then Chac had piloted the trawler into view. . . .

Nhung awoke and joined the adults. The girl wore a sleeved shirt that drooped to her knees. Was she aware who the shirt belonged to? Did Nhung even remember last night, remember that her older sister had pulled her hands from her face, held her close, and then stripped off her bloodied top and replaced it with a clean piece of man's clothing? Hia had to suppress a wild, irrational rage.

"I'm so hungry!" the girl said.

"Make us some food."

"Coconut rice?"

"Good," Hia answered.

But she could not bring herself to eat. Smells—of rotting fruit and garbage, an unidentified odour that almost choked her—filled her nostrils, no less raw for being imaginary. She tried to rest, but the heat, the inexorable sea, made it impossible. When a cramp gripped her abdomen, she assumed the pain was from hunger. Her breathing became irregular. She stood, swayed, dropped to her knees. The second cramp was like a blow. Her bowels loosened; she feared she would defecate in her pants. Glancing down, Hia noticed drops of fresh blood on the deck. She wanted to check between her legs, but was mortified; Dung My Chung was staring at her, and Bon Dran Ly had left the wheel to see what was the matter.

Hia begged them to look away. They complied, and she lowered her trousers. Her thighs were bloody. She loosened the cloth that served as a sanitary napkin. Believing she was about to expel her stomach, Hia gripped the gunwales to keep from toppling backwards.

The pain intensified. Her insides shuddered.

She came to twenty minutes later. Dung My Chung and Nhung crouched over her. Someone had dressed her in a pair of men's trousers, the legs rolled up.

"Was Chac your husband?" the widow asked.

"Not married yet."

"*Chua hoan!*"

Unwed mother? Hia paled. Her confusion was sincere, and the older woman softened.

"What did you think it was?"

"My period . . . ," Hia sputtered. "Iwasn't sure. . . . "

"Children having children," Dung My Chung said. "What kind of life would the baby have had?"

Hia did not answer. Nhung raised a cup of water to her sister's lips and then, at a loss, sang another verse of the welcome song:

You'll float through the sky in four directions,
East and west, north and south;
But you'll never know all these things, my son,
Unless you get out of your house.

Eventually, Hia slept again.

Chapter 11

The knock shatters my concentration but fails to rouse either Carolan, a moraine on the chair, or Pat, a drumlin atop the bed. Lowering the artifact, I cross the front room. It is Jimmy Sullivan, in a housecoat and slippers. Given that he spends most nights with Eily, this familiarity should not be so unwelcome. Jimmy notices my disapproval.

"I won't come in," he promises.

"Pat is asleep."

"Still?"

"Late night."

"He was jarred, I'd say."

"Jarred?"

"Drunk."

"Definitely."

Jimmy's eyes walk over the room. A month ago, I was certain he and I were going to become friends. Since then, however, circumstances have steered us elsewhere. I stare at his spindly legs and pink footwear.

"Excuse the apparel," he says. "I've only the loan of the slippers."

"Do you want tea?"

He ignores the question. Suddenly he ignores me, squinting at the wall beside the bathroom door. "What in the world . . . ?"

"You mean the fiddler?"

"Where did you get this?"

"Pat made a photocopy of album cover. I can't pronounce the man's name. His music is very squeaky."

"Whose music?"

"This guy," I say, indicating the sketch. "Sean somebody."

"Does Pat think the drawing is of O Conchuir?"

"But the album—"

"Sure I know about the album," he interrupts. "Didn't I post the record to Francine myself?"

"You sent it?"

"You mean—?"

"He has no idea."

Jimmy glances at the bed. "We've done the boy an injustice," he says softly. "All of us."

He relays two messages—one for the boy, one for us both—hands me a sheet of paper and a key, then negotiates the stairs.

I throw open the curtains.

"Please. . . . "

"We're going to the island!"

"Show mercy, Hia."

"You have an interview with an old farmer today?" I ask, crossing to the bed.

"Near Ventry. Jimmy's going to drive me."

"Wrong."

"I don't have an interview?"

"Jimmy can't drive you."

I hand him the key.

"What's this?"

"Bicycle lock."

He curses.

"Map," I add, offering the piece of paper.

He curses again.

"More news," I say, enjoying myself. "We've got an invitation to a birthday party!"

I wait until the shower is running before resuming work. A half-hour later Pat commences his morning routine: whistling kettle, popping toast, sizzling eggs. I try to ignore the racket, and easily ignore his offers of a fried breakfast. Still, my concentration is destroyed.

"I had a dream last night," I say.

He pours tea.

"Ghosts were floating through the village, through the burnt houses and over the flooded fields. They sparked and crackled, like electric currents. I stood on a path to receive them. The ghosts filled my eyes and ears. They rushed into my nose and mouth. I couldn't breathe. I couldn't see or hear."

"Same dream," he says, scooping up an egg.

"How can you say that?"

"Same setting, same motifs."

"But the spirits were entering me, filling up my person. Don't you know what that means?"

"What does it mean?"

"You are disgusting."

He lowers his knife and fork. "And what did *you* have for breakfast?"

"Food."

"Details, details."

"Biscuits and tea."

"What kind of biscuits?"

"Oatmeal and raisin."

"How many?"

"A few."

He repeats the question.

"Six."

"How many spoons of sugar in the tea?"

"For three years I cooked noodles. Cooked them all day, seven days a week, then served bowls to peasants who laughed at me, made rumours behind my back. Eat your greasy bacon," I summarize.

He eats his greasy bacon. I pretend to study my drawing. In fact, I listen to him chew and to Carolan wheeze. Pat reads my mind.

"Is that cat still dead?" he asks.

Shifting topics, he compliments me on the sketch. I break my own rule and explain the panel to him. "It tells a Hindu creation myth. On left side is Ravana, god of the underworld. He has twenty-one heads. I try showing this with lines, like a—" I gesture.

"Halo."

"—a halo above him. On right side are gods of the sky and their leader, monkey god Hanuman. Vishnu is in the middle, recognized by his many arms."

"Vishnu looks worried."

"Not worried. He is organizing the twisting of the serpent Vasuki."

"They're tugging on a snake?"

"Twisting Vasuki produces a liquid that creates life. Both sides struggle to control the liquid."

"What are those midgets doing?"

"Those are *apsaras*," I answer patiently, shading some lines. "They are born in the sea of milk and fly away to entertain the kings."

"*Apsaras* are born in milk?"

"The milk is special."

"Special milk?"

"Must I use the word?"

"What word?"

He is kidding me.

"The milk is creation," I blush.

"The milk is homogenized," he replies, holding up a carton.

"Sea-men, silly!"

"The milk belongs to sailors?"

He is not kidding me.

"Semen!" I repeat.

"I heard you. But why would *apsaras* be born in—"

He stops eating.

"The panel is called 'Churning in the Sea of Milk,'" I add, for effect.

Pat swallows.

"Creativity and creation are same thing. Creativity is act of reproduction. Each art is newborn child; inheriting certain traditions, but also able to develop uniqueness. . . . Are you okay?"

"My tongue feels swollen."

"Bite your words lately?"

Making fun of Pat is definitely the best medicine for a foul mood!

"Did the *apsaras* really guide you to the panel?"

"I have memory."

He pauses over his next question. "Of one panel in a huge temple complex?" he asks, substituting thoughts.

"You doubt me?"

"I'm just astonished. The *apsaras* must be doing a great job."

"They try."

"This sketch is—"

"Only a practice."

"Of course."

"I am working towards the entire structure, a drawing that will capture the totality of it."

"I like the struggle motif," Pat says, pressing his hand atop mine. "The tug-of-war between two players, both committed, both after the same thing, with a hapless God trying to mediate from the centre."

Am I being made fun of? "You should get going," I say.

"But the interview isn't for—"

"You should get going."

Our eyes do not meet.

"You are keeping these preliminary drawings, aren't you?" he asks, returning the chill.

"None of your business."

"Hia. . . . "

"I have all the pages from the pad."

"Don't throw them out."

"Is this an order?"

"Don't throw them out."

It is an order.

"Maybe," I say.

The flat is mine all evening. Perfect environment for work: the shouts of kids in the park, the screeches of seagulls, a lemony light across the floor. Pencils have been sharpened, charcoal sticks pared, a page lies open on the table. I have my tea. I have my sugar. No one will drop by tonight (Eily went to Tralee with Jimmy). No letters to write. No shadows against the wall.

I breathe the bracing air. My nostrils dilate; my chest heaves. The blend of sea smells and burning turf, even cow dung, is invigorating. Maybe I need some television as background. Crazy: I have always worked in silence. Maybe I need a lamp. Crazy: natural light is best.

Atop the TV are the chalices I bought as prayer pots. Remembering the photographs, which I planned to rescue from my suitcase weeks ago, I unbuckle the case in the closet, and remove an envelope. A package of incense, purchased on Dundas Street, remains hidden. Four photos fall onto the coffee table. I glance at each snapshot, chastise myself, return to the kitchen.

My pencil moves.

Her profile is moonlit. The sheen is of a Rodin sculpture: deep and natural, unpolished. Her head is downturned and her gaze is introspective. Eyelids are heavy, lashes are lush, brows have been plucked. The line of her forehead eventually joins her cheeks and chin; the curvature of her hair matches that of her entire face. Her lips are delicate. Sadness informs her mouth, exhaustion her eyes. She is not young, not a girl: a woman of forty, loving parent of three (her son was born when she was only eighteen), dutiful wife, weary worker.

How could you die, Mother?

Forgive me!

Pat shakes me awake. My upper body, slumped over the table, blocks the sketch. He switches on a light.

"What time—?"

"Almost midnight."

"No!"

"I have to wash up," he says, breathless with excitement. "Read the notes, listen to the tape, then I'll explain."

He disappears into the washroom. I tear the top page from the pad, fold it into quarters, hesitate, then stuff the portrait under the pad.

Joe John Sheedy lives on a five-acre farm a mile inland from Ventry harbour. He was born there in 1923, emigrated to England after the war, and returned to Dingle in 1964 on the death of his father. Though a tall, robust man who manages a small herd on his own, he walks with a cane and coughs phlegm into a handkerchief. We sit in the front room of a two-storey farmhouse built adjacent to the original family cottage, now a cow pen. The room is plain, with a blazing fire beneath a mantelpiece adorned with family portraits and a crucifix. A television flashes soundless images in the corner—he seems unaware it is on—and a wooden clock keeps a lulling beat. After expressing disappointment that Jimmy Sullivan could not join us, Joe John brings out a tray of tea and sliced bread. I intercept the tray in the doorway, for which he is grateful. A very old fiddle rests in his lap.

PK: When did you start to play?

JJS: Sitting and listening as a child. That's how I got into the music. Listening to the local men my father brought to the house.

PK: Your father played?

JJS: He was a good old man, and a fine fiddler, my father. The music in the family was on his side of the house. My mother sang, mostly at church or while preparing the tea. She died when I was still a boy.

PK: Did your father teach you?

JJS: A little. Picked it up mostly scraping for myself. Hearing others, and going to the odd dance in Ventry or Ballyferriter.

PK: There were dances then?

JJS: I recollect a few, oh yes. We're talking the 1930s now. Way, way back! I took up the fiddle, started scraping for myself.

PK: Tell me about the dances.

JJS: Just country dances, you know, in a barn or more likely the house itself. The very rare occasion they were big events, when a relation was home from America. The normal night was in the kitchen, a half-dozen musicians by the fire and a great number of people on the floor dancing and drinking. I only went to a few, mind—you'd do best to ask Sean O Conchuir about them.

PK: Sean O Conchuir would know?

JJS: He would, sure he would. I recollect him officiating at one or two. Very rare these days, you know. House dances, kitchen sessions—unheard of, really. Few remember them at all.

PK: Were you playing the fiddle by the time you left for England?

JJS: A good lot. I went up to Killarney during summers to find work in the hotels. Big business in the hotels during the war. The father wasn't pleased, but I went still. Carrying my fiddle, keen to learn. Many of the greats were up that way. Fabulous music to be heard around Castleisland.

PK: Was your style influenced by that music?

JJS: It was, oh sure. Listening to Padraig O'Keefe in Charlie Horan's pub, for instance, was an experience I'll not forget. Crystal-clear sound the man got, each note perfect.

PK: When was this?

JJS: Summer of 1944 or '45. Way, way back!

PK: Then you emigrated?

JJS: Seventeen years I was in England. Missed your father's playing entirely. Missed him by a good while. But I heard from others. Sean O Conchuir tells the well-known story—

PK: You heard about my father in England?

JJS: He was meant to be brilliant. The real thing. Likely I play a few of his tunes.

PK: Can you think of any names?

JJS: Names? I can't recall many of those. Mostly reels, I think, though I have it in mind there's a slow air that belongs to him. But ask Sean—he's the man with the memory.

PK: Did you play in England?

JJS: I did. Good fill of music in the Irish pubs around Manchester. No shortage of Irishmen in England.

PK: Would you play English music?

JJS: English? No, but the odd Scottish tune. A lancer or a highland reel. . . . They were big on the polkas and slides in East Kerry. Played a queer, driven sort of polka, not what you'd imagine.

PK: You're known for playing slow airs. Do you prefer them?

JJS: There's a story in that, and I'll tell you it. When I returned to Dingle in 1964, I was none too content. My father was dead, may God have mercy on his soul, my brother was on his way to Baltimore, and if the farm wasn't to pass out of our family then I had to stay on. I'd left a lot behind in Manchester, and what was I gaining in return? Dingle wasn't the lively place it is now. Oh, you saw a few tourists about in July, and plenty came down from Dublin at Christmas, but, all in all, life here wasn't such a gay affair. I took it in my head to play the slow airs and laments, the great melodies of lost times and lost ways, and to play the music as a man who had lived it.

PK: Because you were isolated?

JJS: Possibly. What I was, of course, was furious! Now, in recollection, I realize I acted the fool. I'm still here, aren't I? The farm, the land—it's all still here.

PK: Were you trying to revive a tradition?

JJS: Not that, oh no. It was personal. . . . Listen, will I play you a tune?

PK: Sure.

JJS: I'll have a go at "O'Donnell's Lament", an air Padraig O'Keefe made his own. Not saying I'll match his playing, but it's a lovely melody.

(JJS raises the fiddle. He presses his chin against the rest and guards the instrument close to his body. The position is suggestive of a private, filial relationship with the music. He begins an air that is simple, its elegance grounded in the understatement and devotion of the playing. JJS uses a long stroke, allowing certain notes to linger for twice their quaver values. He also uses vibrato.)

PK: That was beautiful.

JJS: Grand stuff.

PK: You don't often hear vibrato in traditional music.

JJS: And I wouldn't be one to recommend it for dance music. But the right air is a different matter. A narrow, relaxed vibrato can have great effect. O'Keefe would draw the length of his bow across the strings, stretching the note so far you imagined it would sound even after the fiddle was out of his hands!

PK: I noticed you avoid decoration.

JJS: The odd note might be decorated. Mostly with the right hand, the bow rather than the fingers. That's another thing I learned from the greats. Use the *bow* to vary the sound. Remember the tune is likely better known as a song; it's up to the fiddler to distinguish what a voice can't do but a fiddle can.

PK: Is tone important?

JJS: A slow air wants a clear and rich tone. But there's more. . . .

PK: Yes?

JJS: If a man is to do the music justice, he has to *feel* what he's playing.

PK: Could you explain?

JJS: Not easily, no.

PK: Do you mean the fiddler has to understand the music?

JJS: I play an hour or two most evenings. Sit in the kitchen with the fiddle, watching the sun set over the mountain and listening to the birds, the wind, the rain lashing against the window. . . . Does that thing have to be going? *(indicates the tape recorder)*

PK: Does it bother you?

JJS: Oh no, I mean—

PK: I'll turn it off.

The kitchen is suddenly hollow. Air prickles my skin. What time is it again?

"The notes," Pat calls from the front room.

"What?"

"The rest of the interview is in the notes."

"Why do you sit in the dark?" I ask, peering through the doorway at the couch.

He does not answer.

I shuffle the notes until I locate a sheet headed "JJS". Pat's loopy handwriting is barely legible.

JJS: *(flustered)* Where was I?

PK: You sit in your kitchen. . . .

JJS: Playing by myself and thinking on the music I heard a half-century ago in our front room, and the music I listened to in Castleisland and Manchester and even at O'Connor's in Ballyferriter, and I play those soft airs—"The Enchanted Valley", "The Dark Slender Boy"—along with a few jigs and reels, for hours on end, and I forget where I am, who I am, forget even what it is I'm doing. . . .

PK: Does playing laments make you sad?

JJS: Maybe now, maybe now. . . . Listen, what am I going on about? You've got me blathering!

PK: Do you use many grace notes, Joe John?

JJS: Grace Sheppard—are you asking about her?

PK: I'm asking—

JJS: Grace Sheppard was the Manchester girl I was engaged to when my da passed away. That was, oh, some twenty-five years ago. Worked in a hair salon in the centre of town, Grace did, lived with her family on an estate near where I was staying. Great sense of humour, great sense of fun. A lively girl, Grace! Only she wouldn't, well, she wasn't inclined to join me in West Kerry. Rang her several times to plead my case. . . .

PK: Tell me more about her.

JJS: Music can make matters more manageable,

yes it can. Make living day to day more . . . graceful, say, easier to reconcile. Keep the cold off your back. Keep the lonely nights, the lonely. . . . Will you have a drop more of tea, Pat?

PK: Please.

JJS: I'm not looking after you proper, am I? I should have done a few sausages and a bit of dry potato.

PK: This is fine.

JJS: Sure I'm no good at talking about myself. Will I play just one more tune?

PK: Play as many as you like.

"He played for two more hours," Pat says, filling the doorway. "At first he introduced each tune and asked if I wanted to hear it. But after a while he forgot I was there. I had joined the audience he performs for each evening—gravestones and photographs, memories from a half-century ago."

My rejoinder is bland. His expression is concentrated; I am suddenly aware of an eloquence in both his language and his person. The change is, frankly, disconcerting.

"By eleven o'clock, Joe John's hands were trembling and his every other word was slurred. He offered to drive me back to Dingle. I declined, telling him the sky was light enough."

I wait.

"Only it wasn't," Pat continues. "It was actually black outside, and I had to bike home blind. At one bend I was trapped in headlights. The driver noticed the reflector below my handlebars, and swerved. Then I came upon a cluster of lights across a huge field. That was Dingle Harbour. By the cemetery I was pedalling furiously. Had I hit a rock, I would have gone over the bar. Had I run into a fence. . . ."

He smiles to himself.

"I was willing to take the risk, Hia. Tonight, finally, I

was willing."

"Riding a bike like a stupid boy is a good risk?"

"Don't you know what I'm talking about?"

"Sure."

"Even after listening to the interview, and reading the transcript, and hearing my explanation—even still, you don't know?"

Pat stares at me. I don't blink.

Twenty minutes later, he is asleep on the far side of the bed and I am seated upright, blankets to my waist, hands folded. No lovemaking tonight. No snuggling. No suggestion of anything except the contented rest that Pat, until recently an insomniac, now enjoys for eight-hour stretches. I know the sleep intimately because I monitor his breathing and count the dragging hours until dawn parts the curtains. It is coldest then, bone-chilling even in May.

Chapter 12

When Manila Bay had not come into sight after two more days, Bon Dran Ly steered a wide loop and followed a flock of seagulls heading southwest. The birds vanished during the night; at daybreak the trawler was still surrounded by water. As a precaution, the colonel asked Hia to help him erect a sail with the tarpaulin. But then the young man with the chest wound stopped breathing, and Dung My Chung, herself failing, demanded it be used to cover the corpse. Bon Dran Ly agreed without argument and the tarpaulin, split in half with a knife, became a wrap.

"Half a tarpaulin is useless," Hia complained, once the body had been disposed of.

"It will serve a purpose," the widow said.

"What purpose?"

"A respectful burial."

"Burial for who?"

They ran out of fuel in the afternoon.

Dung My Chung slipped into a coma that evening. Her leg had swollen frightfully and stank of bad meat. Hia and Nhung continued to apply wet rags to her forehead, but stopped when Bon Dran Ly felt no pulse. The stench was so overpowering that they carried out the ceremony immediately, aided by a muslin moon and a phosphorescent sea.

"I have no wife," he said.

"She was your wife?" Hia asked, startled.

"My wife was killed in 1969."

"Then—?"

"I have no wife, you have no husband, and poor Nhung has no parents."

"Not in front of the girl," she warned.

Bon Dran Ly smiled bitterly. "Worst of all for our nation," he added, "is the loss of the baby."

Hia swung at him. He did not flinch at her blow, nor the blows of Nhung, who fell upon the colonel with a startling fury. The girl screamed as she hammered his chest, then broke down, squatting on the floor. Hia cradled her. Having no real function, Bon Dran Ly set himself up on the foredeck; except for brief exchanges, he did not speak to the sisters again for thirteen days.

Hia spent her time watching clouds. Fair-weather formations were the most various, and on the afternoon they cut water rations to a cup per person, she discerned a shape among the flat-based clouds billowing into the heights. The configuration stood apart, advancing across the sky at a processional pace. She framed the structure between her hands, examined it, identified the church: Santa Maria del Fiore, Florence, Italy, from *Les grandes cathédrales du monde.* Hia even recalled the page number, which made her wonder if she had studied the book more closely than she remembered.

"The world is flat," she informed Nhung.

The girl nodded.

"It must be," Hia said. "Otherwise, how could it fit beneath the dome of heaven?"

Several more days passed. Though dominated by turbid seas and monotone skies, the days also featured late-afternoon weather spells, when the surface began to roll, clouds drooped, and the trawler teeter-tottered. It was during one such spell that Hia noticed the second church.

Heaven was roofed that evening by high-altitude formations, narrow, fleecy clouds furrowed with light. Among the threads was an outline she recognized at once as St. Stephen's Cathedral, Vienna, Austria, page 13 of *Les grandes cathédrales du monde*. The building was a whirl of spires and traceries, with a hunchbacked main hall and irregular twin towers. The shaft of the main spire tilted slightly before thinning into invisibility, a frailty that could only have been by design. Though the church was stunning, it disturbed Hia; the sensibility seemed reckless, almost wild.

The cirrus clouds did herald a minor storm, but the trawler remained upright and its passengers remained on board. More dead days and nights followed. Everyone suffered: from delusions of rescue, ships in the distance, on the horizon, ships shrinking, receding, until they fell off the earth or were swallowed by waves; and bitter arguments, sister sniping at sister, Hia punishing Bon Dran Ly for his comment about the baby. And then there were the shakes, the fits of weeping and bursts of laughter, the stomach cramps from starvation and muscle spasms from dehydration, and the feeling in Hia not so much that dying was preferable, but that, in some way, it was already over, if only due to fatigue.

Then Nhung spotted a freighter off the stern. Distant at first, the ship doubled in size every few minutes, until it was across their path. Bon Dran Ly ended up sprawled on the cabin floor. Hia and Nhung held on, the artifact tucked under Hia's arm. When the freighter came at them again, Hia told her sister to get ready to jump. The colonel regained the narrow foredeck and spread his arms wide, inviting the ship to finish them off. Hia shielded her eyes.

An hour later, the sisters joined a handful of Japanese crew members at the railing. Two men had climbed down into the trawler and sawed holes in the bottom of the hold. Water gushed onto the deck. First the gunwales sank; then the cockpit disappeared. When the bow vanished, the cabin collapsed. Bubbles and white water, a few eddies on the surface, and the boat was gone.

"Chac," Hia said.

Chapter 13

Light drains from the harbour. The withdrawal takes an hour, and the result is shadow and haze, dimming into night. Pat's daily pilgrimage to the pier reflects his peculiar interest in commercial fishing. I am reluctant, but still accompany him out the jetty, where we keep to one side of trucks and bins and stubbly-chinned fishermen who pepper their catches with cigarette ash. On evenings when the sky is tall, the surface shades gradually. Otherwise, the harbour is injected with ink, and blackens. Those sunsets are hardest to take, and I drag Pat home before the wind rises and the rain falls.

"An ancestor shrine can look like almost anything," I explain while drying my hair in the front room. "Physical objects are not important. You need pots and incense, candles to be lit during commemorations, and photos."

"Are we set?"

"Almost. Did you ask—?"

"You know I didn't. Did you?"

"Eily Murphy has no photos of your father," I say. "She thought Jimmy might, but said he would probably never admit it."

I plant cut joss sticks in each cup, stack the photographs on the windowsill behind the shrine.

"Where did you get the incense?" Pat asks.

"Eily bought it in Tralee," I lie.

He examines the wedding portrait of my grandparents. "When did they die?"

"Nineteen sixty-seven."

"And your brother. . . . "

"Nineteen seventy-four."

"He looked like you."

I shiver. "You have seen this photo many times," I say. "Why now does Bo—?"

"The resemblance has grown."

Two white candles are positioned at the front, with a vase of primroses and buddleia in the centre. I light the candles first.

Pat studies my parents' wedding shot. Actually, he fingers the surviving portion of it; last week I did what I had wanted to do for years—censor my father with scissors. Thanks to the composition of the portrait—her seated, him standing stiff behind her—it was easy to snip around the chair and lop off the top third. Eliminating Than Van Loi did not exorcize any demons. It was done out of—

"Respect for her memory?"

"Her spirit."

"Which you believe in now?"

"I always believed. I always not believed. I am consistent in my thinking."

"She was very beautiful," he says.

"Not like me?"

"In a different way."

"Different, sure. She was beautiful, I am ugly. She was elegant person, I am undignified."

Pat picks up the army photo of Bo again. "Your brother had her cheekbones. Your face is shaped more like—"

"Stop!"

"But it's true."

"I forbid you to say it."

"You forbid me?"

"This is funny?"

Trying to act sobered, he reaches for the fourth photo. "Why have I never seen this before?"

"I just found it."

"In Dingle?"

"In my suitcase."

"Cousin Chac," he says.

"Chac Dinh Che," I correct unthinkingly.

"How old was he?"

"Twenty-one. This was taken maybe a month before we escaped. That is the village dock. At twilight, I think."

The photograph shows Chac standing on a wooden dock with his back to a channel of bowed reeds. His sunburnt face is handsome, his rugged brow and jawbone are softened by dimples. He is slim, but more solid than most Vietnamese (there was Khmer blood in the family). Chac wears wide-bottomed pants, a white t-shirt, and an unmarked baseball cap that presses down his wavy hair. He addresses the camera with an expression I recall vividly, a proclamation that he would give all he could: would be forthright, trustworthy, unafraid. One thing I failed to notice until now: his shadow, too long for the wood, continues out into the water, shading the surface. A superstitious Vietnamese would have foreseen a bad end, a watery grave, in this innocuous detail.

I light the incense sticks. The scent is not a scent; it is the first nineteen years of my life. I cannot inhale the odour without feeling overwhelmed and lost.

"Cousin Chac," Pat repeats.

How long has he known?

"We were so young," I say quietly.

"Were you ready?"

"For leaving Saigon, not ready. For having my father put in jail, not ready. For watching my mother insulted by country people, not ready. For watching her carry pails of water to her stall, boil noodles, and serve them to dirty men who wanted sex with her, not ready. For a boyfriend who didn't abuse me, who liked me—yes, I was ready."

He studies the photo.

"For sex with him in his boat," I add, squirming, "in the evening, with bugs and wood slivers—no, for that, I was not so ready."

"It's okay."

I do not answer.

"It's okay, Hia."

"Okay that I lie to you for years?"

"I don't mind."

"What else have I lied about, Pat? What other deceptions do I keep in my heart?"

"How about the sixth pot?"

I am staggered.

"You've put out one pot for my dad, but that still leaves another. Whose spirit resides there?"

"*Con troi nuoc,*" I mutter.

"Translation?"

I didn't put out a sixth pot. "Why are you messing me!" I shout.

He has no idea what I am talking about.

"You think *I* hide things?"

"I never said—"

"Tell me about the letter you got yesterday."

"From my mother?"

"Tell me."

"I got a letter from Francine yesterday," Pat says.

"It was many pages long. Many pages of small writing. I know Francine. She never writes long letters. What secrets did she tell you? Secrets about parents and children, secrets you will not tell even me!"

He goes to speak, then hesitates. I am ashamed of myself; my anger is, in part, from jealousy—Francine chose to write her son.

"I think I'll take a walk."

"But we have not begun commemoration."

"You've put me off ancestor worship for today."

"Like I have put you off lovemaking?"

He halts, jacket half on, in the doorway. Pat examines his feet for clues as to how he should answer. "You've stopped wanting me."

"I have stopped wanting," I clarify.

I shift my mother's pot to the middle of the shrine, next to the empty container for Pat's father, like the king and queen on a chessboard. The sixth pot, whose presence honestly I cannot account for, is left alone. A breeze puffs the curtains on either side of the television.

"Did you love him?"

"I was eighteen."

"Did you think you loved him?"

"I did not know how to. Children loving children—like drawing in darkness," I say.

Do *not* cry.

"I have started wanting things, Hia. For the first time in ages."

"I am steadfast—"

"I know you are."

He starts back across the room. I order him to leave.

"Carolan!" he says suddenly.

"What?"

"The sixth pot is for Joan McGreevy."

"Why didn't you—?"

"I just remembered."

He leaves.

I love the shape of Pat's crescent-moon eyes. I love the shape of his lanky torso and crooked leg. I love the shape of his laughter, his humour; more and more, I love his quickening imagination. I love the way he taps his foot to conversation. I love his shy smile.

But we no longer make love. No longer create and then

cast shadows. Still: everything is so still, so fixed. Angkor shimmers in a haze, distant and unassailable. Temples hover over the steaming earth. Near Dingle, a butterfly perches on the wall of a Norman ruin. Try to touch it. The butterfly eludes contact. Try to force it to take flight. The butterfly clings to stone. Steadfast. Steadfast Hia.

Pat, Pat, will you help me?

Part III

A LAMENT FOR MY FATHER

A LAMENT FOR MY FATHER

Chapter 1

It happened just a week ago, but I can barely remember the details. The incident involved a dinner, a snipe from a moody companion, a harsh exchange; the bitten hand finally fought back. I have stopped cooking for Hia. I no longer cook her meals, except breakfast, and refuse to boil water for tea unless I plan to drink it too. An overreaction? Possibly. But I am patient, and my patience has been tried; I am mild, and my mildness has been taken advantage of.

I am also half kidding.

Tonight, fixing myself an omelet, I sink happily back into my own thoughts. Able to consider ideas that once alarmed me, I feel not so much changed as expanded, still myself, but also someone else. My father? Definitely not. I ponder these notions with curiosity and concern, not ardour. I have no ambitions. I am in no danger.

Ecstasy becomes possible, I think, when the musician ceases to feel separate from what he is playing; when he becomes the piece, and the piece assumes, in a sense, the fluidity of life itself. The experience must be thrilling. Akin to harmony; akin to God. Hia can't understand this because she can't understand why the sky has no ceiling and the sea is fathomless. My father, in contrast, seemed only too familiar with the dimensions of pure being. As an adult, he was a disaster. But as an artist he attained, I am beginning to understand, the status of visionary. Hia would say he played the fiddle best with his eyes closed; I suspect he could play it only when he thought he was going to die afterwards. Must one be solitary, even imperilled, to capture great harmonies? The work does appear most easily done in isolation: man to fiddle, woman to sketch pad. Alone with your thoughts, you subsume those thoughts; detached from others, you forget yourself.

Sharing that wonder with another person ought to be even more transcendent. In lovemaking, the vital moment is all; the act is both instinctive and faintly perilous. At least, it should be. I wish relationships weren't so inhibiting, so wilful. I wish being with another person weren't analogous to two starlings trapped inside a cathedral, absorbed in senseless ditherings, oblivious of the incarcerating splendour. I wish I weren't thinking of Hia and me, and I wish Hia weren't thinking constantly about Angkor.

She is steadfast in love.

For her mother.

My fear is that the business of making art out of memory and memory out of loss comes down to a gift. My father, whom I cannot respect, possessed the wild, fearful gift of freedom, while Hia, whom I want to love and respect me, is merely genuinely talented, and no one can help that.

These days, she spends less time with her sketch pad than amid the statuary in St. Mary's. Hia visits the church every afternoon. Marching up the centre aisle to the altar, she genuflects, then stops before the bronze statue of the Virgin Mary with Baby Jesus on her knee and a girl reading a book by her side. She never kneels, never bows her head. All Hia does is stand there, her eyes heavily lidded, her lips pursed. I recognize the gaze, the nervous hands, and keep expecting her to stretch across and map Mary's features with her fingertips.

"How do you know I am not praying?" she whispers to

me one afternoon.

"I don't."

"You don't know what I do, what I don't do. Therefore, quit speculating."

"Who said I was—?"

"How would you know what I am thinking? You have no knowledge of your work!"

"Pardon me?"

"Your fiddle research—why?"

"I'm interested."

"Maybe one month ago. Maybe one week ago. Now it is different. Now you are aggressive and confident."

"It's going well."

"What is going well?"

"Whatever it is I'm doing," I answer playfully.

"Do you intend to write an article about Irish music?"

"No."

"A book?"

I laugh.

Hia should stop, but can't. "How can a plan that is no plan work so well? You have success without any shape. I have failure despite having *only* shapes. You are—"

"Don't compare us."

She flushes.

"It's the right thing," I say. "Trust me."

Though St. Mary's dates from 1865, it underwent a major renovation a century later. The red sandstone exterior was refinished; a masonry interior had to be excavated from beneath plaster. The altar received a new ambo, a tabernacle plinth in limestone, a sail-shaped apse suspended on wires. The apse contains a slanted window. Light permeates the church even in dull weather, bathing the tabernacle and tiers of wooden pews. St. Mary's two principal icons are frequently illuminated. Hia's statue hardly merits the spotlight. Mary has the bony legs of an old man, and both the Infant Jesus and the girl are stiff, curiously unrealized.

Though more idiosyncratic, the cross over the altar is, in contrast, compelling. The Christ it depicts is a sallow man who could be dying of starvation. His expression is vacant, and he hangs limply on a blue pole flecked with blood.

I linger near the back. St. Mary's is rarely without worshippers, mostly elderly people saying the rosary or flaring candles. Their murmurs and chattering beads are amplified into a pleasing susurration, along with another sound—music, played soft—I sometimes hear, no less affecting for being inside my head.

"The Virgin is so sad," Hia says from the front steps. "So filled with understanding."

I nod.

"She understands everything, can change nothing. Her peace is total. Her child will be well."

Her child ends up on a purple cross."

"Don't mock me."

"I didn't carve the statues," I say, prepared to argue. "Someone else imagined Mary and the crucifixion in those terms. Someone else in Dingle thinks the figures are worth reconsidering."

"You know nothing about Dingle."

"No?"

"You come here to your past, then ignore it. Jimmy and Eily, who care so much about you, who could be your friends—you treat them as strangers."

"You're right."

"You say you want—" She pauses. "I'm right?"

"I thought this trip would be for you and me to strengthen our relationship," I say. "I thought we could deal with serious things. I guess I was wrong."

She blanches.

"All these people," I continue, gesturing out at Green Street. "I should try and meet them instead. I should interview the whole town. Maybe my father is here somewhere. Maybe I can—"

Hia flies down the church steps. For the first time since I have known her, she wears an expression of vulnerability clouded by hurt. On the bottom step she stumbles. I take her arm.

"Worry about *me*," she says fiercely. "Talk with *me*. Never mind the others."

"Even him?"

She sighs.

"I thought you'd be—"

"It's too late now."

"We'll go to the island."

"What island?"

I ignore her response. "Take the ferry from Dunquin," I say. "Have lunch in the ruins of my grandfather's house. Explore the perilous cliffs. The whole thing—just like you wanted."

Noting the wisps of smoke around the church spire, I quicken our pace. The street empties.

"I thought you'd be happier," I admit.

"I don't feel well."

Arriving home safely, I order her to the couch and then fill the kettle. My offer to transfer Carolan from his chair to Hia's lap is premature; only after repeated shakes does the cat revive. I pull back his lids. Both eyeballs are now sealed beneath a gauze. Carolan's bird-watching days are over, and I let him resume his slumbers.

"I dreamed your dream last night," I say, moving the armchairs against the wall.

"What?"

"I dreamed about Angkor."

"Angkor is my work," Hia answers, blinding herself with her forearm. "I am awake when drawing it."

I make tea for both of us.

"If all my dreams were this vivid," I continue, "I'd try to have more of them. It was as if I were a movie camera moving through the site. Angkor was engulfed in jungle.

Vines and roots, flowering trees and choked streams—everything was dense and verdant."

"Verdant," she echoes.

"You were there, Hia."

"Was I verdant?"

"You were lost. You wandered through courtyards and over terraces, down corridors and up staircases. I remember you wore white pants, a white blouse, and sunglasses."

"With mirrors?"

I ask.

"The glasses—were the lenses mirrors?"

"I saw only ruins in our eyes," I confirm, leaving the tray on the table. "Reflections. Externals."

I return to my other task. "After a while the dream changed from a rolling camera to snapshots. You struck poses in the temples. Perched on the balcony of a tower, your face sacrificed to the sky. Squatting in a doorway with your forehead on your knees. Leaning against a treetrunk outside Angkor Wat. That was the dominant pose, the one I recall—"

"What are you doing?"

"Moving the buffet beside the TV."

"Why?"

"Let me finish."

She covers her eyes again.

"The roots of the trunk were mossy knuckles, which you fit perfectly between. The entranceway was full of carvings, and a marble god extended his hand to welcome visitors. But you just stood there outside the temple, your face blank, your thoughts inscrutable."

Even recalling the dream makes me shiver. I sit in a chair, until recently across from the couch, now beside a flower stand in the corner.

"So? . . . " Hia asks.

"You don't like it?"

"I feel like we are in a church basement, for coffee and cookies after mass."

"It's less cluttered."

She stares at me.

"In case we have guests," I say.

"Pour the tea, please. Eily is taking me to the doctor in twenty minutes."

"You really don't feel well?"

"Eily is my friend."

"Yes she is."

"It is nothing serious."

I pour her tea.

"No sugar," Hia says, blocking the spoon in midair.

"It's serious," I correct.

That evening, after another solitary dinner—I hear Hia's voice in the sitting room downstairs, but do not call to her—and a whimsical scrutiny of my interior redecoration, I launch my first assault on the village green. The gate to the park, a few doors from us, is chained and the lock is rusted. Nocturnal merrymakers must climb a wall or slip through a broken fence. The clouds dissolved at sunset, and light from a half-moon swims silvery in the air. Grey Lane soon intersects Dykegate Lane, and I turn onto the narrow street where my father lived for twelve years, according to Eily Murphy, with his Aunt Moira. Dykegate Lane has a cinema, several bed and breakfasts, rowhouses whose parlour windows press against the sidewalk. The gurgle of rushing water colours my thinking. The stream, flowing down from the Conor Pass, runs parallel to the lane, but is mostly buried in bushes or channelled beneath houses. I study the doors and windows, the blurred castings of light on the pavement, and wonder, for the first time, which building he lived in. A curtain parts and a girl peers out at me. She is eleven or twelve, chubby-cheeked, curly-haired, eyes the shape of almonds. Peters the Pig, Peters the Pig, a face like an ass and an ass twice as big!

I smile at Ellen Peters. She draws the curtain.

The green lurks somewhere behind these homes. An alley divides the buildings, but it is dark, marked Private Property. A dog emerges from shadow to bark at me. Main Street, where I head north, climbs steeply uphill. I make sure to nod at each passerby, the nod I learned from watching Jimmy—left to right, locking eyes with the other person—but have so far avoided using. The nod comes naturally, and locals respond with smiles and good-nights, one or two references to my given name. I am known in Dingle, or at least my lanky torso and distinctive saunter are known, my soon-to-be craggy face—even, apparently, some quality of my gaze. I had thought the gaze belonged to my mother, like my height, like everything else about me. Now that I am being forced to partition these qualities more evenly, it makes sense to pay attention to the environment that coloured his psyche, the faces that sculpted his face.

I complete the rectangle—up Main Street to Green Street, back down past the church—without locating an entrance. Which is fine. I am worrying less about Hia, less about us, and thinking more about where we are, and will be for just three more weeks.

Chapter 2

Seamus O Suilleabhain answered a knock on the door the morning of May 1, 1958, and stood gaping at a ghost for a full minute before inviting it inside. The ghost shook Seamus's hand, crossed the room to the table, poured himself a cup of tea. For the thirteenth straight day, the Dingle sky was dour and the air was damp. The roof muffled the rain but permitted occasional drops to stain the floor. The thatching needed repair. The walls required masonry. The chimney was partially blocked and the windowpanes, plumbing, and electrical wiring—afterthoughts in such an old house—all begged attention.

"Michael?"

"It's good to be back, Seamie."

"For the life of me I don't—"

"You look well."

"Think so?"

"A little heftier in the gut, maybe. Have you been getting along?"

"Barely."

Michael eyed the loaf of bread. "I'm famished," he said, cutting into it. "Hitched a ride out from Tralee at sunrise. Got drenched waiting for a lift."

"I'm delighted to see you again," Seamus offered. He

suppressed a desire to embrace his friend.

"Same here."

"Very sorry about your father."

"Could you drop me out at the cemetery?"

"Now?"

"If you could manage it."

"I'd be lying if I didn't say I'm surprised."

"Francine forgot to send the telegram?"

"I got her message."

"Wasn't my date of—"

"Of course."

"I should have flown," Michael agreed. "Ten days at sea, brooding senselessly, is an awful waste."

He buttered a second piece of bread.

"There's a girl I'd like you to meet," Seamus said.

"James O'Shea's youngest?"

"You know her?"

"I read your letters."

"You'll take to Eily, I'd say. She's grand. You and she will become fast friends."

"I'm sure."

They were silent.

"Would it be too much to ask?" Michael repeated.

The men dashed from the cottage to an Austin Mini parked by the road. The car, bought in 1955 from a cousin who was emigrating to the States, started most mornings and climbed most inclines; like the house, however, it was worn and decrepit and largely beyond repair. A single wiper, squealing with each pass, granted the driver a view but left the passenger blind. Michael rubbed the windshield with his cuff.

Buildings in Dingle town gleamed in the rain, and pedestrians, huddled in doorways or scurrying from shop to shop, were similarly dreary. Michael recognized no one; no one paid attention to Seamus O Suilleabhain's car racing along Strand Street, its tires slushing water. He drove past the pier, past an unlit T. Daly's, through Milltown, over the bridge, and onto the road towards Ventry.

"Congratulations on the marriage," Seamus offered. "She's only brilliant, I'm sure."

"A French Canadian girl," Michael answered. "You'd like her. You *will* like her, when you two meet."

His comment heartened Seamus. "Come here a minute. What's the story with—?"

"Patrick John," Michael interrupted.

"It will be a boy?"

"Surely."

Dunmore Head lay wreathed in mist. Of the islands, only the Great Blasket was visible, and then just the village. Michael rolled down his window and peered across the sound. His disorientation, etched onto his mouth and around his eyes, was so great that he asked his friend why there was no smoke from the chimneys, and didn't several of the roofs look collapsed? He continued to stare. Then, slowly, like a hologram catching the requisite light, Michael saw what was plainly there. His lips moved without producing words.

He climbed to the cemetery. Near headstones bearing the names O Beaglaoich and O Cathain, O Dalaigh and O Maoileoin, was a mound of earth. The grave was worse for the weather: along the uneven top was a landscape of muddy lakes and streams that spilled down sheer slopes. No flowers or wreaths commemorated the dead, and the stone wouldn't be ready for a month. Michael stood before his father for fifteen minutes.

Seamus, meanwhile, switched off the motor. The windshield fogged over almost immediately, but he neither wiped it nor cracked the window. Instead, he closed his eyes and daydreamed about his friend Michael O Cathain ("Michael Keane" in Canada), who lived at 211 Bishop Avenue, Willowdale, Ontario, and was employed in the Toronto Underground. While this friend did not write letters, Seamus had heard from others: Michael had steady work (Seamus only managed odd jobs), Michael was married (Seamus had taken ages to find a girl), Michael's wife was expecting (Seamus would make a proud parent). He thought less happily about the Michael O Cathain who had played the fiddle in Tom Daly's one afternoon six years before. The music, combined with the foul weather, had so unsettled Seamus that he had begged him not to board the trawler, not to abandon the coast, not to venture beyond the shelter of the Great Blasket. *Leave Dingle, Mickey,* he should have said that afternoon. *You are not in control of yourself.* If the memory of Michael playing the fiddle was unhappy, Seamus's next recollection—of him hauling lobsters beneath the cliffs of Inis-na-Bro—was terrifying. Who was this man? A stranger, a mad—

He started. Unrolling the window, Seamus discovered Michael on the driver's side, his gaze fixed beyond Blasket Sound. His friend's features were shorn in concentration. Though his expression hinted at anger, most prominent was a stark avidity for what he was observing.

"We should head back to your aunt's," Seamus shouted. "She'll be thrilled to see you."

"Is it not miserable bleak out here?"

Seamus nodded.

"I'd forgotten the desolation. . . . Who could ever live in such a place?"

"There are a few old ones left in Dunquin."

"I could never have recollected this. No matter how hard I tried—and I did—my mind couldn't have summoned such ferocity."

Seamus grew more anxious. "I've the fiddle still, Mickey," he said.

"Where?"

"In my bedroom closet."

"Did you check . . . ?"

"New strings, and it should be grand."

Michael walked around the hood and opened the passenger door. His knuckles were ivory. "Good man, Seamie," he said.

A LAMENT FOR MY FATHER

Chapter 3

Eily Murphy's dining room table is only slightly smaller than the chamber it centres. Like the arborite hockey rink in my mother's kitchen, the table was designed to seat a Catholic clan. (It belonged, Eily explains, to her parents. The youngest of eight O'Sheas, she was the only childless child when her mother died.) But unlike Francine's suburban setup, the piece of mahogany furniture in Grey Lane was worth preserving. The surface is dark-stained, so polished it reflects chandelier light, and the legs are ornately scrolled. Underneath is a pedestal thick as a treetrunk, with roots extending in every direction. Exploring down there is impossible: my creaky chair is pressed to the wall; a fat man wouldn't fit into the space.

The wood smells like apples.

Happily, there is an aisle along the other side of the room, and Hia, perhaps out of mischief, or because she is florid with alcohol, tips her seat back much of the evening. Eily and Jimmy occupy either end. Behind Eily, near the door to the kitchen, is an upright piano whose keys are never touched. (We would have heard the music upstairs.) The ceiling is low and the chandelier, its glass beads jangling, appears to draw closer to the yawning candles, until I discern a blue genie at the confluence. It is ten o'clock, and the surface is awash in plates and glasses, platters and bowls. Near me is a half-eaten birthday cake; within Hia's grasp is a third bottle of wine.

"It's time," Jimmy announces. He looks dapper tonight in a starched white shirt and brown tie. His oiled hair glistens; his aftershave slaps the air. Jimmy presses both palms over the table top, a cigarette between his fingers. "Too much gloss and buff. Too much saying but not saying. Am I right, Eily?"

Eily smiles into her glass. "If you insist, James. But please keep the melodrama to a minimum. And for God's sake don't exaggerate—Homer this is not."

"Would you rather tell it yourself?"

"You know I couldn't."

"If you put your mind to the task. . . . "

"Could I do a proper job with the story, Hia?"

Hia ponders the question. "It would take hours," she admits. "Days, maybe."

"Weeks," Eily agrees.

"Leisure we haven't got," Jimmy says. "Not with these two heading back to North America shortly. Then what? Another generation to wait for?"

Eily sighs and settles in her chair. She is, I now acknowledge, a gentle person; I wish she had emigrated to Canada and become my mother's friend. Her silver brooch, which I once thought was a phoenix, is actually a wide-winged butterfly bought, apparently, from a mail-order catalogue specializing in jewellery made in Indonesia and Thailand. I find myself staring at it.

"Do you know who I am?" Jimmy asks suddenly.

His face warns me not to joke.

"I think so."

"What did Francine tell you?"

"Nothing, I swear. I had to—"

"I believe you," he says, showering ash over the tablecloth. "Body or no body, your mother laid Michael to rest deep in the earth, and even deeper in her heart, with an abruptness that was shocking."

"She had no choice," Eily offers. "The woman was about to—"

"I'm not criticizing. Merely making a point. By way of explanation for the woeful gaps in Pat's education in these matters."

"Which you really helped fill."

"Tonight will be different."

"I didn't say I wanted to be educated," I comment, the old anger rising. "I'm not asking for anything."

Everyone looks at me.

"But I'm interested," I add quietly.

Jimmy accepts my terms with a nod.

"How well do you know my mother?" I ask him.

"Only by post. Only for a time, and not in recent years. Some relationships fade. Others burn brighter and brighter, who knows why?"

"Melodrama," Eily says.

"Truth," Hia asserts.

"In 1956," Jimmy begins, "three years after Michael emigrated to Canada, I, Seamus O Suilleabhain, asked for the hand of Eileen O'Shea in marriage."

"Hoping for more," Eily says.

"A leg," I suggest.

"Two arms," Hia says.

"Quiet!"

We are quiet.

"Hoping for more? I'd say I was. A good deal more, in fact. And this Eily O'Shea, yet in middle school, the brightest, loveliest girl in town, skilled at drawing and music—she accepted my proposal with enthusiasm, with delight. Are my words too strong, Eily?"

Her smile broadens.

"She did, however, express concern as to how her parents would take to the idea. What did James O'Shea, respected shopkeeper in John Street, think of my proposal? Not much. Not much at all. I lacked steady employment. I was unsettled, unskilled, a man of no visible means. All of which made me, according to local wisdom, a less than first-class match."

"Bah," Eily says.

"Bah?"

"Not the reason. You know it."

"Do I?"

"My father wasn't blind."

"Nor mute."

"You were like a child waiting on Dingle pier for his parent to return from sea. You attended on the postman each morning. Your sights—"

"I was thinking of emigrating," Jimmy says.

"He was waiting for a letter from your father."

I shift in my chair, unsuccessfully. The room temperature climbs.

"He was hoping—"

"To join Michael, perhaps," Jimmy explains. "In Canada, in the Toronto Underground. What youth in West Kerry wasn't thinking of leaving back then? There was nothing for a man here."

"Small wonder my father opposed the match," Eily says. "Would any parent have reacted differently?"

"My mother opposed Chac," Hia informs us.

I refill her glass.

"She would never give reason, but I knew: he was a peasant, and I should have found a middle-class guy."

"All mothers want the best for their child, Hia," Eily says. Her tone suggests the two of them have been over this ground before.

"I told her such thinking was dead. Killed by Dien Bien Phu and the Vietcong. Besides, we were noodle-sellers in delta village! Who could be so picky?"

"I'm a middle-class guy," I say. "Maybe your mother

would be satisfied."

My comment is not appreciated.

"In any case," Eily says wisely, "my Seamus had his sights fixed across the Atlantic Ocean, too distant to be much good to anyone here. Worse, the object of his fixation never wrote his supposed best friend. Never wrote, never tried to ring. Simply appeared on Jimmy's doorstep one morning, nearly two weeks after the funeral."

"My father missed his own father's funeral?"

"By a few lengths," Jimmy admits. "Michael had an aversion to flying that was, on the surface, illogical. I understood it better later on."

"I didn't know."

"His appearance after the fact was much discussed around town. Everything he did, or didn't do, was perceived of as relating to us all."

"Were you two married by then?"

"Engaged," he answers. "As ever."

"Waiting."

"For your father's approval?" I ask Eily.

"For *your* father's approval."

"Bah," Jimmy says.

"*My* father?"

"Whose father?" Hia asks.

"Don't be daft, Eily."

"Jimmy adored—"

"Mind your words."

"Adored, even revered—"

"Hush!"

We all jump. Jimmy coughs.

"More wine?" I suggest.

"Michael was a man of some presence," he tells me, holding out his glass for the first time, "some stature. The accident devastated us. The loss was communal, despite his years away from Dingle. I took it badly, I'd say. Fell apart. Fell apart completely."

"Softly, James."

"Leaving was the best I could manage. Desertion, flight, exile: were these the responses of a worthy man?"

No one answers.

"But I had to leave," he adds to himself.

"I knew it," she replies.

"You thought—"

"I was so very young."

"You thought I was a coward. Which I—"

"Now *you* mind your words."

"Do you know, Pat, that I only summoned the courage to write to Eily a year later? My shame choked the words. What would I have said? That I'd forsaken a marriage, crushed a tender love, disappointed the community that had nurtured me, merely to mourn a friend?"

"It was the rejection that caused the most pain," Eily says to Hia. "How could an eighteen-year-old have understood such a thing? One is never properly equipped to deal with human complexity, I suppose. . . . I decided, wrongly, that Seamus wasn't the man I had thought he was. I decided 'they' were right: he was idle and anchorless. I decided I was better off—"

"Which you were."

"No."

"By half."

"Hush!"

The lighting suddenly dims. I become aware of the beat of my own heart. Across from me, Hia glazes over in sadness and consumptive reverie

"I met another," Eily says.

"One of the Murphys in Milltown."

"Paddy waited two full years before asking for my hand, in case Jimmy reappeared. He and I were married in St. Mary's on July 6, 1961. I was telling you about the wedding, wasn't I, Hia? . . . Hia?"

"Solid man, Paddy Murphy," Jimmy interjects. "Hard

worker, excellent in the boats. No one had a bad word about Paddy. Eileen couldn't have done better."

"Ours was a good marriage."

"Blessed, but then not."

"There's no need, James, to talk about that."

Both raise their hands to their temples, as if each other's mirrors.

"Meanwhile, I was in Liverpool, up to my neck in horses and Englishmen. What a crowd, the English. One listen to my accent and they were convinced I was an expert with horses. See many horses around Dingle?" He pauses to permit himself a smile. "Not that I had any intention of correcting their mistake," he says. "The money was decent and Liverpool was mostly Irish, anyway."

"Is that where you became Jimmy Sullivan?"

"Who, outside the Gaeltachts, can even pronounce the names? Michael changed his; I could too. Even here, people started switching to English. Now, of course, it's fashionable again for Peter to be Peadar, George to be Seoirse. What about you, Pat? Anxious to re-establish your proper name and rightful position in West Kerry society?"

"I want to know Hia's English name," I say, determined to drag her, even by trickery (Vietnamese names do not translate), back into the conversation.

"Hia," she offers in puzzlement.

"In English, dear," Eily corrects.

"Hia."

"Not Joan?" I ask.

"Hia!"

"Not Lucy?"

Her eyes widen. They are so radiant, her eyes, especially when she is angry.

"I think, Pat," Eily says, "that Hia's name, in any language, may just be Hia."

"I was talking about England, . . . " Jimmy complains.

She gestures for him to proceed.

"Bet on the horses over the years, you see, and managed to save a few quid. That paved the way for my return to Dingle as a man of means, a member of the shopkeeping class—someone Hia's mother would have approved of."

"Jimmy bought my father's grocer," Eily provides, "which had been closed since his death in 1963."

"A revenant performing a resurrection," he says.

Hia frowns at the vocabulary.

"Word of his reappearance spread within hours. It was John Garvey, wasn't it, who spotted Jimmy Sullivan, or his double, washing up in the kitchen of his parents' house, more than a decade after he'd dirtied the dishes. John Garvey was the younger brother of the TD for this area, a man who served both parties, I believe. Once, many years ago—"

Jimmy clears his throat.

"Right, yes," Eily agrees. "What was I saying? . . . People spoke of little else for weeks. Imagine the shock: a man presumed lost to the town, to himself, simply returning and taking up his life, like he'd never left. I didn't see Jimmy until Sunday mass. . . . "

"My legs shook the whole way up Green Street to the church," he says. "Kept my eyes fastened to the missal, then slipped away before the final blessing. Had Eily spoken even a word to me that morning, I'd have broken down in public. But she didn't."

"For some time."

"Ten more years, less twenty-six days."

There is a silence. I steal a glance at our hosts; they have ceased addressing each other with their gazes, a detail at odds with the apparent familiarity of the story-telling. Their blitheness masks pain, and I am cautious. A revitalized Hia, in contrast, decides it is question time.

"Your husband got sick?" she asks Eily.

"Cancer, in spring 1979. Paddy was barely fifty when the disease spread. The end was quick, small mercy."

"A tragedy," Jimmy says.

"One of several."

"You were living in Dingle?" she asks him.

"You might call it that. I'd sold my parents' house, which was promptly razed to build a gas bar, and had a flat above the shop. Worked regular hours and took meals with Pat's great-aunt, Moira Lynch."

"Where did she live?" I ask.

"Dykegate Lane. With your father, until he left."

"What number?"

Jimmy crooks his eyebrow into a circumflex. "Across from the cinema," he answers quietly. "Her house was redone five or six years ago. There's a bed and breakfast there now."

"Mrs. Lynch!" Hia exclaims.

"Her daughter-in-law."

"Did she know him?" I say.

"Who?"

"The daughter-in-law."

"As a child, surely. Not as well as others in town. Not as well as myself, or Tom Daly, or Eily here."

I nod, satisfied.

He retraces the thread of his narrative. "But aside from the grocery shop, my first decade back in Dingle was devoted, in all honesty, to—"

"Drinking," Eily provides.

"In excess, in Tom Daly's, in the snug."

"Where he wouldn't likely run into me."

"Only on the streets," Jimmy concurs. "And then say hello, when politeness required. My cheeks burned after each greeting, let me tell you."

"Did you still love her?" Hia asks.

"Surely."

"How romantic."

"How fucking awful. No melodrama here, Eily—just the truth." Then, to Hia: "Dingle is only a slip of a town, Hia, and affords a man neither privacy nor diversion. How stupid a manner to conduct your life. One long, mournful lamentation for mistakes made and opportunities let slip."

Hia is contrite.

"Jimmy waited still another year after Paddy's funeral," Eily says, covering for her gaffe "—a funeral at which he served as a pallbearer—before making his feelings known again. As if I didn't already know! His politeness was uncalled for, and, to my way of thinking, quite exasperating."

"Nearly made a hames of it the second time out as well," Jimmy says.

"Why not get married?"

"Old birds like us?"

"I would have liked children," Eily offers, addressing Hia in an almost stern voice. "Very much so. Children are the link, it seems to me, between our failed lives and a sturdier, more coherent vision of the future. Without them. . . . " She sighs, spins her glass by the stem. "I loved Paddy Murphy as best I knew how, but I *should*—may Paddy forgive me—have married Seamus in 1958, and we *ought* to have begun a family together. I feel certain we could have, and that this table would be more worn, better used, than it is. These are the mistakes we made. These are the tragedies that befall ordinary, unexceptional people."

The room is sweltering. My back is drenched, my mouth arid from the wine.

"When did you stop drawing?" Hia asks.

Eily is surprised by the question. So am I. So, probably, is Jimmy, though he has withdrawn from the conversation, his features sullen.

"I never had any real talent. That was my burden: enthusiasm, but no gift. Most of the sketches in the house date back to the 1960s. Those upstairs, or at least the drawings that were on the walls, were among my last."

"I tell Pat not to take down the drawings," Hia claims,

avoiding my bemused stare. "I tell him they are too interesting, too good. He didn't listen to me."

"What do I know about art?" I say.

"Possibly my best sketch was also one of my first," she adds. "Of a musician, done in his presence. Beginner's luck, I now suspect."

"What happened to it?" I ask.

An uncomfortable silence follows. For some reason, both Hia and Eily look to Jimmy for an answer. He speaks, but on, as far as I can tell, a different subject: "Everyone is unexceptional, Eily," he says irritatedly. "That's hardly the point of the story."

"I like being unexceptional," I say.

"*He* wasn't," she insists.

"It was circumstance."

"It was Michael."

"God's will."

"Michael's will."

Eily turns to me. "No offence, Pat. Your father hurt no one intentionally. He was—"

"A monomaniac," I interrupt.

Jimmy coughs again.

"But he was."

"Where's the good in saying it?"

"The truth is good."

"Some things you can't change."

"Some things you can't forgive either."

"I hardly see what there is for you to forgive, lad."

"Bah," I say.

"In the camp in Hong Kong," Hia announces, "the officials asked me to tell my story to a journalist who was writing a book on boat people. I said, why I should do this? The man said that talking would help me forgive those who did harm to me and my family."

Did I miss something here?

"And you agreed?" Eily asks.

"I thought Nhung and me would be sent back to Vietnam if I refused. But I could think of only simple, foolish thoughts. I told the man that my sister and me wanted to change worlds, because our old world was too harsh. This change is not natural for humans, not in our natures. So it is hard, and harmful to our hearts, and we do not know how to act, because no one can teach you about doing what is new, and never done before."

The women exchange purposeful smiles.

Eily turns to me: "I promised to show you those photographs," she says, rising so abruptly that she knocks into the table. She made no such promise—I made no such request—but the timing seems right, and so we all rise, bump against the wood, watch the chandelier tremble.

In the front room, ill lit by a solitary lamp, I examine her photo collection, nodding at each explanation of the story behind the snapshot and the story, or a tangent to it, behind the story. Jimmy and Hia continue through to the street. Among the out-of-focus faces is that of Paddy Murphy, a compact man with unruly hair and sideburns. Another shot, barely discernible beneath a patina of dissolution, offers a youthful Seamus O Suilleabhain. He stands in the cockpit of a trawler, gesturing—his left arm is a blurry pendulum—to a figure outside the lens, encouraging him (or her) to be freeze-framed. Seamus has a high forehead and smooth skin stretched over the peaks of his cheekbones. His smile is self-effacing, and though his features are in shadow they still convey anxiousness, a desire to please. Eily holds the photo beneath the tasselled shade. Finally, she retreats into the kitchen for her glasses.

The glasses dangle from a string around her neck, but I let her go. Examining the photo myself, I try to read the name on the prow of the trawler: M –S– R – EL is all I can distinguish. I also inspect the left margin for any evidence of the figure positioned between Seamus and the photographer. My father was notoriously camera shy—a solitary, unflattering wedding shot exists, taken by an amateur—and I have trouble conjuring up his face. Frustrated, I hold the photo at an angle and run my finger down the glass. At the frayed bottom corner is a date: October 11, 1952. Eily returns, waving the glasses and laughing at her own absent-mindedness.

I join the others. Hia has already gone upstairs; Jimmy is outside, a curved plinth of shadow beneath a streetlamp. Wreaths of cigarette smoke waft up into the light. I wish him good-night.

"Happy birthday, Padraig," he answers.

Hia confronts me at the top of the landing.

"Only child keeps everything to himself, right?" she says. "Too selfish to share?"

I am perplexed.

"You are not the only child here, Pat. Not just you and your empty graves and fiddle memories."

"Take it easy."

"Me too! I am here. I am your sister."

"My sister?"

A tear clings to her cheek. I reach out to brush it. She swats my hand.

"Francine's letter," she shouts. "You must share it."

"Sure."

"Don't condescend."

"I wasn't hoarding the letter. I just didn't think—" She slams the bathroom door.

"Who exactly are our parents, anyway?" I call.

Hia turns on the shower.

Chapter 4

Michael had a proposition for Seamus. The men sat by the fire after an evening meal of sausages and potatoes, a loaf of Moira Lynch's brack, bottles of stout. The hearth had recently been relaid with bricks but the fireplace, a soot-blackened hole shaped like a cave mouth, was the original masonry. Turf ash spilled onto the floor, a cast-iron kettle dangled from a beam. Seamus stored the kettle over the flames for convenience; he had bought a gas cooker the year his father died and his mother moved to Tralee. With his brother and three sisters in America, the family house had passed into his hands, along with a shed and two fields. His first decision as property owner was to sell the cows, and the fields, to a neighbour. The money was then used to make the cottage livable. Now it had a cooker, fitted glass in the windows, electricity. Still no indoor plumbing, though, and floors, walls, and a roof that were nearly a century old. Equally ancient, for that matter, were many of the cracked dishes and handleless mugs, the uneven table and oak settle, the tattered couch Seamus had slept on as a child. Some money had remained to improve furnishings. But Seamus had hesitated, and then paid cash for his cousin's car, and opened a bank account with funds for a transatlantic airplane ticket.

Kitchen Music

Twilight seeped through the latticed windows as Michael outlined his plan. He had in mind an evening of music, a gathering of players, dancers, and those who might enjoy a listen, for a session—including, possibly, a few tunes by himself. Seamus was pleased. Where would the session be held? he asked. His friend's gaze circled the kitchen, and he cleared his throat.

"It used to be common, you know," he said. "In the kitchen of a house, like this. The furniture moved aside, creating space for dancing. Both routine occurrences and special occasions, apparently."

"I don't recall any in Dingle."

"Further out, Seamie. Ventry, Ballyferriter, Dunquin. Sure, they were part of daily life then. No one had to organize them; they just happened, like the weather. It must have been lovely, don't you think?"

"I'd say."

"I'm almost ashamed to try one now," Michael continued. "Too self-conscious about it, as I am about everything I do in Canada."

Seamus asked.

"I keep watching myself, as if I'm outside my body, observing this character give out that he's a transit worker, a husband, a Canadian. I half expect to see my face on the television, a news special about immigrants struggling to make the new country their own."

"Even with Francine?"

"She's grand, of course. . . . " Michael paused. A turf brick in the fire hissed as it split, revealing flames already devouring the material from within. "People over there," he said slowly, as if the thought was exhausting, "are forever planning. Fran and me, we live in a suburb that's miles from the city, because the city will surely grow to it, and we buy a house that's way too large, because we'll surely parent a brood, and she doesn't quit her job when she's pregnant, in case she needs it back later, and we go to shops and pick up dishes for six and silverware for eight and a table for a dozen, all for the future, you see, always for the future. . . ."

Seamus thought of the chipped plate he had served Michael his meal on, and the pocked kettle he had boiled the water in, and the frayed sheets and mouldy blankets he had provided as bedding for his friend; and he counted the jobs he had worked that winter—a few days of fishing, some bartending for Tom Daly, two weeks of laying electricity lines in October—and the countless days he had not found work at all; and, swallowing scalding tea, he remembered the night at the O'Shea's, when Eily's father had shook his head in resignation and announced that he had *better find a job in the shop for poor Seamus, if the boy was ever going to marry his Eileen*, and Seamus had only ground his teeth, rolled his cigarette in the ashtray, and then bid the family good-night before dessert, before he grabbed the carving knife from the platter and plunged it into James O'Shea's heart. . . .

"Right," he said.

They discussed the details. Seamus offered to do the bulk of the organizational work, and to get Eileen to help collect the guests. Some of the people Michael wanted to invite had died during the interim. But the rest still lived in communities west of Ventry, men and women who had known Tomas O Cathain in the 1920s and 30s and played music with his son, Michael, in the late 1940s and early 50s. Most were elderly; several were infirm. Would they consent to being driven all the way to Dingle for a few hours of nostalgia? Michael, who seemed embarrassed by his own plan, asked the question elliptically. Seamus thought for a moment. Privately, he was indifferent to traditional music, preferring big band jazz on RTE Sunday evenings and the monthly classical concerts in Tralee. Still, even the thought of hearing Michael play the fiddle again quickened his pulse.

"They'll come, Mickey," he replied. "Make no mistake

about it."

The date was set for the following Saturday.

Michael commandeered the house. For eight hours a day he exercised his fingers, reasserted his feel for the bow, his mastery of positions the length of the neck. Cataloguing his repertoire, he sketched the opening bars of the hundred tunes he knew by name, including the dozen he had, as far as he could tell, composed himself. He also outlined the hundred melodies he couldn't identify but played easily, and the scores of jigs, reels, and hornpipes he simply had access to, like childhood memories.

Airs were a different matter. He knew each title, each lineage, and found himself less concerned with getting the notes right than with relocating the space the melody inhabited. The going was hard at first. But Michael, never known for his discipline, trained systematically, quitting for the night not when his fingers cramped or his back muscles seized up but when he sensed, dispassionately, an equilibrium between physical dexterity and mental concentration. At that point, anything might happen: phrases could appear without warning, tunes might change in mid-bar, drones so raw that he had to close his eyes would surge from the instrument, altering the surface of the tune the way a wind altered the sea. Only then did he feel ready; only then, he explained to Seamus, was his playing free.

Though Michael visited his aunt every afternoon, and dropped by Tom Daly's after closing one night, he otherwise avoided the town. People wondered. Rumours of the session had surfaced—Seamus removed himself to the pub most afternoons, to be out of the way—and the list of guests exasperated as many as it pleased. One rumour was electric, and Seamus had no choice but to confirm it. Yes, Michael had invited Sean O Conchuir to the session. Yes, O Conchuir had accepted, but only if Michael promised to play. Yes, the two men would surely perform together.

Chapter 5

I leave the letter with Hia while Jimmy and I drive out to Dunquin for the final interview.

May 1, 1990

My Pat,

Hia's letter makes me write to you. So many things to say, so many thoughts run through my head each night, leaving no chance for sleep. Knowing you are there, where Michael was—he was never really elsewhere, I think—this is complicated, and I feel worry, excitement, distress. When you left, I thought, foolishly, that I was losing more love. (I am terrified of Dingle.) That is why I kept details from you, why I hid connections. Now, I understand that what I lose, you and Hia gain. I accept this happily.

When Moira Lynch called me with the news thirty-two years ago—my only ever conversation with your great-aunt—I was baking a pie for some ladies who were coming the next afternoon. Dagmar Johnson and Agnes Murray; do you remember our original neighbours? (The street was more friendly back then, everyone living the same life, sharing the same dreams.) I went to the phone, picked it up, then told the person to wait while I checked the oven. Moira said she had been baking bread for a wedding—she probably said a "wake", but I did not know that word—which I thought funny: two women, separated by the ocean, both cooking foods. Then her voice cracked. What she told me next, I heard only fragments: an accident . . . on the island . . . no body . . . authorities are assuming . . . the whole town is in mourning. . . . She also talked about Michael's friend Seamus, who had also disappeared, but I hung up.

I have never told you these things. Never told you that the minute I got off the line, you, a watermelon in my belly, due to be born any day, suddenly started making somersaults again!

Impossible: your head was almost in the birth canal. I called Dr. Reynolds. "My child does not want to be born," I told him. "I do not want to live." An ambulance came and took me—us—to Branson hospital. They were astonished; you had retreated from position. Not turned around—climbed back into the womb. Dr. Reynolds asked me what had happened. "A phone call," I said, "and an apple pie. The child's father does not eat desserts."

I was admitted, and waited in bed for a week until you reconsidered. Other friends phoned the house, of course—Davey stayed here for me—and I had visitors, but I remember nothing except your birth. Twenty-eight hours I laboured: you were a reluctant child. Timid Pat, from the start. Want to know what I thought about during those hours? Michael's dream, a horrible, recurring dream that he told me only once—in Allan Gardens, before we married—but I guessed he had often, from his red eyes and sweaty hair in the mornings.

Do you know the dream? Happily, I think not. Except for those accidents in the tree—a strange period, when I felt him in the house, seated at the table, drumming his fingers on the surface—Michael has failed to reach you. I wouldn't let him. You are my only child.

Some people said afterwards that I hated my husband for doing what he did. That I was too selfish to mourn him, show him respect. Maybe. What I remember is that in May 1958 I was a twenty-four-year-old widow with a new baby. Our savings had gone for his trip home. Mortage payments were due. I would not give up the house. I would not give up my career and move back with my parents. It was my life—and yours—and I would still live it as I wanted, no matter the difficulties. Besides, going back to work was a good activity. Agnes Murray looked after you during the week. (Everyone bottlefed in those days, so my guilt was manageable.) Davey Russell helped on weekends. Slowly, with much pain, we constructed a life.

You were my Lonely Boy.

I was exhausted, day and night.

Do I hate Michael? No, I don't. I wanted to love him until we both died, grey and forgetful. I wanted to give him my heart and soul and, together, fly into the sky. But he would not have me. Some other passion controlled him, excluding all else. So driven. So destructive. He was only half human (forgive my bitterness), the half of us that is alone on this planet with death and eternity. The other half, the good half—our relations with others, our hunger for love and friendship—was unknown to him. His birth must have been strange. A baby from the womb thinking he is an old man at the grave.

Now I weep.

People should not be puzzles. Should not be unknowable. God, yes, he is unknowable. Not us.

I must stop. Tomorrow, I will—

May 2

I will not apologize for what I wrote yesterday because it is how I feel, have always felt, and for so long

I did not share these things with you, so you would not be hurt, not feel worse, but now, well, it is late: you are an adult, and soon, I hope, a husband, a father. I slept heavy last night, perhaps from the weeping, and dreamed. (Like you, I almost never dream.) I dreamed— Oh, never mind.

Okay, I drank a little wine before. Davey was here, and he saw no harm in it. You know that Davey and I have been intimate for many years—nine, to be exact, since you moved into your apartment—and that, had the choice been mine, we would have become a couple decades sooner. Only an Irishman would wait so long. Only an Irishman would insist the son of the deceased be out of the house. Davey would be furious if he knew I was writing this. Even now, he wants us to be—what word does he use?—"discreet". Like we are in some small village, where privacy is impossible. But Davey is, maybe you will agree, everything Michael was not: open, easy to laugh, suspicious of solitude.

(Sorry: I suppose you cannot agree. Some days, I forget you never knew him. How, I wonder sometimes, could Pat Keane, who looks so much LIKE Michael Keane, know nothing OF him?)

Davey revered your father. Seamus—who you now know, Hia informs me, as Jimmy—was equally respectful. Michael received the spontaneous, genuine respect of everyone who encountered him, like he was a king. For thirty years I have struggled to earn the respect of my colleagues at work. I guess I was not fit to be his queen.

My English is better today. More relaxed and playful. At the office, even now, I dictate letters to my secretary; who wants to read broken language? Davey says I should take a course. At my age! Hia and I share this trouble. Like so much else, I often think. Such a lovely girl. So full of love and honour. Her struggles with her past are efforts at wholeness, for herself, for her family.

Remember this, please; she is trying to look outward. My piece of mother's advice? Try and refocus Hia onto that which she can build, not rebuild, construct, not restore. (My English is snappy!) Stable things, affirming things; do I have to be specific?

Your father never understood. He drowned in history.

Hia asked me about a record album I gave you for your eighteenth birthday. I'm afraid I can't be much help; the record was sent by Jimmy Sullivan, and I know nothing about it. (I had the impression you never liked the music.) Actually, that was among the final exchanges of letters between Seamus and me.

Today will be a lovely spring day. Davey and I are going for a drive and a picnic, in celebration of our wedding at city hall this morning. Don't be mad with me, Pat. We had booked six times for the ceremony, cancelled five times. I had forgotten today's appointment until last night, when Davey and I drank wine and talked about you and Hia, and all our lives, and memories. Old hen! he called me. Le vieux maquereau, I taunted back.

Your mother

PS Slip-Jig died two weeks ago. We counted: the cat was nineteen, and lived two years longer than his parent. Davey buried him in the backyard, in the shadow of the tree.

Sean O Conchuir welcomes Jimmy and me into his house. The view from the front room takes in farmland, Dunmore Head straining into the sea margin, a choppy sound, the smaller islands, and finally the Great Blasket shrouded in rain. The rawness of the air extracts the islands from their settings. The eye traces lines that are both bold and vague, firm and indeterminate. Jimmy stays in the house just long enough to introduce me as "Padraig O Cathain". His preamble on O Conchuir, which stressed the man's hermeticism and steely intelligence, was intimidating, and I am prepared to endure his sarcasm in exchange for his presence. Jimmy notes my silent entreaties before departing.

Sean O Conchuir was born in the village of Ballydavid. His ninety years have been spent exclusively on the stretch of peninsula west of Dingle town, where he worked as a postmaster in Ballyferriter and Dunquin. O Conchuir first gained fame as a fiddler through a series of radio programs in the 1950s, his skills being hailed by, among others, Sean O Riada and Seamus Ennis. His refusal to record in a studio or even perform into a microphone limited, however, the availability of his music while, paradoxically, enhancing his reputation. Finally, in 1972, a diligent record company executive managed to tape him during a single session in O Conchuir's kitchen. The resulting album is considered a classic.

O Conchuir is a tall bony man with white hair and sunken blue eyes. He walks slowly and grips both arms of the chair to disguise, or perhaps simply contain, his trembling. His manner is unselfconsciously patrician; I am treated like one more in a string of musicologists and admirers who have flocked to his home over the years. The room is tasteful, featuring an oriental rug, bookshelves, and landscape paintings on the walls. Also on the wall is the original of the album cover: the outlined fiddler, minus the musical notation. Sean O Conchuir's wife of fifty years, Maire, was a well-known painter. (Though the sketch resembles, if anything, the collection in Eily Murphy's house.) Maire Bean Ui Conchuir died in the autumn of 1985. People around Dunquin, remarking on O Conchuir's failing health, assume he will not be long in joining her.

PK: Thank you for agreeing to this interview.

SOC: Out of respect for your father.

PK: You knew him well?

SOC: Michael was my peer, one of the finest fiddlers I've ever heard. The manner in which he lived his life constituted a waste of great talent, of a great, God-sent gift. What about yourself?

PK: Myself?

SOC: Musical structure is causal. Melodies fixed in the memory *become* the memory, weaves of brilliantly dyed wools that refuse to be unstitched. What about yourself?

PK: . . . I don't know. . . .

SOC: "A Lament for Paudeen Bawn" doesn't know his own mind?

PK: Sorry?

SOC: You are familiar with *The Drunken Butterfly?*

PK: Every note of every tune.

SOC: You know the lament—

PK: Yes.

SOC: It's yours, after all.

PK: I don't understand.

SOC: Michael had another name for the melody, true. I only heard him play it once, and chose to recall the notes rather than the name.

PK: Michael Keane wrote "A Lament for Paudeen Bawn"?

SOC: He would never admit to it; hence, my calling it "traditional" on the liner notes. But I heard the tune first from his fiddle, and then never again, and I know the music well enough to distinguish what is new. Over the years, I took to calling the piece "Paudeen Bawn", a private allusion. . . . Son?

PK: Huh?

SOC: Ask the obvious.

PK: My father wrote—?

SOC: A private allusion to his name for you. . . . During his fateful visit Michael would, when asked about your mother's state, refer to the unborn child as either Patrick John or, among Irish speakers, Paudeen Bawn—fair-haired Paddy. He guessed your gender more accurately than your hair colour.

PK: My hair is black.

SOC: Did you not—? Ah, I see. . . . Wait one moment. . . .

(SOC rises very slowly and goes into the adjoining room. He returns with a magnificent fiddle, its sycamore back polished, its ebony neck black as coal. His bow seems unusually long; the strings are definitely not of metal, as preferred by most musicians. The hairs have been rosined and the fiddle is, judging from SOC's down-bow, already in tune.) I have always played this melody from the memory of that one listen. You are about to hear your father, pure and simple, and *that* is immortality.

(SOC plays "A Lament for Paudeen Bawn", beautifully, but with a dropped note in the final bar. Except for his imperceptible movements over the fingerboard and the action of the bow, the music emerges from a point of absolute stillness—as if, ironically, from a stereo speaker. SOC has Hia's spindly fingers, and favours a long, classical stroke. The music sucks all air from the room. SOC sinks into his chair before the final note has abated. Playing for even fifty-eight seconds is clearly too much for him.) Congratulations.

PK: For what?

SOC: You are the first person to hear me play since Mary died, what, four years ago. . . . Here, by the way, is the score.

(He offers me a sheet of music folded on the table beside his chair.)

PK: Thank you.

SOC: Another first for me. I have never before jotted down a tune in my repertoire.

PK: I'm grateful.

SOC: You should be.

PK: It sounded different.

SOC: Different from . . . ?

PK: The record, I guess.

SOC: Albums are second-hand experiences: eviscerated, unsatisfying. The reason I dislike giving interviews and refuse to speak into a tape recorder—today I make an exception—is no different from the reason I am reluctant to have my music recorded. You and I are chatting. That's grand. Like myself playing a few tunes, say—grand also. But to see the sentences in strange books or to hear the notes on black discs: not correct, to my way of thinking. Not the truth, if you like.

PK: Why is an album or a book less truthful?

SOC: Both forms fail to satisfy the deep longings in a person for music and company.

PK: But I've been told you play only by yourself now.

SOC: *(ignoring the question)* The finest moments in my musical career involved the house dances and kitchen sessions of the 1920s and 30s. Pubs today are noisy and smoky and full of foreigners who gawk at the musicians like they are exotic birds. I haven't performed in public since, well, since Dingle was declared a scenic wonderland. One of the last occasions I played *for* other people, as opposed to *with* fellow musicians, was in the house of Seamus O Suilleabhain, along with your father and a piper, one of the MacDonaghs from Lispole.

PK: Really?

SOC: The night was extraordinary. Michael

played with genius. I understood that he hadn't touched a fiddle all those years in Canada—part of the tragedy, in my view, a confusion in his mind of place with self that made *dis*placement a disaster—yet on that occasion his tone and pitch, the quality of his bowing, were impeccable. I recall him tuning his instrument to a lower octave at the end of the session, as musicians did in the last century, to produce a deep sonorous sound, like a viola. He proceeded to play the lament with consummate pathos and sorrow. The music—

PK: Did you just play it in a lower octave?

SOC: *(insulted)* Of course.

PK: I didn't see you adjust the pegs.

SOC: The fiddle was already tuned.

PK: Do you always keep it—?

SOC: I lowered the tuning in anticipation of your visit, just as I wrote out the score for "Paudeen Bawn". Do not make me say what should be apparent, son. Do not overstep—

PK: Sorry.

SOC: The music Michael played was pure and evocative, a window onto a world none of us had experienced but all knew had once existed. The whole evening, artificially planned though it was, constituted a threnody of sorts. Thus, it was rife with mutability, despite Michael's touching attempt to use the gathering to celebrate values he held the dearer, perhaps, for possessing more in his imagination than in his past or, indeed, future life. Still, the night resembled those sessions from before the war. Music then was communal and secular, in the best senses of those words. No hierarchies; the musician was an equal with the dancer and singer, the listener supplying accompaniment with his feet. No church, either; the modest kitchen of a house, tables and chairs pressed against the walls to create a centre—the centre of the community, if you like. I am not romanticizing these events. My memory is acute. I am simply recalling the once vibrant capacity of music to serve as a cohesive force in the lives of people. During those times, it was a pleasure and an honour to play, and play well, in public. Kitchen music was music of celebration, of joy and unspoken conviction. . . . Now, well, I play solely by myself, for myself, in the presence of the Lord. I play at his bidding, in thanks, of course, but without the fervent joy I once felt.

PK: You said these sessions were common before the war. *Which* war?

SOC: Only your father's death, now that I think of it, only his death did any justice—in a dreadful Old Testament manner, like Jonah or Ahab—to the passion and commitment of his music. An artist's life can only be a bundle of contradictions, only be a disaster waiting for a circumstance. Will you remember that?

PK: Yes.

SOC: I'm asking you. . . .

PK: I'll remember it.

SOC: Well done. Now, let's be talking of more cheerful matters!

PK: I just want to clarify the time period of these—

SOC: In his playing, his relationship with the music, Michael was an ancient. Worse, he possessed a dying tradition within himself. That is a terrible burden for a young man to carry.

PK: What about yourself?

SOC: Michael O Cathain is dead, Johnny Doherty is dead, and I am feeling none too well, thank you.

PK: I don't mean to be so aggressive. . . .

SOC: You are more self-possessed than I had imagined Michael's son could ever be. That is good. The men of your father's generation lacked confidence and self-esteem. They had endured too much deprivation, too much isolation. . . . But allow me to redirect the conversation. . . . *(clears his throat)*

The music in our family was on my father's side of the house. He could trace a lineage of fiddlers, and before that pipers, to the early years of the nineteenth century. My own father, Aodan O Conchuir, was a big man, a droll man, hailing from the village of Ballinknockane at the foot of Mount Brandon but resident most of his sixty-five years in Ballydavid. I was born and reared there. Our house in those days, the time of the original Troubles, was frequented by musicians from every corner of the peninsula. These men held my father in high esteem, and I've been assured more than once that he was a fiddler, and story-teller, of great refinement.

PK: I was told—

SOC: It was natural I would take to the fiddle myself. My father's style, very clean and precise in note-making, and his insistence on having what he called the right "setting" for a tune, greatly influenced my development. By the age of fifteen, sixteen at the latest, I had assimilated the technical points of the instrument, the techniques a player used to individualize a tune, but I was already restless with the predetermined constrictions of form in traditional music. I agreed, yes I did, that a musician had to *play* the tune, give it shape, if you like, yet to my mind much of the music I heard lacked emotional resolution, lacked a compelling sense of notes being stirred into thought and sensation. Music was the discovery of structure. I demanded then, as I demand now, a blending of serious-mindedness and technical fidelity with the artist's desire to communicate every manner of thing—love, splendour, awe, devotion—through his or her chosen medium.

PK: I was—

SOC: I can speak about improper settings for tunes, or the ill thinking behind the current vogue of grouping together reels, or the failure of many musicians to adhere to the discipline of the piece, the intrinsic modality of it, just as easily as I can discuss the wisdom of a phrase or the beauty of a single note. All the one, don't you know.

PK: But aren't you famous for changing tunes in the middle of a bar and mixing two and three reels together?

SOC: What of it?

PK: And on your record, during the jig "The Salamanca", don't you insert two bars from a Bach fugue?

SOC: I had been listening to Bach that morning. Natural enough it would still be on my mind in the evening, when the man from the record company appeared at the door.

PK: Listening to Bach? On what?

SOC: The phonograph, of course.

PK: Oh. . . . But is it true that you sometimes deviate from the tune by adding phrases from classical composers?

SOC: I have never deviated from a piece of music in my life.

PK: Okay.

SOC: Every tune has a line of thought and a line of feeling. Once the musician is tapped into those lines, is reading the music, then he is incapable of deviating from the integrity, the truth, of the piece, regardless of which notes he plays. To mistake the flat reproduction of a melody for the interpretative flights brought on by the sweeps of colour and emotion one feels while playing it would be akin to agreeing that GOD is, indeed, simply DOG spelt backwards.

PK: Is it lonely playing by yourself?

SOC: Is it lonely praying by yourself?

PK: I said "playing".

SOC: And I said "praying".

PK: I find praying extremely lonely, yes.

SOC: Then perhaps you should take up a musical instrument.

PK: The legend is that you play the fiddle only in your kitchen and only at night, with the lights off, and that by sunrise there is often a drying puddle of tears where you've sat. . . .

SOC: I've long stopped denying those stories.

PK: Music must be exhausting when you feel it so deeply.

SOC: The exhaustion is superseded by exhilaration. You must try and comprehend the nourishment music provides me. My wife is four years in the grave. My friends too have all passed on. I have nothing in my life, except the music. I have always wanted to play perfectly. Originally, I sought perfection out of respect for my father. Then it was to benefit my community. During the period that I allowed that man to record the session—an action I regret, for the album is pitiable—I was playing for myself, perhaps in an egocentric manner. Now I play for the Lord. He is a good listener. I need fiddle only softly, in my kitchen, at whatever time of the day suits me. I need no longer worry about the exigencies of reputation and repute. I have a gift, son. I'm as appreciative to God as I can be for that

> gift. And I am rendering it back unto him through playing. The mind is at peace when one is active. The bow over the strings, the fingers up and down the fingerboard—these movements are the energy of life, of enlightenment. When one is using the gifts God gave, then there *is* enlightenment, along with a gentle, hushed ecstasy. I see the fiddle as a faint echo of the unbroken music in heaven. While on this earth, one can do no harm playing music for God.

Hia is not working, not rendering back unto God the gift of her talents, when I say good-night to Jimmy and climb the stairs. She claims to be reading. A book lies open in her lap, my mother's letter folded between the pages. But the room is hazy, lit by a solitary candle, and the book teeters on her thigh. Hia is neither drawing nor doting over Carolan. She has spent the evening reading, she assures me, reading the book and Francine's letter: the words on the printed page, the words in Mother's tidy script. The book, which she borrowed from Eily, is a history of the great Irish families before the conquest. And the letter, I ask. What's it all about?

"You don't know?"

"I'm asking your opinion."

"The letter is to you."

"She knew you'd read it, Hia. You could tell by the tone of her writing. It was for us both."

"You didn't share it until—"

"What do you *think* of it?"

"I am glad she and Davey made their love official."

"And?"

"I am sorry about Slip-Jig."

"And?"

"I think Francine made mistakes with your upbringing."

Hia does not enquire about the interview, does not enquire if Jimmy and I used the car ride to make amends. She sits in the gloom studying a swimming text. Why don't I pop the cassette into the tape player and share Sean O Conchuir's mystical ruminations with her? Better, why don't I put *The Drunken Butterfly* into the machine, fast-forward to the final cut on the first side, and then announce casually, neutrally, that the Lament for Fair-Haired Paddy was written by my father and is, moreover, being performed by O Conchuir using Michael's own style? Why instead do I cross to our ancestor shrine—the room is easily navigated with the middle open—and, not even checking the corresponding photos, fire two more candles, hold the match over the joss sticks until they also catch, fan the embers with my breath, linger a moment over the gyres of sweet smoke, and then, still silent, still neutral, walk into the kitchen to fix toast and tea?

Chapter 6

The kitchen was jammed by nine o'clock, and already stifling, despite the opened door. Seamus had spent the afternoon rounding up the guests, and now he and Eileen O'Shea were arranging furniture and serving refreshments. John and Moira Hoolihan had come from Rahinnane, Paud Quinn from Ventry, the singer Bridget O Murchu from Dunquin, Dingle residents Cathal and Mary Farrell, the bachelor Sheedy brothers from Lateevemore, Michael's sole surviving uncle, Maurice O Cathain, Breda O Beaglaoich of Ballydavid, John O'Connor from Tiduff, the Brosnan clan—Paddy, Tomas, and Barra—also from Ballydavid, and a seventy-year-old Lispole piper named Jimmy MacDonagh. Sean O Conchuir arrived alone and crisscrossed the room like a politician, greeting men with a handshake and women with a slight bow. A chair awaited him beside the hearth, across from Michael.

O Conchuir wore a three-button jacket over a white high-neck, grey pants, and black shoes. His fiddle case was also black, curiously unscuffed. Michael had just rolled up the sleeves of his sweater and hitched his trousers. A cigarette burned in a tea saucer; a glass of whisky glistened on the mantelpiece.

"How did the instrument survive the years in storage?"

O Conchuir asked.

"The D peg is loose. I've jimmied a match to keep it from slipping."

"Might I have a look?"

Michael passed him the fiddle. O Conchuir raised the body to his ear, plucked all four strings, then lowered it upright to his knee, the scroll in his left hand. For ten minutes he tuned and retuned, a frown creasing his forehead. Though many eyes followed the operation, no one dared speak with him; chatter was church-hushed. Finally, O Conchuir pronounced the instrument playable. Michael went to take it back. He received instead Sean O Conchuir's own fiddle, along with his bow.

"But Sean—"

"I will insist."

Michael turned the fiddle over. "I recalled the tone of this even in Canada," he confessed. "It has a sweetness I've heard in no other."

"Yes it has."

"There's no way I could—"

"Many of the great itinerant fiddlers didn't even own their instruments. They borrowed from the house they were to play in. It was the home that possessed both the means and, if you like, the motive for making music. Without an audience, what need had the man for a fiddle?"

Guests nearest the fireplace strained to follow the conversation. The majority, though, chatted among themselves. They spoke Irish and English, often switching languages in mid-sentence to better express a thought. While some had seen each other at the funeral two weeks before, many more, separated by long country miles, had years of news to catch up on. Certain guests assumed the night was in homage to Tomas O Cathain. Others took it to be a celebration of his son's good fortune in Canada. Still others, noting the arrangement of the kitchen, the position of the fiddlers across from each other, with Jimmy MacDonagh in the background, believed they were about to witness a session of rare quality. Those people tended to wait quietly, glancing at Michael for a clue as to when it—whatever "it" might be—would begin.

Everyone was slightly anxious. While nearly all the guests could recall similar events, almost no one could remember when they had last attended one, much less been formally invited, and collected in an automobile, and served tea and bottled beer, and felt so shy, even self-conscious, about spending an evening in a house with friends.

Everyone, that is, except Michael. He sat with O Conchuir's fiddle in his lap, tapping the bow to the strings in rhythm with the banter.

"God bless your da, Michael," John O'Connor shouted. "Tomas was a grand man."

"He was," Michael agreed.

"A grand man, and a good talker," his uncle said.

"All the old names are gone now," Breda O Beaglaoich sighed.

"I recall your own mother, Breda," Michael said.

"You don't."

"She taught in the island school one year, when you were away in Dublin."

"Did she learn you anything?"

"Probably not."

There was a chorus of laughter.

"And your sister, John," he continued, addressing John Hoolihan. "She worked in Dingle hospital during the war, didn't she?"

"That's right."

"Sister Bridget," Michael said with a grin. "Miss McGreevy marched the entire class up Goat Street for an inoculation one spring morning. Your sister was wicked with the needle, I recall."

"I'd imagine she was."

"Give us a tune, Michael," Bridget O Murchu requested.

"It's only proper," someone else said.

"I'd rather chat a while."

Sean O Conchuir nodded to himself.

"You were hardly known for your chatting, Mickey," Maurice O Cathain pointed out.

"Was I not?"

"You drove your da to distraction with your silences. He swore more than once that his only child was mute."

"I was listening."

"Closely, I would venture," O Conchuir said.

Paddy Brosnan, who had attended middle school with O Conchuir four decades earlier, asked him about a former teacher who had ended up in New York. O Conchuir's answer was lengthy and entertaining. More questions followed, more laughter, until it was past ten o'clock. Michael let the conversation flow around him; he grinned, made the odd comment, brushed the strings with the bow. A command from Bridget O Murchu drew him back.

"Your glasses, boy."

"Bridget?"

"You're squinting your eyes closed."

"But I don't wear glasses."

"Is Michael squinting or isn't he?" Bridget asked Mary Farrell.

"He might be."

"Your face gets all narrowed, son," his uncle said.

Michael shifted in his chair. He inquired if everyone was comfortable. Everyone was. He wondered if the kitchen wasn't warm. Seamus offered to put out the fire.

Silence descended.

"Michael, . . . " Sean O Conchuir advised.

"Will I have a go at a tune?"

"That would be appropriate."

Michael announced the first notes of "The Star of Munster" in a hush so singular he momentarily confused the tapping of feet on the floor with his own heartbeat. The bow was a feather in his hand; he swore it barely skimmed the strings, yet they resounded, beautifully. All his unease flowed into the instrument, leaving him relaxed, almost drowsy.

Only when Michael slid in mid-bar into a Clare jig known by various names, including "The Whipeen", did Sean O Conchuir position his fiddle. He joined in with a flourish, droning an octave above the line, then levelling off. O Conchuir's flamboyant style, typified by his signature lifting of the bow to blunt a note and landing back in the melody without a slur, like a diver breaking a pool surface cleanly, complemented Michael's playing. The men made eye contact, ending the jig the exact moment before it normally would have ended.

The audience stirred. John O'Connor offered a compliment and Maurice O Cathain, nearest the hearth, patted Michael on the knee. Otherwise, guests folded their hands and sipped their drinks. Seamus noted the discomfort from the doorway, where he was busy discouraging interlopers from peeking through the windows. He cracked a joke about who might be called upon to sing, initiating a dialogue between Bridget O Murchu and Mary Farrell that had to be both repeated and translated, due to deafness and poor English. Bridget promised to perform, then promptly fell asleep.

A consultation between musicians produced a solo by Sean O Conchuir, a dizzying interpretation of a Kerry slide that varied phrases and inverted parts. The line was elusive, possibly random, yet Michael calmly joined the second round and straightened the slide out. His entrance brought a smile to O Conchuir's face. The boisterous drone of Jimmy MacDonagh's pipes—both bows paused in the air as MacDonagh opened a tune—dissolved any lingering tension in the room. John O'Connor shouted, "Good man, Jimmy!" and Moira Hoolihan, winner of a Munster dance competition in 1926, made a spontaneous whirl around the floor before collapsing back in her seat. The fiddlers fell in halfway; the applause afterwards came from both within the kitchen and outside, where, Jimmy reported, the crowd had swelled to include Father Leahy, Naill Walshe, and the local *garda* officer, Pats Farrell, patrolling the town on his bicycle.

"Now, lads," Sean O Conchuir said.

Most guests, including Seamus, assumed the evening had found its rhythm: exchanges of solos and duets between Michael and O Conchuir, with the piper providing accompaniment. Sean O Conchuir alone was neither surprised nor disappointed by what transpired. Retiring the fiddle to his lap, Michael encouraged the other musicians to take solos and cajoled audience members, whose accomplishments he catalogued with exactitude and evident pride, into performing. Moira Hoolihan felt sufficiently recovered to lead a half-set. Sean O Conchuir played, calling out the changes, while Michael cautioned dancers to keep to the middle of the floor. Once the room stopped spinning, he asked Paddy Brosnan to tell a story. Brosnan's tale lasted twenty minutes and wandered from the drinking of bad liquor to an American wake that ended up a genuine wake when the young man, destined for relatives in Philadelphia, drowned in Dingle Bay the morning of his departure. Once he had finished, Paddy switched to English to explain that it had been many years since he'd told a story, and many more still since he'd told one well.

Sean O Conchuir provided a musical addendum: the slow air "An Fhallaingin Mhuimhneach". Adopting his public voice, O Conchuir related how the tune was believed to be of Spanish origin, brought to Kerry in the sixteenth century by survivors of the *Santa Maria de la Rosa*, the Armada ship wrecked off the Great Blasket. While the story was likely apocryphal—the British executed any Spaniard who reached the shore alive—it was a lovely tune nonetheless.

Next, Michael convinced Bridget O Murchu to sing. He reminisced about the first time he heard Bridget, at a fair in Ballyferriter in 1940, and how his father had spent a week afterwards explaining the subtleties of the song she had performed—"An Bonnan Bui"—to his son. Michael asked if she remembered that song. Bridget confessed to only a partial memory, and offered "Cath Cheim an Fhia"instead, taught to her by her aunt Mary McCann of Waterville, and prepared for three days in anticipation of the evening. The song was long and she sang it standing, using a heavy nasal drone to emphasize the emotion of the lyrics. Twice she stopped: once to reorder a stanza, once to insert two forgotten lines. Towards the end, Michael walked over to her. Bridget slumped, and he helped her back into her seat.

"That was lovely, wasn't it?" he asked the room.

Another chorus of agreement sounded.

"Are you all right, Michael?" Breda inquired.

"Grand, Breda."

"Your eyes look—"

"There's a sting," he admitted. "Must be the smoke."

The kitchen, now suffocating, reeked of cigarettes and sweat. Guests yawned and scrubbed their faces, dozed until jarred awake by laughter or an elbow. Seamus kept an absent watch over them. He had devoted much of the evening to observing Michael; by midnight, his puzzlement was complete. His friend had picked up the fiddle exactly once since the opening tunes, preferring to act as host and champion of performers whose skills, Sean O Conchuir's excepted, hardly matched his own. An obvious question had preoccupied Seamus during the preparations. Asking it aloud had seemed unnecessary; surely the session would provide the answer. It hadn't, and he suddenly felt foolish, vaguely offended.

People rose to leave. Those with cars shook Michael's hand and wished him continued luck back in Canada. Several asked about the child, saying that Patrick John was a fine name.

"All the old names are gone," John O'Connor lamented.

Michael agreed.

"But your father, now, he was a grand lad."

Michael agreed again.

"Gone, gone, gone," Bridget offered.

"You were very gracious to come down tonight," he said. "I won't soon forget it."

"Go away," Maurice O Cathain said.

Guests awaiting a lift eyed Seamus expectantly. He was fetching his coat when Michael returned to the fireplace and began to tighten the nut on O Conchuir's bow. Seamus crossed to him.

"Are you going to play?"

"I thought I might."

"But I have to drop these people back out."

"Right, Seamie."

"I wouldn't mind listening."

"Brilliant evening, wasn't it? The kitchen had a lovely feeling to it. Warm and friendly. Like I always imagined it would be, you know?"

Seamus fumed.

"Had you imagined it this way?" Michael asked.

"Imagined what?"

He positioned the fiddle. Seamus was about to protest when Eily O'Shea demanded the ignition key from him. She had no permit, but had been driving for two years; he wasn't about to argue, and requested that Michael wait until he had seen her to the car. Michael agreed, taken aback by his friend's tone.

Sean O Conchuir overheard the exchange. "Seamus has worked mightily to see this evening succeed," he said.

"The music was brilliant."

"I doubt very much Seamus cares one whit for the music, Michael."

"No?"

O Conchuir shrugged.

"It was meant . . . ," Michael began.

"There's no need to tell me, man."

"Right."

"But you will play a few tunes more?"

"You'll join in?"

"Absolutely not."

Michael down-bowed the strings. "The sound is astonishing. I'm reminded—I don't know why—of a shallow brook, each stone clear under the water."

"It is a flawless instrument," O Conchuir said. "Played, sadly, by flawed hands and hearts. I have never been able to reconcile these truths."

Seamus returned, closed the door, and chose from among the dozen empty chairs one halfway down the room. O Conchuir also relocated, leaving Michael isolated at the hearth, the fire at his feet.

He opened with a series of jigs in a higher position, then performed "The Salamanca" in a minor key. Two-part reels were transposed, the final section raised a half-tone. Hornpipes became fugues as he counterpointed phrases a third above and below the line. During "The Steampacket", a tune played almost exclusively by pipers, his bowing duplicated the rhythms of a chanter. Dance music alternated with airs and laments. Michael's fiddling was typically remote, but unusually audacious; his imagination seemed to reconstruct each melody, recast each phrase, to play hundred-year-old tunes with fidelity and abandon, as if he were making it all up as he went along. He performed in a trance, hesitating only a few seconds between numbers and answering O Conchuir's queries with impatience. Seamus's offers of tea were ignored.

At some point during the night, Eily O'Shea slipped into the house and sat at the back. She opened a sketch pad, took a pencil from her purse, and sketched, as a beginner would, a fiddler consumed by his craft.

Towards daybreak, with light seeping through the curtains and under the door, Michael started to attack the music. Phrases emerged gnarled, the rhythm lurching in and out of time. His mumbled apologies, directed at O Conchuir, implied that these variations were accidental. Sweat streamed into the crevices of his cheeks; his shirt collar was stained. At last, rubbing his left arm, he stopped.

"Enough, Mickey," Seamus surprised himself by saying.

"Maybe one more tune."

"But you're wrecked."

"What have you in mind?" O Conchuir asked.

"Nothing. I've had an empty mind since shortly after midnight."

"How does it feel?"

"Like itself."

"There you go," Seamus said. "There isn't any—"

"He'll play one more, Seamus," Sean O Conchuir said sternly.

Chapter 7

Friday starts poorly. I roll over and nestle against Hia, kiss her salty neck. It has been two weeks since we made love, and I am anxious to communicate my willingness. At this stage, I would forgo lustier ambitions and simply snuggle, reconcile our estranged bodies. But she only sighs and murmurs in Vietnamese.

I dress in the kitchen. Carolan, dozing atop his throne, is definitely still dead. His perpetual slumber has been punctuated of late by cries that resemble the quavers Eily reported hearing through the ceiling before our arrival: baleful and impatient, suggesting in timbre a habitual grievance. He is, in other words, far too busy communing with Joan McGreevy to bother with the flat's current occupants. I pet him on the head. Getting no response, I draw the stroke into a caress, including both a levitation of the eyelids and a ruffling of the hairs near the tail. Still he ignores me. I squat and press my lips to his ear. Carolan? I whisper. Anybody home?

Twice rejected, I descend the stairs and head up Grey Lane. The morning is literally funereal. Green Street, Dykegate Lane, even sections of Strand Street are lined with cars. Men in suits and women in dresses climb to St. Mary's. The mourners advance against a backdrop of storm clouds that engulf the upper village. I lower my gaze out of respect for the dead and resignation about the weather. The wind is a *pilbroch* at the end of the pier. Breakers explode against concrete and covens of gulls consort in mid-draft. I allow the music to fill my ears and the sky to press down upon me. It has always been this way here, I now suspect. The volatility, skittish as a bow across unrosined strings, the weight of chance, everything random: didn't I sense it would be like this?

In the parking lot behind Strand Street, I seek out the derelict trawler, certain the boat is called the *Munster Reel* and once belonged to Seamus O Suilleabhain and Michael O Cathain. Though the idea is crazed, it is lodged clumsily in my brain. At the spot, I find dead grass where the blocks once rested, gouged earth where a truck must have spun its wheels before lurching forward with the vessel in tow. The tracks disappear at the pavement.

Back in our kitchen, I find Hia hunched over her pad. The Angkor Wat artifact, relegated to a suitcase for two hopeful weeks, is once more on display. Its primary function is an open secret: she caresses the sandstone with her hand as she draws. We exchange hellos and I fix myself breakfast, ignoring the snarl of a page being torn.

"Want some eggs?" I ask.

"Tea only."

"Have you eaten anything today?"

"You refuse to help."

"Why don't you cook for yourself, Hia?"

"I am working," she says. "Cannot you see this?"

"I can see you are fretting. That's obvious. I can see you're punishing yourself. That's—"

"No eggs for me."

Hia pretends to resume drawing. "The water table at Angkor Wat is too high," she announces. "The temples were built without deep foundations. The Khmers had canals and moats to drain excess water, but now these are choked in weeds and hyacinth. Stability is not so sure any more. Everything could collapse."

"But Angkor would still be there, wouldn't it?"

"How?"

"In dream."

She orders me to the table. "Watch," she says, folding the pad to a fresh page. "Watch me fail."

Hia takes up a pencil, studies the surface, and then executes a series of single-line sketches. "Phnom Bahkeng," she explains of the first outline. "The original temple of Angkor. It is composed of four hundred small towers that are symbols of movements of heavenly bodies."

She fills the space below.

"Ta Keo, from 1000 AD. Made of sandstone. Five towers are built, I mean laid, in the pattern of a cruc— cruci— I cannot speak English!"

"Cruciform."

"Ta Keo is dedicated to Siva."

The next line resembles a wave-length.

"Phreah Khan," she says. "Built by Suryavarman II. Enormous interior to this temple, filled with pavilions, halls, and chapels."

"Don't press so hard."

"What?"

"You're grinding your pencil into the paper."

She continues.

"Here is the Bayon. Fifty towers, every one rounded, supported on pillars with complex, I mean ornate, portals and gates. Here is where I once saw priests burning incense. Also birds and butterfly clouds."

"The *apsaras* showed you these things?"

"I see them no longer."

"You will again."

"I was mistaken."

"I'm sure you'll—"

Hia surveys the remaining space, turns the pad sideways, pauses to make contact with the artifact, then draws an outline down the page.

"Angkor Wat?"

She drops the pencil.

"It's big," I manage.

"I can draw you the smaller temples also. I can draw statues and bas-reliefs and imagined gardens filled with elephants and monkeys and jungle birds. I can outline a sky view of the whole temple-city. Every proportion, every dimension, all scales and shapes I know, and can do. But I cannot, cannot, bring it together!"

"Remember when I asked you to keep the preliminary sketches?" I say, ignoring her outburst. "How many pages did you complete before you started destroying them?"

"Twenty, thirty—how should I know?"

"Do you have a stapler?"

Her expression hardens.

"Get the stapler, assemble the sheets, make sure the edges meet, then staple them in the corner. Next, take a piece of charcoal and title the top sheet ANGKOR. That way you will have brought your wonderful work together, Hia, and can move on to something else, something that isn't so corrosive and. . . . " I leave the thought be.

Her eyes shine with tears.

"You didn't do anything wrong," I add.

"Except kill my mother."

I stifle a groan.

Hia rises and drags herself into the living room. Exhausted, she flops on the unmade, unfolded bed. "I dreamed something new last night," she says, her voice quavering. "It begins at the waterfall where Bo and I once swam. But I am now the adult, climbing the slope beside the waterfall to go into the jungle. It grows dense and dark, full of loud, hidden birds, until I reach some open fields. The land rolls in waves; in the distance is a large wat. In the heat, the temple floats above the ground, very strange. I cross the paddies, the rice stalks red and gold."

I sit in a chair.

"The wat is a monastery, protected by tall trees with umbrella tops and a canal. The canal is dry, though, as at Angkor. . . . " Hia pauses at the congruence. She rolls onto her side, pillowing her head with her hands. Despite her listlessness, she has never looked more striking, or more desirable.

"I enter and study the main temple. It is made of stone, with four towers. At each corner are statues of animals. Incense burns in pots around them. Prayer flags hang like drying clothes. An outdoor altar has many Buddhas on top, but also photos and postcards and bottles of liquid. A monk crosses the courtyard. He has a wide face and dark skin, and speaks the same language as the woman who once gave me a coconut. I am in Cambodia. I am with monks who live outside society, outside time."

"When were you there, anyway?"

"Pardon?"

"I mean, when did you actually *see* Angkor?"

"See it?"

"In person, . . . " I say, remembering the doubts I once harboured about Hia having ever been to Cambodia, even as a child. "I had always assumed, wrongly, that you made, you know, a trip. . . . "

"Family vacation?"

"I guess I didn't—"

"In the station wagon? Stay in motels with swimming pools?"

"Okay."

"You really thought that?"

"I suppose I knew."

"If you knew . . . ?"

"I wasn't sure what to do with the knowledge."

Hia closes her eyes. "A beautiful woman crosses the ground to me," she resumes. "She wears a robe of brilliant orange, and no shoes. 'Hia,' she says. 'I have waited so long for you.' I try to speak. 'Don't talk,' she says. 'Only say you will stay here with me, now and for ever.'"

She chokes.

"'How can you be—?' I say. 'Alive?' she replies. 'I am not alive. I am not dead. Here, we all pray.' 'Can I pray?' I ask. 'You must,' she answers. 'Take one life, give another back.'"

"Great advice," I murmur, unable to contain my impatience.

"Your father died . . . ?" Hia asks coldly.

"Francine's letter explained it."

"He died . . . ?"

"Seven days before I was born."

"If I had had this information. . . . "

"What information?"

"You never had a father, Pat. You never lost anything. I always was comforted by our sharing of this tragedy. Now, I say we share little."

Crossing to the shrine, I grab the two newest members of our gallery and hold them up for inspection. "Did you see Joan McGreevy?"

"That old woman?"

"Eily Murphy found the snapshot in a newspaper. Can you believe Eily has copies of *The Kerryman* dating back to the 1950s? She cut the photo out and mounted it on cardboard for us. They say pets and their masters grow to resemble each other. Don't you think she looks like Carolan?"

Not even a smile.

"And here it is . . . ," I hasten to add, displaying the other photo.

"Jimmy Sullivan is not dead."

"Not Jimmy. The figure he is gesturing to. The man outside the camera frame."

I am expecting at most her congratulations, at least her recognition that this *is* a significant moment for me. Instead,

Hia stands up and announces she is going for a walk.

"In the rain? Visit Eily instead."

"Don't tell me what to do."

I grab her arm and smile. "You're beautiful," I say foolishly.

Rather than strike me—her first impulse, I gather—she spins around, marches to the table where we keep our wallets and keys, and returns with her sunglasses. Without a word, she stretches up and jams the glasses over my eyes, nearly poking the left one out. I accept the disguise, the darkened light, with the same smile, the same inexplicable buoyancy. Hia slams the door behind her.

A LAMENT FOR MY FATHER

Chapter 8

"Peadar Guiheen asked me to have a look at his flock," Michael informed Seamus. "I couldn't very well say no, could I? Not to my own cousin."

"Peadar asked you to mind his sheep?"

"That's right."

"In Dunquin?"

"The Guiheens still graze their animals on the island."

"Mickey. . . . "

"Could I say no?"

Seamus massaged his eyelids. Since retiring Sean O Conchuir's fiddle to its case six hours earlier, Michael had been on a ramble: breakfast at his aunt's, a visit with his former Irish teacher, a stroll out the pier to inspect the *Munster Reel*, and a two-pint lunch at Tom Daly's, where he was hailed by the regulars as an Odysseus returned from sea. Seamus had trailed after him obediently, swallowing yawns, trying to ignore the weariness in his legs. When Michael had insisted they retreat into the snug, he had agreed: at least he could put his feet up.

"Peadar asked you to go out to the Blasket to check on his flock? He asked you to board the trawler on your second-to-last day in Dingle, make the journey, land her, all for a look at a few bloody sheep?"

Michael was silent.

"I'm not stupid," Seamus said.

"He's my cousin."

"How many times have you spoken to Peadar Guiheen in the last ten years?"

"What are you saying?"

"I'm saying there's more—"

"I mentioned it to him."

"Mentioned what?"

"That I might be going out. . . . "

"To the Blasket?"

"For the day. I ran into Peadar in Green Street and mentioned that I might, we might, be heading out."

"Might we?"

"That's what I said."

Seamus stared into Michael's red-rimmed eyes. Then, backing off, he scuffed the floor with his boot. The snug window swung open unexpectedly.

"My hard men. . . . "

"Tommy," Michael said.

"Eily O'Shea was asking after you a minute ago, Seamus. I told her you weren't to be seen."

"Why did you tell her that?"

"Was it a lie?"

"You could have just showed her back here."

"I figured you two wanted a moment in private. This town rarely provides such privileges. Sure, why else would you have taken to the snug?"

The bartender, a young man with a mop of black hair and a bandage over his nose—he had broken it playing hurling—complimented Seamus. "Eily's a lass," he said. "You deserve far less."

"Cheeky bastard."

"If I wasn't ugly as sin, . . . " Tommy offered with a whistle, "I'd be all over her."

"Fair play to you."

"Are you lads right?"

"My eyes are throbbing," Seamus admitted.

"A pint, please," Michael said.

The slot closed.

"Aren't you knackered?" Seamus asked in exasperation.

"I'm too far gone to be tired, Seamie. Each tune I played destroyed me. Each melody did me in."

"Do you go on like this with Francine?"

"Huh?"

"She wouldn't put up with it, I'd say. It's Dingle that's talking—nothing else."

A pint arrived.

"Are you—" Tommy began.

"Shut the window," Seamus said.

The slot slammed.

"You bought the ticket?"

"You know I did."

"Train to Dublin tomorrow? Flight from Dublin to London, London to Toronto? Home in plenty of time to be with Francine when she—"

"Right."

"I drop you in Tralee in the morning? You board the train for Killarney, then switch for—"

"Don't go on about it."

"I will go on until I'm sure."

"You can be sure."

"Can I?"

"Half the money for the ticket is yours, isn't it?" Michael said irritably.

"It's your money now."

"I'll pay it back."

"I don't want it back. I want you on the airplane for Toronto. I want you with your wife and baby."

"Two flights, should I survive them, and I'm there."

"It's not so frightening as you imagine."

"You've been in the sky?"

"You know I haven't. But thousands cross the ocean every day. Do they mind it? I'd say not."

"Have you asked them?"

"You give a man cause to worry," Seamus said.

"I only want an hour on the Blasket. Wander the village and maybe up the path. It's been ages since I was there." Michael paused, glanced at his friend. "The day looks fine, doesn't it? We should land her easily. Is the *Munster Reel* seaworthy?"

"She'll manage."

"Then it's settled?"

Seamus crushed his cigarette against the heel of his shoe, fighting a tremor in his hands. "It's far from settled, Michael. My honest opinion is that we should *not* go to the Great Blasket today."

"Your honest opinion?"

"Correct."

"Not open to discussion?"

"It's for the best," he said, sensing victory. "We'll drop around your aunt's for a sandwich and tea."

"A scone or two?"

"I'm famished."

"And your mind is set?"

"I am resolved," Seamus answered.

Kitchen Music

A LAMENT FOR MY FATHER

Chapter 9

From the sidewalk outside Tom Daly's, I take in a grim pub-life tableau: a line of tweed sentinels at a bar, jackets rucked in the armpits, trousers wrinkled. Rough faces stand in profile, melanin-spotted hands grip pints, sooty nails pinch cigarettes. Only after closing the door do I recognize Jimmy next to the snug. He is dressed in black. Noting his puffy eyes, I approach cautiously.

"I'll have to tell Hia," I say.

"Tell her what?"

"The calendar—it's up to date."

The Bank of Ireland calendar that is not a museum piece has been changed again: has, in fact, been replaced by a new calendar, one displaying the days and weeks of May 1990.

"When was it corrected?"

"It was never wrong."

I digest this thought.

"Who died?" I ask.

"Think it's a joke?"

"I saw the funeral this morning. I was just wondering—"

"Where's Hia?"

"In the church, staring at that weird statue of Mary. Staring, and brooding."

"Eily's up at St. Mary's also," Jimmy says, returning his gaze to the counter. "They're probably together."

"They have their secrets."

"Which you don't?"

"If I have any secrets left," I say, "then they're secrets to me too."

I am pleased by my own wit. Jimmy is less impressed. I press on. "You have a whisky in your hand, right?" I ask, examining the bar side of the slot.

"Apparently."

"And these other men here—they all have drinks?"

"No secret there."

"And there's no one behind the bar: no Tom Daly, no other barman?"

"The area is vacant."

"Okay. . . . "

We are silent.

"Am I missing something?"

"No secret there," he repeats.

"Suppose I wanted a beer," I continue, "even just a Britvic. How would I go about ordering it?"

"I am not in the mood. . . . "

"I'm serious, Jimmy. Some basic principle isn't—"

"A woman has just died," he hisses. "A woman dearly loved not only by her family but the entire town. Will you shut your gob, or won't you?"

I shut my gob. Wordlessly, I retreat to where the snug wall ends, step to the right, open the door, and enter the chamber. From the bench I observe the form on the other side of the glass. A minute passes. The clock tick-tocks. The doorbell clangs. Another minute goes by. Finally, he traces my route.

"What's your game?"

"Watch."

I rap on the slot.

"What do you think—?"

"Wait."

We wait.

The slot opens.

"Lads?" Tom the barman asks.

"Just wanted to say hello," I say.

"How are you, Pat?"

"Great."

"We're all a touch sad around here. In a town the size of Dingle, even a single death is deeply felt."

"Am I having too much fun?"

"It's possible."

I wipe the grin from my gob.

"I'll leave you two in peace," Tommy says. He withdraws, but the slot stays open.

"Well?" Jimmy demands.

"Tell me about the *Munster Reel.*"

"What about it?"

"Was it up on blocks by the harbour?"

"So?"

"Until recently?"

"How recent?"

"Yesterday."

"Yesterday what?"

"Was the trawler up on blocks behind the shops on Strand Street until some time yesterday?"

"Have you lost your mind?"

"I just thought—"

"The boat went for scrap in 1972."

"Then I guess we won't be taking it out to the Great Blasket on Friday," I say quickly, covering my embarrassment.

Jimmy's expression is murderous. "Your second-to-last day in Dingle, and you're still determined to make this trip?"

"Hia has been nagging me since we got here."

"All her doing, eh?"

I shrug, unwisely.

"Do you think he could face it either?" he asks. "Do you think he understood any better the difference between constriction and commitment? You are the image of him. In every respect." Jimmy examines me. "The eyes. The gestures. The way you walk. But most especially the manner: keeping everyone at arm's length, letting no one inside."

"You don't know who I am."

"Don't know who you are? I've known you all your life. You are just about my son. You *are* my son, come to think of it, returned from long years in exile to bring his father contentment in his old age."

His own words nearly topple him. He lowers both elbows to his knees, his shoulders sagging. "I asked your mother to marry me once," he whispers.

I am dumbfounded.

"In 1960, an engagement letter to a woman I'd never met. To provide her with a husband, her son with a father. To provide me an excuse not to find a bridge and jump off it."

"What did she say?"

"Her reply was kindly. Must have thought me insane. Still, we corresponded. Until a decade ago, we exchanged the odd letter. Francine Keane," he adds. "A lovely woman, I'd say."

"I never knew."

"You know nothing."

"True."

"Nothing about this place."

"It could be anywhere," I say.

"What?"

"What you're telling me. What happened. Why not Scotland or Spain? Births are accidents. Personalities are made up, not bequeathed."

"Yours, maybe."

I appreciate the gesture. "Hia is a little different," I agree.

"Hia? I'm talking about the rest of us."

"All of you?"

"By my reckoning," he says.

We are silent for several minutes. The light alters outside, and in the pub: dim to dark, sombre to depressing.

"Weeks we waited for you," Jimmy announces in a different voice.

"Oh?"

"For the body to wash ashore. It should have turned up in Ferriter's Cove or Sybil Head. Even the Blasket Strand itself. Even that would have been—"

"Easy," a voice commands.

I glance at the window. No face appears.

"Where were you?" Jimmy asks.

"Canada?"

He stares.

"Lost?" I clarify, feeling the skin tighten over my skull.

"It was a disaster. No body, no proof. Do you understand the agony we endured? Do you understand the pain?"

"You had to leave Dingle," I answer, mouthing a stranger's words. "Your flight was from a static, closed world to one that was active and open. No one harboured any anger. No one blamed you."

Jimmy stands. "I was there in Tralee the afternoon you and Hia arrived. Waiting at the station to see if I'd recognize you."

"You didn't have to—"

"I didn't want to. When you stepped off, I knew immediately it was Michael. It was Michael, the year was 1958, and I was poor, pitiful Seamus all over again. I could barely keep from blabbering right there and then."

"Why didn't you introduce yourself?"

The question is stupid. Jimmy ignores it.

"I won't take you," he says.

"To the island?"

"Dunquin, even. You need a lift to the launch? But I will *not* participate in this insanity."

"You're sure?"

"I am resolved."

"Why didn't you tell me about the lament?" I ask.

He frowns.

"When you sent the record to my mother fifteen years ago—why didn't you explain that Paudeen Bawn was me?"

"You?"

"Isn't it?"

"The lament is only for you?"

"I'm Padraig or Paudeen, aren't I?"

He punches me. When he first lunges, I assume it is a flimsy embrace. But Jimmy's fist is hard, and my jaw burns. I drop to a knee.

The snug door opens.

"Would it have been any different with him?" Jimmy asks.

"Easy, lad," the voice repeats.

"Would the great Michael O Cathain have fared so much better than those of us who stayed on, who endured the hardship, the wasted years?"

"Get up, Pat."

I glance at the black shoes and dark trousers, the rumpled shirt and thick neck, and finally the battered face and tousled hair of a sixty-year-old Dingle publican. The man extends a hand; I am yanked unceremoniously to my feet.

"Tom Daly?"

"Who the fuck else would it be?"

Jimmy is still in the chamber. He sinks back onto the bench and folds his arms over his head, like an animal blocking the light. I look to Tom Daly. His narrow eyes blaze dismay, but also instruct me to leave. A minefield of beer kegs, transferred to the middle of the main room for pickup, slows my retreat. I weave my way to the door.

"Son," Jimmy calls behind me.

It is night now. I am addled, and chart a path out the pier between the lamplight and the shadowy edges, skirting pyramids of lobster pots, middens of fish carcasses, nets. At the end of the jetty sits a young man who gazes into the encircling dark, a reddish throb moving from his waist to his lips. The man wears a suit and tie. A gesture he makes—holding the cigarette by the filter and raising it before his eyes for inspection—reminds me of someone, though I cannot be more precise.

"It's himself?" he says.

"Sitting on the dock of the bay, Francis?"

"There you have it."

"You're dressed very sharply tonight," I say, anxious for a friendly conversation.

"Who are you, anyway?"

"What?"

He twists around for a better look. "Do I know you at all?" he asks.

"Pat Keane. Remember?"

Francis shrugs, as if my name has no bearing on whether he knows me. His attention reverts to the embers. "This bogwater is surely the arsehole of the universe. What in the world am I doing in such a kip?"

I am silent.

"Once you take in the desolation, call it home, you've fucking bought it. How could a body last a lifetime, like she did? Was the woman mad? Was she raving mad?"

"I should leave you be."

"I'm twenty-eight years old," Francis explains.

"I'm thirty-two."

"There aren't but a dozen people my age in Dingle. Even fewer decent women. I tried chatting up this Asian bird in a pub last week. She blew me off like that—"

He flicks the cigarette into the water. "What am I to do with myself? Where am I to go?"

"I understand."

"You do not."

"I don't understand."

"My mother was a tiny woman," he says abruptly. "Like the China girl I was mentioning. Incredibly small: five foot tall, hands of a doll, porcelain feet. You and I, we're practically giants. Behemoths, belching and farting, full of fight. But her, now—she was altogether different, altogether special."

"Sure."

"Imagine how fragile her heart must have been. Trapped inside a child's frame, knowing all along it was a strain, a risk. Small people make fucking explosions. Both coming and going, explosions. Small people compensate for the misshapen bullocks like us. Compensate for the ugliness."

"Yes they do."

He pivots again. "Do I *know* you?"

"No."

"You don't sound Irish."

"I'm just a tourist here."

"Right."

I retreat.

"I've a few jars in me," he adds. "All in a muddle from the drink. Ignore me, whoever you are."

Francis bends forward to imprison his face behind his forearms, rocking gently. I am beginning to understand how people grieve in Dingle.

"I'm sorry," I say.

He nods, and I retrace my steps to the foot of the pier, where I check the pub to make sure a certain villager isn't leaving for home to sleep off his shame and disappointment. The road is empty, and I hasten up Green Street. The main entrance to St. Mary's is locked but the vestibule door is open, the chamber lit by a reading lamp crooked over the announcements board. I scan the notices:

Wednesday, May 24
MEMORIAL SERVICE FOR
MARY LOUISE WALSHE
of Green Street
10 AM

The sanctuary is dark, perfumed with funeral wreaths, and I rest in the last pew. The rustle of someone near the altar revives me. A figure genuflects, makes the sign of the cross, then walks, head bowed, into the light. It is a China doll, hopelessly undersized. Smiling in anticipation, I watch as she marches right past me with a cursory glance that is bereft of recognition. Her face is flushed, radiant.

Chapter 10

Michael needed three tries to land the *Munster Reel* in the island harbour. A natural cove, the harbour was sheltered by a breakwater erected to slow the currents that could sweep a boat back out to sea. The cove was one of many carved into the Great Blasket's eastern flank, but the only accessible landing. Vessels had to be both shallow and sufficiently light to be dragged onto solid ground. A trawler would not normally have anchored there, except in ideal weather. Seamus had planned to mention this to Michael (who knew it well) before they landed, along with a few other equally urgent thoughts. But he had lost his will somewhere between Dingle Harbour and Blasket Sound and, resigned to going against his better judgement, brooded instead. When his partner veered from the mouth the first time, narrowly avoiding a standing rock, Seamus made no comment. On the second attempt, where Michael steered into the jaws only to feel a wave lift the hull—during that crisis, Seamus lit a cigarette. With the third go, he took note of their success, fetched the rope, leapt ashore to secure the mooring.

"She'll be right for an hour," Michael said, watching the *Munster Reel* scrape against rock.

Seamus shrugged.

"Hard landing," his friend admitted.

"Did you do much fishing in Toronto, Michael?"

"What do you think?"

"Judging from the way you handled her, I'd say not."

"You could have taken the wheel."

"I want no part of this."

"One hour, Seamie—where's the harm?"

Seamus examined the half-dozen *naombogs* abandoned upside down near the landing. The canvas on the canoes had rotted in places, exposing their oak ribbing. A week before Michael's return, Seamus had come upon the corpse of a massive fish in a cove near Reenbeg Point. Most of the flesh had decomposed, but the skeleton was still wrapped in papery skin, and the skin in swarming insects.

"Let's get on with it," he said grimly.

At the top of the cove Michael stopped, surveyed the sea, then pointed out a school of porpoises rounding a headland. The animals moved in a pack, raising their fins out of the water, like synchronized swimmers.

"Do you hear it?"

"I hear only surf."

"Listen!"

Seamus had to concentrate to distinguish the squealing of the porpoises.

"They'll mind the trawler for us," Michael said.

The path from the harbour to the lower village was steep and uneven. The men fought a stiff breeze and a blazing sun that made them adjust their caps. As they climbed past the buildings, Michael rhymed off each family name, often linking a relative or a childhood friend with a stone foundation, a grassy shell. To the north of the trail stood a *clochan*, a bush sprouting from its roof. Behind the hut was the whitewashed home, still thatched, of a famous, long-dead islander. Michael told Seamus that once all the houses in the village had looked that way: simple and sturdy, proud. Seamus received the information silently, hurt that Michael would treat him as an outsider, despite his frequent trips to the island over the years to visit Tomas O Cathain. He kept yet another thought to himself: the scene reminded him of a famine village, one of those eerie ghost hamlets one still came upon, up a mountainside or deep in a bog, in the more remote corners of the west.

Out of breath, Seamus paused before a house near the top of the village only when it became apparent Michael had no intention of stopping. Though in better condition than many, the house still had no windows or door. The thatching had caved in. Grass grew through the floor.

"Roof's gone," Michael commented.

"Will we have a glance inside?"

His friend stayed on the path.

"It's your own bloody house!" Seamus complained.

"Kind of looks like it caught fire, doesn't it?" Michael answered, making a cursory inspection.

"I need to rest a minute."

"The ground levels at the top."

"It does not."

"Levels a bit, then."

Seamus strode ahead to the well near the summit, sweat trickling down his spine. Michael climbed without apparent strain, hands in his pockets, back straight. Seamus knew where his friend intended to go, and suspected Michael *knew* he knew, which only increased his hurt, and his desperation.

The men paused at the spot where the footpath, reaching its highest elevation, shifted north. Once they were beyond a final ridge, the village and harbour would vanish. Again, it was Seamus who hesitated, visoring his eyes to take in the landscape. Michael waited with his head bowed. He began to fidget, then to mumble; finally, he turned and strode over the crest. Seamus was staggered by a gust at the rise.

"I won't go with you," he shouted.

Michael kept walking.

"You're headed to the rocks, aren't you?"

He slowed.

"Lochar?"

"A quick stroll, there and back," Michael said.

"No chance."

"Fine."

"Fine?"

"Wait at the boat. I won't be long."

Seamus caught up.

The weather deteriorated during the hike to the Lochar Rocks. Clouds suddenly skirted the hilltop. The wind suddenly tasted of rain. Not that Michael paid attention to the conditions. His concentration was unwavering: his feet might be on the path, but his gaze hovered where the cliff ended and the sea began. Except for a few monosyllables naming a bird, he kept mute; kept a few metres ahead; kept to himself.

Seamus was equally preoccupied. For him, the sky had sunk too close—he felt smothered by it. The path was too banked and strayed too near the precipice. Even more terrifying was the breeze that blasted down from the summit, threatening to topple him.

"Where are Peadar's sheep, then?" he said.

"Sheep?"

"Aren't we out to check his flock?"

"Peadar wouldn't want his animals on this side of the island," Michael replied. "Half of them would tumble off."

A moment later he left the path. Michael descended into a gully so sheer it swallowed him from the shoulders down. Below his outline was a horizon evenly partitioned between dark clouds and blue-grey ocean. Though he understood it was an illusion, Seamus was stunned: his friend appeared ready to render literal a longstanding disengagement from the earth.

Michael craned his upper body over the cliff. The wind

whipped his clothing, exposing his lanky torso and spindly legs.

"Down here, Seamus."

Seamus shook his head.

"There's a porpoise on the shelf," he shouted, a curious expression animating his features. "Just like when I was a boy."

"Please, Mickey."

"You have to look."

"Please."

"Have I ever told you about my great-uncle Sean-Phats?" Michael called, turning his back to the precipice.

"I can't move!"

"Sean was known for his cliff-walking. Fearless he was, wandering Fatal Cliff or even Ceann Dubh without concern. Sometimes he was after a stray sheep or a bird's nest. But my great-uncle was mostly a man of pleasure, you see, and the air, the wind, the motion of the sea—those drove him to such wild spots."

Seamus brushed a tear from his cheek.

"I was only a wee lad, mind, but was still—" Reeling from a blast, Michael thrust both arms into the air. "Terrible shame what happened to Sean," he continued calmly. "We were all dismayed."

"He fell?"

"Hit by a car."

"Michael?"

"Sean-Phats left Dingle for the only time in his life in 1937, to visit a daughter in Liverpool. The same day he stepped off the boat, the poor man tried to cross a road without checking traffic, and was struck by an automobile. Died in hospital a week afterwards. Never knew what hit him, no matter how many times his son explained it."

Seamus slumped on the path. Michael was, he realized, unaware of what he was doing; unaware, moreover, of what he was capable of doing, accidentally.

"Stay there," Seamus called. "I'm coming down!"

Michael, clearly delighted, began to pace back and forth along the bluff, his arms teeter-tottering, his body a pendulum. Guillemots wheeled over him.

Seamus begged him to wait.

"Isn't it lovely here?" Michael said. "So open, so welcoming?"

The birds screamed *scraw! scraw!*

Seamus, on his backside, slid halfway down.

Michael reached the crest. His face clouded momentarily, and he jammed a finger into his ear, as if to clear it. Then he smiled at Seamus—the same shy, pained smile—before disappearing over the rise.

Chapter 11

Viewed from the bottom of Grey Lane, the creature perched on our windowsill could be a sentinel guarding a shrine. The animal is majestic: bolt upright, paws curled over the edge, whiskers scanning the air for wing tracings. In a curious gesture, Carolan raises his right paw to swat at an invisible barrier, cocking his head in surprise. Hia drops a bag of groceries and sprints to the house. I listen to the clump of her shoes on the stairs and the crack of the door. Her upper body crowds the frame.

"Be careful," I warn.

She sweeps the cat back inside. Eily Murphy appears on the doorstep.

"Carolan was acting reckless," I say.

"He hasn't gone out onto the windowsill in years. Not since Joan McGreevy took ill."

I am reminded of something else.

"Did Joan McGreevy teach Irish?"

"She did, yes."

"Could my father have been her student?"

"She was the Irish teacher in Dingle for decades. Her lessons influenced generations of local children."

I nod.

Eily touches her hair. "Pat," she says. "I was wondering

if, well, if you and Hia have had the opportunity lately to have a leisurely chat."

"We prefer curt arguments."

"I am so sorry."

"Me too."

"A proper conversation on matters of some urgency would be wise, don't you think?"

"I thought I'd break my cooking embargo tonight," I say. "Prepare a special dish."

"Oh?"

"Something Hia likes. As a peace gesture. I'll also sing to her, if she'll listen."

"And about Jimmy, . . . " she continues.

"Jimmy tried to break my jaw last night."

Eily winces.

"Not that I mind," I add.

"You don't mind?"

"I understand."

"You're not angry?"

I answer honestly.

"What a curious man you are," she decides.

"I feel easygoing about things these days. Stuff doesn't bother me any more."

"Hia questions your conviction."

"I haven't explained myself well enough. But we'll work it out, I promise."

We enter the house together.

"Jimmy, I'm afraid, is refusing to drive you to Dunquin in the morning," Eily remembers with a smile. "Be ready by nine o'clock, in case he changes his mind."

I open the door onto a terrible scene. Hia is curled on the couch, weeping. She wears the same dress she has worn the last three days, with grey leggings and running shoes, and looks, with her bangs recently grown long enough to obscure her eyes, like a forlorn teenager. Beside her is the body of Carolan. I cross the room, glance at the corpse, go to her. She rejects my embrace.

"I'll find a box," I say.

I empty a cardboard box in the closet, and transfer Carolan into it.

"I have lost too much, Pat," Hia says, her face buried in a pillow.

"I'm sorry."

"Five pots for me, one for you."

Five pots?

"A person with five pots cannot live with a person with only one."

This is hardly the time to question her count. "I'll fix dinner," I say.

Leaving the coffin in the stairwell—Hia demands a proper burial, possible only after nightfall—I prepare a version of her favourite dish. Hampered by a lack of spices, I boil up a bland noodles-with-beef. She sits at the table long enough to swallow a few bites and sip broth from the bowl. Privately, I remark her high colour and bright eyes. Either she can no longer feign inscrutability or else her emotional life has blossomed so suddenly she is unable to disguise the flowering. I am desperate to have her tell me about the changes.

I sing, as threatened:

In the narrow lanes of Dingle
Where young men stay single
I first asked for the hand
Of sad Hia Thi Loi.

Expecting no reply, I am not too disappointed.

Later that evening, I knock on Eily's door to borrow a shovel. The muffled tones of her and Jimmy talking (arguing, more likely) were audible from our kitchen, but no one answers. Giving up, I stroll into the alley marked Private with a genuinely dead cat in my charge, hoping the lane opens onto the green. It does, through a crumbled wall, and I slip at last into Dingle's forgotten centre. A solitary streetlamp, positioned in the far corner, bathes a circle of grass in haze. Otherwise, the edges of the park are illuminated by cantings of window light from houses. Under a tree near the caravan I dig a grave with a flat rock, aided by the sodden earth. Carolan, now stiff, slides from the box. The soil covers him, as it does my hands, until there is only a bulge beside a trunk, like a root burrowed underground.

The caravan appears empty, and I step through its doorway. At first the night feels dense, malicious; I flash back to a closet in a suburban bungalow, and almost panic. But then, allowing my eyes to adjust, I inspect my surroundings and discern the sky—largely overcast, fringed in black—through the torn roof. The floor is strewn with bottles and the air is rank. Amid the debris hulks a couch, its coiled springs exposed, a dresser laden with rain-mulched newspapers, a chair to a missing kitchen table.

Vowing to give Hia an hour to calm, I sit on the chair. It absorbs my weight, but the floor underneath sags. I am more tired than I realized, and strangely comfortable with the enclosure. Tension flows from me. Thoughts jump, scramble, then abate.

I remain awake.

And think about him. Whom I don't know. Who doesn't know me. Who died here, while I was born there. How far apart are these places? An ocean. A world. A world lost? I might ask. A world destroyed, he would probably answer.

But he would be wrong. If my father were present, and I do sense him nearby, a little shy, a little ashamed, I would pose a single question, then answer it myself. Where does a tradition begin to die? The same moment it is born.

Whose words are those? My own, I suspect.

In the apartment, moonlight widening across the floor,

I make a mental note of how silly the room looks with all the furniture against the walls, and how unfitting it is to locate a shrine atop a television. Nevertheless, I strike a match and light the candles and incense sticks. At the sixth pot, owned by Carolan, I hesitate, unsure of the propriety.

"Did you—?" a sleepy voice asks.

"Under a tree in the park. He'll be fine."

She thanks me.

I sit on the edge of the bed. Hia props herself up on her elbow.

"Should I remove the extra pot from the shrine?"

She pauses for so long I wonder if she has heard me. "Leave it," she says.

"Unlit?"

"As you think best."

Solemnly, intuiting a profundity to the gesture that belies appearances, I light the sixth pot—for unknown, but still respected, loved ones. A thought comes to me for the first time with the ease of a child skipping through an open door: I would like to be a parent.

Hia starts to cry.

A LAMENT FOR MY FATHER

Chapter 12

Seamus stared at the spot where Michael had vanished. The longer he gazed, the more the gully tilted; the steeper the tilt, the greater the blurring of sky with earth, cloud with sea. Eventually, he slid the rest of the way down to the cliff edge, tearing up clumps of heather with his hands. At the bottom, the blood pounding in his skull, he crawled across the ridge to the next gully, where he found a similar funnel of land. Seamus dared not glance at the drop. For a moment he decided he would never find the courage to ascend back up the slope, which now seemed impossibly sheer. Trapped, his limbs refusing to respond, he collapsed, shuddered.

Returning to himself, Seamus shifted his upper body. With his backside above him, he felt a little safer exploring the crumbling precipice. A breeze rasped his cheeks. He advanced a few centimetres. Would the earth support him? He resolved to retreat. Then came the dizziness—his imagination insisted on forecasting what would happen next—and he paused, tried to calm his breathing.

He was not Michael.

He lacked the courage, the fortitude. He was an ordinary, unspecial man.

He was not Michael.

It was impossible for him to—

He thrust his head over the ledge.

The drop was a hundred metres and the cliff was concave, meaning Seamus hung above the water. At first he saw only shades: white, grey, dark blue. Then he distinguished floating carpets of mist, wisps of cloud, a rain shower further along the face. He saw gulls warring in midair, spray explosions in coves, whitecaps frilling the surface. He heard the roar of thrashing waves and the whistle of wind in cracks. And he detected a voice. It reached him as a whisper: soft and intimate, as if the creature was close by. Seamus searched the rocks. Something black perched in a cove. From so far up, he could not be sure. Then the animal called again, clearly, for his ears only.

He envisioned the precipice tilting and himself falling so fast his eyes bulged, so hard his eardrums burst, until he was swallowed by the ocean, and sank like a stone.

The next thing Seamus remembered, he was back on the path, his clothes torn, a cut over his left eye. The descent back into the village was delirious: he sprinted until pitching face first into the mud, squatted to clear his mind, froze in his tracks for minutes in deranged terror. Below the ruins he shouted a name until he was hoarse, then staggered onto the *Munster Reel.* The trawler had nearly capsized. Though the hull was badly scraped, the engine started. Twice the boat was repelled at the opening; with the third launch, the prow squeezed through the gap.

Only one man spotted Seamus O Suilleabhain mooring the vessel by himself on Dingle pier that evening. Liam Daly recalled that Seamus walked with difficulty and stopped to lean against a lamppost. The same figure also managed to cover the length of Strand Street unnoticed. Pats Farrell, the officer on duty, recorded that Seamus entered the *garda* station at 7:33 p.m. but was either too drunk or too disoriented to make his statement intelligible. Farrell ordered him home with instructions to come by again in the morning.

But the next morning he disappeared. Abandoning a

pot of tea and an uneaten breakfast, forgetting even the radio, Seamus climbed into his automobile and drove to Dublin. There, he left the car beside the ticket office for the Liverpool ferry. Before boarding the night sailing, he rang Pats Farrell to explain what had happened. A police vessel was dispatched to the Great Blasket. Suspicious, the *gardai* searched the O Suilleabhain house, where they confiscated a fiddle, a half-packed suitcase, and a Canadian passport belonging to the man Seamus claimed had fallen to his death. Inside Michael O Cathain's passport was a ticket voucher from a Tralee travel agency. The voucher was valid for a flight scheduled to depart Dublin that same day, with a connection to London and then Toronto.

Chapter 13

I am awoken by a rumble that rattles candlesticks and prayer pots. The thunder is out over the ocean, but still repercussive. Sliding up to Hia, I inhale her scent, whisper *please* and *it doesn't matter* and *I need your help*. Her objections diminish and we kiss. I trace her eyelids with my fingertips, her cheekbones, the curve of her chin; I sketch her shoulders, her swollen breasts, the line down her spine. When it seems right, I ask her to come on top, saying *please* again and holding her by the hips. I insist we move slowly, move together, and that our eyes remain locked. Once she is settled, I lower a hand to her belly, which I gently massage, around and around, until a smile curls her mouth. *I am dizzy*, she admits.

We are waiting in the doorway at nine o'clock. The storm has passed on; the clouds are tall and fleecy. Jimmy's car is parked outside. He emerges from Eily's house without apology or excuse. "Too rough," he says immediately.

"You can tell?"

"They wouldn't risk it with tourists when the sea is high."

"Can you take us out, just in case?"

"I'm going that direction anyway," he replies, opening the car door for Hia.

Silence reigns the entire ride to Dunquin. Jimmy is a mess of nervous tics—dry coughs, tugs on his ear—but he neither smokes nor glances in the rear-view mirror. Hia, Buddha-like in the back seat, rests her eyes.

"Francis Walshe has gone missing," he eventually says.

"Since when?"

"His mother's funeral. One or two people spotted him near the pier two nights ago, but Naill said he hasn't come home at all. They called the guards this morning."

In Dunquin, Jimmy bypasses the path to the launch and continues on to Sean O Conchuir's house. The road near the house has been narrowed by cars parked on both sides. He stops at the foot of the driveway and asks Hia to wait. We weave around groups of elderly men smoking and talking in ill-fitting, out-of-fashion suits, then enter the front door. The room is jammed. My initial hope—that a crowd has gathered to hear O Conchuir play—fades as I examine faces.

I ask when he died.

"Wednesday."

"Why didn't you tell me?"

"You seemed busy."

Jimmy's ambush succeeds. I am in jeans and a sweater. I am also the only non-local, a fact made plain by the way attention shifts to us and a pathway to the coffin widens. Their stares read like accusations, and I blanch, feel my limp worsen as we cross the room. The casket is half open. O Conchuir's chin is thrust forward and his eyebrows are arched in displeasure. His mouth too is set, lips pursed to refrain from criticism of the ungifted. Even his thin hair seems severe, judgemental.

I am staggered, and beg Jimmy to leave. On our way back through the house I am assailed not by jibes but, to my astonishment, smiles and slaps on the back. Mourners pronounce my name and call me "son". Their tone is baffling. Before I can make any sense of it, we are once again on the lawn. Two men approach us. One is Joe John Sheedy.

He has aged since I interviewed him, and leans heavily on his cane. Joe John wishes me all the best. The second man is Charlie MacDonagh, squirming in a sports jacket and platform shoes. MacDonagh grinds a cigarette into the grass.

My memory clicks in. "Going to buy a video machine now?" I ask him.

"No fucking way," he answers.

We reach the car.

"What?" Hia says.

"I'll explain later."

"You cry?"

"No."

"Isn't that a tear?"

The ferry to the Great Blasket departs Dunquin pier at ten o'clock every morning, weather permitting. We pull up to the area above the launch a few minutes early, and Jimmy accompanies us to the walkway. A wind, blowing off the water, plasters our clothing to our bodies. Hia grips my hand.

"Too rough by far," Jimmy shouts.

"If the boat doesn't show up, we'll hitch a ride back to Dingle. Don't worry."

"I'll worry."

"When were you last on the Great Blasket?" I ask.

"When do you think I was?"

"Not since . . . ?"

"I wouldn't set foot on that island to save my life," he answers. "Or yours." Then, noting Hia's puzzlement: "Sorry, Hia."

She and I descend a corrugated path. At the bottom are five inverted *naombogs* surrounded by lobster pots and gas tanks, rubber boots and wetsuits. Outboard motors cower beneath canoes; a rusted anchor, still attached to a line, rests against a rock. A sign is posted:

–INSEARAC TAR
–N —INNTE SEO

DANGEROUS
BEYOND THIS POINT

The pier extends only a few metres into the water and displays the name TOMAS KEANE painted on the wall below the walkway. I take silent note of the coincidence. Even at the end of the launch, we are still beneath the cliff; a glance upward at glistening rocks and whirling gulls induces, in me at least, a first taste of vertigo.

Gazing at the sound isn't exactly calming. Near the pier the water is a greenish brine, tendrilled with seaweed. Further out it darkens and swells. Five hundred metres off shore, where the surface crests, the sea is menacing. Happily, the launch is protected by a line of rocks that reduce most breakers to harmless volleys.

"Here it comes," I say.

The trawler-ferry has rounded Dunmore Head and is advancing on the pier. Though apparently riding the waves, the boat still bobs madly. It looks, from a distance, like a bathtub toy.

All colour drains from Hia's face.

"Only a few minutes now," I say.

I climb onto the breakwater, in case the skipper hasn't noticed us. Once the trawler has drawn to within a kilometre of the shore, however, it appears to stop. Behind me, a man is readying a dinghy.

"I'll be with you in a minute," he promises.

"Isn't it too rough?" Hia asks him.

"Rough, but not impossible. You'll be the first to make it out this season."

He raises up an outboard motor. "Three Germans waited most of last week for a calm sea," he says. "One morning we almost took them. Lucky we didn't; the weather turned, and they'd have been trapped overnight."

Hia leans against a *naombog*, then slides onto the cement. I cross to her. "I'm sorry," she says.

I have been expecting this.

"I didn't think it would be so bad. The memories hurt my eyes. I was sick the whole period at sea. Sick even worse than I am now."

I apologize to the man.

"No bother," he says, signalling the trawler. "There's still a day of fishing."

"You make the trip," Hia tells me.

"By myself?"

"If it is important. . . . "

"Nothing in the world matters less to me."

The ferry vanishes around another headland. Immediately, Hia's face eases.

"There's a pub up in the village, . . . " I suggest.

"Let's stay here for a while. Can I eat those sandwiches, please?"

I borrow a wetsuit, spread it over the surface, and Hia and I picnic, not towards the sheltered back of the landing, but—at her insistence—near the front.

"I miss him," I say. "Isn't that funny?"

"I miss her, too."

"But this," I continue, indicating the island, the ocean, the sky, "has nothing to do with me. Michael has nothing to do with me either. There's only you, and Francine, and the people we know here."

An hour ago the Great Blasket was sunlit and the village ruins were so sharply outlined they resembled models on a board. Now, with the weather worsening, the island seems remote, an iceberg drifting out to sea.

I insist Hia wear my poncho. I also rub her hands. "Hia's lovely hands," I comment. "Good for shadow puppets. Perfect for fiddling."

"I am sorry you cannot play."

The rain starts.

"I've never wanted to play," I tell her truthfully. Then, risking it: "Maybe it will be generational. Maybe our daughter will be a master violinist."

She considers rising, but her fingers are still webbed in mine. I tighten my hold while studying her face: she is determined to drag this out.

"I will marry a Vietnamese," she says.

"Why not me?"

"Chac."

"He's dead."

"His spirit is unsettled."

"So are most spirits."

"You don't understand my mind."

I resist.

"In the hold of the trawler," Hia says in a calmer voice, "where I hid for hours, not thinking of my mother, not thinking of anyone—in there, my imagination died. *I* died, maybe." She pauses. I release her. "The terrible things that happened afterwards made this death certain. I could help no one. I could create nothing."

"That was a decade ago."

"That is today."

"Your mother forgives you, Hia."

She struggles to her feet.

"But your child won't," I add sternly.

Unnoticed by us, the island has vanished. It was there, now it isn't; I am already having trouble recalling the contours that should be carved, according to the local code, into my memory with the permanence of a bas-relief in sandstone. Blasket Sound thrashes and heaves. Even an experienced fisherman would find these waters dangerous. Surprising myself, I offer a silent prayer for the men who were to ferry Hia and me, in the hope that they have turned back, and are safely in harbour.

Eventually, a spitting rain drives us from the launch.

She insists on walking backwards, so as not to miss a final study of a shape no longer visible.

"Could you remind me why we came here in the first place?" I ask her.

"To succeed or fail," she replies, her eyes narrowed into the wind. "Nothing in between."

"But suppose there only *is* in-between."

"For you, maybe."

"So arrogant!"

"And you still want to marry me? Have a family together?"

"I respect you more than anyone else in the world," I answer simply. "You are dignified and strong and slightly ruined. I wish I had half your passion."

That earns a smile. "To respect is one thing," Hia says, "to love is another."

It is. It isn't. Unable to explain myself, I don't try.

Before climbing the path, I tighten the hood on her poncho. Gulls, catching updrafts off the cliff face, hang in the air over us like haloes. Our ascent is cautious, slowed by Hia's glances to make sure the Great Blasket hasn't suddenly reappeared. My heart pounds.

"This won't solve anything," she says at the top. "Same ghosts will haunt us. Same tensions will keep us apart."

"There's no end to it," I agree.

We stand by the road waiting for a lift. I hold my head high and scan the face of Mount Eagle for the source of the music flooding my ears. So resonant and so natural is the sound that I cannot separate it from the landscape or the weather. I am hearing the first part of Sean Ó Conchuir's "The Drunken Butterfly" and thinking of the slope of the Great Blasket that stretches through space to attach itself to the cliffs of Dunquin; and of Hia's fear of water, Michael's fear of his impulses, and my own fear of repeating patterns as ephemeral as bird prints in sand. Then I am hearing the orotund phrases of the second part and thinking of a windsheared hillside and a dissolving sky; of television shrines and faces missing from photographs; and of Francine Keane and Thuy Thi Ngo, Eileen O'Shea the morning she learned that Seamus O Suilleabhain had fled her, and Dingle, to mourn his fallen idol. And I am hearing the third part too, the flourish of notes that intimate the butterfly's intoxicated flutter, and thinking of seabirds who sketch with their wings, sketch churches and temples too complex ever to be re-created by our trembling hands. Finally, I am hearing the moment when the closing phrase encounters the original sequence, the contraction of certain notes, the expansion of others, the announcement that form dictates that all must begin again—no finale, no crescendo; that only through repetition can we comprehend structure, comprehend harmony and counterpoint and the sadness, the ecstasy, of beautiful sounds.

O Conchuir's treatment of the slip-jig is typically terse. The version in my head, in contrast, is rhapsodic, grounded in modulation and strong bows. A question haunts me, as Hia predicted it would. Who is playing this music?

CODA

CODA

The kitchen was hazy with first-dawn light. Only Seamus and Sean O Conchuir were awake, slouched in their chairs amid glasses and bottles, a grate overflowing with ash. Michael was retuning O Conchuir's fiddle to duplicate the pitch he'd heard one night in 1947, he explained, when an itinerant musician—an eighty-year-old from Gloutane—performed in a Tralee pub. The tuning was an octave below, and rarely used. O Conchuir asked about the melody.

"It's a lament," Michael said, "written by a son for his father."

"Why for him?"

"To commiserate, or celebrate, the passing of things. I can never tell the difference myself."

"Who are we talking about?" Seamus asked wearily.

Sean O Conchuir glared at him.

"Will I not bother?"

"You'll bother," O Conchuir said.

"Grief is useless, sure."

"Play the tune, Michael."

"It's only brief."

"Is it yours?" Seamus thought to ask.

Michael raised the fiddle. "'A Lament for My Father,'" he said, resting his gaze on the neck.

Acknowledgements

Kitchen Music is indebted to many sources and individuals. Books consulted on Irish music and society include *The Northern Fiddler* by Allen Feldman and Eamonn O'Doherty, *Traditional Music in Ireland* by Tomas O Canainn, *Our Musical Heritage* by Sean O Riada, *Inishkillane* by Hugh Brody, and, among numerous works on Blasket culture, *The Blasket Islands* by Joan and Ray Stagles. Le Ly Hayslip's *When Heaven and Earth Changed Places*, and *Hearts of Sorrow*, edited by James M. Freeman, were used for information on Vietnam and Vietnamese refugees. *Angkor* by Michael Freeman and Roger Warner was the principal source for details regarding Angkor Wat.

Individuals owed thanks include Barra O Seaghdha, Mark Abley, Linda Leith, Carol TenBrink, Mary Ladky, Vicki Ross, Than Nguyen and, most emphatically, David Manicom. I am also grateful to the Explorations Program of the Canada Council for its support.